Also by Christian Cameron

THE TYRANT SERIES

Tyrant
Tyrant: Storm of Arrows
Tyrant: Funeral Games
Tyrant: King of the Bosporus

THE KILLER OF MEN SERIES

Killer of Men

OTHER NOVELS

Washington and Caesar

Marathon

CHRISTIAN CAMERON

First published in Great Britain in 2011 by Orion Books,
an imprint of The Orion Publishing Group Ltd
Orion House, 5 Upper Saint Martin's Lane
London WC2H 9EA

An Hachette UK Company

1 3 5 7 9 10 8 6 4 2

A CIP catalogue record for this book
is available from the British Library.

ISBN (Hardback) 978 1 4091 1408 6
ISBN (Export Trade Paperback) 978 1 4091 1409 3

Typeset by Deltatype Ltd, Birkenhead, Merseyside

Printed in Great Britain by CPI Mackays, Chatham ME5 8TD

The Orion Publishing Group's policy is to use papers
that are natural, renewable and recyclable products and
made from wood grown in sustainable forests. The logging
and manufacturing processes are expected to conform to
the environmental regulations of the country of origin.

www.orionbooks.co.uk

For the craftspeople who bring history to life — from vases to swords, horn cups to armour, kitchen knives to jewelry.

Glossary

I am an *amateur* Greek scholar. My definitions are my own, but taken from the LSJ or Routeledge's *Handbook of Greek Mythology* or Smith's *Classical Dictionary*. On some military issues I have the temerity to disagree with the received wisdom on the subject. Also check my website at www.hippeis.com for more information and some helpful pictures.

Akinakes A Scythian short sword or long knife, also sometimes carried by Medes and Persians.

Andron The 'men's room' of a proper Greek house – where men have symposia. Recent research has cast real doubt as to the sexual exclusivity of the room, but the name sticks.

Apobatai The Chariot Warriors. In many towns, towns that hadn't used chariots in warfare for centuries, the *Apobatai* were the elite three hundred or so. In Athens, they competed in special events; in Thebes, they may have been the forerunners of the Sacred Band.

Archon A city's senior official or, in some cases, one of three or four. A magnate.

Aspis The Greek hoplite's shield (which is not called a hoplon!). The *aspis* is about a yard in diameter, is deeply dished (up to six inches deep) and should weigh between eight and sixteen pounds.

Basileus An aristocratic title from a bygone era (at least in 500 BC) that means 'king' or 'lord'.

Bireme A warship rowed by two tiers of oars, as opposed to a *trireme*, which has three tiers.

Chiton The standard tunic for most men, made by taking a single continuous piece of cloth and folding it in half, pinning the shoulders and open side. Can be made quite fitted by means of pleating. Often made of very fine quality material – usually wool, sometimes linen, especially in the upper classes. A full *chiton* was ankle length for men and women.

Chitoniskos A small *chiton*, usually just longer than modesty demanded – or not as long as modern modesty would demand! Worn by warriors and farmers, often heavily bloused and very full by warriors to pad their armour. Usually wool.

Chlamys A short cloak made from a rectangle of cloth roughly 60 by 90 inches – could also be worn as a *chiton* if folded and pinned a different way. Or slept under as a blanket.

Corslet/Thorax In 500 BC, the best *corslets* were made of bronze, mostly of the so-called 'bell' *thorax* variety. A few muscle *corslets* appear at the end of this period, gaining popularity into the 450s. Another style is the 'white' *corslet*, seen to appear just as the Persian Wars begin – re-enactors call this the 'Tube and Yoke' *corslet*, and some people call it (erroneously) the *linothorax*. Some of them may have been made of linen – we'll never know – but the likelier material is Athenian leather, which was often tanned and finished with alum, thus being bright white. Yet another style was a tube and yoke of scale, which you can see the author wearing on his website. A scale *corslet* would have been the most expensive of all, and probably provided the best protection.

Daidala Cithaeron, the mountain that towered over Plataea, was the site of a remarkable fire-festival, the *Daidala*, which was celebrated by the Plataeans on the summit of the mountain. In the usual ceremony, as mounted by the Plataeans in every seventh year, a wooden idol (*daidalon*) would be dressed in bridal robes and dragged on an ox-cart from Plataea to the top of the mountain, where it would be burned after appropriate rituals. Or, in the *Great Daidala*, which were celebrated every forty-nine years, fourteen *daidala* from different Boeotian towns would be burned on a large wooden pyre heaped with brushwood, together with a cow and a bull that were sacrificed to Zeus and Hera. This huge pyre on the mountain top must have provided a most impressive spectacle; Pausanias remarks that he knew of no other flame that rose as high or could be seen from so far.

The cultic legend that was offered to account for the festival ran as follows. When Hera had once quarrelled with Zeus, as she often did, she had withdrawn to her childhood home of Euboea and had refused every attempt at reconciliation. So Zeus sought the advice of the wisest man on earth, Cithaeron (the eponym of the mountain), who ruled at Plataea in the earliest times. Cithaeron advised him to make a wooden image of a woman, to veil it in the manner of a bride, and then to have it drawn along in an ox-cart after spreading the rumour that he was planning to marry the nymph Plataea, a daughter of the river god Asopus. When Hera rushed to the scene and tore away the veils, she was so relieved to find a wooden effigy rather than the expected bride that she at last consented to be reconciled with Zeus. (Routledge *Handbook of Greek Mythology*, pp. 137–8)

Daimon Literally a spirit, the *daimon* of combat might be adrenaline, and the *daimon* of philosophy might simply be native intelligence. Suffice it to say that very intelligent men – like Socrates – believed that god-sent spirits could infuse a man and influence his actions.

Daktyloi Literally digits or fingers, in common talk 'inches' in the system of measurement. Systems differed from city to city. I have taken the liberty of using just the Athenian units.

Despoina Lady. A term of formal address.

Diekplous A complex naval tactic about which some debate remains. In this book, the *Diekplous*, or through stroke, is commenced with an attack by the ramming ship's bow (picture the two ships approaching bow to bow or head on) and cathead on the enemy oars. Oars were the most vulnerable part of a fighting ship, something very difficult to imagine unless you've rowed in a big boat and understand how lethal your own oars can be – to you! After the attacker crushes the enemy's oars, he passes, flank to flank, and then turns when astern, coming up easily (the defender is almost dead in the water) and ramming the enemy under the stern or counter as desired.

Doru A spear, about ten feet long, with a bronze butt-spike.

Eleutheria Freedom.

Ephebe A young, free man of property. A young man in training to be a *hoplite*. Usually performing service to his city and, in ancient terms, at one of the two peaks of male beauty.

Eromenos The 'beloved' in a same-sex pair in ancient Greece. Usually younger, about seventeen. This is a complex, almost dangerous subject in the modern world – were these pair-bonds about sex, or chivalric love, or just a 'brotherhood' of warriors? I suspect there were elements of all three. And to write about this period without discussing the *eromenos/erastes* bond would, I fear, be like putting all the warriors in steel armour instead of bronze . . .

Erastes The 'lover' in a same-sex pair bond – the older man, a tried warrior, twenty-five to thirty years old.

Eudaimonia Literally 'well-spirited'. A feeling of extreme joy.

Exhedra The porch of the women's quarters – in some

cases, any porch over a farm's central courtyard.

Helots The 'race of slaves' of Ancient Sparta – the conquered peoples who lived with the Spartiates and did all of their work so that they could concentrate entirely on making war and more Spartans.

Hetaira Literally a 'female companion'. In ancient Athens, a *hetaira* was a courtesan, a highly skilled woman who provided sexual companionship as well as fashion, political advice and music.

Himation A very large piece of rich, often embroidered wool, worn as an outer garment by wealthy citizen women or as a sole garment by older men, especially those in authority.

Hoplite A Greek upper-class warrior. Possession of a heavy spear, a helmet and an *aspis* (see above) and income above the marginal lowest free class were all required to serve as a *hoplite*. Although much is made of the 'citizen soldier' of ancient Greece, it would be fairer to compare *hoplites* to medieval knights than to Roman legionnaires or modern National Guardsmen. Poorer citizens did serve, and sometimes as *hoplites* or marines, but in general, the front ranks were the preserve of upper-class men who could afford the best training and the essential armour.

Hoplitodromos The *hoplite* race,

or race in armour. Two *stades* with an *aspis* on your shoulder, a helmet and greaves in the early runs. I've run this race in armour. It is no picnic.

Hoplomachia A *hoplite* contest, or sparring match. Again, there is enormous debate as to when *hoplomachia* came into existence and how much training Greek *hoplites* received. One thing that they didn't do is drill like modern soldiers – there's no mention of it in all of Greek literature. However, they had highly evolved martial arts (see *pankration*) and it is almost certain that *hoplomachia* was a term that referred to 'the martial art of fighting when fully equipped as a *hoplite*'.

Hoplomachos A participant in *hoplomachia*.

Hypaspist Literally 'under the shield'. A squire or military servant – by the time of Arimnestos, the *hypaspist* was usually a younger man of the same class as the *hoplite*.

Kithara A stringed instrument of some complexity, with a hollow body as a soundboard.

Kline A couch.

Kopis The heavy, back-curved sabre of the Greeks. Like a longer, heavier modern kukri or Gurkha knife.

Kore A maiden or daughter.

Kylix A wide, shallow, handled bowl for drinking wine.

Logos Literally 'word'. In pre-Socratic Greek philosophy the word is everything – the power beyond the gods.

Longche A six to seven foot throwing spear, also used for hunting. A *hoplite* might carry a pair of *longchai*, or a single, longer and heavier *doru*.

Machaira A heavy sword or long knife.

Maenads The 'raving ones' – ecstatic female followers of Dionysus.

Mastos A woman's breast. A *mastos* cup is shaped like a woman's breast with a rattle in the nipple – so when you drink, you lick the nipple and the rattle shows that you emptied the cup. I'll leave the rest to imagination ...

Medimnos A grain measure. Very roughly – 35 to 100 pounds of grain.

Megaron A style of building with a roofed porch.

Navarch An admiral.

Oikia The household – all the family and all the slaves, and sometimes the animals and the farmland itself.

Opson Whatever spread, dip or accompaniment an ancient Greek had with bread.

Pais A child.

Palaestra The exercise sands of the gymnasium.

Pankration The military martial art of the ancient Greeks – an unarmed combat system that bears more than a passing resemblance to modern MMA techniques, with a series of carefully structured blows and domi-nation holds that is, by modern standards, very advanced. Also the basis of the Greek sword and spear-based martial arts. Kicking, punching, wrestling, grappling, on the ground and standing, were all permitted.

Peplos A short over-fold of cloth that women could wear as a hood or to cover the breasts.

Phalanx The full military potential of a town; the actual, formed body of men before a battle (all of the smaller groups formed together made a *phalanx*). In this period, it would be a mistake to imagine a carefully drilled military machine.

Phylarch A file-leader – an officer commanding the four to sixteen men standing behind him in the *phalanx*.

Polemarch The war leader.

Polis The city. The basis of all Greek political thought and expression, the government that was held to be more important – a higher god – than any individual or even family. To this day, when we talk about politics, we're talking about the 'things of our city'.

Porne A prostitute.

Porpax The bronze or leather band that encloses the forearm on a Greek *aspis*.

Psiloi Light infantrymen – usually slaves or adolescent freemen who, in this period, were not organised and seldom had any weapon beyond some rocks to throw.

Pyrrhiche The 'War Dance'. A line dance in armour done by all of the warriors, often very complex. There's reason to believe that the *Pyrrhiche* was the method by which the young were trained in basic martial arts and by which 'drill' was inculcated.

Pyxis A box, often circular, turned from wood or made of metal.

Rhapsode A master-poet, often a performer who told epic works like the *Iliad* from memory.

Satrap A Persian ruler of a province of the Persian Empire.

Skeuophoros Literally a 'shield carrier', unlike the *hypaspist*, this is a slave or freed man who does camp work and carries the armour and baggage.

Sparabara The large wicker shield of the Persian and Mede elite infantry. Also the name of those soldiers.

Spolas Another name for a leather *corslet*, often used for the lion skin of Heracles.

Stade A measure of distance. An Athenian *stade* is about 185 metres.

Strategos In Athens, the commander of one of the ten military tribes. Elsewhere, any senior Greek officer – sometimes the commanding general.

Synaspismos The closest order that *hoplites* could form – so close that the shields overlap, hence 'shield on shield'.

Taxis Any group but, in military terms, a company; I use it for 60 to 300 men.

Thetes The lowest free class – citizens with limited rights.

Thorax See *corslet*.

Thugater Daughter. Look at the word carefully and you'll see the 'daughter' in it ...

Triakonter A small rowed galley of thirty oars.

Trierarch The captain of a ship – sometimes just the owner or builder, sometimes the fighting captain.

Zone A belt, often just rope or finely wrought cord, but could be a heavy bronze kidney belt for war.

General Note on Names and Personages

This series is set in the very dawn of the so-called Classical Era, often measured from the Battle of Marathon (490 BC). Some, if not most, of the famous names of this era are characters in this series – and that's not happenstance. Athens of this period is as magical, in many ways, as Tolkien's Gondor, and even the quickest list of artists, poets, and soldiers of this era reads like a 'who's who' of western civilization. Nor is the author tossing them together by happenstance – these people were almost all aristocrats, men (and women) who knew each other well – and might be adversaries or friends in need. Names in bold are historical characters – yes, even Arimnestos – and you can get a glimpse into their lives by looking at Wikipedia or Britannia online. For more in-depth information, I recommend Plutarch and Herodotus, to whom I owe a great deal.

Arimnestos of Plataea may – just may – have been Herodotus's source for the events of the Persian Wars. The careful reader will note that Herodotus himself – a scribe from Halicarnassus – appears several times ...

Archilogos – Ephesian, son of Hipponax the poet; a typical Ionian aristocrat, who loves Persian culture and Greek culture too, who serves his city, not some cause of 'Greece' or 'Hellas', and who finds the rule of the Great King fairer and more 'democratic' than the rule of a Greek tyrant.

Arimnestos – Child of Chalkeotechnes and Euthalia.

Aristagoras – Son of Molpagoras, nephew of Histiaeus. Aristagoras led Miletus while Histiaeus was a virtual prisoner of the Great King Darius at Susa. Aristagoras seems to have initiated the Ionian Revolt – and later to have regretted it.

Aristides – Son of Lysimachus, lived roughly 525–468 BC, known later in life as 'The Just'. Perhaps best known as one of the commanders at

Marathon. Usually sided with the Aristocratic party.

Artaphernes – Brother of Darius, Great King of Persia, and Satrap of Sardis. A senior Persian with powerful connections.

Bion – A slave name, meaning 'life'. The most loyal family retainer of the Corvaxae.

Briseis – Daughter of Hipponax, sister of Archilogos.

Calchas – A former warrior, now the keeper of the shrine of the Plataean Hero of Troy, Leitos.

Chalkeotechnes – The Smith of Plataea; head of the family Corvaxae, who claim descent from Heracles.

Chalkidis – Brother of Arimnestos, son of Chalkeotechnes.

Darius – King of Kings, the lord of the Persian Empire, brother to Artaphernes.

Draco – Wheelwright and wagon builder of Plataea, a leading man of the town.

Empedocles – A priest of Hephaestus, the Smith God.

Epaphroditos – A warrior, an aristocrat of Lesbos.

Eualcidas – A Hero. Eualcidas is typical of a class of aristocratic men – professional warriors, adventurers, occasionally pirates or merchants by turns. From Euboea.

Heraclitus – c.535–475 BC. One of the ancient world's most famous philosophers. Born to an aristocratic family, he chose philosophy over political power. Perhaps most famous for his statement about time: 'You cannot step twice into the same river'. His belief that 'strife is justice' and other similar sayings which you'll find scattered through these pages made him a favourite with Nietzsche. His works, mostly now lost, probably established the later philosophy of Stoicism.

Herakleides – An Aeolian, a Greek of Asia Minor. With his brothers Nestor and Orestes, he becomes a retainer – a warrior – in service to Arimnestos. It is easy, when looking at the birth of Greek democracy, to see the whole form of modern government firmly established – but at the time of this book, democracy was less than skin deep and most armies were formed of semi-feudal war bands following an aristocrat.

Heraklides – Aristides' helmsman, a lower-class Athenian who has made a name for himself in war.

Hermogenes – Son of Bion, Arimnestos's slave.

Hesiod – A great poet (or a great tradition of poetry) from Boeotia in Greece, Hesiod's 'Works and Days' and 'Theogony' were widely read in the sixth century and remain fresh today – they are the chief source we have on Greek farming, and this book owes an enormous debt to them.

Hippias – Last tyrant of Athens, overthrown around 510 BC (that is, just around the beginning of this series), Hippias escaped into exile and became a pensioner of Darius of Persia.

Hipponax – 540–c.498 BC. A Greek poet and satirist, considered the inventor of parody. He is supposed to have said 'There are two days when a woman is a pleasure: the day one marries her and the day one buries her'.

Histiaeus – Tyrant of Miletus and ally of Darius of Persia, possible originator of the plan for the Ionian Revolt.

Homer – Another great poet, roughly Hesiod's contemporary (give or take fifty years) and again, possibly more a poetic tradition than an individual man. Homer is reputed as the author of the *Iliad* and the *Odyssey*, two great epic poems which, between them, largely defined what heroism and aristocratic good behaviour should be in Greek society – and, you might say, to this very day.

Kylix – A boy, slave of Hipponax.

Miltiades – Tyrant of the Thracian Chersonese. His son, Cimon or Kimon, rose to be a great man in Athenian politics. Probably the author of the Athenian victory of Marathon, Miltiades was a complex man, a pirate, a warlord and a supporter of Athenian democracy.

Penelope – Daughter of Chalkeotechnes, sister of Arimnestos.

Sappho – A Greek poetess from the island of Lesbos, born sometime around 630 BC and died between 570 and 550 BC. Her father was probably Lord of Eresus. Widely considered the greatest lyric poet of Ancient Greece.

Simonalkes – Head of the collateral branch of the Plataean Corvaxae, cousin to Arimnestos.

Simonides – Another great lyric poet, he lived c.556–468 BC, and his nephew, Bacchylides, was as famous as he. Perhaps best known for his epigrams, one of which is:

Ω ξεῖν᾽, ἀγγέλλειν Λακεδαιμονίοις ὅτι τῇδε
κείμεθα, τοῖς κείνων ῥήμασι πειθόμενοι.
Go tell the Spartans, thou who passest by,
That here, obedient to their laws, we lie.

Thales – c.624–c.546 BC The first philosopher of the Greek tradition, whose writings were still current in Arimnestos's time. Thales used geometry to solve problems such as calculating the height of the pyramids in Aegypt and the distance of ships from the shore. He made at least one trip to Aegypt. He is widely accepted as the founder of western mathematics.

Theognis – Theognis of Megara was almost certainly not one man but a whole canon of aristocratic poetry under that name, much of it practical. There are maxims, many very wise, laments on the decline of man and the age, and the woes of old age and poverty, songs for symposia, etc. In later sections there are songs and poems about homosexual love and laments for failed romances. Despite widespread attributions, there was, at some point, a real Theognis who may have lived in the mid-6th century BC, or just before the events of this series. His poetry would have been central to the world of Arimnestos's mother.

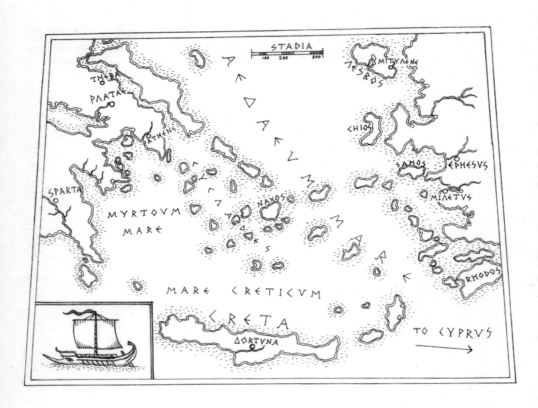

STADIA
100 200   500

THEBA
PLATAE
ATHENS

LESBOS   MITYLENE

CHIOS

SAMOS   EPHESVS

SPARTA

MILETVS

MYRTOVM
MARE

NAXOS

RHODOS

MARE CRETICVM

CRETA

DORTYNA

TO CYPRVS

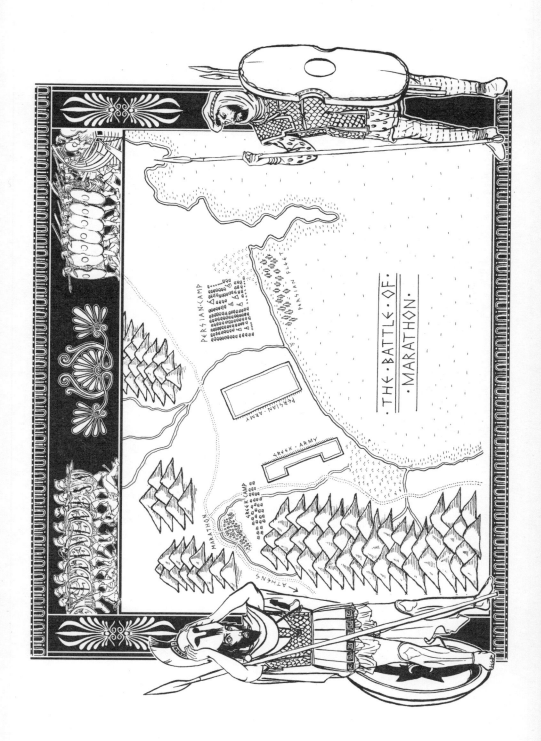

THE · BATTLE · OF · MARATHON ·

PERSIAN CAMP

PERSIAN FLEET

PERSIAN ARMY

GREEK ARMY

GREEK CAMP

MARATHON

ATHENS

I'm not any younger, and that's a fact. But I gather my story's a good one. Or you young people wouldn't cluster around so eagerly to hear my tale.

Honey, you've brought your scribbler back to me. He's promised to write it all out in the new way, although if I was allowed, I'd rather hear a *rhapsode* sing it the old way. But the old ways died with the Medes, didn't they? It's all different now. The world I'm telling you about is as dead as old Homer's heroes at Troy. Even my *thugater* here thinks I'm the relic of a time when the gods still walked abroad. Eh?

You young people make me laugh. You're soft. But you're soft because we killed all the monsters. And whose fault is that?

And the blushing girl's come back – ah, it makes me younger just to see you, child. I'd take you myself, but all my other wives would object. Hah! Look at that colour on her face, my young friends. There's fire under that skin. Marry her quick, before the fire catches somewhere it oughtn't.

It looks to me as if my daughter has brought every young sprig in the town, and some foreigners from up the coast as well, just to hear her old man speak of his fate. Flattering in a way – but you know that I'll tell you of Marathon. And you know that there is no nobler moment in all the history of men – of Hellenes. We stood against them, man to man, and we were better.

But it didn't start that way, not by as long a ride as a man could make in a year on a good horse.

For those of you who missed the first nights of my rambling story, I'm Arimnestos of Plataea. I told the story of how my father was the bronze-smith of our city, and how we marched to fight the Spartans at Oinoe, and fought three battles in a week. How he was murdered by his cousin Simon. How Simon sold me as a slave, far to the east among the men of Ionia, and how I grew to manhood as a slave in the house of a fine poet in Ephesus, one of the greatest cities in the world, right under the shadow of the Temple of Artemis. I was slave to Hipponax the poet and his son Archilogos. In time they freed me. I became a warrior, and then a great warrior, but when the Long War began – the war between the Medes and the Greeks – I served with the Athenians at Sardis.

Why, you might ask. My thugater will groan to hear me tell this again, but I loved Briseis. Indeed, to say I loved her – Hipponax's dark-haired daughter, Artemis's avatar and perhaps Aphrodite's as well, Helen returned to earth – well, to say I loved her is to say nothing. As you will hear, if you stay to listen.

Briseis wasn't the only person I loved in Ephesus. I loved Archilogos – the true friend of my youth. We were well matched in everything. I was his companion, first as a slave, and then free – and we competed. At everything. And I also loved Heraclitus, the greatest philosopher of his day. To me, the greatest ever, almost like a god in his wisdom. He, and he alone, kept me from growing to manhood as a pure killer. He gave me advice which I ignored – but which stayed in my head. To this day, in fact. He taught me that the river of our lives flows on and on and can never be reclaimed. Later, I knew that he'd tried to keep me from Briseis.

When her father caught us together, it was the end of my youth. I was cast out of the household, and that's why I was with the Athenians at Sardis, and not in the phalanx of the men of Ephesus to save Hipponax when the Medes gave him his mortal wound.

I found him screaming on the battlefield, and I sent him on the last journey because I loved him, even though he had been my owner. It was done with love, but his son, Archilogos, did not see it that way, and we became foes.

I spent the next years of the Ionian Revolt – the first years of the Long War – gaining word-fame with every blow I struck. I should blush to tell it – but why? When I served at Sardis, I was a man that other men would trust at their side in the phalanx. By the time I led my ship into the Persians at the big fight at Cyprus, I was a warrior that other men feared in the storm of bronze.

The Greeks won the sea-fight but lost on land, that day at Cyprus. And the back of the revolt should have been broken, but it was not. We retreated to Chios and Lesbos, and I joined Miltiades of Athens

– a great aristocrat, and a great pirate – and we got new allies, and the fighting switched to the Chersonese – the land of the Trojan War. We fought the Medes by sea and land. Sometimes we bested them. Miltiades made money and so did I. I owned my own ship, and I was rich.

I killed many men.

And then we faced the Medes in Thrace – just a few ships from each side. By then, Briseis had married the most powerful man in the Greek revolt – and had found him a broken reed. We beat the Persians and their Thracian allies and I killed her husband, even though he was supposedly on my side. I laugh even now – that was a good killing, and I spit on his shade.

But she didn't want me, except in her bed and in her thoughts. Briseis loved me as I loved her – but she meant to be Queen of the Ionians, not a pirate's trull, and all I was in those years was a bloody-handed pirate.

Fair enough. But it shattered me for a while.

I left Thrace and I left Miltiades, and I went home to Plataea. Where the man who had killed my father and married my mother was lording it over the family farm.

Simon, and his four sons. My cousins.

Your cousins too, thugater. Simon was a wreck of a man and a coward, but I'd not say the same of his get. They were tough bastards. I didn't hack him down. I went to the assembly, as my master Heraclitus would have wanted me to do.

The law killed old Simon the coward, but his sons wanted revenge.

And the Persians were determined to finish off the Ionians and put the Greeks under their heel.

And Briseis kept marrying great men, and finding them wanting.

The world, you know, is shaped like the bowl of an *aspis*. Out on the rim flows the edge of the river-sea that circles all, and up where the *porpax* binds a man's arm is the sun and the moon, and the great circle of earth fills all between. Medes and Persians, Scythians and Greeks and Ionians and Aeolians and Italians and Aethiopians and Aegyptians and Africans and Lydians and Phrygians and Carians and Celts and Phoenicians and the gods know who else fill the bowl of the aspis from rim to rim. And in those days, as the Long War began to take hold like a new-started fire on dry kindling, you could hear men talking of war, making war, killing, dying, making weapons and training in their use, all across the bowl of that aspis from rim to rim, until the murmur of the bronze-clad god's chorus filled the world.

It was the sixth year of the Long War, and Hipparchus was archon in Athens, and Myron was archon for his second term in Plataea. Tisikrites of Croton won the stade sprint at Olympia. The weather was good, the crops were rolling in.

I thought I might settle down and make myself a bronze-smith and a farmer, like my father before me.

Ares must have laughed.

Part I

Lade

The time will come, Milesians, devisers of evil deeds
When many will feast on you; a splendid gift for them,
Your wives will wash the feet of many long-haired men,
And other men will assume the care of my temple at Didyma

Oracle of Apollo to the Men of Miletus
In Herodotus, Book 6:19

I

Shield up.

Thrust overhand.

Turn – catch the spear on the rim of my shield, pivot on my toes and thrust at my opponent.

He catches my spear on his shield and grins. I can see the flash of his grin in the *tau* of his Corinthian helmet's faceplate. Then his plumes nod as he turns his head – checks the man behind him.

I thrust overhand, hard.

He catches my blow, pivots on the balls of his feet and steps back with his shield facing me.

His file-mate pushes past him, a heavy overhand blow driving me back half a step.

The music rises, the aulos pipe sounding faster, the drums beating the rhythm like the sound of marching feet.

I sidestep, faster, and my shield rim flashes like a live thing. My black spear is an iron-tipped tongue of death in my strong right hand and I am one with the men to the right and left, the men behind. I am not Arimnestos the killer of men. I am only one Plataean, and together, we are *this*.

'Plataeans!' I roar.

I plant my right foot. Every man in the front rank does the same, and the pipes howl, and every man crouches, screams and pushes forward, and three hundred voices call: *The Ravens of Apollo!* The roar shakes the walls and echoes from the Temple of Hera.

The music falls silent, and after a pause the whole assembly – all the free men and women, the slaves, the freedmen – erupt in applause.

Under my armour, I am covered in sweat.

Hermogenes – my opponent – puts his arms around me. 'That was ...'

There are no words to describe how good that was. We danced the *Pyrrhiche*, the war dance, with the picked three hundred men of Plataea, and Ares himself must have watched us.

Older men – the archon, the lawmakers – clasp my hand. My back is slapped so often that I worry they are pulling the laces on my scale armour.

Good to have you back, they all say.

I am happy.

Ting-ting.

   Ting-ting.

The day after the feast of Ares, and I was back at work – planishing. Planishing is when you use a hammer to smooth out finished work – *tap-tap, tap-tap*. The hammers need to be polished, and the anvil needs to be crisp and well surfaced, and you need a stake of just the right shape with a polished surface, and your strokes need to be perfectly placed, crisp and all the same strength. It was not my strong point.

I remember it well, because I was making myself a new helmet, and thinking of Miltiades. All my other orders were completed, winter was coming and there was no reason that I shouldn't play with my equipment. My barns were full, my people fed and I had a sack of silver buried under the shop floor – without having to send to Miltiades for my gold. I had decided I would not go back to Miltiades.

Miltiades of Athens – the tyrant of the Chersonese – was my father's patron, and sometimes mine. I'd fought and killed for him, but I'd left him when the killing became a habit I had to break. And when Briseis said she would not have me. Hah! One of those is the true reason.

But Athens, mighty Athens – the bulwark of the Hellenes against the Persians – was deeply divided. Miltiades was no hero back then. Most Athenians saw him as a fool and a tyrant who was bringing the wrath of the Great King of Persia down on Greece. Rumour came over the mountains from Attica and Athens that he was to be declared *atimos* and lose his citizen rights – that he would be exiled – that he would be murdered. We heard that the faction of the tyrant-slayers – the Alcmaeonids – was ascendant.

I have to tell you, as an aside, that calling the Alcmaeonids tyrant-slayers is both incorrect and laughable, but a fine example of how easily fooled mortal men are by good orators. The mighty Alcmaeonids, the richest family in Attica and perhaps all of Greece

– one of their many scions killed one of Pisistratus's sons in Athens. It was a private quarrel, but we still call the overhand sword cut the 'Harmodius blow', and most men think that the dead man was the tyrant of Athens.

In fact, the only reason that the Alcmaeonids would have arranged the death of the Pisistratids was so that they could seize the city and rule themselves. They were all in the game – all the great men of Athens. They prated about democracy, but what they wanted was power.

In the early days of the Long War, I was bitter – disillusioned, even – to find that the heroic Miltiades was a pirate and a thief, not a freedom fighter. Oh, he was brave as Achilles and wily as Odysseus, but beneath his aristocratic manners lurked a man who would kill a beggar for an obol if it would finance his schemes. After a while, I took to hating him for his failure to be the man I wanted him to be. But I'll tell you this, my children – he was a better man than any of the Pisistratids or the Alcmaeonids. When he wanted something, he reached for it.

At any rate, it was late summer and the rumours of open conflict in Athens, our ally, had begun to disturb even sleepy Plataea. As the saying went, when Athens caught a cold, Plataea sneezed.

I recall all this, because I was thinking of Miltiades while I was working on my helmet. I thought about him a lot. Because, to tell the truth, I was already bored.

I'd shaped the helmet twice – first, I'd made the bowl far too deep, and the result looked so odd that I'd melted the bronze, added a little more tin and poured a new plate on the slate where Pater had done the same. I made a wine bucket from that bronze. I didn't trust twice-forged stuff for armour.

The second time I was more careful with my prayers and I made a real invocation to Hephaestus, and I took time to draw the curve in charcoal on a board as part of the invocation. I raised the bowl of the helmet carefully, for an hour or two each day after propping the vines and gathering olives with my slaves and my household, and this helmet grew like a child in a mother's belly. Like a miracle. So on that day, I remember I was growing afraid – I, who feared no man in the meeting of the spears, was afraid. Because the object I was making was beautiful, and better than I ever expected of my own work, and I was scared that I might ruin it.

So I planished slowly.

Ting-ting.

Ting-ting.

The anvil rang like a temple bell with every blow. My apprentice, Tiraeus, held the work and rotated it as I requested. He was older than me, and in some ways better trained, but he'd never settled with one master, and before he met me, he'd never even learned the signs that any man can learn who dedicates to the smith god. I'd had him a month, and he'd changed. Just like that – like molten metal settling into the mould. He'd been ready to take a new shape, and he was no work of mine, but it still felt odd to have an older man – and in many ways a better smith – as my apprentice.

He raised his head, as if listening.

Ting-ting.

Ting-ting.

Like a temple bell, my anvil called aloud to the gods.

I was deep into it – the focus that the gods send to a man intent on a task – when I heard what Tiraeus heard. The same focus, to be honest, that comes in combat. How Aristides would writhe to hear me suggest a link between the two.

I ramble. I heard a horse in the yard.

'Don't stop,' my apprentice ordered. That'll give you an idea of his actual status. He gave me orders.

Behind me, Bion, my father's former slave apprentice and now almost a master smith in his own right, was rewelding a pot. His hammer rang on his own anvil – heavier blows than mine.

'What the man says,' Bion grunted. 'Never stop once you're in a task.'

That was a long speech, for Bion. But I was young, and a horse in the yard promised adventure. As I said, months of farming and smithing had left me – bored.

I took water from the bucket by the door and saw a young man in a fine wool *chlamys* slip off his horse's neck, showing a lot of leg and muscle, as pretty young men are wont to do.

'I have a message for Lord Arimnestos,' he said portentously. His disappointment showed in every line of his body. He'd expected better.

Pen – my sister, Penelope – came down the steps from her eyrie with the women, and Hermogenes, Bion's son and my best friend, came in from the fields, both drawn by the horseman. I let Pen have the boy. He was handsome, and Pen needed some suitors or my life was going to become very difficult indeed.

My mother stayed in the women's porch and didn't emerge – probably because she was drunk. Hades – for a certainty she was drunk. She was the only child of the *basileus* of Hispae – a small place west of Plataea. She ran off with my pater – a smith, but a powerful man in his own right. She thought he'd become a great man. He did – but not in the way she wanted. He became a great smith. She became a drunk. Did I say this was a pretty story?

Back to it, then. The handsome boy with all the muscles paid me no attention at all. I had a rag wrapped around my groin and was otherwise naked. I was covered in soot and looked like a slave, and he'd have had to be a careful observer – not something usually found in handsome boys – to note that I had the muscles of an athlete, not a farrier.

'I am Lord Arimnestos's sister, Penelope,' she told the young sprig. 'My brother is busy. May I take your message, sir?'

That flustered young Paris, I can tell you. 'My message – is for the lord himself.' He looked around for a social equal – someone to punish all these slaves and women.

I laughed and left Pen to the enjoyment of his discomfiture. My helmet was calling me. I drank another dipper of water and got my hammer back in my hand.

Ting-ting.

Ting—

I realized that there was a boy in my workshop. Where in Hades had he come from? He was Styges – the dark boy from the hero's tomb. No one was clear whether he'd been a prisoner or a bandit – he'd become part of Idomeneus's retinue. I think he'd been a thief – he was silent as the grave.

So much to explain! Idomeneus was Cretan – a soldier and archer who had been my hypaspist – my squire – in the fighting for years. When I cleared out my father's house, Idomeneus made himself priest of the hero's tomb. I had trained at that tomb as a boy, and it was my place – my sacred place. And Idomeneus, for all his madness and his delight in killing and his debauchery, was my friend. And a member of my *oikia*, my household, my own retinue of trusted men and women.

Styges was in Idomeneus's oikia. He was the Cretan's lover, his *eromenos* and his hypaspist too, as they do things in Crete.

'My master needs you, lord,' the young man whispered, his eyes downcast.

My hand hesitated, the head of the iron hammer high in the air. I let it fall – *tang* – and cursed. A clear mis-stroke, and I'd left a small flaw in the surface of the helmet.

Tiraeus put his hand to my mouth. 'Curses won't change the metal,' he said.

See? He had ten more years than I had. In many ways, I was an overgrown boy with a talent for ripping men's souls from their bodies. He was a mature man – a man who'd seen enough hardship to learn to make better choices.

'Fuck,' I said. But I didn't throw the helmet across the shop. I'd learned that much. Nor did I gut Styges with the heavy knife I always wore – even in the shop, or lying with a slave girl – although the red rage flashed over my eyes.

Instead, I placed it on a leather bag, washed my hands in the basin and nodded to Styges.

'I need a cup of wine, and I'll be happy to give you one as well.' I did my best to imitate Achilles and be a man of warm hospitality. Even to a catamite-thief who had just caused me to miss a hammer stroke. I was growing up.

Styges bowed. 'I am honoured, lord.' Of course, in Crete, men who were called 'lord' were seldom covered in soot and bronze scale, with hands so black that the skin couldn't be seen. But in Boeotia, things were different. Besides, I had a great deal more respect for Styges than for the perfumed boy in my courtyard.

My sister, Penelope, came out of the house with wine. She poured a libation to Artemis, as was right for her, and then to Hephaestus, for me, before serving the rest of the pitcher of wine to Tiraeus, Bion, Hermogenes, Styges and my guest. Of the crowd, only the guest and Pen could be said to be wearing clothes. I just want you to see this in your heads.

Only when Styges had a cup of wine in his fist did I question him. 'Why does Idomeneus need me?' I asked.

'He killed a man,' Styges replied.

'What man?' I asked. 'A Plataean?' By which I meant: *A citizen? Or a man of no account?*

'No, lord,' Styges said. 'In fact, we killed two men. One, a soldier at the shrine, the other,' and Styges smiled, 'I killed myself, one of the bandits, lord. They knew each other – were planning to escape or perhaps take the shrine. Lord Idomeneus thinks they meant to kill all of us.'

He had a fresh cut, I realized, running from his shoulder to the middle of his side. He saw me looking at it and nodded, beaming with pride. 'He had a knife and I did not.'

This sort of heroic understatement was the rule of the Greeks, and Idomeneus, for all his blood-madness, ran a tight ship up there on the mountain.

'The soldier we killed was Athenian,' Styges said, his smile fading. 'My master is afraid that he was a man of consequence.'

That got my attention.

'My lord, is it nothing to you that I have travelled here from Sardis?' the beautiful young man asked. In truth, they were both quite handsome – the aristocrat like a statue of an athlete, and Styges a more practical, down-to-earth set of muscles, scars and smooth skin.

I could tell that Pen was pleased by both.

I smiled at the aristocrat. 'Young man, I apologize for my rude dress and quick welcome, and I ask that you stay a day or two. This matter concerns my honour, and must be dealt with immediately.'

He blushed – I hid a smile – and his eyes flickered to Pen's. 'I would be honoured to be a guest here. But I have an important message—'

'Which I'll hear when I return.' I nodded to him. The gods were blinding me. If I had paused a moment to listen to him ... But I thought my duty was calling me, and I didn't like him or his airs.

'Mind that they don't put you to work in the forge,' Pen muttered.

'I'll be back by midday,' I said, and ordered the slaves to saddle my horse.

The gods were laughing. And Moira spun her thread so fine ...

It was the edge of darkness by the time I rode up the hill to the shrine. It may seem comic to you lot, to hear that I rode a horse. Now I'm lord of a thousand shaggy Thracian ponies and half a hundred Persian beauties, but in Boeotia in those days, the ownership of a horse was a matter for some remark, and I had four. Laugh if you like – four horses made me one of the richest men in Plataea.

Styges ran by my side. He'd fought a mortal combat, run thirty stades to fetch me, drunk a horn of wine and now he'd run thirty stades back to the shrine. Later, when I tell you of the deeds of arms my people performed, think on this – we made hard men then. We

13

bred them to it, like dogs to the hunt. In Sparta, they trained aristo-crats to be superb. In Attica and Boeotia, we trained every free man to be excellent. Calculate the difference if you like.

I could smell the blood at the tomb, even over the night air. I took the leather bottle off my shoulder and poured a libation to old Leitos, who'd gone to windy Troy from green Plataea – and come back alive, to die in old age. Now that, my friends, is a hero.

At the tomb, we have a tradition – that it was Leitos who stopped bold Hector's rush at the ships, not by clever fighting or mad courage, but by getting lesser men to lock their shields and stop his god-sent killing rage. Not a mighty killer, but a man who led other men as a shepherd tends sheep. Who kept his men alive and brought them home.

So men come to the tomb from all over Greece – men who have seen too much war. Sometimes they are broken past repair, but if they are not, the priest feeds them wine, listens to them and gives them work, or perhaps a small mission. And the completion of that work makes them clean, so that they can go back to the world of men who are not killers.

Sometimes, though, a man comes to the tomb with the mark on him. How can I tell this? It is the mark of evil, or of a soul past saving. And then the priest, who is always a retired killer himself, must face the man and kill him on the precinct wall, so that his shade screams as it goes down to nothing, lost for ever, and his blood waters the souls of the dead and feeds the hero.

Heh, heh. Boeotia is a tough place, and no mistake. And we've little tolerance for those men who've lost their way. Can I tell you a hard truth, friends? If a killer goes bad, the best the rest can do is put him down. Wolves know it, dogs know it and lions know it. Men need to know it too.

Even when the man is your friend. But that's another story.

More wine here.

Idomeneus came out and held my horse as I slid down.

'Sorry to call you all the way here, lord.'

The dent in my perfect helmet still rankled, and I couldn't get the thought of a messenger from Sardis out of my head – Sardis, the capital of Lydia, the satrapy of the Persian empire closest to Greece. Who would send a messenger from Sardis? And why in the name of all the gods hadn't I stopped to ask?

But Idomeneus was a man who'd saved my life fifty times. Hard to stay angry with him. 'I needed to come out, anyway. If I stay at the forge too long, I might forget who I used to be.'

'Used to be?' Idomeneus laughed his mad laugh. 'Achilles reborn, now hammering bronze?'

'So, you killed a man?' I asked. One of the women pressed a horn cup into my hand. Watered, spiced wine, just warmed. I drank thankfully.

'We just killed us an Alcmaeonid,' Idomeneus said. His eyes glinted in the last light. 'He stood there on the precinct wall and proclaimed his parentage and dared us even to think of killing him. He thought that big name would protect him.'

I shook my head. The Alcmaeonids were rich, powerful and nasty. Their wealth was boundless, and I couldn't imagine what one of them was doing at the tomb of the hero. 'Perhaps he was lying?' I asked.

Idomeneus produced something from under his chlamys. It flashed red-gold in the last beams of the sun. It was a clasp belt, the sort of thing a very rich man wore with his *chiton*, and every link was beaten gold. It was worth more than my farm, and I have a good farm.

'Fuck,' I said.

'He had the mark of evil,' Idomeneus said. 'What could I do?'

I went and looked at the corpse, stretched over the precinct wall in the traditional way. He had been a big man – a head taller than me, with a bell cuirass of bronze as thick as a new-flayed hide.

He probably weighed twice as much as wiry Idomeneus. He had a single wound, a spear-thrust in his left eye. Idomeneus was a very, very dangerous man. The Athenian nobleman must have been too stupid to see that – or the mark truly was on him and the hero needed blood.

The armour was of the best, as was his helmet.

'Fuck,' I said again. 'What was he doing here?'

Idomeneus shook his head. Behind him, men and women were lighting the lamps. There were six huts now, instead of just one, as there had been in my youth. My Thracians had one, and former bandits were four to a hut in the others, except the last, which was for the women. They were clean and orderly. Dead deer hung in rows from the trees, and there was a whole boar, and piles of salted skins, rolled tight. Idomeneus ran the tomb like a military camp.

'He was recruiting,' I said aloud, answering my own question. Perhaps the grey-eyed goddess stood at my shoulder and said the

15

words into my head, but I saw it. He was in his best armour because he wanted to impress. But he'd challenged Idomeneus – somehow – and the mad fuck had killed him.

These things happen.

My problem, I thought, was how to clean it up. They were all in my oikia, so I bore the responsibility and it was my place to put it right. Besides, I knew most of the big men in Athens. I knew Aristides, and he was related to the Alcmaeonids by marriage and by blood. I was sure he could make it right, if anyone could.

I considered the alternative – I could do nothing. It was possible that no one knew where this man was, or what he had intended. It was possible that even if his people found out, they would take no revenge.

'In the morning, I'll cast an augury,' I said. 'Perhaps the *logos* will offer me an answer.'

Idomeneus nodded. 'You'll stay the night?' he asked.

'Just as you wanted, you mad Cretan,' I said.

'You need to get away from the farm before you turn into a farmer,' he said.

I had the glimmer of a suspicion that my mad hypaspist had killed a powerful man merely to get me to come up the hill and drink with him. I sighed.

Styges put a warm cup in my hand and led me to the fire circle, where all the former bandits sat. We sang hymns to the gods while the bowl of the heavens turned over our heads. The firelight dappled the ancient oaks around the hero's tomb. Styges took out a *kithara* and sang alone, and then we sang with him – Spartan songs and aristocratic songs – and I sang Briseis's favourite, one of Sappho's.

My eyes kept meeting those of a slave girl. They weren't precisely slaves – their status was not simple. They'd belonged to a farmer – a widow – and the bandits had killed her and taken her chattels. Then I'd killed the bandits. Whose were they? Were they free? They slept with all the men and did too many chores.

She was short, almost pretty, and one of her legs was twisted. Our eyes kept meeting, and later she laughed aloud while I was inside her. Her breath was sweet, and she deserved better than a hero who thought only of another woman. But despite her limp and her odd face, she stuck in my head. In those days I must have mounted fifty slave girls a year. Yet I remember her. You'll see why.

*

In the morning, I hunted on the mountain with Idomeneus, but if he'd left any deer alive within half a day's walk, I didn't see them. But we did cross the trail where we'd ambushed the bandits a year before. The road goes as high as it ever does on Cithaeron's flank, then drops down into a mud-hole, after which it climbs a little before starting the long descent, first to the tomb and then to Plataea herself.

There was a cart abandoned by the mud-hole, and tracks.

The cart was loaded with weapons and leather armour – good, strong stuff. And there were a few coins scattered on the ground.

'He had servants,' I said.

'And they ran,' Idomeneus said. 'No need to cast an augury, is there?'

The abandoned wagon meant that the rich man had had attendants – men who even now were running back to the family estates in Attica with a tale of murder.

'We could chase them down and kill them,' Idomeneus said, helpfully.

'Sometimes, you really piss me off,' I said. And I meant it.

'I feel bad,' he admitted. 'What are you going to do?'

'I'll ride into Attica and make it right,' I said. 'Send to the farm, get Epictetus to fill a wagon with my work, and have it head for Athens. I'll meet the wagon in the Agora in Athens in ten days. Before the Herakleion. Then my whole trip won't be wasted fixing your fuck-up.'

Idomeneus nodded sullenly. 'He had the mark on him,' he said, like a child who feels a parent's law is unfair. 'The hero wanted his blood.'

'I believe you,' I said. And I looked at him. He met my eye – but only just. 'You can't come,' I said. 'Not unless you want to die,' I added. He shrugged.

My entertainment of the night before was standing a little apart. I palmed a coin to give her, but she shook her head and looked modestly at the ground.

'I want to go,' she said. 'I can be a free woman in Attica. I'll warm your bed on the trail.'

I considered it for a while. 'Yes,' I said.

The other two women cried to see her go.

I'd have done better if I'd stopped to cast the auguries. But who knows? The gods like a surprise.

★

We made good time up Cithaeron's flank. Up where the oak trees falter, I killed a young boar with my bow. From there, and with that as an omen, I took the old road and we climbed all the way to the top of the ancient mountain, and made camp in the wood of the Daidala, the special place of all the Corvaxae, where the crows feast on meat we provide for the god.

I made a good camp, with a wool sheet as a tent and a big fire. Then I left the slave girl to cook meat from the hero's tomb and I climbed up to the altar. In our family, we say that the altar is to Cithaeron himself, and not to Zeus, who is, after all, an interloper here.

There was a sign on the altar, the remnants of a burnt offering and a hank of black wool. So – Simon's sons lived. And they had come here in the dark of the moon to curse someone. Not hard to guess who. I smiled. I remember that smile – a wolf's snarl. Hate comes easily when you are young.

It was a clear night, and I could see out to the rim of the world, and everywhere I looked, I could see fire. And I thought: *War is coming*. The thought came from the god, and his eyes helped mine to see the girdle of fire all around the world, standing there on the summit of the mountain.

I heaped brush on top of the pile of ash on the old altar, and I rolled the boar's hide, hooves and bones around the fat, then lit the fire. That fire must have been visible to every man and woman from Thebes to Athens. I set the boar to burning and made my prayers. I fed the fire until it was so great that I couldn't stand near it naked, and then I went back down to where the slave girl waited.

She served me food. 'Will you free me,' she asked, 'or sell me?'

I laughed. 'I'll free you,' I said. 'With that twisted foot, you're not worth selling, honey. Besides, I keep my word. Do I not?'

She didn't laugh. 'I wouldn't know.' She stuck out her bad foot and stared at it.

'Your barley broth is delicious,' I said, and it was. That's all the flirtation a slave gets. 'I was a slave, honey. I know what it's like. And I know that all my talk isn't worth shit until you have your freedom tablet in your hand. But I give you my word, by the high altar of my ancestors, that I will free you in the Agora of Athens and leave you twenty drachmas as dowry.'

Every god in Olympus must have been listening. A man needs to be careful when he swears, and careful what he promises.

'The sons of men lie,' she said, her voice hollow, so that just for a

18

moment I wondered what goddess was sharing my campfire. 'Will you be different?'

'Try me,' I said with a young man's arrogance. I moved towards her, and as I put a hand behind her head, the ravens came, a great flock, and they alighted in the trees around my fire – the same trees where the Corvaxae feed them, of course – and they knew me. I had never seen so many. The fire reflected their eyes – a thousand points of fire – and when I put my mouth over hers, her eyes glowed red in the fire, too.

We made love anyway. Ah, youth.

We were five days crossing Cithaeron, at least in part because I became infatuated with her. Sometimes one body just fits another – hard to describe to you virgins. Suffice it to say that despite her twisted foot and odd face, my body adored hers in a way I have seldom experienced. I wanted her every minute, and the wanting was not slaked by the having, as it is so often with men, especially young men.

After we had made love on a rock by the trail, where you can first see the rich blue of the sea over Attica, she rose from my best efforts, smiled and threw her chiton over her shoulder and strolled on, naked, by my horse.

'Don't you want to get dressed?' I asked her.

She smiled and shrugged. 'Why? It will only come off again before the sun goes down a finger's breadth.'

And she was right. I could not have enough of her.

She wouldn't tell me her name, and sometimes I called her Briseis. That got a bitter laugh and a hard bite. I begged her and tickled her and offered her money, but she said that telling her true name would break the spell. So I called her Slave Girl, and she resented it.

After the slowest trip over the mountain in the history of the Greeks, we came down by the fort at Oinoe, where my brother had died. I poured wine to his shade and we rode on, the horse useful now. We didn't camp in Attica – I was a man of property, and we stayed in inns or I claimed guest status from men who I knew a little, like Eumenios of Eleusis, who was happy to see me, toasted me in good wine and warned me that he'd heard that the Alcmaeonids were out for my blood.

I sneered. 'They don't even know who I am,' I said. 'I'm just some hick from Boeotia.'

Eumenios shook his head. 'No. You're a warrior and a friend of Miltiades – and Aristides. It's said in the city that you can lead three hundred picked men of Plataea over the mountain whenever Miltiades snaps his fingers.'

I shook my head and drank my wine. 'Who the fuck would say that? Myron is the archon – Hades' brother. In Plataea we care very little for who lords it in Athens, as long as the grain prices are good!'

But then I thought of the black wool on Cithaeron's altar. Simon's sons would spread that story, if it would help them to revenge.

In the morning, Eumenios pretended he'd missed a night's sleep because of my antics with my slave girl. He saw me mounted, poured a libation and sent me on my way. But before I'd turned my mare's head out of his gate, he caught my ankle.

'Go carefully,' he said. 'They'll kill you if they can. Or bring you to law.'

Nine days on the road, and we came to Athens.

My daughter, and young Herodotus, have both been to Athens – but I'll tell you about the queen of Greek cities anyway. Athens is not like any other city in the world, and I've been everywhere from the Gates of Heracles to the Mountains of the Moon.

Most men come to Athens from the sea. We came down from the mountains to the west, but the effect is the same. The first thing you see is the Acropolis. It was different then – now they have new temples a-building, fantastic stuff in white marble to rival anything in the east, but it was impressive enough in my day, with the big stone buildings that the Pisistratids, the tyrants, had put up. New temples, and new government buildings, and power in every stone. Athens was rich. Other cities in Greece were stronger – or thought they were stronger – Thebes, and Sparta, and Corinth – but any man with his wits about him knew that Athens was the queen of cities. Her Acropolis had held the Palace of Theseus, and men from that palace went to the war in Troy. She was old, and wise, and strong. And rich.

More people lived within the precincts of Athens than in the whole of Boeotia, or so men said. The city was bigger than Sardis, and had almost twelve thousand citizens of military age.

Athens had bronze-smiths and potters – the best in the world – and farmers and fishermen and sailors and oarsmen and perfumers and tanneries and weavers and sword-smiths and lamp-makers and men who dyed fabric and men who whitened leather and men who did nothing but plait hair or teach young men to fight. Moreover, they had women who did most of these things. The world was turned on its head in Athens, and in my time I've met women who played instruments, women who coached athletes, women who wove and women who painted pots – even a woman philosopher. It was the city.

The City.

They're a greedy, rapacious, foxy lot, the Athenians. They lie, steal and covet other men's possessions, and they argue about everything.

I've always liked them.

I'd never been to Aristides' house, but he was a famous man, even then, so it was easy enough to ask directions. But I had to turn down a dozen offers on my slave girl – the truth is, she shone with some power, and no man who saw her cared an obol about her limp – and for some reason men fancied me, too, and even offered for my horse and my saddle blanket and my sword and anything else visible.

We should have passed around the shoulder of the Areopagus and walked on, down the hills to the cool countryside on the east side of the city. Instead, I paused for a cup of cheap wine. What I really wanted was to walk down the street of the bronze-smiths, so I left my horse with Slave Girl and headed to the Agora. Now, there's a fancy new temple for Hephaestus. Back then, it was a much smaller affair, with tiny cramped streets all over the low hill and a small shrine to Athena and Hephaestus at the top – just one priest and no priestess. But I went, made a small sacrifice and left the meat for the poor, as befitted a foreigner, and then I walked down into the smiths' quarter. I'd have done better to take the Boeotian dog-cap off my head – but I didn't.

I gave the sign to the priest, of course, and he passed me the sign for Attica, so that other smiths would treat me as a guest. Then I worked my way down the hill, looking at their shops, admiring their bellows or their tools – or their hordes of apprentices. I finally stopped where an iron-smith was roughing out spear-points – beautiful things, long as my forearm with light sockets and heavy ribs for punching straight through armour.

'You look like a lad who can use one of these,' the smith said. 'For a dirt-eating Theban, I mean,' he added.

I spat. 'I'm a dirt-eating Plataean,' I said. 'Fuck Thebes.'

'Fuck your mother!' he said with pleasure. 'No offence meant, stranger. Any Plataean is welcome here. Were you in the three battles?'

'Every one,' I answered.

'*Pais!*' the master called, and when one of his boys came, he said, 'Get this hero a cup of Chian.'

'You?' I asked politely.

'Oh, I stood my ground once or twice that week,' he said. He extended his hand and we shook, and I passed the sign.

'You're a smith!' he said. 'Need a place to stay?'

That's how it was, back then. Sad, to see those old ways go. Hospitality was like a god to us – to all Greeks.

I had started to explain that I was on my way to see Aristides when a well-dressed man leading a horse leaned into the stall.

'Did I just hear you say you were a Plataean?' he asked.

I didn't know him from Oedipus, but I was courteous. 'I have that honour. I am Arimnestos of the Corvaxae of Plataea.'

The man bowed. 'You've just saved me quite a journey, then,' he said. 'I'm Cleitus of the Alcmaeonids of Attica. And you are under arrest, for murder.'

2

The law of Athens is a complex, dangerous monster, and no foreigner like myself could possibly master it. I stood there with my mouth agape, like a fool, and the smith came to my rescue.

'Says who?' he asked. 'I haven't missed an assembly since the feast of Dionysus, and no one has voted a capital charge.'

The Alcmaeonid shrugged. 'You don't look like the kind of fellow to vote on the hill,' he said casually. What he meant was that iron-smiths didn't get invited to join the Areopagitica, the council of elders, mostly old aristocrats, who ran the murder trials. I think my smith might have let it go, except that this Cleitus was such an arrogant sod that he gave offence by breathing.

'I don't have to be a sodding aristo to know the law,' the smith said. 'Where'd the charge come from?'

'None of your business,' Cleitus said. He reached for my chlamys. 'Best come along, boy.'

Some men claim that the gods play no role in human affairs. Such statements always make me laugh. Cleitus and I have crossed wits – and swords – often enough. He's as wily as Odysseus and as strong as Heracles, but on that day he couldn't spare the time to calm the ruffled plumage of an iron-smith. What might have happened if he had?

The smith stepped around the counter of his shop with a speed that belied his bulk. 'Where's your wand, then?' he asked.

Cleitus shrugged. 'With my men, in the Agora.'

'Better go and get it, rich boy,' the smith said. 'Hey, sons of Hephaestus!' he called. 'Down your tools and come!'

Cleitus rallied his wits instantly. 'Now – master smith, no need for that. I'll get my wand. But this man is a killer!'

'A killer of Athens's enemies,' I said. A good shot – and it went right into the bullseye. 'Not an unlawful killer.'

By then, there were fifty apprentices looking for a fight, and a dozen smiths, and every hand held a hammer. Cleitus looked around. 'I'll be back with my men,' he said.

'Bring your staff of warrant, or don't bother,' my new friend the smith called. Then he turned to me. 'Tell me your tale, and make it swift. Men are missing work.'

So I told him. I left nothing out – not even the dimple I'd left in my helmet.

He sent an apprentice for Aristides.

I sat on a folding stool that was provided for me – fine ironwork, and very elegant – and began to breathe more easily.

And then I heard the screams. There were a fair number of screams in Athens – high-pitched, often in fun, sometimes in earnest. But by the third scream, I realized that this was my slave girl. I rose to my feet.

My smith looked at me. 'Where are you going?' he asked.

'That's my slave,' I said.

He shook his head. 'I've pledged my people to this,' he said. 'You aren't going anywhere.'

'I've made her an oath to free her,' I said. 'Send a boy – send a pair of men with hammers. Please. I ask you.'

He spat orders at a couple of shop boys – big ones – and they hurried out of the door.

'Arimnestos, eh?' he asked. 'I've heard of you. Killer of men, right enough. Thought you'd be bigger.'

I tried to sit still. The screams had stopped. Time passed.

More time passed.

Finally, the boys came back.

'Cleitus has left the market,' the bigger of the two said. 'He's got your horse and your girl. He talked a lot of crap about what you took from his brother. Did you kill his brother, mister?'

I shook my head. 'No,' I said, and I felt tired. Did I say I loved Athens? Athens makes me tired. They have a great many rules. 'Can he really take these things from me?' I asked the smith.

He shrugged. 'Alcmaeonids do what they like,' he said. 'Most commoners won't even try to stand against them.' He grinned. 'Lucky you're a smith.'

'He's no smith,' said a voice behind my chair, and there was Athens's leading pillar of justice, the greatest prig ever to lead warriors in the field. A man so driven by fairness that he had no space left for ambition.

I embraced him anyway, because I loved him, despite the fact we had nothing in common. It was Aristides. He was still tall, lanky, graceful like a man who's had the best training the drachma can buy all his life.

'I gather you've turned to crime,' he said. I like to think it was a rare show of humour, and not a statement of fact.

'Not true, my lord. This scion of the Alcmaeonids was killed by a man in my service – at a shrine, for impiety. I've given orders for his body and his armour to be brought here, and all his possessions that weren't looted by his own servants. They will be here in a matter of days.' I shrugged. 'I am a man of property, not a freebooter, my lord.'

Aristides nodded solemnly. 'I'm pleased to hear it.'

'He's a smith, right enough,' the iron-smith said. 'He knows the signs.'

Aristides looked at me under his bushy eyebrows. 'Always more to you than meets the eye, young man. So you are a smith?' Young man, he called me. He was less than ten years my senior. But he had the dignity of an old man.

'A bronze-smith,' I said. 'And a farmer now. My property brought me three hundred *medimnoi* this autumn.'

Aristides laughed. 'I never expected you to rise to the hippeis class,' he said.

'I'm not sure that I still qualify,' I returned. 'The Alcmaeonids just stole my best horse and my slave girl.'

Aristides' smile was wiped off his face. 'Really?'

Smiths and apprentices pressed around him, each telling his own version of the story.

'Come to my house,' Aristides said. 'I'll send to the council and announce that I have you in my custody and that I'll represent you at the trial. Then everything will be legal.'

'What about my horse?' I asked. 'And my girl?'

He didn't answer.

I shook hands with every smith who had aided me, thanked them all and walked off into the evening with Aristides and a dozen young men he had about him – all armed with heavy staves, I noticed. When we were clear of the industrial quarter, Aristides wrinkled his nose.

'I've seen you in the storm of bronze, Plataean. You are a man of worth. How do you stand the stink of all that commerce?' He didn't slacken his step, and he was a tall man.

25

I shrugged. 'Money smells the same, whether earned at the point of the spear or in the sweat of a shop,' I said.

Aristides shook his head. 'But without virtue. Without glory.'

'You're arguing with the wrong man,' I answered. 'My master taught me that "War is the king and master of all, some men it makes lords, and others it makes slaves."' I laughed, and then my laughter stopped. 'What's happening here? Your lads are all armed, and those Alcmaeonids were out for my blood.'

'Later,' he said.

We walked around the steep hill, its rock worn smooth from hundreds of men climbing to the top, where criminal trials were held, and then past the slums on the east side and back up a big road, the road to the Temple of Poseidon at Sounion. The moon was up by the time we came to a big gate.

'My farm,' Aristides said with pride. 'I don't sleep in the city any more. I expect I'll be exiled soon, if not killed.' He said it with the flat certainty you hear from a veteran on the night before he takes his death blow.

'You? Exiled?' I shook my head. 'Five years ago you were the golden boy of Athens.'

'I still am,' he said. 'Men think I seek to be tyrant, when in fact I seek only to provide justice – even to your friends the smiths.'

'There are noble men – men of worth – even in the forges and the potters' shops,' I insisted.

'Of course! Democracy wouldn't function if there were not. But they keep trying to insist on increased political rights, when any thinking man knows that only a man of property can control a city. We're the only ones with the training. That smith could no more vote on the Areopagitica than I could dish a helmet.'

Aristides shed his chlamys and chiton, and I noted he was still in top fighting trim. As we talked, slaves attended us. I was stripped, oiled and dressed in a better garment than I'd worn since my last bout of piracy – all while listening to Aristides.

'Helmets are raised, not dished,' I said.

'Just my point,' he said.

I shook my head. 'Allow me to disagree with my host,' I said.

He smiled politely.

'Perhaps it is that the perfection of any trade – war, sculpture, poetry, iron-smithing, even tanning or shoe-making – provides a man with the tools of mind to allow a mature man to take an active part in politics,' I said.

He rubbed his chin. 'Well put. And not an argument I'd heard put in exactly that way before. But you are not proposing that all men are equal?'

I sneered. 'I've stood in the haze of Ares too often to think that, my lord.'

He nodded. 'Just so. But an equality of excellence? I must say that I admire the notion. But that equates politics and war, which are noble pursuits, with ironwork and trade, which are not.'

I took wine from a woman who had to be his wife. I bowed deeply, and she smiled.

'Arguing with my husband?' she said. 'A waste of breath, unless it's about the running of this house, and then he loses all interest. You are Arimnestos of Plataea?' She had gold pins in her chiton and her hair was piled on her head like a mountain. She was not beautiful, but her face radiated intelligence. Athena might have looked so, if she were to dress as a matron.

'I am he, despoina.' I bowed again.

'Somehow, from my husband's stories, I thought you might be bigger. On the other hand, you're as beautiful as a god, which he somehow forgot to mention. Every slave girl in the house will be at your door. I'll just go and lock them away, lest we have a plague of the nine-months sickness in my house, eh?' She smiled.

'Women are not allowed in the assembly,' Aristides said, 'because if they were, we'd be left with nothing to do but move heavy objects. This is my dear wife Jocasta.'

She twirled her keys on her girdle and stepped out of the room.

'Tell me your notion then,' Aristides said. 'You speak well, and men seldom face me in debate.'

I shrugged. 'I am as outmatched as a boy with a stave would be against me in the phalanx, lord. But, as you are so polite as to hear me out ... You assume that war and politics are noble. You assume that they are ends to themselves. But you cannot make war without spears, and we have no spears without iron-smiths.'

'My point exactly – the iron-smith is less noble than the warrior because his craft is subordinate.' Aristides smiled as he made his point – his kill-shot, he thought.

'But my lord, if you will accept my expertise,' I said carefully, because I did not want to anger him, 'war is a terrible end unto itself.

I have made more war than you, although I am younger. War is a terrible thing.'

'But without it, we could not be free,' Aristides said.

'Ah, so *freedom* is the higher goal.' I smiled. Aristides frowned, and then he grinned.

'By the gods,' he said, 'if all smiths were like you, I'd replace the council of elders with smiths tonight!'

I shrugged, and then met his grin. 'Remember, lord, I was the pupil of Heraclitus.'

He nodded. 'Yes, in truth, you are an aristocrat – as you were educated as one!'

'While being a slave,' I added. And drank my wine.

But Aristides did not laugh. 'This is no matter for light talk,' he said. 'Athens is an experiment – an experiment that may mean life or death to her. We're attempting to push responsibility for the city *down* – as far down as we feel that free men have the power to think and vote. The further down we push these rights, the more fools we must tolerate—'

'And the more shields you have in the phalanx,' I said.

'And the harder it is for the Pisistratids or the Alcmaeonids to restore the tyranny,' he countered.

'Is that what this is about?' I asked. 'The tyranny of Athens? Again?' I'd had four summers of listening to Miltiades plot to take the city. Frankly, I couldn't imagine why any of them wanted it.

Aristides nodded. He sat down. 'The Medes are coming,' he said.

That was news, and no mistake. I sat on a couch. 'When?'

'I have no idea, but the city is arming and preparing. You know we are at war with Aegina?' he asked.

I shrugged. Athens and Aegina and Corinth ruled the waves – so of course they were not friends.

'It's not much of a war, but we're using it as an excuse to arm. The Great King is coming. He's appointed a satrap of Thrace – of Thrace, by the gods, on our very doorstep! Datis is his name, or so we're told. We're to be the target as soon as Miletus falls.'

I started. 'Miletus falls?' I asked.

'Every man in Athens – every *political* man,' Aristides corrected himself, ignoring my interest in Miletus, 'is gathering a retinue. Many – I name no names – have pledged themselves to the Great King.' He shrugged. 'Both factions are gathering warriors – citizens and non-citizens.'

I put my wine cup down and laughed aloud. 'You – are allied with Miltiades.'

'Well might you laugh,' Aristides grumbled. 'He would be tyrant here, if he could. Only men like me stand between him and power. But he can't abide the Persians and he's in the field fighting, while we sit here.'

'Piracy for his own profit, you mean,' I said. 'I served with him for four years, my lord. And I might serve him again. But it is not the greater good of Athens that drives Miltiades to battle. More likely, it is his attacks on the Great King's shipping that have brought the Medes down on Athens.'

'Politics,' Aristides said, ignoring me again. He held up his cup to a slave for a refill, and I was annoyed that his slave got a glance and a smile, whereas I was merely a sounding board. 'Doubtless some busy plotter among the Alcmaeonids thought to hire your men for their side and leave you powerless – thinking that otherwise your men would serve me or Miltiades.'

I snorted with disgust. 'I was at home in Boeotia, tilling my fields,' I said. 'Please do not take it ill, my lord, but I care very little who is lording it in mighty Athens, so long as my bills are paid and my barns are full.'

'You disappoint me,' Aristides said.

I shrugged. 'You have seen a couple of handsome boys wrestling by a public fountain?'

Aristides nodded.

'Because there are young girls around the fountain?' I went on.

He laughed. 'Yes. Every day.'

'Ever notice that the girls don't even *glance* at the boys? Because such posturing bores them silly. Eh?' Now we were laughing together.

'Of course. You have the right of it, my well-spoken friend.' Aristides glanced away, at Jocasta, and they shared such a smile. It was a pleasure to see them together.

'Well then. We Plataeans are the girls by the fountain. Come back and talk to us when you have learned to listen and to play tricks that please *us*. Until then, you and Miltiades and all these Pisistratids and Alcmaeonids are just boys wrestling by the fountain.' I chuckled.

'Who made you so wise?' he asked.

I laughed. 'A generation of girls at fountains in Ephesus,' I said. 'Now, how do I get my horse and my slave girl back?'

Aristides shook his head. 'Ask after the trial,' he said.

I coughed. 'Trial? My trial? When is that? I thought you'd fixed that for me?'

He shook his head. 'The law is the only glue that binds Athens,' he said. 'You will have a trial. I'll be your speaker.'

'When?' I asked again.

'Tomorrow,' he said.

The idea of a trial drove news about Miltiades and the siege of Miletus out of my head.

In Athens, a foreigner cannot speak or defend himself at a trial of any kind. Without a 'friend', a *proxenos*, to represent him, a foreigner, even if he's a metic who lives in the city and has a trade and serves in the phalanx, cannot utter a word in his own defence.

Actually, I approve of this law. Why let foreigners speak in your assembly? A pox on them. All they'll do is stir up trouble.

Aristides walked with me as far as the first public fountain. 'You are not permitted to speak,' he said. 'But that changes very little. You can still smile, and frown, and raise your eyebrows – you can control your emotions or give them free rein. Men know who you are – and if they didn't yesterday, they will by this morning. The jurors will watch you. Comport yourself like a man. Ask yourself – what would Achilles do?'

I laughed. 'Sulk in his camp until provoked, and then kill anyone who offended him.'

Aristides frowned. 'The law is not a matter for levity. I must leave you – I have stops to make, and men to see. Be on the hill of the Areopagus by the middle of the day.' He handed me a three-leaf wooden tablet with wax pages. 'Keep this by you,' he said. 'I've written out the charges and your counter-charges, just in case another man has to speak for you. And I want you to understand. We're suing young Cleitus for the civil loss of your chattels – that is, the girl and the horse. Of the two, the horse is by far the most valuable – and will, I think, trip young Cleitus up handily at the trial. Understand?'

I read the tablet quickly. The writing was tiny and precise, but I am a literate man – I was taught my letters early.

'Will the trials go on at the same time?' I asked.

'Zeus! You know nothing of our laws. No. Your trial is for the *murder* of a citizen. That will be tried by the Areopagitica – the elders of the city. Friends of the Alcmaeonids, every man. In fact, more than

30

half of them *are* Alcmaeonids.' He nodded gravely. 'The civil trials will be held when the roster allows – probably early in the spring. We'll need a jury of at least four hundred.'

I swallowed some rage. 'Spring? I promised that girl her freedom.'

Aristides shrugged. 'I doubt you'll ever see her again, frankly. I'll see to it that you receive chattel of equal value.'

I shook my head. 'Aristides, I trust you. But I will have that girl back, and I will free her. I swore it. It may seem a little thing to you—'

He shook his head in turn. 'No – oaths to the gods are weighty matters, and you are a pious man. I apologize. I will do my best. But if they cannot kill you, these men will seek to hurt you – even your woman and your horse.'

I spat. 'This is your democracy? Aristocrats hitting out at better men through their chattels?'

He went down into the Agora with the rest of his followers, leaving me two young men with staves: Sophanes, who already had a name as a warrior, and Glaucon, his friend. They were both aristocrats, both followers of Aristides and both very serious. They wanted me to tell them about Miltiades.

'I want a good *krater* to take home,' I said, ignoring them and shrugging off my rage. I put the tablet into the back-fold of my chiton – a beautiful garment of natural wool. 'Something with a hero on it. Will you take me to the potters' quarter?'

I had an errand on the way, and so I walked them down past the cemetery and took them to visit Cleon, my hoplite-class friend from my first campaign.

He met me in his doorway, and he barked like a dog, howled and threw his arms around me. Sophanes and Glaucon watched wide-eyed as we drank a shared cup of wine – terrible wine – and traded tales.

'You, Sophanes,' he said, 'you have the name of an athlete. Do you know that this big lummox charged the Persians single-handed at the Pass of Sardis?' Cleon was proud to know me, proud to show me off to passers-by.

I shrugged. 'Eualcidas of Euboea led the way, and there were ten of us.'

Cleon laughed. 'It froze my fucking blood just to watch, by Aphrodite's burning cunt.' His face was red, and I thought that he'd had too much wine already. 'You look rich and pampered,' he went on.

I thought he looked like a broken man. 'How are things with you?' I asked. He had told me that his house was smaller than the stern-gallery on a trireme, and I could see it was true.

'My wife died,' he said. He shrugged. 'And both of my children. Apollo sent some affliction, and they were gone in a week.' He looked at the floor. Then he straightened his spine. 'Anyway, how are you? Famous, I note.'

Talk of my fame made me nervous.

'I'm here because Idomeneus killed one of the Alcmaeonids,' I said, to cover the pain in his eyes with facts. Men do these things. Men are cowards when it comes to sorrow.

'Good for bum-boy. For a kohl-eyed catamite, he's a fine man. Killed an aristocrat? That's something,' he said.

I laughed nervously. Cleon was drunk, and difficult. Sophanes and Glaucon were both aristocrats, and they were not pleased.

I shrugged. 'I have an appointment,' I said.

'Damn, you remind me of better times. I'm not even a hoplite any more, eh? Failed the property qualification.' He looked at the floor, and then hugged me. 'Damn, listen to me. All whines and self-pity. Come and see me again.'

I hugged him hard, took my two guards and left for the potters.

My two aristocrats clucked and muttered, and finally Glaucon spat that I had a friend of no worth.

I stopped and put a hand on his shoulder – older man to younger. 'Cleon looked a little drunk. His wife and children have died.' I held his eyes and the boy flinched. 'He stood his ground and kept men off me – many times in the rage of Ares. When you have done as much, then you may speak of him in that way in my hearing.'

Glaucon looked at the ground. 'I apologize.'

I liked him for that. The young are superb at disavowing responsibility – Hades, I was myself, so I know what I speak of. But this one *was* a better man.

We walked east into the morning sun and I lightened the atmosphere between us with tales of Miltiades. I was beginning the tale of the fighting in the Chersonese, and the Tearless Battle, where we took all the enemy boats with the loss of a dozen men and smashed the Phoenicians, when we crossed the festival road and found ourselves in the midst of a forest of brothels and taverns and free men's houses. Only Athens could so hopelessly over-commercialize something as simple as sex. I remember losing the thread of my story as I contemplated – well, I'll gloss over what I was contemplating, as you virgins would probably expire on the spot.

'So we took fishing boats,' I remember saying. 'There was a fair fishing fleet at Kallipolis—'

The dagger punched into my back just above the kidney. The blow was perfectly delivered and had a great deal of force behind it. I staggered, fell to my knees and felt the blood leak out over my arse.

I should have been dead.

But I wasn't. So I rolled through the fall and rose, my chlamys already off my throat and around my arm. As I came up, I had my knife in my right hand. Glaucon was down, but Sophanes was holding his own, his stick against two bullies with clubs. Even then, at seventeen, he was a foe to reckon with.

My man was big – titanic, in fact. I hate fighting big men – they don't feel pain, they have a natural confidence that is hard to break and they are *strong*.

My man was still trying to figure out why I wasn't dead. I shared his confusion, but I wasn't going to dwell on it.

It crossed my mind that I probably didn't want to kill him. Legal troubles, and all that.

I sidestepped, got down in my stance and flicked my chlamys at his eyes.

Behind him, Sophanes landed a blow with a crack that must have been heard at the peak of Cithaeron, and his man went down. The other backed away.

My opponent had a club and a knife. He cut at me with the gross ineptitude of the professional bruiser.

I killed him. It was no big deal – he was big, not skilled, and as the club rose I put my knife in between the shoulder muscles and the throat. Interesting point – I can remember that I had been planning a much more complicated feint when he left himself wide open from sheer folly and I took him. That's single combat.

I threw my chlamys over Sophanes' second opponent. It had corner weights and the gossamer wool settled like a net. Sophanes stepped in with his stave in two hands and broke the man's head as if we'd planned the move for weeks in the *palaestra*. That was the fight.

I felt much better. When you are enraged at injustice and humiliated by your helplessness in the face of towering bureaucracy, killing a couple of thugs is deeply satisfying. At least, it is to me. Sophanes must have felt the same, as he flashed me a grin and we embraced.

Then he went to his friend, who was starting to stir. I stripped the bodies of cash. Each had a little purse with a dozen silver owls – quite a sum.

The *daimon* of combat was wearing off, and suddenly I thought: *Why am I alive?*

The first blow should have been the last. I never saw it coming. And I was bleeding – just a little – from a deep puncture above my hip. A prostitute fetched water and cleaned my wound and said a prayer for me. Meanwhile, I cast around the ground, trying to find the dagger. All I could think was that the blade must have snapped.

The dagger was under the dead titan – lost things are always in the last place you look, I find. Glaucon was getting colour back in his face, and a pair of local girls were stroking him while a doctor felt his skull. Sophanes helped me roll the dead man over, and there was the dagger – a single finger of bright steel sticking out of Aristides' wax tablet.

Sophanes whistled and made a sign of aversion. 'The gods love you, Plataean.'

I'd fought with pleasure, but the sight of the tablet with the dagger right through it made me shake for a moment – just a moment.

That close.

I gave the girls five owls – a fortune – to make the body vanish. Sophanes was, I think, both appalled and thrilled.

The morning was young, and I found a brothelkeeper and had him take the other two thugs and lock them in his cellar, which was cut straight into the rock of the hillside. I paid him, too. The free-spending habits of a life of piracy instantly conquered a few months' attempt to be a farmer. Kill people, take their money, spend it recklessly.

Yet I had changed – because another part of me registered that I'd just spent the value of thirty-five medimnoi of grain at current prices – merely to get rid of a body.

We left Glaucon to recover – ostensibly to watch the prisoners. I went and bought a wine krater. It's that one, right there – Achilles and Ajax playing polis. It tickles my fancy, that it wasn't all war. Men had time to gamble at Troy.

The sun was high, but not yet noon, when we got back to the brothel. Glaucon looked like a dog with too many bones – he'd had his flute played, I could tell – but the two men were both in the cellar. One was dead. Blows to the head can have that effect. Sophanes didn't like that – that he'd killed a man.

I shrugged. 'If you fight, you will kill,' I said.

The other was terrified. He wasn't a citizen and the punishment for his crime would be the silver mines until he died. Nor was he brave. But all he knew was that some men and women, all veiled, had paid the titan to find me and kill me. They'd been paid at sunrise, in the grove of Pan.

That's all he knew.

I looked at him, tried a few more questions, listened to his tears – and cut his throat. Sophanes was shocked. I stepped back to avoid the flow of blood, and then handed the brothelkeeper five more drachmas.

He nodded to me, as one predator to another.

The two boys who had been sent to 'guard' me were spluttering.

'Listen, lads,' I said. I caught their arms and held them. 'All he had coming was to be worked to death as a slave. Right?' I looked at both of them. 'And now the only story that will ever be heard is ours. Hard to cook up a lie if none of your witnesses can speak.'

'You ... killed him!' Glaucon got out, after some muttering.

'He tried to kill you,' I pointed out.

'That was in the heat of battle,' Sophanes said. 'By Zeus Soter, Plataean, this was murder. It's different.'

I shrugged. 'Not when you've killed as many men as I have,' I said. 'Console yourself that he was a foreign metic, probably an escaped slave, and a man of no worth whatsoever. He wasn't even brave.' I wiped my knife on the dead man's chiton, poured a little olive oil from my *aryballos* to keep it bright, sheathed it and headed up the rock-carved steps.

We were a silent crew as we walked to my murder trial. I was pretty sure that my two companions were no longer in the grips of hero worship.

Athenian justice is swift. I arrived a little early, but most of the Areopagitica was already on the hill, and the last of the old men made their climb just behind me. Aristides was there. He had a bruise on one shoulder that he hadn't had that morning.

'Tried to kill you?' I said quietly.

'Yes,' he said. 'And you, I take it?'

I handed him the tablet with the dagger through it. Heads turned all over the summit.

He was angry. 'This is not Athens,' he spat. 'What are we, some court of Medes? Some soft-handed Lydians? Next, men will turn to poison.' But then he calmed. 'This will tell in your favour. I'll hand it around. The symbolism is so clear, it's like an augury – the dagger through the law!'

So I watched the tablet passed from man to man, and the muttering must have helped me a little.

Aristides was calm and forceful when the trial started. Let me digress a moment: you've noticed that I wandered the city without much trouble. I could have run. But of course I didn't. That's how it was then – Athens assumed that I would come to my trial, and I did.

In a murder trial, each side gets one speech – a couple of hours by a water-clock – first the prosecution, then the defence. And the verdict is delivered immediately after the defence delivers its argument. We're much the same in Plataea, although it's years since we had a proper murder trial. Simon, my cousin, killed himself rather than face the tribunal.

So we all stood in the blazing sun, and Cleitus of the Alcmaeonids began his speech. I can't remember all he said, but I know it was damning and at the same time utterly inaccurate.

'I accuse Arimnestos of Plataea, the man who stands before you, of the murder of my cousin Nepos. Nepos was murdered within the precincts of a shrine – foully murdered, with impiety – unarmed, standing making an oration to the gods.' Cleitus had a good voice.

I couldn't speak. But I could roll my eyes. So I did.

'All of you know of this man – a notorious pirate, a man who serves with the vicious cut-throat Miltiades. With Miltiades, he sacked Naucratis. With Miltiades, he attacked the Great King's ships, and those of our allies at Ephesus and other places – over and over again. It is men like this who bring the just wrath of the Great King down on our city.'

Well, I couldn't really disagree with that, so I smiled genially.

'Don't let this man's reputation as a fighter cloud your vision, though, gentlemen. Look at him. This is no Achilles. This is a fighter trained in the pits of slavery – a man who has neither *arete* nor generosity. He is merely a killer. Is the look on his brow more than that of a bestial destroyer? Is he different from a boar or a lion that kills the men who tend our crops?

'This is a man bred to slavery, and what he has now, he has stolen from better men – first through piracy and then through open theft of a farm in Plataea. No man in Plataea dares act against him – they fear his wrath. But here in Athens we are better men, with a better strength of law.'

There was more – much more. Two hours of detailed (and fallacious) vilification. Cleitus knew nothing of me save some highly coloured details from Plataea – and it was obvious where they came from. Because my cousin Simon, son of Simon who hanged himself, was standing a little to the left of Cleitus, with a look of joyous hate stamped across his features.

I locked eyes with him, and gave him some bland indifference.

By the time Cleitus was finished, many of his audience were asleep. He had, after all, repeated the charges and the assaults on my character fifteen or twenty times. His arrogance showed through too plainly. Heraclitus would have taught him better. At Ephesus, one of the things we learned was not to annoy a jury – nor to bore it.

On the other hand, none of the men in that jury were my friends, and most were bored only because they had made up their minds before they put a sandal on the slippery rock of justice.

Slaves came and refilled the water-clock. I leaned over and pointed out Simon to Aristides, who looked at him and nodded to me.

Aristides stood up slowly. He walked gracefully to the speaker's podium and turned to me. Our eyes met for a long time.

Then he turned back to the jurors.

'My friend Arimnestos cannot speak here today as he is a foreigner,' he said. 'But although his tongue cannot speak, his spear has spoken loud and long for Athens – louder and longer than any of you Alcmaeonids. If deeds rather than words were the weight of a man, if the price of citizenship were measured in feats of arms, not barley or oil, he would sit in judgment, and none of you would even qualify as *thetes*.

Ouch. Powerful rhetoric – but a damned annoying way to win over a jury.

Aristides walked across to Cleitus. 'You maintain that my friend is a slave? Or some sort of penniless foreigner?'

Cleitus stood. 'I do.'

Aristides smiled. 'And you have received my suit against you for the theft of a horse and a woman?'

'I have taken them against the man's indemnity,' Cleitus said.

'In other words, you admit yourself that my friend was the *owner* of the horse and the slave.' Aristides stepped back, just like a swordsman who administers the killing blow and now avoids the fountain of blood.

Cleitus flushed red. 'He probably stole them!' he shouted, but the archon basileus pointed his staff.

'Silence!' he roared. 'Your time is done and you speak out of turn.'

Aristides turned to the jurors. 'My friend is the son of Technes, head of the Corvaxae of Plataea. My friend could, if he might speak, tell you how his father was murdered – by the father of that man standing by Cleitus – and his farm stolen by the same man, and how Arimnestos later returned from ten years of war – war at the behest of Athens, I might add – to find his enemies in possession of his farm. He might speak of how the assembly of Plataea voted to punish the usurper – that man's father – and he might speak of what a twisted claim has just been made – accusations void of truth. Any man of Plataea would tell us, if called to witness, that my friend is master of a farm that provides three hundred measures of grain and oil and wine.'

Aristides had them listening now.

'But none of this matters. What matters is simple. My friend did not kill Cleitus's useless cousin. In point of fact, Cleitus's case is already void, because he has spoken – and he may not speak again – yet he has not troubled to prove that his cousin is dead.'

Cleitus had missed the matter entirely. His head snapped up, his mouth worked.

'Really, cousin – for we are cousins, Cleitus, are we not? – you are too young to plead before this august body. You needed, first, to prove that your cousin Nepos is dead. Second, you needed to demonstrate that my friend was in some way linked to his death, beyond the circumstance that he is from Plataea. If you had remembered, you would have maintained that your cousin died at the shrine of Leitos on the flanks of Cithaeron. But like a young man, you let spite carry you away, and you forgot to mention the place of this supposed murder, or any other facts relating to it. What you have not told these worthy men is that your whole knowledge of this matter comes from two panicked slaves who returned to you, claiming that their master had been killed. You have never been to Plataea, you have no idea if the claim is accurate, you have acted on the word of two treacherous slaves, and in truth, as far as you know, at any moment your cousin Nepos may stroll into the crowd and ask what this is about.'

Cleitus rose again. 'He *is dead*. He was killed at the shrine—'

The archon rose. 'Silence this instant, puppy.'

'Listen to me!' Cleitus spat.

The archon waved and two gaudily dressed Scythian archers took Cleitus by the arms and carried him off the hill.

Aristides looked around in silence. 'I claim that my opponent has made no case. He has not shown a body. He has not offered a witness. There is nothing for me to answer but the slander of a traitor's son. I call a vote on the evidence presented.'

Stunned silence greeted him. The water-clock was running noisily – it was still almost full.

The archon looked them over. 'I cannot direct you,' he said. 'But if you pretend that Cleitus has a case, I'll make you pay.'

I was acquitted, twenty-seven to fourteen. A carefully arranged vote, as it meant that I could not claim damages from Cleitus.

Several men tried to force through a different vote that would have made me stand trial again if more evidence could be gathered. They were still arguing when the sun set and Aristides led me off the hill.

'You are the very Achilles of orators,' I said.

Aristides shook his head. 'That was bad. I used arts to win. Had I argued the case on its merits, they would have found a way to kill you.' He rubbed his nose. 'I feel dirty. Perhaps I should exile myself. This is not law. This is foolishness.'

'The archon was just.'

'The archon hates the Alcmaeonids as upstarts and posturers. He's no friend of mine, but he'd raise me to Olympus if it would hurt the new men. All I had to do was put Cleitus in a place where his arrogance would count against him.'

'What now?' I asked. 'I want my horse and my slave girl.'

Aristides shook his head. 'Perhaps in the spring. And if you stay here, you'll be dead. I don't have enough wax tablets to keep you alive.'

We walked to his farm and Jocasta served wine. I told her the whole of the trial while Glaucon and Sophanes sulked. They didn't love me any more.

Aristides noted them. He inclined his long chin in their direction and raised an eyebrow at me.

'Hmm,' I said.

Jocasta was looking at her husband with her eyes shining. 'Should I invite this pretty foreigner to live in our house, so that I can finally hear what happens at your trials, love?' she asked. To me, she said, 'He never tells me a word of his speeches.'

The great man looked down his nose. 'If I told you my speeches, you would only seek to improve them,' he said. 'I could not bear that.'

Their eyes met, and I felt a twinge of jealousy – not bodily jealousy, like a boy feels when a girl leaves him for another, but something in the soul. Those two had something I had never had – something calm and deep.

'Why are the boys on edge?' Aristides asked quietly.

'I killed some thugs,' I said. I saw the effect my words had on the lady. Killing was part of life for me. Not for her. 'Sorry, despoina.' When Aristides shrugged, I clarified why the two young men were upset. 'One I killed in cold blood.'

Aristides shuddered in revulsion. 'How can you do such things?' he asked.

'It's much like killing a man in a fight, only quicker,' I retorted. His squeamishness – did I mention that he was a prig? – offended me.

'I cannot have you under my roof while you are tainted with such a crime,' Aristides said.

I all but fell over in shock.

'They *attacked* us.' But I could see it on his face. This was Athens. I had spent too long in the camp of Miltiades. Men didn't simply cut other men's throats here. I had, unwittingly, committed a crime – and offended my host and patron.

I'm no fool. I got to my feet. 'I understand, my lord. But the man – what was before him but death in the mines? And he might have been used against us in law.'

Aristides kept his head turned away, as if breathing the same air as me would hurt him. 'A thug – a metic? He could never have been used in a trial. And you should know better. Are you a god, that you may choose who lives and who dies? You killed him because it was *easy*.'

Alas, he was right.

'A god, or one of the fates, might well say that this man had no future but a straight trip to the mines and a few months of wretchedness.' Aristides pulled his chlamys over his head in disgust. 'You have no such knowledge. You killed him for convenience. Your own convenience. Now I am beginning to doubt my wisdom in defending you.'

Jocasta was standing as far from me as possible. They were a very religious household, and my bloody pragmatism now looked to me, as it did to them, like selfish crime.

I had two choices – the amoral outrage of the pragmatist, or admission that I had acted wrongly. Rage rose within me, but Heraclitus was there, too.

'You are right,' I said. I clamped down on my anger. It was wrong – ugly, unworthy.

Aristides raised his head. 'You mean that?'

'Yes,' I said. 'You have convicted me in the court of my own mind. I should not have killed him, though he was of no use, even to himself.' I shuddered. It was so easy to fall back into the habits of the pirate.

'Cleanse yourself,' he said.

'I need my horse and my woman,' I said. 'I swore an oath.'

Aristides shook his head. 'Cleanse yourself, and perhaps the gods will provide.'

There were, in those days, a number of temples that offered cleansing from the stain of death and impiety. Even the shrine to Leitos, in Plataea, although that was open only to soldiers.

But the principal places of cleansing for crime were Olympia, Delphi and Delos. And of the three, Delos was easiest to reach, though most distant in stades, I suppose. And the Apollo there was the most ready to listen to a common man.

'I will go to Delos,' I said.

'You can be in Sounion by morning,' Aristides said. 'Have you money?'

I didn't tell him I still had twenty drachmas from the dead men. 'Yes,' I said.

'Gods speed you there,' Aristides said. He stood by me while I rolled my blankets and an old bearskin, then followed me out of his gate. 'Listen, Arimnestos. You may take me for a pious fool, or a hypocrite.'

'Neither, my lord.' We were alone in the dark.

'You need to be gone – before your wagon arrives with the corpse and the goods, and they find an excuse to take you again. I will try to find your girl. But this murder is a stain, and you must be clean before you come back here. It may be that some god led you to it – because you do need to be gone, and tonight is better than tomorrow.' He shrugged. 'They will kill you if they cannot convict you.'

41

'I don't fear them,' I said, but I wasn't telling the truth.

'In a year, the balance will change. Right now, you cannot be here. Even Plataea might prove dangerous for you. Go to Delos, and do as the god bids you.' He held out his hand. 'I do not fear pollution so much that I would not clasp your hand.'

And then I was walking in the dark, down the rocky road to Sounion.

3

I managed to find a ship at Sounion, practically on the steps of the Temple of Poseidon. He was a Phoenician bound for Delos with a cargo of slaves from Italy and Iberia. I didn't think very highly of slavers and I dislike Phoenicians on principle, even though they are great sailors, but I took it as a test from the gods and I kept my eyes open and my mouth shut.

All the slaves were Iberians, big men with heavy moustaches, tattoos and the deep anger of the recently enslaved. They eyed my weapons and I kept my distance. They all looked like fighting men.

The navarch, a man with a beard trimmed the Aegyptian way, curling like a talon from his chin, made them row in shifts between his professional rowers. He was training them so that he'd get a better price. He planned to sell the best of them at Delos and the rest at Tyre or Ephesus.

'Ephesus?' I asked. Ephesus always interested me.

'The satrap of Phrygia has an army laying siege to Miletus,' he said. 'His fleet is based at Ephesus.'

That was news to me. 'Already?' I asked. The fall of Miletus – the most powerful city in the Greek world, or so we thought – would be the end of the Ionian Revolt.

Once again, I have to leave my tale to explain. In those days, most of the cities of Ionia – and there were dozens, from beautiful Heraklea on the Euxine, down along the coast of Asia to mighty Miletus, then to Ephesus, the city of my youth, richer than Athens by a factor of five times – across the Cyprian Sea to Cyprus and Crete – more Greeks lived in Ionia than lived in Greece. Except that most of those Greeks lived under the rule of the King of Kings – the Great King of the Persians.

While I was growing to manhood in the house of Hipponax, I lived under Persian rule. The Persians ruled well, thugater. Never believe the crap men say today about how they were a nation of slaves. They were warriors, and men of honour – in most cases, more honour than we Greeks. Artaphernes – the satrap of Phrygia – was the friend and foe of my youth. He was a great man.

In those days – in my youth – the Greeks of Ionia rose up to throw off the shackles of Persian slavery. Hah! Now, there's a load of cow shit. Selfish men seeking power for themselves cozened the citizens of many Ionian cities to trade the safety and stability of the world's greatest empire for 'freedom'. To most Ionians, that freedom was the freedom to be killed by a Persian. None of the Ionians trusted each other, and every one of them wanted power over the others. The Persians had a unified command, brilliant generals and excellent supplies. And money.

The Ionian Revolt had lasted for ten years, but it was never much of a success. And when this story starts, as I was sailing as a passenger on a slave ship, it was entering its final phase, although we didn't know it. The Persians had seemed at the edge of triumph before, and each time, the revolt had been rescued – usually by Athens, or by Athenians acting as surrogates for their mother city, like Miltiades.

But Athens had its own problems – the near civil war I described. Persian gold was pouring into the city, inflating the power of the aristocratic party and the Alcmaeonids, and the Pisistratids were backed by Persia to restore the tyranny – not that I knew that then. Persian gold was paralysing Athens, and the Persian axe was poised over Miletus.

To the navarch of this slave ship, all this meant that he could make a handsome profit selling half-trained rowers to the Persian fleet anchored on the beaches around Ephesus, supporting the siege of Miletus.

I listened and managed not to speak.

We were fifteen days making a three-day voyage, and I hated that ship by the time we landed. His long, black hull was swift and clean, and for a light trireme he was the very acme of perfection – yet this Phoenician cur sailed him like a pig. The Phoenician was afraid of every cup of wind, and he stayed on a coast to the very end of a headland and crossed open water with visible reluctance. I've never loved the Phoenicians, but most of them were brilliant sailors. Every pack has a cur.

I sat alone in the bow, sang the hymn to Apollo as we sing it in

Plataea – I have Apollo's raven on my shield – and prepared myself to meet the god of the lyre and the plague. I tried not to think of how easily I could take this ship. Those days were gone. Or so I thought.

The last night at sea, I had a dream – such a dream that I can remember wisps of it even today. Ravens came to me and carried my good knife away, and one of them set a lyre in my hand as a replacement. I didn't need a priest to tell me what that meant.

The most dangerous of the Iberians – you could see it in his eyes – had a raven tattooed on his hand and another on his sword arm. When the slaver's stern was set in the deep sand of a Delian beach and his people were moving cargo, I dropped my heavy knife into the blackness under the Iberian's bench, while he lay watching me, exhausted from rowing.

Our eyes met. I nodded. His face was completely blank. I wasn't even sure he'd seen the knife, and I went ashore, poorer by a good blade.

Priests are priests the world around – I've noted a certain similarity from Olympia to Memphis in Aegypt. Many of them are good men and women; a few are remarkable, genuinely blessed. The rest are a sorry lot – people who probably, in my opinion, couldn't make a living any other way, except as beggars or farm labour.

The man who met me as I kissed the rock by the stern of the slave ship was one of the latter. His hands were soft and his hand-clasp was limp and unpleasant, and his soft voice wished me a speedy encounter with the god in a voice that seemed all too ready to wheedle and plead.

'You are Arimnestos of Plataea,' he said.

Well, that took me aback. I was naive then, and didn't know the effort to which the great priesthoods went to be informed. Nor did I suspect how carefully engineered this might be.

'Yes,' I allowed.

'Brought here by the god to hear your penance for murder,' he said in the same voice that a man might tease a girl into his blanket roll. I didn't like him. But he had me, I can tell you.

'Yes,' I said.

'The god has spoken to us of you,' he said. He leaned his chin on the head of his staff. 'What have you brought as offering?'

Just like that. My feet were still in the sand of the beach and the priests of Apollo wanted their fees.

I sighed. 'I have served Apollo and Hephaestus all my life,' I said. 'I revere all the gods, and I serve at the shrine of the hero Leitos of Plataea.' This by way of my religious credentials, so to speak.

He said nothing. His eyes flickered to the purse in my hand.

'I have twenty drachmas, less the one I owe as passage to that slave trader.' Need I mention that the priests of Apollo played an active role in the trade?

'Nineteen silver owls? That is all the duty you pay to the god, you who are called the Spear of the Greeks?' He shook his head. 'I think not. Go back and return when you intend to give the god his due.'

Now, lest you young people miss the accounting, nineteen silver owls was the value of a farm's produce for a year. But of course, it was as nothing next to the profits a man might make trading – or as a pirate.

I didn't know what to say. I had more respect for priests in those days – even venal creatures like this one. 'These nineteen drachmas are all I have,' I protested.

He laughed. 'Then Lord Apollo will give you nineteen drachmas' worth of prophecy – I can feel his words in my heart. Go – and come back when you have learned enough wisdom to pay your tithe.'

Perhaps at eighteen, I'd have obeyed.

But I was older. 'Out of my way,' I said. 'I need to find a priest.'

He oozed insult. 'I am the priest the god has assigned.'

I shrugged and pushed past him. 'I suspect the god can do better.'

He followed me up the rock and his voice became increasingly shrill as he demanded that I speak to him, but I continued up the steps to the temple complex. At the gate, he was still shouting at me as I asked the porter to find me a priest.

The porter grunted and I gave him a drachma, and he sent a boy.

'Arimnestos of Plataea!' the priest from the beach persisted. 'This is not the way a gentleman behaves!'

'Only eighteen drachmas left,' I said. 'And by the time I get a new guide to the altar, there will be *none*.'

'Your arrogance will be your death,' he said. 'You seek to cheat the god!'

'I do not,' I said. 'I am a farmer in Boeotia, not a pirate in the Chersonese. These coins are a fair share of my fortune in the last year.'

I said so – but I began to be afraid. Those coins were, as you know, taken from the corpses of men who tried to kill me. Perhaps the

46

coins were polluted. But essentially my words were true ones. The eighteen coins in my purse were more than a tenth of all the coins I had in the world.

'Why have you requested a second guide?' a hard voice asked. This priest was older, dressed in a simple wool garment that had seen better days. 'Thrasybulus? Why have I been summoned?'

'You may go back to your cell,' the oily man behind me answered. 'This arrogant Boeotian is attempting to bargain with god.'

'I wish to be washed by the god for a murder committed in Athens,' I said. 'If the god has words for me to hear, I would laugh with delight to hear them. But this man asks me for money I do not have.' I pointed at the younger priest.

The older man rubbed his beard. 'What price have you offered?' he asked.

'He is—'

'Silence, Thrasybulus.' The older priest seemed a different kind of man.

'I have offered eighteen drachmas,' I said. 'It is all I have.'

'The cost of three new bulls?' He looked at me.

'He can do better. Much better.' Thrasybulus pointed at the metalwork on my empty scabbard.

The older man sighed. 'This is unseemly. The priesthood of Apollo does not bargain like fishwives on the beach.'

The porter's laugh suggested that this statement was not entirely true.

'I am Dion of Delos,' the older man said. 'I am principally a scholar, and I seldom lead men to the gates – but Thrasybulus has, I fear, earned your displeasure.' The older man glared at the younger. 'You will need silver for food – and passage home, as well. Will you not?'

I nodded.

'Give me twelve drachmas for your sacrifices, and I will lead you to the god,' he said.

Thrasybulus spat. 'You are a liar before the god,' he said, pointing at me.

Not an auspicious start to my time on the island of Apollo.

That evening, I made the first of my three sacrifices – this one on the so-called altar of ash. I sacrificed a black lamb, a symbol of my crime, and I told the god and all the other men waiting to sacrifice how I had come to kill the thug in Athens and what my sin was – the sin of hubris, in feeling that I was as fit to decide his fate as the gods.

Other men sacrificed for other crimes. One, from Crete, had killed his son with a javelin – an error, a grievous miscast while hunting. Another had slept with a foreign woman during her courses and felt unclean. I almost laughed, but everyone else seemed to feel this was a serious thing. Several men were soldiers – mercenaries – who had come to atone for killing other Greeks – over dice, or in battle. Two men were guilty of gross impiety.

My sacrifice was refused. I took the animal to the altar and killed it, but the fire would not accept the beast. I saw it myself.

The same happened to one of the men guilty of impiety, and the man who had killed his son.

My priest – Dion – led the three of us from the altar. He took us to a hut made of brush on the cliff high above the beach. 'You will remain here for a week, eating clean food and drinking only water. Consider how you became unclean. Consider your life. I will return for you.'

That was a long week.

The Cretan was called Heracles. He was tall and strong, noble in his carriage, and so broken by grief that it was hard to speak to him. He felt the guilt that I did not feel. He felt that he had killed his son and deserved the wrath of the god, while I felt that I had acted hastily – selfishly – but that I had now learned my lesson and did *not* deserve the wrath of Apollo. Yet I had enough sense to see that I had far more culpability than this Cretan lord.

In fact, he was mistaking sorrow for guilt. I sat with him, night after night, held his hand and spoke to him of hunting, and of Crete, a place I knew well. I could get him to listen, and I could make him smile, and then some chance of speech would cast him back into the pit.

'I am cursed,' he said. 'I have killed my son, and now my wife is barren.'

'Take a concubine,' I said, with all the arrogance of youth.

'I cannot replace eighteen years of my life and his, just by making another squawking babe,' he shot back – with more spirit than I'd seen so far.

'Lord, you can. And then you must toil for as many years again, until he comes to manhood, so that your patronage is secure.' I spoke carefully, for I felt I might be speaking wisdom.

He sighed. 'Perhaps,' he said. 'You are young. When you have seen fifty winters, tell me how you feel about lasting through another fifteen seasons of war and the hunt. My joints hurt just lying here.'

The other man was a blasphemer. I could tell this because he swore by various gods every hour on the hour, and cursed the gods for setting him on Delos. He was a little man – in mind, not stature – and a lesson to anyone who would listen about the vices men can get into through idleness and superstition. I might have been a foolish young man, but I was the very king of piety next to Philocrates.

'If you care so little for the gods, why did you come here and confess?' I asked him.

He shrugged. 'I swore an oath – nothing big – just part of a business deal. I never meant to pay the bastard – he was cheating me. But the priest of Zeus in Halicarnassus will not let me do any business in the agora until I atone.' He shrugged. 'All mummery. No greater liars or thieves than those priests.' And grunted. 'And now I have to put up with this. My money is as silver as everyone else's. Fuck the gods. Why am I singled out? Because they think I should pay more.' He spat.

I didn't like his attitude, but I had to agree with the sense of his complaint. 'You are hardly repentant,' I said.

'What are you, some kind of aspiring priest?' he asked. 'Fuck off. I'll eat my bread and water for a week, and if they don't take my sacrifice, I'll sail away and let them dance for the money.'

'But the god?' I asked.

'How much of a bumpkin are you?' he asked me. 'Listen, there's a pair of bellows behind the altar – they manipulate them to decide which sacrifices are accepted and which rejected. Right? You understand, boy, or are you too thick? There are no gods. All you get is what you *take*.'

I felt the sort of shock that a man feels when lightning strikes too close at sea. I had thought of myself as a man of the world – I was a hardened killer, a soldier of fortune, a former pirate. But that men would manipulate the sacrifices of the gods? Or that this man would claim there were no gods?

Heraclitus told us that such men were contemptible, but very brave. 'Only small men are incapable of seeing something greater than themselves,' my master once said.

So I shook my head at Philocrates. 'You are a sad case,' I said.

He just smirked. 'Bumpkin,' he shot back.

The week was hard. I drank water and watched the sun, and I sang a hymn to Apollo every day. I set myself a task – to remember all the men I had killed. Of course, there were men I couldn't remember – the Carians at Sardis and Ephesus had died in the anonymity of their armour, and the Phoenicians I'd killed on my ship during the mutiny didn't even have faces in my memory – but I was able to conjure up fifty men in the theatre of my head, and that seemed a great many. And I had probably killed twice that, or even three times.

A week of consideration, and it seemed to me that the god was right to refuse my sacrifice. I killed too easily, I decided. It wasn't a hard decision to reach. After all, Heraclitus had said as much most of the days of my youth.

When old Dion came for me, he was leading another black ram. 'Did you dream?' he asked.

I shrugged. 'I had dreams,' I said. 'I dreamed once of a man I killed – a boy I put out of his misery on a battlefield. And I dreamed of a woman I love.'

Dion led me to the highest headland on the island – ten stades or more from our hut. The ram followed along obediently. Then he sat me down on a seat carved from the living rock.

'And why do you think the god refused your sacrifice?' he asked.

I looked out over the sea. There were a dozen ships on the beach below me. Two of them I knew, and I sat up with a start.

'That's my ship!' I said. It was *Storm Cutter*, and he still had the raven of Apollo on his sail, the first ship I had ever owned, spear-won from the Phoenicians. Even now, his navarch was likely to be one of my chosen men.

Dion raised an eyebrow. 'Men have been asking for you for three days,' he said. 'But you are in the god's hands. Answer my question.'

'The god refused my sacrifice because I kill to easily, and for little things,' I said. 'And yet, even as I say this, I wonder what the god asks of me. I am a warrior.'

Dion nodded. 'I thought you were a farmer and a bronze-smith?'

Dion was a decent priest. So I said what came to mind. 'The sight of that ship raises my heart in a way that my anvil never does,' I confessed.

'So,' Dion said. Now he smiled. 'So now you are confused?'

I laughed. 'Yes,' I said. 'Answer me a question, priest.'

He shrugged. 'It is my place to ask. But I'll answer one question, if I can.'

I pointed at the temple. 'Is there a pair of bellows mounted in the altar of ash to control the flame of the sacrifices?'

Dion nodded. 'When you work bronze, do you use bellows?' he asked.

I nodded.

'And do you pray to Hephaestus to guide your hand when you work?'

'Of course!' I said. 'Before I started my helmet, I omitted the prayer, and my work failed.'

Dion nodded again. 'And yet you had bellows and a hammer and an anvil, I expect.'

'I did,' I said, seeing his point.

'And if you sought to work bronze, and you prayed, and yet had neither bellows nor an anvil?' he asked.

'I'd be a fool,' I agreed.

'Some of us here are fools,' Dion said. His eyes narrowed. 'I am not one of them. Are you?'

'I'm still not sure I understand what the god asks of me,' I said.

'The confession of confusion is often the beginning of wisdom,' he said, and slapped my knee. 'Let's make sacrifice.'

My ram died well, and the god accepted him in a blast of fire, and I walked down the steps of the altar, my bare feet treading on the burnt remnants of thousands of animals sent to the heavens here, so that I wondered for a moment what a herd they'd make, and what the first animal to die here had been.

Let me also note that the god accepted the sacrifice of the impious trader and rejected the sacrifice of the Cretan lord who had killed his son. My confusion deepened.

'There is more to god than a pair of bellows and an altar,' Dion said. 'He's a good man, and the god will send him home when he is ... ready.'

The next morning, in the first blush of dawn, I waited in the cleft at the base of the altar, clad in simple white linen without so much as a stripe woven in. The cleft smelled of almonds and honey, and I was afraid. Hard to say why, exactly.

Dion held my shoulder while the first supplicant crawled up and into the cleft. He was gone for a long time, and when he returned he was as white as a corpse and couldn't stand up, so that three acolytes had to carry him. When he was able to speak, priests gathered around him like sharks around a kill, demanding to know what words the god had spoken.

Then it was my turn.

Men were known to die confronting the god in the cleft. No amount of spear-craft on my part could avoid death if the god intended it for me, and I was afraid.

The cleft itself was odd. A big shelf of rock overhung another, and the cleft was between them, so that a man had to climb *up* first, as if into a hearth. I could *just* get my head and shoulders through the gap, and I banged my knees badly, and the smell of almonds grew stronger all around me. The priests had told me not to flinch and not to stop climbing, so I felt in front of me with my hand – all black, and me lying on my back – and I found the next handhold and pushed myself up with my legs, crouching and pressing myself flat against an invisible rock surface. My head bumped rock, and I felt a breeze on my face. I got a knee up, and scraped it again, but the pain was far, far away, and then I was up on the second shelf, breathing like bellows ...

'Eh-eh-eh ...' said the dying man at my elbow.

I looked at him, and he was younger than me – and kalos, even at the point of death, with big, beautiful eyes that wanted to know how his world had turned to shit. His skin, where it was not smeared with sweat and puke, was smooth and lovely. He was somebody's son.

I drew my short dagger, really my eating knife, from under my scale shirt where I keep it, and I put my lips by his ear.

'Say goodnight,' I said. I tried to sound like Pater when he put me to bed. 'Say goodnight, laddy.'

'G'night,' he managed. Like a child, the poor bastard. Go to Elysium with the thought of home, I prayed, and put the point of my eating knife into his brain ...

I tried to stand, and my head hit the rock.

I whirled, and I couldn't find the cleft any more.

I knelt and my knees were bleeding.

How strong are you, Killer of Men? a voice said.

To be honest, I suspect I may have whimpered.

I have no memory past that, until I was kneeling on the sand of the beach, puking my guts out like a babe.

Dion held my hand. 'You are clean, and the god has spoken through you,' he said gently. 'I will send word to Aristides.'

'You know Aristides?' I asked.

Dion smiled. 'The world is not so big,' he said.

'Did the god have words for me?' I asked.

Dion nodded. 'Simple words, simply obeyed. You are lucky.' He patted me on the head. I was that weak. 'When you leave the temple, obey the first man you meet. Through obeying him, you will do a service for the god – it will come straight to you, like an arrow.' He held out his hand and I got to my feet. A slave brought me water and I drank it. 'Are you ready?'

My head was spinning, but the world was growing calmer by the moment. 'Yes,' I said.

'I add on my own account,' the priest said, as he led me up to the altar, 'that if you were to hold your hand when you could kill, each time you acted so would count as a sacrifice to Lord Apollo.'

'Hmm,' I said. But I knew that this was the most important message, and the lesson I had come to Delos to learn. The stuff about the first man outside the temple – I had seen Miltiades' ship on the beach. I knew who would be waiting for me outside the temple, and I was cynical enough to wonder how much my former lord had paid for me.

I sacrificed at the low altar and the high altar, and then I changed my temple garments for my own Boeotian wool, with my own sturdy boots and my own felt hat. And the hilt of my own sword under my arm. I looked for my knife, and then I remembered that I'd given it to the slave – or it was lost in the bilges of a Phoenician slaver, rusting away.

I kissed Dion on both cheeks. I couldn't help but notice that Thrasybulus was standing by the portico, eyeing me the way a butcher eyes a bull.

'Thank you,' I said.

'You doubt,' Dion said. 'I, too, doubt. Doubt is to piety what exercise is to athletics. But the god spoke to you, and in a day or less, you will see.'

Then I walked down the steps of the portico. I contemplated briefly a dramatic assault on my fate. I wondered what would happen if I ran to the left, accosted the slave sweeping the steps and demanded that he order me to do something, so that I might obey.

But some things are ordained. Whether the hand of man or the hand of the gods is in it matters little, as the petty hands of men may well be the tools of the gods as well. Dion's lesson. So I walked down the steps to where Miltiades stood, his arms crossed over his magnificent breastplate of silvered bronze. His helmet was between his feet, and his shield was being held by his hypaspist. His son Cimon stood behind him, also arrayed for war.

In truth, my heart soared to meet them.

'Command me, lord,' I said.

'Follow me,' he said, as his arms embraced me, and he crushed me against his chest. Just those two words, and my fate was sealed.

Again.

Miltiades had had a bad season, and he'd lost two ships in the fighting. He had three ships on that beach: his own, with Paramanos of Cyrene as his helmsman, whom I embraced like a brother; Cimon, with a long, low trireme he'd taken himself; and Stephanos of Chios, a man my own age, who had served under me every step of the ladder and now had my own *Storm Cutter*.

'Take command,' Miltiades said, as I embraced Stephanos.

I looked at Stephanos.

He shook his head. 'I can't afford to run a warship yet,' he said. It was true – it took treasure to keep a ship at sea, scraped clean and full of willing rowers.

I turned to Miltiades. 'All my money gone?' I asked. I'd left him my treasure when I went back to the farm.

The Athenian shrugged. 'I'll repay you,' he said. 'It's been a bad season. We've been fighting Medes and not taking ships. More losses than gold darics.' He shrugged. 'I lost two ships in the Euxine. I need captains.'

'Who told you I was on Delos?' I asked, curious. Not even angry. Fate is fate.

'I did,' Idomeneus said. He stepped out from the crowd of rowers as if produced by the machine in a play. 'I came to Athens with a wagon of goods and a corpse. Aristides took it all off my hands and told me to follow you.' He grinned. 'I thought you were going back to the real world.'

'Who's tending to the shrine?' I asked.

'Ajax, who served against us in Asia, and Styges,' he said. My hypaspist had an answer for everything.

I nodded. 'Will you be helmsman?' I asked Stephanos.

He grinned.

'Captain my marines?' I asked Idomeneus.

He grinned too.

I didn't grin. I sighed, wondering why it was so easy to fall back into a life I thought I'd put behind me. Wondering why the god who asked that I avoid killing men would send me back to the life of a pirate.

But before the sun slipped any farther down the horizon, our stern was off the beach and we were at sea. We weren't particularly elegant – my lovely *Storm Cutter* was unpainted, unkempt and down thirty rowers from her top form. Neither of Miltiades' other ships was doing any better.

Stephanos followed my eyes and nodded. 'It's been bad,' he said. 'Artaphernes is no fool.'

That I knew. And hearing his name brought to mind the messenger I'd left waiting in the courtyard of my house in Plataea. I turned to Idomeneus.

'Did you stop by my home before rushing after me?' I asked.

'Of course, lord,' he said. 'Where do you think I got the wagon or all the bronze?'

'Any messages?' I asked.

He laughed. 'Despoina Penelope says that if you make money, you had better send some home. Hermogenes says that he'll sit this one out. And here's a message from the satrap of Phrygia.' He held out an ivory tube slyly, knowing that he was causing me a certain consternation.

I took it.

Inside was a letter from Artaphernes inviting me to come and serve him as a captain, at a rate of pay that made me gasp. I knew he would remember me – I had saved his life. And he had saved mine. This was the message I had spurned in Plataea.

As I contemplated the ways of the gods, a single curl of milk-white parchment fluttered in the breeze, peeking out of the scroll tube. I almost missed it. And when I saw it, I plucked at it and it escaped me and flew away, but Idomeneus trapped it against the mast.

On it, in a strong hand, was written:

Some men say a squadron of ships is the most beautiful but I say it is thou who art beautiful. Come and serve my husband, and be famous.
Briseis.

That night, we landed on an empty beach on the south coast of

Myconos. After we had eaten cold barley and drunk bad wine, I approached Miltiades.

'Hear anything of Briseis?' I ventured. I'm sure I asked with the attempt at casual disinterest for which the young strive when they really want something.

'Your sweetheart is married to Artaphernes,' he said. He shook his head and made as if to rest it in the palms of his hands, too weary to go on. He was mocking me. 'She's always by his side, or so I hear.'

Cimon nodded. 'She wanted to be the queen of Ionia,' he said. 'It seems she's chosen her side. And her brother is no longer with the rebellion, either. He's been restored to all his estates in Ephesus. She may have been the price of his return to the fold.'

I didn't weep. I took a deep breath and drank more wine. 'Good for her,' I said, though my voice betrayed me, and Cimon was a good man and let it rest.

'What's the plan?' I asked Miltiades after some time had passed.

'We do what we can to rebuild,' the tyrant of the Chersonese said. 'We prey on their shipping and use the proceeds to rebuild my squadron, and then we retake some of the towns on the Chersonese.'

'You've lost all the towns?' I asked.

Cimon stepped between his father and me. 'Arimnestos,' he said, 'this is it. This is all we have.' He put his arm around my shoulder. 'And unless we convince Athens to get off its arse and help, Miletus will fall, and the Persians will win everything.'

When I had left Miltiades, he had four towns and ten triremes. I nodded. 'Well,' I said, 'I guess there's a lot of work to do.'

Morning found us at sea south of Myconos, our sails full of wind as we bore north by east for Chios, now the heart of the rebellion and the only island on the coast whose harbours were open to us.

About the time the sun rose clear of the sea, Stephanos spotted a sail on our bow. We watched it incuriously until it stood clear of the water with a hull beneath it, and then I recognized my Phoenician slaver.

I closed with Miltiades, stern to stern. 'See that ship?' I said. 'Phoenician slaver full of Iberians, to be delivered to Artaphernes.' I remember grinning. It was as if the god had sent this gift to me. 'Legitimate prize of war!' I shouted – not that we were ever too precise about such stuff. Any Phoenician was fair game.

Miltiades whooped. 'Yours if you can catch him!' he shouted, and I was away.

October is not the best month for a long chase in the Ionian Sea. October is the month when the winds change, and the rains become cold, and Poseidon starts to reckon on his tithe of ships. But it was a beautiful day, with a golden sun in a dark blue sky, and I'd spent fifteen days on that dark hull. His oarsmen hated the slaver, and he was undermanned like all men who made a profit selling their oarsmen.

On the other hand, the ship carried more sails than I could, and his hull had a finer entry. *Storm Cutter* had started his life as a Phoenician heavy trireme, and nothing in his build was for racing. Even fully crewed, he was not the fastest. He had one great point – he was strong.

I took *Storm Cutter* to windward under oars, as if I was departing the rest of the squadron, heading north across the wind for Thrace. When I was over the horizon, the sun was already high in the sky, and now I put my oarsmen to work, pulling hard while the sails were up so that we piled speed on speed. Sometimes this works, but this particular set of oarsmen – not the same men I'd left in this hull, I'll add – weren't up to it, and in the main their oars served only to slow the rush of water down our side.

I cursed and put the wind directly aft. The wind was stronger than it had been in the morning, and the sky at my back was growing dark, and many of my oarsmen were muttering.

All afternoon we raced along, until I had to brail up the mainsail to keep something from carrying away, and still we had no sight of our prey, or even of Miltiades. 'Now I feel like a fool,' I said quietly to Stephanos.

He made a face. 'We should be up with them now,' he said.

I couldn't figure it out. 'We lost time on our first leg,' I said. 'But unless he turned south—'

'Miltiades made chase as soon as we went over the horizon,' Idomeneus said. 'He needs rowers too.'

I grunted. I'd forgotten what a rapacious bastard my lord was. 'Pushed him south and *didn't* catch him,' I added.

'Can we stay at sea with this crew?' I asked Stephanos.

'What, in the dark?' He shook his head. 'No. All the good men ran or took their treasure and walked. Or they're dead. Nobody wants to tell you this, but your friend – Archilogos of Ephesus – he came against us with eight ships, caught us beached and made hay.'

I had a hard time seeing Archilogos, one of the founding voices of the Ionian Revolt, as a servant of Artaphernes, who had cuckolded his father and shamed his mother. On the other hand, his father had been a loyal servant of the King of Kings before the little incident of his mother's adultery.

'You escaped?' I asked.

'I had *Storm Cutter* off the beach. We were washing the hull when your friend came. I lost most of my rowers.' He was ashamed.

'So what?' I said. 'You saved the ship.'

Stephanos turned his head away. 'Not the view of everyone concerned,' he said bitterly.

We beached for the night and I went from fire to fire, getting to know my rowers. There were half a dozen men I knew – a couple of survivors of the storm-tossed days of my first command, and they were happy to see me. A few former slaves I'd freed for a year's rowing, now rowing as free men for wages.

The rest were riff-raff. I watched them land the ship at the edge of night and almost get her broached in the surf. I was angry, but instead of showing my anger, I walked around and talked. I offered them an increased wage on the spot. That helped a little.

Next day we rose with the last light of the moon and we were away before rosy-fingered dawn touched the beach. We rowed on an empty sea, bearing north and east. The wind was fitful, and the clouds to the north were thickening and looked like a shoreline in the sky, an angry dark purple. The oarsmen muttered as they rowed.

About noon, the sun vanished behind a wall of cloud, and Stephanos spoke up from the steering oars.

'Time to beach, navarch,' he said formally.

I shook my head. 'Lots of time, Stephanos. A little chop won't slow us. This is when we gain on Miltiades.' I had abandoned any thought of my chase now – I was just aiming to get back with the squadron, or at least get into Chios on the same day.

By mid-afternoon we were out in the deep blue between Samos and Chios. The sky to the north and east was that terrifying dark blue-grey – so dark as to approach black, and the sky over the bow was distant and bright, like a line of fire.

I'd misjudged my landfall – or misjudged the rate of our drift on the wind. Chios was over there, past the bow – somewhere. It should have been a low line punctuated by mountains, with the island's coast

58

inviting me in for the night. I couldn't understand – we were hurtling along as if pushed by the very fist of Poseidon, and yet I wasn't up with Chios yet.

The muttering of the oarsmen grew. We didn't have a proper oar master, and we needed one. If only to protect them from me.

'I missed this!' I shouted over the wind. 'Take in the mainsail and strike the mainmast down on deck.'

Under the boatsail alone, we ran into the line of fire.

The sun began to set red, and the dark clouds behind us swallowed the red light and looked more ominous yet.

Just against the white line of the last of the good weather, my lookout spotted the hull of our slave ship.

He had his masts down, and his oarsmen rowing for all they were worth. He was more afraid of the storm than of pirates.

We came up on him fast, as our boatsail was enough in that wind to throw foam and spray right over the ram in our bow and on to the rowers, who sat silently, cursing their fates and looking at the madman who stood in front of the helm.

I summoned Idomeneus aft. 'We'll have to take him fast,' I said. 'We'll strip him of rowers and add them to our own, and then we'll live the night.'

Idomeneus shook his head in admiration. 'I thought you'd gone soft,' he said.

'Don't kill the Iberians,' I said. I poured a libation to Poseidon for his gift, because I knew that it was no seamanship of mine that had caught the fast slaver.

When we were five or six stades astern of our prey and the storm line was visible behind us, a long line of rain flowing in the last light of the sun, the Phoenician changed tactics and raised his boatsail.

But Poseidon accepted my libation and spat the slaver's back. Before it could be sheeted home, his boatsail whipped away on the wind, the ship yawed badly and we gained a stade.

Who knows what happened in the last moments as we closed? He was a slaver, and most of his rowers were slaves. And one of the slaves had a knife – a wickedly sharp raven's talon.

By the time Idomeneus went aboard, the deck crew was dead and the Iberians were loose, severed ropes hanging from their ankles, and their leader had an axe and was cutting their fetters. The Phoenician was pinned to the mast with a knife through his chest. We left him there, because sometimes Poseidon likes a sacrifice.

I took every extra slave out of that ship that I could, left them undermanned but not desperate and set them a landfall.

Stephanos stepped up. He was Chian, and he wanted his reputation back.

'They'll die in the dark,' he said. 'Send me aboard and give me a handful of marines and I'll get them through the night.'

Idomeneus nodded.

'Do it,' I said. I stepped across to my new ship even as the rain began. I walked down the main deck and touched hands with a few of the Iberians, meeting their eyes and nodding at the men I remembered from my trip to Delos, and many nodded back. A couple smiled. The dangerous one clasped my hand – hard, testing me – and then threw an arm around me.

Aft of the mast, a voice spoke up in Doric. 'By the gods! Arimnestos! Get me out of here!'

It was the blasphemer, Philocrates.

I leaned down. 'You want to be thrown over the side?'

'No! I want – fuck. Get me out of here!' He was pleading.

'You want to live?' I said. 'Row harder.' I laughed at him. 'Pray!' I suggested.

The Iberian on the opposite bench showed me his teeth. 'Fucking coward,' he said.

I pointed at the Iberian. 'If you don't row, these men will certainly kill you,' I said. 'Now, rationally you must know that if you *do* row, you may live through the night.' I stepped up on the bench, stepped up again to the rail and balanced there as the swell raised the stern. 'But I don't have to be an aspiring priest – isn't that what you called me? – to suggest that this might be a good time to examine your relationship with the gods.'

I leaped down from the rail into the midship of *Storm Cutter*, feeling immensely better. The storm was coming in behind us, but I had done my service for the god, and I knew I could weather the storm.

We turned north and rowed all night, and we constantly lost sight of the other ship, and as often found him again, so that the first fretful grey light, shot with lightning, found the eyes over his ram just a short stade to windward. And about the time that dawn was shining somewhere – it was a grey morning for us, and lashed with rain – I swung the great steering oars to starboard to put the wind astern. I could see a great rock, the size of a castle or the Acropolis, rising from the water to starboard, and I thought that I knew where we were.

Somehow we had come two hundred stades north of our target, and we were off the west coast of Lesbos. That rock marked the beach of Eresus, where Sappho had her school.

Best of all, the beach there was wide and deep, and the rock would break the wind and rain long enough for me to get my ship ashore.

My oarsmen were spent – used up, long since. The Iberians had put some strength into them, and they weren't bad men, but I wasn't going to get a heroic burst of power from them. Not in a month of feast days.

No way to signal Stephanos, either. But he knew this anchorage as well as I – better, no doubt. So I waved at him and turned my ship, hoping that he would read my mind.

I got Idomeneus to come aft. Only a few hundred heartbeats left before the crisis.

'Go down the benches and get every man ready. I intend to put him right up the beach, bow first.' I pointed at the lights shining in the acropolis, high above the beach. 'Hard to miss.' I waited until I saw him understand.

Idomeneus shook his head. 'You'll break his back,' he said.

I confess that I shrugged. 'We'll live.' I nodded towards Asia, which loomed ahead, ready to catch us on a much less kind coast if we failed to land on the sand of Eresus. 'We're out of sea room.' I pointed again. 'Every oarsman has to be ready to *back water*. Tell them to dip lightly, so that they don't get killed by the oars.'

Idomeneus nodded and headed forward, shouting as he went.

I hesitate to say how fast *Storm Cutter* was moving when we came in under the lee of the rock, but I'd say we were faster than a galloping horse. It's less than a stade from the rock to the beach. We were going too fast.

'Oars out!' I shouted across the gale. 'Back water!'

It was ragged. I was as scared as the next man – now that we were in flat water, our speed was shocking. The oars bit, and I couldn't see that we were slowing at all – but the ship yawed and an oarsman screamed as his backed oar bit too deep and slammed into him, breaking his arms.

Like a wool blanket that unravels in the wind, his failure spread, so that the whole port-side loom of oars began to fall apart. Men struggled to keep their oars clear, but the ship rolled from the mis-strokes, and the port-side oars bit too deep, and men died, or were broken. We turned suddenly, and the port side dipped so low on the roll that we took water. We still had so much way on us that we were racing *sideways* into the beach.

The port-side rowers – those still in command of themselves – finally got all their oars clear of the water. The starboard-side rowers were at full stretch and the hull pivoted again, rotating on the starboard oar bank, and the bow hit the sand a glancing blow as the bronze-plated ram caught the trough of gravel just shy of the beach and skipped along it.

Then we could hear the ram ploughing a furrow in the gravel and suddenly the boatmast snapped with a crack as loud as the lightning, and every man not sitting a bench was thrown flat on the deck as a wave picked up the stern and tossed us – the kindly hand of Poseidon, I like to think – up the beach, stern first.

'Over the side!' I roared, although I was lying half-stunned. 'Get her up the beach!'

It was the ugliest landing I ever saw – we'd been rotated halfway round by the sea, men were badly hurt all along both sides, and I could see broken boards where my ram ought to be.

But when I jumped over the side, my feet barely splashed.

We were ashore.

Stephanos didn't even try to land. He watched us, and he assumed we were lost in the waves, and he put up his helm and coasted by, a few oar-lengths offshore. In seconds he was past the beach, and before we had our broken hull clear of Poseidon's reaching tendrils, his ship had gone around the promontory to the north of Eresus.

I lay by the rope I had been hauling and cursed, because the loss of Stephanos hurt me more than I'd expected. I hadn't seen him in a year. I wanted him back.

Idomeneus had his marines in hand and was driving oarsmen to work, gathering wood to put supports under the hull timbers. We propped *Storm Cutter* on sand that was only wet with rain, and then we drove the oarsmen into the sea to fetch the ram before it got buried in storm-wrack and sand. The ram was heavy bronze plate, but with thirty men helping we hauled it above the tide line. Then we collapsed.

I sent Idomeneus to the citadel to get us help and hospitality, then I sat in my sodden chlamys and watched the storm, and sang a hymn to Poseidon and prayed that Stephanos might live.

The news came back that Sappho's daughter had died – an old,

old woman, but a great teacher, as awe-inspiring and god-touched in her way as Heraclitus in his – and had been succeeded by another woman, Aspasia, who now led the school of Sappho. So much had changed in just a few years. But Aspasia was supported by Briseis's largesse, and she accepted me without question when I told her who I was, and she lodged my men and fed them.

I let myself into Briseis's house and sat by her shuttered window, drinking her wine and eating her food. Surely it was she, and not Artaphernes, who had sent me that message. Hence, she must have need of me, I reasoned. And not a need she dared commit to paper. I reasoned – with a brain clouded by Eros, let me add – that she must need me.

I would find Miltiades soon enough. But if I could get *Storm Cutter* rebuilt, I would cross the straits and run down the coast to Ephesus and visit my love, and see why she had summoned me.

The storm took three days to blow out, and my men praised me openly for bringing them to such a safe haven, with lamb stew every night and good red wine for every man, as if they were a crew of lords. The folk of Eresus treated us like gods – as well they might, since it was Briseis's gold that kept the school going, and her political power that kept it free of outside control. And they feared us.

When the storm was gone, we had beautiful weather for autumn. I put men on the headlands to keep watch, and I prayed to Poseidon every day and gave offerings of cakes and honey on the Cyprian goddess's altar, too – anything to bring back Stephanos. We cut good wood on the hillsides east of the town and rebuilt the bow, with two carpenters from the town helping us with the main beams that had cracked. We stripped the hull clean and rebuilt the bow, and found a fair amount of rot in the upper timbers. I built a marine platform – like a box, with armoured sides – into the new bow, and a little shelf where an archer or a lookout could stand high above the ram.

I borrowed from the Temple of Aphrodite, and spent the money on tar and pine pitch, and blacked the hull, a fresh, thick coat so that he was armoured in the stuff, watertight and shining. I gave him a stripe of Poseidon's own blue above the waterline, and we painted the oar shafts to match, all in a day, and the women of the town washed our great sail so that the raven was fresh and stark again.

In such a way we propitiated Poseidon, but there was no sign of Stephanos. So after a week of good food and freely given aid, we prepared to sail away in a fresh ship. I was sombre at the loss of a friend, but the crew was wild with delight.

'Boys are saying their luck has changed,' Idomeneus said.

I had appointed two Iberians who could speak some Greek to be officers. My new oar master was Galas, and he had more tattoos than a Libyan, for all that his skin was fairer than mine. He had blue eyes and ruddy hair and his scalp was shaved in whorls, but he knew the sea and his Greek was good enough. And he had taken command of the port-side oars during the disaster of the landing.

My new sailing master had the same tattoos and his name was too barbaric for words, something like 'Malaleauch'. I called him Mal, and he answered to it. He spoke a pidgin of Greek and Italiote and Phoenician.

I had thirty of the former slaves on my benches now. I'd lost more than a dozen men in that horrible landing – dead, or so badly injured that they still lay in Lady Sappho's Temple of Aphrodite, waiting to be healed or to die.

The Iberians all viewed me as the author of their freedom. I explained to Galas how small a role I'd played, and how much they owed to the gods, but I was not sorry to benefit from their gratitude.

At any rate, we heaved *Storm Cutter* into the surf and got the rowers in position as if we knew what we were doing, and then we were away. Galas brought more out of the rowers than I had, and we spent two more days rowing up and down the sea off Lesbos to drill them until their oars rose and fell like the single arm of a single man.

Then we rowed around to Methymna, and I put her stern on the beach and asked after Miltiades and my friend Epaphroditos, the archon basileus of the town. But the captain of the guard told me that Lord Epaphroditos was away at the siege of Miletus.

I needed money, and Epaphroditos's absence left me no choice. I had to take a prize, and a rich one. My men needed paying, and I was down to no wine and no stores. I got one meal out of Methymna based on their memories of me and my famous name, but we sailed from that town like a hungry wolf.

We ran south along the east coast of Lesbos, and the beaches were empty at Mytilene, where the rebel fleet ought to have been forming up. And just south of Mytilene, we saw a pair of heavy Phoenicians guarding a line of merchantmen – Aegyptians, I thought as I stood on the new bow.

'Get the mainmast up,' I called to Mal, and motioned for Galas, who was steering, to take us about. We could no more face a pair of heavy Phoenicians than we could weather another storm. 'Fuck,' I muttered.

They were none too happy to see us when we put on to the beach at Mytilene, but men remembered me there, and I arranged for a meal and some oil and wine on credit – Miltiades' credit.

I was sitting alone at a small fire on the beach, cursing my fate, or rather, my ignorance of events and my inability to accomplish anything, when a pair of local men – traders – came up out of the dark.

'Lord Arimnestos?' the shorter one asked.

'Aye,' I answered, and offered them wine.

In short, they had a cargo of grain – several cargoes, in fact – and they wondered if I'd like to have a go at smuggling it into Miletus. The rate of exchange they offered was good – good enough to give me some slack. So I loaded grain at their wharf and filled the ship, so that she sat deep in the water and my rowers cursed.

'We're fucked if we have to run,' Idomeneus said.

'Really?' I asked, as if the thought had never occurred to me.

We sailed at sunset, ran along the coast of Lesbos before full dark fell and were off Chios in the light of a full moon. My oarsmen were none too happy with me, because this was flirting with Poseidon's rage and no mistake, or so they said.

I made my sea-marks off Chios, and we passed silently along the beaches I had known like family homes in my youth. Just past false dawn, we passed the beach where Stephanos had lived before he went away to sea to be a killer of men.

There was a long, low trireme beached there.

My heart rose in my chest, and I abandoned my plan and put our stern to the beach, and we went ashore.

'I thought you were done for,' Stephanos said. 'And I thought I could weather the cape by Methymna and run free in the channel, with the two islands to break the fury of the storm.' He shrugged. 'Those Iberians don't know how to row, but they have a lot of guts. I got us around the corner, and they kept the bow into the seas, and we determined to land at Mytilene, but there was a current – I've never seen anything like it. We went past Mytilene in the blink of an eye, and north of Chios we hit a log that was drifting, broke a board amidships and started to take on water.' Stephanos was a big, plain-spoken sailor who had grown to manhood as a fisherman, and his hands moved like an actor's as he told the story.

His sister Melaina was beaming up at him. She, too, was a friend of my youth, from the heady days when I was newly freed, just finding my power as a man-at-arms. We kept grinning at each other.

'Then what happened?' Idomeneus asked.

'The back of the ship snapped like a twig, we sank and the fishes ate us!' Stephanos laughed. His sister swatted him, and he ducked. 'One of the rowers shouted that we weren't done yet – a Greek fellow, Philocrates. He put some heart in the boys and we got the head around, then the wind let up for a few moments, and in that time we got into a cove on the north shore – it was as if Poseidon agreed to let us live. I put the bow on the shingle, and to Hades with the ram – which took a right battering, and we've been a week repairing her. But we lived!'

'As did we,' I said, and we embraced again. I looked at his ship. 'What do you call him?' I asked.

Stephanos grinned his easy grin. 'Well, we thought of calling him *Storm Cutter*, but that's taken, so we opted for *Trident*.'

The sign of Poseidon. 'A fine name.'

He grinned again. 'So – how do we make some money?' He kissed his sister and pointed up the beach. 'Go and find Harpagos, dear.'

Harpagos proved to be Stephanos's cousin. Melaina brought him down to the beach, and he was no smaller than Stephanos and his hands were hard as rock. Stephanos introduced him with flowery compliments.

'This is my useless layabout cousin Harpagos, who wants to ship with me. He's never been to sea.' Stephanos spat on the sand and laughed.

Harpagos had the look of a man who'd kept the sea his entire life. His hair was full of salt. But he stood, abashed.

I winked at Stephanos. It was like old times. 'You're a trierarch now, my friend. No need to consult me on every raw man.'

'I've been helmsman on a grain ship,' Harpagos said.

'I want him as my helmsman,' Stephanos admitted. Then he said, 'I need him where I can see him.'

I liked Harpagos. His embarrassment at all this attention shouted of the sort of solid, quiet confidence that makes a man able to go to sea and fish every day for forty years. 'On your head be it,' I said. 'Harpagos, can you fight?'

He shrugged. 'I wrestle,' he said. 'I teach the boys in the village. I can take this big fool.' He indicated Stephanos.

'Hmm,' I allowed. 'Well, he can take me, and that would be bad for discipline. Ever used a spear and shield?' I asked.

Harpagos shook his head. 'Can't say I have.'

'Ever killed?' I asked.

Harpagos looked out to sea. 'Yes,' he said, voice flat.

We all stood together in silence, and the fine wind blew across us. 'Well,' I said, 'welcome aboard. We're pirates, Harpagos. Sometimes we fight for the Ionian rebels, but mostly we take other people's ships for profit. Can you do that?'

He grinned – the first grin I'd seen. 'Yes, lord.'

Melaina listened to this exchange and brought more wine, and we ate fresh sardines and a big red fish I hadn't eaten often – with flesh like lobster. We drank too much wine. Melaina pressed herself on me, and I flirted with her, smiled, even held her for a time while standing by the fire on the beach. But I didn't take her into the dark. My head was full of Briseis, and Melaina wasn't a beach girl. She was Stephanos's sister, and she dressed like a woman of property. Somewhere, she had a man she was going to marry. And to bed her would have been to betray my guest-friendship with Stephanos.

In the morning, I gave him half the grain, and the next evening, full of food and a little too much wine, we were off the beach, rowing soft in the moonlight for Miletus.

Our plan was simple, like most good plans. We both had Phoenician ships – both newly repaired and looking fairly prosperous. We sailed due south, got behind the coastal islands, west around Samos, rowing all the way, and came into the Bay of Miletus from the south-west – that is, from the direction of Tyre and Phoenicia – as the sun set in the west, mostly behind us. We stood straight down the bay, bold as brass, apparently a pair of their own ships bound for the blockade fleet at Tyrtarus on the island of Lade.

The fishermen of Chios had been able to lay the whole siege out like a scroll for us, because they smuggled fish to the rebels and sold them openly to the Medes, Persians, Greeks and Phoenicians who served the Great King, too. Miletus is an ancient city, founded before Troy, and she stands at the base of a deep inlet of the sea, just south of Samos, although the bay over towards Mycale is starting to silt up. Miletus has a steep acropolis, impregnable, or so men used to say, and her outer town is protected by a circuit of stone walls with towers. The Persians began by moving their fleet to Ephesus, just a hundred stades up the coast. Once they had a base there, they moved in and stormed Tyrtarus, a fishing village with a small fort, and used it as their forward base, so that ships from there could easily launch into the narrow channel and catch any vessel heading into Miletus.

Mind you, it is possible to row north around Lade. The problem is that anyone holding the fort on Lade can see you coming fifty stades away, and when you turn north, they're waiting – and the currents around the island favour the side that holds it.

Once the Persians had the fort at Tyrtarus, they brought up their land forces on the landward side of the peninsula. Artaphernes came in person, and they built a great camp in the hills overlooking Miletus. After a few weeks of skirmishing, he started on the siege mound.

Men tell me the Assyrians invented the siege mound, and perhaps they did, although as usual the Aegyptians claim they invented it. Either way, it was not the Greeks, who prefer a nice flat field and a single day of battle to a year's siege. But the Ionians and Aeolian Greeks have fortified cities, and when the Lydians or the Medes come against them, they fight a war of shovels. The Persians dig a giant hill that runs from the flat of the plain to the top of the walls, and the Greeks in the city counter-dig, trying either to raise the wall by the mound or to destroy the Persian mound. And while both sides dig, the men outside make sure that the men inside receive no help, no weapons and, most of all, no food.

Sometimes the men inside the walls triumph, boring their opponents into backing off. And sometimes a single load of grain can be a mighty weapon. First, because the men inside the walls can eat, and their hearts rise; second, because the men outside the walls know they must struggle for so much longer each time a cargo reaches their enemies.

But in my experience, sieges are rarely settled by the hand of man. Usually, the Lord Apollo hurls his fearsome arrows of disease into one side or the other – or sometimes into both – and the dead pile up as if Ares had reaped them with a sword, but faster. Sieges *eat* men.

I didn't know that then, as the sun set over my stern. I was twenty-five years old, and I had never seen a siege.

South of Samos, and no guard ship came to look at us. We stood straight on, and as we entered the Bay of Miletus, we bore up and sailed along the south coast of the bay, as if bound for the island of Lade. We were sailing in light airs, but every bench was manned and we were ready to run.

In the last light of the day, two of their ships headed out to meet us. They took a long time coming off the beach, and we didn't hurry towards them.

'Oar-rake and past,' I called softly to Stephanos, and he nodded and repeated my orders to Harpagos, whose hooked nose could just be seen above the stem of the ship. We could see Miletus in the distance now, rising on the next headland, due east down the channel.

There's a world of difference between being ready for action and expecting nothing to happen, and that world of difference separated our ships and theirs. They came out thinking we were Phoenicians. We knew exactly what we intended to do, and when we were at hailing distance and the lead ship called to us in their Phoenician tongue, I clapped my hands once – I remember that the sound carried over the water and made a little echo against the nearer enemy hull – then every back bent on my ship, and the oars twinkled in the setting sun. If they had been ready, they'd have leaped into action right there, but many heartbeats passed while their navarch and his officers tried to work out why we were rowing so hard.

The lead Phoenician was so ill-prepared that his crew caught a crab and he fell away from his course, which was almost the end of my plan. I wanted to oar-rake the pair, Stephanos taking the port-side enemy and I the starboard, and my plan was that we'd crush their oars and race through before any other ships could launch off the beach.

But the lead Phoenician turned broadside on to us, and we had no choice but to ram him or abandon our attempt. The channel was too narrow to avoid him, so I caught him just aft of amidships and Stephanos caught him a few heartbeats later, well forward, and together we rolled him over, dumping his rowers in the water.

We'd turtled one ship, but the impacts tested our bows and cost us all our speed and hard-earned momentum, and we were all a-stand for the second ship.

He knew his business, and now that he'd had a moment to think, he was ready. He loosed a flight of arrows, and some of my rowers were hit, but Galas had them in hand and we were moving forward.

'Oars in!' I called.

It was sloppy, but we had all our oar shafts in as our bow slammed into the second ship. We weren't moving fast – neither was he – and the two ships didn't have the power to get past each other. As we came to a dead stop, broadside to broadside, Idomeneus got grapples over the side, but at the cost of three marines. The Phoenicians were poling us off while their archers flayed us. Galas went down with an arrow in him, and my deck crew was melting – men were taking cover behind the masts, behind screens, anything. And this from four or five archers.

I had the helm, but we had stopped. On the beach, men were pushing ships into the water – a dozen slim hulls launching all together.

'Fuck,' I said aloud. I remember, because there was a lull, and my imprecation carried clearly across the water.

I drew my sword and caught up my big hide shield, a simple Boeotian I'd bought on the beach at Chios. I didn't have my armour or my good war gear or my new helmet, and I was carrying a shield just two goat hides thick. Even as I raised it, an arrow punched through, tore my hair and carried on to sink into the sternposts.

I ran down our central platform. A running man is a hard target for archers, but that didn't stop them – they knew I was the helmsman. Every archer fixed on me, and two arrows hit my shield, but neither pinked me.

Amidships, Idomeneus had two grapples fixed and guarded by his marines, their big shields covering him and his ropes. Opposite, a pair of Phoenicians sawed with swords at the hawsers that held us fast. I saw all of this in a glance and pivoted on one heel. I leaped from the command platform to the gunwale by Idomeneus, covered for a valuable moment by the two aspides of his marines, and without pause – hesitation would have been death – I was across the gap, my left foot on their gunwale and then both feet firm on a rower's bench, and I started killing.

I took the men who were sawing at our grapples in two blows, and then I cleared the rowing bench by beheading the oarsman. His blood sprayed back on the men behind him, and I punched with the rim of my light shield, caught one of the Phoenician marines who was surprised at the length of my arms and knocked him flat, and I was on their command platform.

'Hellas!' I shouted.

I was fuelled by desperation and the elation of a starving man offered food. I hadn't fought like this in more than a year – and I was better than a mere man, thugater. My shield and my sword were everywhere, as if they had eyes and thoughts of their own. I remember rotating my hips and punching *back* with my shield rim, catching a sailor in the groin, and glowing with the joy of fighting so well. A winter of training the Plataeans had not been wasted. Each blow, each parry, blended seamlessly into another. It was like dance. It might have gone on for ever.

And then Idomeneus was shouting my name, and I raised my hand, and the enemy deck was clear. I had my blade in the air and there was a half-naked sailor under the edge – but I stayed my hand, as Dion had asked.

'Apollo!' I called, and let the man live.

Idomeneus and the marines had followed me aboard. There were a dozen warships in the water, and Stephanos was already past us, rowing hard for Miletus. That's what he was supposed to do.

'Mal!' I called. He turned his head, and I waved at him. At the same time, I cut the grapples that held the two ships together. 'Go!'

It took three shouts, but he got it. He started striking men with his stick, and the oarsmen on the starboard side began to push against our hull with poles and spears and even their oars.

Idomeneus was on the stern of the ship I'd just taken. I saw him grasp the oars, and I picked up a javelin that one of the enemy marines had dropped – or thrown.

'Reverse your benches,' I ordered in Greek. A few men obeyed, and others looked blank, or mutinous.

I threw my javelin into one of those who was refusing his duty, and he fell across his oar. Then I pulled the spear free of his corpse. 'Reverse your benches!' I roared.

They obeyed.

I pounded the oar-beat against the mast with the spear-butt, and they rowed. It wasn't good rowing, but the men coming off the beaches weren't eager to fight in the dark and they weren't any too sure what had just happened, either. We backed down the channel – first a stade, and then another stade – and then the arrows from Miletus began to fall on the enemy ships following us.

One bold ship made a last try. Before the final bend in the channel, a beautiful long trireme with a red stripe went to full speed in half a dozen ship-lengths – a superb crew – and tried to ram us, bow to bow.

Idomeneus had the ship, and he steered well, so that the two rams rang together like a hammer and an anvil, and our ship bounced away, apparently undamaged.

Arrows fell from the near bank, so many that they were visible against the faint light of the sky, and there were screams from the red ship, and it fell away. I could hear a familiar voice cursing and ordering men to reverse their cushions – a Greek voice.

Archilogos's voice. A man I'd sworn to protect – now leading the ships of my enemies.

The men of Miletus greeted us like brothers – better than brothers. We'd killed an enemy ship and seized another right under the eyes of their blockade, in full view of the walls, and we would have been drunk as lords in a few hours if there had been any wine in the lower city.

As it was, my first hours in the siege of Miletus showed me all the things I'd never wanted to know about sieges. The people were as thin as cranes – the children looked like old people, and the women looked like children. A handful of the town's best fighters still looked like men – they got extra food, and they needed it. The rest looked like starved dogs, and Histiaeus, the tyrant of the town, had to set his fighters as guards to get our grain ashore.

I took our pay in gold darics. 'I'll be back,' I promised.

Histiaeus was a tall, beautiful man with a mane of black hair and golden skin and a heavy scar across his face. His brother Istes was another of the same – they had been raised at the Great King's court and spoke Persian as well as Greek, and they looked like gods. I liked Istes better – he was less addicted to power and a better man – but he laughed at me. 'No one comes back a second time,' he called as my men got the stern off the beach. 'But thanks!'

That stung. 'I'll be back in ten days, by the fires of Hephaestus and the bones of the Corvaxae!' I shouted to Istes. I craved his good opinion. In those days, men said Istes was the best sword in Ionia. He was a few years older than me, and we had never been matched against each other. But we were instant friends, that night in Miletus.

So, having sworn my oath before men and the gods, I ordered my men to row. We were heavily laden – I'd filled the ship with all the women and children that dared to come with us. We headed straight back to sea.

It was dark as pitch. I reckoned that Archilogos wouldn't expect me to try again immediately, and I was right. We rowed out of the harbour at ramming speed, made the turn at the harbour-mouth in fine style and tore up the estuary, and the Medes and traitorous Greeks on the beaches at Tyrtarus must have watched us go by and felt like fools, but none opposed us. I stood on my stern and laughed at them, and the sound of my mockery carried over the water and bounced back from the bluffs above the town.

Probably a stupid taunt, but it felt good, and it still makes me smile to think of how Archilogos must have writhed at the sound of my laughter.

And then we were out to sea and running before a freshening wind.

All our rowers were exhausted by the time we made Chios. We disgorged our cargo of refugees, and the people of the fishing villages fed them. But they wouldn't keep them, and we still had them aboard when we headed back north to Mytilene.

I had to give command of the new ship to Harpagos. I was out of officers, and Idomeneus, for all that he was a skilled killer, had no interest in the sea and could no more inspire men than I could play a flute. Harpagos was a good seaman, and his quiet solidity was the sort of thing men trust in a storm or a fight. I gave him a try, and I never regretted it.

I took all three ships back into the great harbour at Mytilene, and still there was no sign of the rebel fleet. Nor had anyone heard a word of Miltiades. It was as if the Persians had already won.

I paid my grain merchants from the gold I'd received in Miletus.

'And I'll buy the rest of your grain,' I said. I offered them a handsome profit, for men who never had to move from the comfort of their own homes, and I filled three ships with grain in sacks and jars. I'll say this for them – for all the Lesbians – they took the shiploads of refugees from Miletus and treated them like citizens.

This time, we sailed in broad daylight. My crew trusted me now. And weeks of action had made them better men. I knew the process and I used it for my own ends. We rowed when we might have sailed, and I hardened their muscles as if they were athletes, and I promised them a gold daric a man if they got us in and out of Miletus again.

I waited for the dark of the moon, and the gods sent me a dark night and heavy seas. We had lights on our sterns, and we rowed across in the dark, with the rowers cursing their ill-luck and praying with every stroke – but after a month of constant adventure, my crew could row in the dark.

We went down the bay with the wind at our backs, under boatsails alone, north around Lade. The wind defeated the currents and allowed us to move quickly, and the Phoenicians were snug in their blankets when we went past, because it was raining and winter had come. But some fool laughed aloud and alerted them, and when we had unloaded and turned our bows to the open sea, they were formed across the bay, fifteen ships waiting for our three. And they were good sailors. I watched them for a while from the safety of the Milesian archers, and then I took my little squadron back into the harbour.

All the gold darics in the world weren't going to save me. I was blockaded in Miletus, and it looked as if our luck had run its course.

4

The Persian fleet didn't actually have any Persians in it, of course. There were Ionian Greeks and Phoenicians and a handful of very capable Aegyptians on those beaches, and I stood in the so-called Windy Tower of Miletus and watched them.

To the south, the Persian siege mound grew every day. No Persians there, either – just slaves culled from the countryside, hundreds and hundreds of agricultural slaves from the Milesians' own farms carrying brush and soil, while fending off rocks and arrow shafts, and dumping it under the walls, so that the siege mound grew the width of a man's hand every night.

The Milesian aristocrats remained confident, however. Their city had never fallen, and they still had stores – they hadn't killed all their animals yet, and only the lower-class people were suffering. When I was taken up to the acropolis, it was as if I'd entered a city free of war – I was bathed by slaves, anointed with oil and served a meal that included thin-sliced beef tongue.

But in the lower city, the people were starving.

My grain put heart into them, and I wasn't the only captain who got through – just the only one who'd done it twice. And this late in the season, my second cargo – three ships' worth – saved the city. Histiaeus and his brother did not hesitate to tell me so.

My second night in the city, Istes led the warriors in an attack out of a postern gate and set fire to a brush pile the enemy had been preparing – brush piled as high as a city wall, intended to help with the last days of the siege mound. But they couldn't burn the soil, and in the morning the slaves were back at work.

Persian archers appeared periodically and shot into the city – fire arrows, sometimes, but mostly just war shafts, carefully aimed. Every day they killed a man or two on the walls. On the other hand, they kept the city supplied with arrows.

Archilogos, or whoever was in command over there on the beaches of Lade, was not giving up either. They formed a cordon every night, and had small boats rowing across the channel, and at least two ships out in the bay north of the island. At dawn and dusk they sortied out with at least fifteen ships, and I didn't see much hope for escape.

But on the third night, the city's defenders sallied out again, and this time I went with them. It is ironic that, once you have the reputation as a great warrior, you must support it constantly. I could no more sit in the acropolis while the men raided than I could abstain from eating.

The city was well appointed with regard to armour, and Lord Histiaeus gave me a bell corslet and a fine Cretan helmet with a magnificent horsehair plume. It was a bit like living in the *Iliad*. I took my marines, and Philocrates the Blasphemer, who had settled into the life of piracy like a veteran. I got him arms as well, a full panoply.

'You look like Ares come to life,' I said to him, when he was dressed in bronze.

'Ares is a myth to frighten children,' he said.

'I see that a storm at sea and a life of war is not enough to restore your respect for the gods,' I said.

He shrugged. 'You can't respect what ain't there.'

I stood back a little and regarded him. There was something frightening about him. He ignored portents, laughed at talismans and called the gods by foul names. At first only the Iberians would eat with him, but as he continued to blaspheme and the skies never swallowed him up, other men began to accept him. That said, I have to say that he *had* changed. I couldn't put my finger on why, but he explained it himself later, as you'll hear, if you come back for more of this story tomorrow.

At any rate, sixty of us went out of the postern gate nearest the harbour. It was pelting down with rain – we slipped on the mud, and I blessed my good Boeotian boots even as the other men cursed their open sandals. The ground in front of the walls had been churned to a froth by the passage of thousands of men, slaves and soldiers, and both sides dumped their waste and filth into that no-man's-land. It was foul.

You'd think that after a hundred of these raids, the Persians would have set a watch, but of all their contingents, only the Aegyptians kept a regular guard. Most of their crack troops were cavalrymen who disdained such rigorous pastimes as guard duty, and who am I to comment? I never knew a Greek who was willing to stand a night watch.

We crossed the mud and the ordure in the lashing rain, and then we went over the fresh brush they'd piled in lieu of a wall around their camp. No hope of lighting a fire on this night, but we had a different goal in mind.

We weren't after Artaphernes. If he'd been at the siege, he might have had Briseis, and my approach would have been very different. Indeed, since I'm trying to tell the whole truth here, I'll add that I didn't feel any particular commitment to the rebels. They weren't Plataeans, for instance. I was loyal enough to Miltiades, but you'll note that I wasn't criss-crossing the seas looking for him. Nor was I sailing up and down looking for the rebel fleet to offer my services. Mind you, once I was trapped in Miletus, my options were limited. But I wasn't an idealist. I was a Plataean, and I was Briseis's lover – or rather, the same, but in the other order.

But neither the satrap nor his new wife was at the siege that autumn. Datis was Artaphernes' lieutenant, and our aim was to kill him. His great red and purple tent showed clearly across the lines by day, and we'd worked out a couple of sea-marks – torches mounted at two different heights in the town – to guide us to his tent. He was a relative of the Great King – Artaphernes was one of the king's many brothers, and this Datis was a cousin, or some such, and a famous warrior, and the rumours were that when he took Miletus, he'd be sent with a great fleet against Chios and Lesbos – and perhaps Athens. Or so men said.

No one expected us to succeed in killing him, but it was this sort of constant pressure that kept the besiegers on edge and encouraged them to pack it up for the winter and head home.

We crept through the dark, soaked to the skin, squelching in mud, turning frequently to get our line of approach from the torches on the walls, and we crept forward, cursed by men in the tents whose ropes we bumped – little knowing, of course, that we were mortal foes. I wondered if this was what Odysseus had felt when he left the Trojan horse to sneak into the town of Troy. The *Iliad* is very real at times – but no one ever seems to be wet or cold, or have the flux. I find that these three are the proper children of Ares, not Havoc and Panic and whatever else the poets ascribe. Who ever had a war without wet and cold?

We were in the middle of the column, so we had no idea what – or who – alarmed the camp, but suddenly we were discovered. It was raining so hard that no one could light a torch, and as soon as the enemy came out of their tents, they lost all sense of the situation.

Our men killed the first to come close to them, then scattered. That's what we'd planned. The Milesians simply vanished. They had raided the camp before and knew it well enough. My marines were not so lucky, and in the dark we followed the wrong men. We thought we were following Milesians and we ended up in the horse lines, where a dozen conscientious Persian troopers had run to protect their mounts. Our men started fighting them with no cue from me. My marines were armoured and the Persians were unarmed, and they died – taking two of my men with them. Persians are *brave*.

'Cut the halters and undo the hobbles,' I ordered. My survivors spread out and caused chaos on the horse lines, ripping pickets out of the ground. I ran to the top of a low hill and looked back at the city, and only then did I realize that we had the whole width of the enemy camp between us.

More immediately, men were boiling out of the camp, backlit by the lights on the city wall. Persians love their horses. My ten men weren't going to last a minute against a regiment of Persian cavalrymen.

I thought of stealing horses and heading inland, but that sort of thing only works in epics. In real life, your enemies have more horses and native guides, and they ride you down. Besides, my men were sailors in armour, not cavalrymen. Most of them had probably never forked a horse.

I was out of ideas, but Poseidon stood by us. Horses scattered in every direction, and I didn't have to be Odysseus to reckon that we could escape with the herd. A few of us mounted, and others simply clung to manes, even tails – and we flowed with the horses, moving west and north, back towards the city. I got mounted, lost my bearings and my companions, and spent a watch among the rocks south of the city, where my horse left me.

The gods help those who help themselves, or so I've heard it said, and while I lay in the rocks watching the city and the force of Persian archers between me and the walls, cursing my fate, I realized that it was a six-stade walk along the ridge of rock to the beach opposite Tyrtarus. And not a sentry on the way.

I took the time to poke along the ridge of rock. Every piece of waste ground has trails, if you know where to look – goats make them, and shepherds, and boys and girls courting or playing at being heroes. The moon came up late and the rain ceased, and I walked to the beach opposite Lade, stripped to my skin and swam to the hulls opposite – really just a few horse-lengths, well less than a stade. I rose up, dripping, by the black hulls, close enough to the enemy camp to hear the snores of Archilogos's oarsmen, or so I reckoned. Then I swam back and picked my way among the rocks. As I had expected, the Persians had gone back to bed. I crawled through the mud and shit to the walls of the town, and wasted another half an hour persuading the sentry to let me climb the wall without gutting me. Oh, the romance of siege warfare!

I was the last man back from the raid, and my sword had not left its scabbard. There were men in the upper city who were of a mind to laugh at me. I let them laugh. I was no longer a hot-blooded boy, and I didn't need a blood feud in the town. I wanted to take my gold and go, although I was keen to show Istes what I was made of. He'd killed three Persians, and brought in their bows and arrows as proof.

I slept well enough. In the morning I ate honeyed almonds in the upper city and took a long bath to kill the smell of the mud. Histiaeus and Istes joined me.

'Your men accomplished a miracle,' he said. 'Not a slave is working on the siege mound today. They're all out searching for the horses.' He smiled grimly. 'We didn't get Datis, but we hurt them – a deserter says we killed fifteen Persians and some others.'

I nodded. None of this interested me much. This war of tiny increments was not something I could really appreciate. To me, the city looked doomed, and I wanted out before I was sold into slavery again.

'Will you raid again tonight?' I asked.

He shook his head. Even he – the best-fed warrior in the city – had circles under his eyes like shield bags, and the lines on his face were as deep as new-ploughed furrows. 'No,' he said. 'We've been out two nights in a row. We can't keep it up. The fighters are exhausted. The real fighters – the men of worth.' His eyes flicked to Istes, who also looked like a man at the edge of exhaustion.

'I'm leaving tonight,' I said.

He shook his head. 'I don't recommend that,' he said. 'Mind you, if you stay much longer, I'll be selling you your grain.'

'I'd appreciate a dozen of your archers to help me get clear,' I said. 'I'd bring them back on my next trip.'

'You plan to shoot your way out?' Istes asked. 'Archers are our most valuable troops.' He shrugged. 'You are the best friend this city has made in many months – but the loss of ten archers would be a blow.'

'I understand. But I need the archers for my diversion, and I'll leave you a trireme as surety – the Phoenician I took on my way in.' I pointed to the hull. 'On a dark night – you might use her to get some people out.'

He shook his head in puzzlement. 'Why leave a ship?' he asked.

I grunted. I didn't want to tell him. As in any siege, the town was riddled with deserters, traitors and double agents, I had no doubt. 'We'll be away in the dark of the moon,' I said.

'Poseidon bless you, then,' the tyrant said. But his eyes flicked to his brother, and something passed between them that I didn't like.

Oh, I was eager to be gone.

I slept most of the day and mustered all my men – marines, oarsmen, deck crews – at dusk. I put my plan to them as the sun vanished into clouds, and enough men volunteered to give me hope. I wish I could say that they all volunteered, but a week on half rations in a doomed city is enough to sap anyone's morale.

I took my party out of the harbour sally port when the rain started. We made the rocks south of town in the end, although I had an anxious time finding them in the dark. It is always easier to go *to* a town than away from it.

We were soaked through and shivering by the time we made the rocks, and then we crept along, spear-butts sounding like avalanches as they scraped the stone. Philocrates cursed steadily. When we were on the beach opposite Lade, we stripped and swam, clinging to our spears as best we could.

We missed our way – the darkness was deep and there was no moon. Let me just say that swimming in the dark – no sight of anything, cold through, so that you shiver, clinging to your weapons – is perhaps the ultimate test of the warrior. Men turned back. And who am I to blame them?

We ended up on the rocks east of the ships, and there was nothing for it but to crawl. I'd explained this part, but the execution was much harder than I'd anticipated. Try crawling on a rainy night, naked but for a wet chlamys, and keeping a spear with you, across broken ground thick with brush.

Hah! We sounded like a herd of cattle. But fools that we were, and inept, the enemy were as bad or worse.

I made the most noise as I was wearing Histiaeus's gift, the bronze cuirass. I wore it swimming, and it wasn't bad, but when I crawled across rocks it was loud and the flare around the hips caught on *everything*.

That was one of the longest, darkest hours of my life. I had not reckoned on losing my way again – we only had a stade of open ground to cross – but I did. In the end, I had to rise to my feet, stumbling like a drunkard, and turn slowly – in full view of the enemy sentries, if there had been any – to realize that I had crawled right past the enemy encampment.

Too late to correct my course. I was well south of my target, but I could see the black hulls of their triremes just to the left, shiny in the darkness. I had at least a dozen men with me – men who had chosen to follow me even when their sense said they'd gone wrong – and now we crept across the dunes, then clattered across the tongue of rock that separated the mudflat from the sea until we were crouched by the ships.

Most of the men had packets of oiled cloth and pitch, or even bitumen – there was plenty of it in Miletus – and we built a pile of the stuff under one hull.

Although there was no moon, the rain abated while we crouched there. The camp had fires – mostly coals – and several Iberians crept between the boatsails erected as tents and lit their torches at the fires. By now there were thirty or forty of my men among the hulls of their ships, and we all called 'Alarm! Alarm!' in Greek for all we were worth. Our Iberians ran through the camp with lit torches before thrusting them into our prebuilt pyre.

And then chaos came.

The fire roared up in the time it would take a man to run the stade – from a few flickers of flame to a conflagration twice the height of a man's head and as loud as a horse race. The ship caught immediately – hulls coated in pitch are an invitation to flame, even in the rain. My sailors ran back and forth, feeding sails and oars into the inferno, and then throwing the lit wreckage into other hulls.

Men came out of the tents, and we killed them. As we were the ones calling the alarm, they kept on coming to us for many minutes, unarmed or with buckets to put out the fire, and we put them down.

By then we had three ships alight, and my two were out in the channel, already running free while the archers on their decks shot fire arrows into the black hulls. A fire arrow is a feeble thing, and none of them caught, but it provided further distraction. The enemy was misled – again – into believing that the fire arrows were the cause of the fires. It took them a long time to realize that we were in amongst them.

I had no idea how many men I had under command, or how much damage we'd done, but I knew that it was time to go. I had a horn – the gift of Istes – and I ran clear of the flame, the men closest to me following, and I stopped in the dark to sound the horn, but the only sound I made was the bleat of an old ewe looking for her last lamb.

'Give me that,' Philocrates said, and he took it and blew a mighty blast. There was the sound of running feet, and we braced ourselves – we had no shields, and we were going to be reaped like ripe grain if the enemy had a phalanx to set against us.

But it was Idomeneus, laughing like a hyena, with fifty of our sailors and marines on his heels. Towards the back of his rout, there was fighting, but so far our enemies were disorganized.

'Get them into the ship!' I called – because the *Storm Cutter* was coming ashore for us.

Some men took some hide boats they found there – Tyche favours the brave, or so they say, and thirty men made it away in the small boats. But the fighting was intensifying, and I could hear the enemy getting into a line, their shields tapping against each other in the dark, and the fires behind them showed me how fast they were building the shield wall.

The enemy hoplites were backlit by burning ships, and mine were hidden by darkness. 'One quick charge!' I told the men I could find. 'On me, on me!' I called, and I picked up a heavy rock. 'Get close and throw,' I said. 'Put one man down, and run for the ship. Don't stay and fight!'

Maybe a dozen men listened to me and obeyed. We ran down the dune out of the darkness, and just a pace or two from their shield wall I threw my rock – a big rock, I can tell you. My rock caught my foe in the shin and he went down, and I jumped through the gap in their line and plunged my spear into the unshielded side of the man next to me.

Then the night was full of shouts. Fighting at night is nothing like fighting by day. Men fall down when no foe assails them – they lose their way in the melee. I turned to run and somehow found myself deeper in their line.

I came upon Archilogos as another ship burst into pitch-soaked flame behind my former friend. I think he recognized me as soon as I recognized him. Neither of us had a helmet on – no one wears a helmet at night.

I knew that if I stopped moving, I was dead or taken, so I shoved him – he had a shield and I had none. I had sworn to protect him, so I couldn't try to harm him – such a thing would haunt me for ever.

He roared and cut at me with a long *kopis* – the sword flared like flame over my head. I tangled his blow with my spear and jumped back, slamming into a man who had no idea whether I was friend or foe. I fell, lost my spear and rolled, and another man fell on top of me.

That should have been the end.

Archilogos called 'Doru! Stand and face me!' and he cut at the man I'd tripped over. That's fighting in the dark. I saw the flash of his blow and heard it thunk home in another man's shield.

I gave up trying to find my spear, or even getting to my feet. I crawled and then I rolled, and at one point a man stepped on my breastplate in the dark. The hinges gave, but held, and he stepped away, thinking me a corpse.

There was shouting behind me, where I'd been. I reckoned that the Ionian Greeks were fighting each other. Later I heard that the Greeks and Phoenicians started fighting. Many men were forced allies of the Persians, and not sorry to kill a Tyrian in the dark, I can tell you, and it may be that we only lived because the Ionians helped us.

At any rate, I got to my feet after what seemed an eternity of being helpless, tore my chlamys from my neck, cast it at my feet and ran to the beach.

Storm Cutter was already backing water.

I was out of my breastplate even as I ran – I cut the straps with my eating knife, running parallel to the ship's course, easily outpacing it as it backed water. I dropped the thing on the sand – a fortune in well-tooled bronze, but a small price to give the gods for freedom – and I ran to the edge of the sea and dived in without pausing on the shingle, my knife still in my hand.

Four strokes out, I got my arms around an oar and called for the rowers to pull me in. Something hit me in the head and I started to go down – I took another blow between the shoulder blades, and my last thought was that their archers had got me.

5

Well, I wasn't dead. Does that surprise you?

Idomeneus and Philocrates hauled me up the side. I'd been hit on the head by an oar, and when I awoke I had a rip on my scalp and a bruise on my side as if I'd been hit with an axe.

We lost sixteen men – heavy casualties from the sixty or so raiders who'd started the night together. Later I learned that six of them turned back from the swim and remained in Miletus. The rest were killed. Two of them were marines, men who had been with me for years.

On the other hand, we were free. In those days, we seldom stopped to mourn the dead, although it was a humiliation to me to have left their bones behind. Greeks pride themselves on retrieving their dead – even on a raid. The sun was well up in the sky before I could think, but my first thoughts were full of joy – joy at the cleanliness of the sea and the blueness of the sky. Sieges are ugly.

The sea is never ugly, even when he means to kill you.

We made our way north, up the Samian channel, and we took our time because we had three crews packed into two ships, with a dozen Milesian archers thrown in for good measure. They were good men. Teucer was their leader – when a father names his son after the greatest archer in the *Iliad*, he must expect the boy to grow to pull a bow, eh? Teucer and Philocrates were friends almost before he had his sandals off, and they could be seen throwing knucklebones by the helmsman's station all through the day, as neither had a station except in combat.

We stopped for meals and we set good lookouts, but the sea remained empty until we were off Ephesus.

There, out in the roadstead, we caught a pair of Aegyptian ships with a pair of Cilicians for escort, or so we thought. Now, the Cilicians were great pirates – they preyed on everyone, but as the Ionian Revolt grew, they took service with the Great King because preying on the Ionians and the Carians promised the richest pickings.

Cilicians seldom use triremes. They are poor men, and they prefer smaller, lighter ships, like the hemiolia, a bireme with a heavy sailing rig and a third half-deck in the stern. The two Cilicians in the distance were hemioliai. Their raked masts marked them for what they were.

My head hurt as if a horse had stepped on it, and I had to sit on the bench by the helmsman and watch as Idomeneus and Stephanos planned our attack on the little convoy.

Closer up, we could see that the two Cilicians were not guarding the Aegyptians. They were *taking* them. One of the low merchant ships had already been grappled and there was blood in the water.

Naturally, the Cilicians thought we were Phoenicians. Not that they cared. Cilicians are against every race.

They ran – north.

We let them go and took the Aegyptians for ourselves. One of their ships had already been taken and abandoned, and he was empty of life, decks red with sticky blood and already breeding flies, but the cargo was mostly intact – raw hides and ivory.

The second ship ran, and Stephanos showed me how fast the former slave ship really was. The sun was not yet at its height when Stephanos caught the Aegyptian over against the Asian coast and brought him back to where we were grappled to the first capture, the oarsmen blessing the gods for the luck of a cargo of ivory and praying that the other ship was as rich. It was, laden with ceramic bottles of perfume and bales of ostrich plumes, an absurdly rich cargo that made us all laugh for sheer joy.

We landed on the beach at Chios with the two prizes in tow and the Aegyptian captain still cursing his poor luck at being attacked twice in a single afternoon. I loaded all the valuables into one ship, gave the hides to the Chians as payment for their hospitality and let the Aegyptian crew take the empty ship south for home, unharmed – my thank-offering to Apollo, twenty-six sailors alive who I'd usually have killed. The Chian fishermen told us that their lord, Pelagius, and his nephews had visited, and that the whole fleet of the rebellion was gathering at Mytilene. Then we were away, up the coast of Chios, across the deep blue to Lesbos.

We made Mytilene under a tower of cloud, and the beaches were lined with ships.

At last, we'd found the rebel fleet.

Miltiades had done the work. He'd gone from island to island, rallying the rebels to make a stand. He'd assumed I was dead, until he heard of my first load of grain going into Miletus.

We were sitting in the great hall, the Boule of Mytilene, and men toasted me like a hero, and it went to my head like neat wine.

'You saved the rebellion,' Miltiades said, in front of a hundred captains. Epaphroditos was there, grinning from ear to ear. Paramanos shook his head and raised his cup to me, and Cimon stood at my shoulder and pounded me on the back, which made my head hurt.

There were other captains and lords I knew well enough – Pelagius of Chios, a few Cretans and a dozen Samian captains. But there were men I'd never seen before. One was a tough-looking bastard called Dionysius, who carried a kalyx krater on his shield and claimed descent from the god of wine. Miltiades took me around the hall and introduced me to all the leaders.

It was like a whole new rebellion. And Miltiades had done it, for all the praise he lavished on me, taking his ship from inlet to inlet all through the autumn, wheedling, cajoling and threatening the Ionians and the Cretans and the Samians until they put together a fleet.

'We drove the Medes from the Chersonese in a week,' Miltiades bragged. 'And you kept Miletus alive at our backs. In a few days, we'll run down the coast and flush out their squadron, and then we'll fill Miletus with grain.'

Everyone smiled. It was a turning point in the rebellion, we all agreed.

Next day, I sold my ivory, my ostrich plumes and my fine Aegyptian glass to the same merchants who had sold me grain. I'd brought two sacks of gold darics from Miletus, and now I added a quantity of lapis, a stack of gold bars and a pile of silver to my hoard.

With Idomeneus and Philocrates and Stephanos and Galas and Mal and Teucer to help, I carried it all across to Miltiades' great ship *Ajax*. I laid it out on the sand and divided it in half.

'Choose, lord,' I said.

He shook his head. 'You are the best of my captains,' he said.

'He says that to all the girls,' Cimon added. 'Thank the gods you earned some gold. We earned nothing but abuse, sailing about like busy mice. I took a good prize over by Cyprus, but it turned out to be the property of one of our "allies", and we had to return it.' Cimon glowered at his father, who shrugged.

'May all the gods bless you, Arimnestos,' Miltiades said.

Then, my debts cleared, I paid my oarsmen. By common consent, we included our Milesian archers in the payout. Most men received a pair of gold darics and some change. I'd seldom managed such a rich payout, and Stephanos and I watched with unconcealed glee as our boys went up the beach, roaring like fools, determined to spend it all in a haze of wine and fornication.

Then I paid the officers. Galas and Mal counted as officers now, and they were unable to believe their good fortune, and young Teucer, a mere archer, looked at his wool hat full of silver and shook his head. Stephanos the fisherman was doing the same. 'Never had so much money in my life,' he said.

'Save it, brother,' I said, putting my arms around him. 'You're a captain now. You'll need to keep treasure against a rainy day – when I take an arrow, or when you go your own way.'

He might have protested, but instead he gave me a serious nod and went off. He sent almost all his money home to his sister in a fishing boat commanded by his brother.

Teucer gambled. When he was poor, it wasn't an affliction, as he and Philocrates played for stones from the beach and shells, but once he had money, he was a terror – the more so as he won. Constantly.

I put a waxed-linen wallet full of lapis and gold and a fine, gold-worked bottle of rose scent into my leather bag, and shook my head. It is easy to be rich, if you take other men's wealth. I had the value of my father's farm and forge in my bag – ten times over. Those Aegyptian merchants had *a year* of the value of my crops in every pair of ivories. But even as I grinned at my wealth, I saw the lawless men on the mountain at Cithaeron – the bandit gang I'd broken – and I knew that I was no different. It was a sobering thought. And one I dismissed as quickly as I could.

That afternoon, we had a council of all the rebel captains and lords at Boule. The seams in the rebellion showed a lot faster when there wasn't any wine to drink. The Samians felt that Miltiades had wasted them, taking them north to the Chersonese. The Cretans wanted a battle, and cared nothing for the odds. The Lesbians and the Chians seemed to me to be the only men who actually cared about the rebellion – they were the one contingent that thought in terms of the good of all. Perhaps it was because they were between the northern Chersonese and the southern Cretans – the men in the middle. Everyone argued about the loot that had been taken.

Demetrios of Samos rose in late afternoon and pointed at me. 'This boy took two ships full of ivory, but he has not shared with the rest of us,' he said.

I hadn't expected it. To be honest, I'm always surprised by the foolish greed of men, and their envy. I thought I was a hero. I expected everyone to love me.

So I just looked at the fellow.

'See something you like, boy?' he sneered. 'Let's have a share of your precious ivory. Or did your lover Miltiades take it all for himself?'

I stood there, angry as Orpheus in Hades, gulping like a fish. I wanted to gut him on the spot, but I couldn't think of a thing to say. Miltiades glared at me. He didn't want to step in – that's what the Samian wanted, to show that Miltiades was my master.

Finally, my head began to work. 'I'm sorry, my lord,' I said, my voice low, to force men to be quiet. I bowed my head in mock contrition.

'You are?' he said.

'If I had understood that we were to share prizes taken *before* we joined the fleet,' I said, 'I owe a great deal more than just two ships' worth of ivory. And painful as I will find it to hand over my gains, I'll comfort myself that at least I contribute something besides hot air!'

He leaped to his feet. 'What the fuck are you saying?' he snarled. 'That I can't earn my keep? Is that it?'

I shrugged. 'I gather you've never actually taken an enemy ship,' I said in my softest voice. 'As you seem to need to pay your crews from my profits.'

Dionysius's great belly laugh carried through the hall. 'Sit down, Demetrios! No man needs to share what he took before he came to the fleet, as our young Plataean knows full well. Don't be an arse. What we need to decide is a strategy.'

Voices came up from every part of the hall. 'Miletus!' some shouted. 'Cyprus!' called others. Not a few insisted that the fleet should make for Ephesus.

Miltiades' son Cimon appeared at my elbow. 'My pater wants to see you tonight,' he said. 'To plan for the future.'

I nodded.

Cimon slapped my back and went out, apparently uninterested in the fate of the rebellion.

A cynic would say that Miltiades had spent the summer and autumn rallying rebels so that he could use them to reconquer his holdings in the Chersonese. And a cynic would be correct. Miltiades needed the power base that the rebellion offered him. He needed the rebellion to continue, so that when he dealt with Athens, he could appear as a great man on the front lines of the conflict.

What Miltiades didn't need was for the rebels to defeat Persia. If the rebellion was victorious, he would suddenly be nothing but the tyrant of the Chersonese. Athens wouldn't need him, and neither would the rebels. Further, his greatest rival among the Ionian tyrants was Histiaeus. Aristagoras had been his greatest rival – but I'd killed him in Thrace. Aristagoras had been Histiaeus's lieutenant, and Miltiades had no reason to want Miletus to be free of siege and powerful in the east. At one level, Miltiades wanted control for himself. At another level, he was an Athenian, and Athens wanted Miletus humbled – Miletus and Ephesus and all the Ionian cities that rivalled Athens for supremacy at sea.

I won't tell you that I really understood all this, that dark autumn and winter, with the rain lashing the shutters and the fires sputtering and smoking, and a hundred bored and angry Greeks fighting like dogs for the leadership of the rebellion. But I understood that all was not as it seemed. And it slowly dawned on me that whatever men said aloud, Samos and Lesbos and Rhodos and Miletus all hated each other, and Athens more than most of them hated Persia.

So you children can see that it's a miracle we ever got a fleet together at all.

Cimon left, but Miltiades and I both stayed, and over the course of hours of debate, it was decided to relieve Miletus for the winter, fill the city with supplies and go back to our homes. We were to rally in the spring on the beaches of Mytilene, find the Persian fleet and crush it. With the main Persian fleet finished, we'd have the initiative, and then we could act against the Persian land forces as we saw fit.

It was a good plan. Dionysius and Miltiades hammered it out, even against their own interests. Miltiades had no love for Miletus, as I have said, and Dionysius had every reason to favour a long war of commerce, as he was a pirate by profession. But the two of them joined together in something like alliance, and the Lesbians and Chians backed them. It is odd – a thing I've seen many times – that men will rise to nobility out of squalor and greed, especially when there is competition and worthy fellowship. On their own, Miltiades and Dionysius were greedy pirates. Together, they competed against one another to be the saviours of Greece.

Their plan left a lot unsaid. There was nothing about rescuing the cities of the Asian coast. Rather, it was the strategy of all those Greeks who had water between them and the hooves of the Persian cavalry. It left the mainlanders as slaves.

It was also the first realistic plan the rebels had ever made.

Dionysius offended everyone by insisting that most of the ships were ill-trained and that we should spend our first months when we rallied together in spring training our rowers and marines. I agreed with him, but his manner of stating this obvious truth was arrogant.

'You aristocrats are like children when you go to sea,' he said. 'My boys do nothing but row. They don't go to sea with their heads full of the *Iliad*. They go to sea to win – to take enemy ships and turn them into silver and gold. Have you seen the Phoenicians manoeuvre? Have you seen how hard they train their crews? Ever face a Cilician in narrow waters? Can your oarsmen row you into a *diekplous*? Turn on an obol and ram an enemy under the stern? No. Hardly one of you. When we come to the day – the moment of truth – there's not twenty ships here that can be trusted in a close action. Let me train your crews. A little sweat now, and liberty is the prize.'

If he'd stuck to that as a theme, he might have won them over, but every one of them fancied himself the greatest captain of the ages, fit to be trierarch on the *Argo*. It is a Greek failing.

So with nothing decided on save action, we loaded grain and root vegetables and ships full of pigs and goats, and we sailed for Miletus in midwinter, which was thought to be daring in those days. Not like now, when we make war in every season. We were so powerful that we went through the Samian channel, caring nothing whether the Persians knew we were coming.

The enemy squadron at Lade had had word of us, and their sails were just notches on the horizon by the time we sailed down the bay, and their camp was a field of burning embers. They hadn't even left a garrison. We took the island and landed the stores in Miletus.

The populace of the lower town hailed us as heroes and we all feasted together, but I noticed that whole families wanted to be taken away when we sailed. Histiaeus frowned, but he didn't forbid any of the lower-class families to leave.

I drank wine with Istes – wine I'd brought myself. We sat on folding stools in the agora, and drank from a *kylix* his slave boy carried, Athenian work with two heroes fighting.

'Ever think of leaving?' I asked.

He watched my ship for a long time, drank his wine and shook his head. 'No. But yes.' He laughed. 'You're a hero. You know the rules. I can't leave. I'll die here – this year or next.'

A stick-figure girl came by with a heavy pot on her head – carrying water. She glanced admiringly at the two of us – fine, well-muscled men, and killers too.

'What's her glance worth?' Istes said. 'What would it be like for you to awaken one day to find that she spits on your shadow?'

I understood all too well. 'But if we take too many of your people away . . .' I began.

Istes shook his head. 'Don't say it, my friend,' he whispered. 'My brother . . . does not feel as I do.'

'How do you feel?' I asked.

'I think we should go to Sicily and start again, far from the Persians, the Medes, the Lydians and the fucking Athenians.' He shrugged. 'I am filled with joy at every citizen family that gets away, to remember what Miletus was.'

I must have looked startled at the force of his expression, because he leaned back and drank more wine. 'You asked. I answered. But my brother – he is determined that we will meet our ends here. All of us. Sail before he makes a law against emigration.' His deep brown eyes locked with mine. 'Take all the families of those archers.'

I looked around. 'Why?'

Istes shrugged. 'He is mad,' he said, and then would say no more.

We sailed that afternoon, as the first of the great winter storms brewed to the east. We were the last to be allowed to take citizen refugees out of Miletus. The city had new heart, and food for the winter.

But the siege mound was not any smaller, and Datis did not decamp, as the Persian army had in other winters. He stayed, and his men built a proper wall around their camp, so that the raids had to stop. And the mound grew higher.

I took sixteen citizen families to Lesbos. Most of them had money, and they offered us – me and Stephanos – a good rate to take them all the way across the deep blue to Sicily.

Miltiades convinced them to come and settle in the Chersonese instead, and before the second Heracleion, we landed them at Kallipolis and settled in for the winter. My red-haired Thracian had found another man, but there were more fish like her in the sea, and I caught one quickly enough with a necklace of gold beads – a delicate blonde with a heart-shaped face and no other heart at all. She spoke Lydian and Greek and another language, too, close enough to what the Iberians spoke to make each other laugh.

It might have been a good winter for me, except that there was a long letter from Penelope about the farm, and it wasn't good – Epictetus the elder was dead, some of our stock had died in a pest and she needed me to come home so that she could be wed – but not a word of whom she might marry.

And enclosed in her letter was another slip of white vellum, written in the same hand.

Some say a phalanx of infantry is the most beautiful thing, but I still insist it is you who is the most beautiful. Come and be rich.

I held the parchment close to an oil lamp, and more words came through on the surface – written in acid, and now burned into the hide.

Come soon.

6

I was able to help Penelope. I sent my gold home to her, with Idomeneus as my courier. He went with a good grace – he wasn't missing any killing, and he knew it.

Briseis was another matter. It is harder, when the first flush of love is past, to understand what value to place on that love. I had gone to her rescue before – more than once – and never been better for saving her. In fact, I was never sure I *had* saved her. Should I cast life aside, crew up my ship and race for Ephesus?

I'd thought about it all autumn. Ephesus is less than six hundred stades from Miletus, and on that night when I'd found myself on a stolen horse, avoiding Persian archers, my first thought had been to ride for Ephesus and find her.

But I was no longer eighteen. I was fulfilling my duty to Apollo, or so I thought. In fact, in my head, it was clear to me that I was one of Apollo's tools in the success of the Ionian Revolt. Apollo was leading the Greeks to victory. The constant luck of the autumn – the escapes from Miletus, the seizure of the two rich Aegyptians – all pointed to the Lord of the Silver Bow's favour. And in my head, the needs of the Ionian Revolt outweighed the needs of a single, selfish woman.

Which tells you two things. First, that I still held her refusal of me against her. Second, that I was as much a fool at twenty-five as I was at eighteen. But I could rationalize my irrationality better.

So I spent the winter calling my blonde Briseis and forging excuses as to why I could not possibly go to her rescue.

Spring, when it came, was the longest, wettest, stormiest spring anyone could remember. I took *Storm Cutter* to sea before the cakes were fully burnt on Persephone's altar, and I brought him right back in when a combination of wind and wave snapped my boatsail mast like a twig.

We spent four weeks locked in the Bosporus when we should have been at sea, and a rumour started to spread that Miletus had fallen. But no real news came to us at Kallipolis, and we fretted and quarrelled with each other, and my decision not to go to Briseis in the autumn began to look shockingly like faithlessness.

We tired of exercising our crews, of painting our ships, of games and contests. We tired of girls and boys, and we even tired of wine. But the wind howled outside the Bosporus, and every attempt I made to round the point at Troy and head for Lesbos was foiled by a cold, dark wind.

Demeter showed man how to plant grain, and the new grain peeped above the earth, and finally the sun leaped into the heavens like a four-horse chariot, and the ground dried, and the sea was blue.

Miltiades had a good squadron. He had two volunteers from Athens who came in with the first good weather – Aristides, sailing a fine light trireme, and his friend Phrynichus, the playwright, with Cleisthenes, the Spartan proxenos and a powerful man in the aristocratic faction who was, nonetheless, a solid supporter of the Ionian Revolt. Aristides had Glaucon and Sophanes with him, but they didn't meet my eyes. I laughed. They were in my world now.

The Athenians brought disturbing news.

'It's all but open war in the city,' Aristides said quietly.

'Are you exiled?' Miltiades asked.

Aristides shook his head. 'No. I thought I'd come and do my duty before I was sent away without having the ability to influence the decision. The Alcmaeonids have almost seized control of the assembly. Themistocles is the last man of the popular party to stand against them.'

Miltiades sneered. 'Our blood is as blue as theirs,' he said dismissively. 'Bluer. Why do they get called aristocrats?'

Aristides shook his head. 'You don't need me to tell you that the colour of our blood is not the issue. Let's defeat the Persians first and worry about the political life of our city second.' He frowned at Miltiades. 'Don't pretend you are a byword for democracy, sir.'

Miltiades threw back his head and laughed. I thought the laugh was a trifle theatrical, but he pulled it off well enough. 'Not much democracy here,' he admitted. 'Pirates, Asians and Thracians all living together? By the gods, we should have an assembly, except that the first debate would be on what language to debate in!' He drank some more wine. 'And you are a fine one to talk, Aristides the Just! For all you prate of this democracy, you distrust the masses, and when you need company, you run away from the aristocrats – to me!'

Aristides bit his lips.

I stood up. 'No one has run *from* anyone,' I said, raising the wine cup. 'Tomorrow, we sail *against* the Great King.'

Aristides looked at me in surprise – a surprise that wasn't altogether complimentary. 'Well said,' he replied. 'You've made your peace with Apollo, or so I hear.'

'Not yet,' I answered. 'But I am working on it.'

'No man can say fairer when he speaks of the gods,' Miltiades answered. Miltiades believed in the gods to exactly the same extent at Philocrates – which is to say, not at all – but he spoke piously and offended no one.

Cimon hid a guffaw and Paramanos winked at me. Don't imagine that because I don't mention Paramanos I didn't see him every day, drink with him every night. He'd gone his own way and left my oikia to be a lord in his own right – a lord of pirates – but he was a fine man and still the most gifted son of Poseidon on the wine-dark.

'Let us drink to the defeat of the Medes,' Miltiades proposed, as the host.

We all rose from our couches and we drank, each in turn – Aristides; Cimon; Cleisthenes; Paramanos; Stephanos; Metiochos, who was Miltiades' younger son; Herk, who had been my first teacher on the sea; the Aeolian Herakleides, who now had a trireme of his own; Harpagos and me. Eleven ships – as big a contingent as many islands sent, all in the name of Athens – not that Athens paid an obol. I remember that Sophanes was there, and Phrynichus the poet, his eyes flitting from one man to the next – so that we knew we were *living* in history, that this cup of wine might be made immortal.

We drank.

In the morning we rose with the dawn and put to sea. We were a magnificent sight, sails full of a good following wind as we passed the cape by Troy and sacrificed to the heroes of the first war between Greeks and barbarians. Miltiades was like a new man – full of his mission, and his place as its leader.

Every night we camped on the headlands and beaches of Ionia – Samothrace, Methymna, Mytilene – and celebrated the unification of the Ionians and the victory we were going to win. Our rowers were at the height of training – a month trapped in the Bosporus had allowed us to work them up as few crews have ever been hardened, and the rich pay of last autumn kept them loyal to their oars. I noted that all the Athenians kept their distance from me.

When we came to Mytilene, the beaches were empty, and in the Boule, the old councillors told us that the storms that had trapped us in the Chersonese hadn't blown on Lesbos. The allied fleet had gathered three weeks before and sailed for Samos. And they had appointed Dionysius of Phocaea as navarch.

If we hadn't had Aristides and the Athenians with us, I think Miltiades would have deserted the rebellion right there, but he couldn't appear petty in front of his Athenian rival, and we sailed south for Samos. Suddenly, we were a surly crew.

Keep that change of daimon in mind, thugater, for we were the best-disciplined of all the Greeks.

We came into the fleet's anchorage on the beaches of Samos a little before dusk, and my breath caught in my throat. I had never imagined that the Greeks would do as well.

I stopped counting at one hundred and eighty black-hulled triremes. In fact, I was later told by Dionysius that at its height, we had more than three hundred and seventy in the fleet – probably the mightiest gathering of Greek ships that there ever was. Everyone had come – Nearchos, my former pupil from Crete, was there with five ships, and the Samians had a hundred. Miletus itself had crewed seventy, leaving the city with a skeleton army to guard it.

And Miltiades was a great enough man to smile and shake Dionysius's hand.

However it had been done, the alliance was the work of gods, not men. Never had so many quarrelling Greeks come together. They filled the beaches of Samos, and the Persians ought to have surrendered in terror.

But both Datis and Artaphernes were made of sterner stuff than that. Datis fortified his camp to an even greater degree and sent out the word all along the Asian coast, demanding the service of every vassal that the Great King had. And Artaphernes gathered his guards and his court, and moved his personal army to Miletus. He was not the kind to lead from behind.

Dionysius was a fine admiral and a great sailor, but he was a poor orator and worse leader of men, and his constant harping on the ill-training of the Ionian and Aeolian oarsmen smacked of racial superiority, as his own men were mostly Dorians. The Samians hated him. They hated Miltiades just as much, and openly pressed for a

Samian – Demetrios, in fact – to take command of the fleet. Let me just say, thugater, that their claims had a certain justice. They had a hundred ships and no one else had nearly that number. Miletus had but seventy, despite being the richest Greek city in the world, and Histiaeus declined to leave his citadel anyway, even though he was the one man who might have taken command without a voice being raised against him.

At any rate, Dionysius instituted his training programme, and as so often happens, the ships that needed the training least volunteered to undertake it, while those who needed it most – the aristocrats from Crete and the soft-handed volunteers from Lesbos, Chios and Samos – were the most reluctant to work.

I'll say this, too. Dionysius knew his business. I thought my crew to be the best-trained oarsmen in the world, but Dionysius quickly disabused me of my notions of arete. When he laid out a course with inflated skins, I told him it was impossible for a trireme to row through it, and he put me to shame by showing me how in his *Sea Snake*.

I spent a week training, and the more of his tricks I learned, the more I disliked his manner of teaching them. He was abusive when he might have been instructional, and abusive when he might have praised. And when I attempted to explain to him how deeply he offended most of his navarchs, he dismissed my criticism as a petty attempt to get back at him for his superior ship-handling.

'You're a quick learner,' he said, 'but in your heart you are no seaman, just another petty lordling. Don't linger on the sea when we've beaten the Medes, boy – it's for better men.'

What do you say to that?

I said nothing. But I was searching for an excuse to sail away, at least for a few days.

My excuse came up quickly enough. I was a captain in my own right, for all that I served Miltiades, and I attended the fleet council when I had time – which was all the time.

While Dionysius focused on seamanship, Miltiades and old Pelagius of Chios wanted intelligence. Miltiades had spies in Sardis but no way to contact them, and what we all needed to know was the progress of the Persian fleet – where were they? Did the fleet even exist? Were they forming at Tyre? Sidon? Naucratis?

We imagined that the Persians feared us.

I knew someone who could answer all those questions. She lay on a couch, just a few hundred stades away.

'Drop me on the beach by Ephesus,' I said.

Every head in the council turned.

'I know the town as if I was born to it. And I have friends there – people who are no friends to the Persians. Perhaps I can even contact one of your spies in Sardis, Miltiades.' I bowed to him. 'Give me the word.'

One of the great advantages of being a hero is that when you propose something daring, no one will stand in your way. It's as if everyone assumes that this sort of thing is your destiny.

By early summer, I was growing a trifle cynical about my role as a hero. But the Greeks were sending me to Ephesus. We had spies in the Persian camp at Miletus, and I knew that Briseis had *not* accompanied her husband to war.

She was alone, in Ephesus.

I set off the next day, free of bloody Dionysius and his sea-wrack tyranny, and free too of the ugly competitions between Miltiades and Aristides and the Samian leaders.

I daydreamed about taking *Storm Cutter* up the river to the city of Artemis, bold as new-forged bronze, but I didn't. Instead, I bought a sailing smack from some Samians, and Idomeneus and Harpagos and I sailed him ourselves, with Philocrates our unpaid passenger. The blasphemer had grown on me, and he'd shown no interest whatsoever in returning to Halicarnassus to trade grain for hides and lie when he swore oaths.

'I was born for this,' he said, not less than twice a day. And he smiled his curious smile of self-mockery. 'I miss Teucer, the bastard. He needs to come back aboard so that I can win back my money.'

Teucer's family were snug in the Chersonese, but the archer himself was back on the walls of Miletus, and we all missed him.

We sailed the fishing boat through easy seas, right around Mycale. We spent the night there, frying fresh sardines on an iron pan and drinking new wine from a leather bag. In the morning we were away again, up the coast and past the ruins of the old town that guard the promontory beyond Ephesus, and in the last light of the second day I could see the Temple of Artemis glow in the sunset, the old granite lit red like sandstone in the setting sun.

They left me on the coast road, twenty stades from the city. I told them to return for me in three days, and I put on my leather bag, checked the hang of my sword and pulled my chlamys about me. I had two spears and a broad straw hat, like a gentleman hunter.

I walked, and no one paid me a second glance.

As I made my way up the road to the city, I thought of my last journey up that road – delirious with fever, a slave bound to the temple, destined to die hauling stone. Ten years or less separated me from that boy. Indeed, the river of time flows in only one direction, as my master loved to say.

In a few hours, I would see him. He, at least, would never betray me, or any other Greek who served the rebellion.

I had determined to go to Heraclitus first, because I loved him, and because I had no idea what to expect with Briseis, nor had I any notion of where her loyalties would lie. She must have heard by now of my encounters with her brother the previous autumn and winter.

In truth, I was afraid of meeting her. But as always, fear forced me to act. I can never abide to see myself as afraid, and even as a child I would drive myself to do things that I feared, only to prove myself – to myself.

Briseis had always seen through this aspect of my character – and used it against me.

I heard her voice as I walked, and I tasted her tongue on my lips, and other parts of her, too, in my imagination. I thought of the first time she had come to me, fresh from humiliating her enemy for her, just as she had expected me to. And of the reward, although at the time I thought her another woman entirely. See? You are blushing, my dear. Boys only think of one thing, and how to get at it.

Boys are predictable, girls.

When I looked up, I had walked to our gate. To the house of Archilogos, which had been the house of Hipponax. To the house of Briseis. I was standing in full view of the gate, like a fool.

I'd like to say that I did something witty, or wily, like Odysseus. But I didn't. I stood there in the sun and waited for her. I suppose I thought that the Cyprian one would send her into my arms.

No such thing happened.

Only when the tops of my shoulders started to burn from the sun did I come to my senses and turn away. I walked up an alley, cut north to the base of the temple acropolis and then went to the old fountain building.

It was gone.

That was a shock. In its place was an elegant construction of Parian marble and local granite, with fine statues of women carrying water, cut so that that hydriai on their heads supported the roof.

I didn't belong there. There were a few free women and a great many slaves, and I was the only free man – the only man armed, and as such, a figure of fear.

Heraclitus's river had flowed right by, and I could not dip my toe again.

I fled.

I went up to the temple, where hunters were never uncommon, although I was a stranger and I was a man in a city where most of the men were at war. I left my spears with the door warden and I climbed to the palaestra, made a small sacrifice to the goddess and looked around the porticoes for my master.

Thank the gods, he was there. Had he been absent, I think my panic might have killed me.

He knew me immediately. His performance was admirable – he finished his lesson, a point about the way Pythagoras formed a right triangle, then he teased a new student, and finally, as naturally as if we'd planned it, he came to me, took my arm and led me away.

'You cannot walk abroad here, my boy,' he said.

'And yet I have done so all day,' I said.

'That others are fools does not make you less a fool,' he said.

Oh, I had missed you, my master.

He sent all his slaves away before he let me take the cloak from over my head, then we sat for hours, drinking good wine and eating olives. He was thin as a stick, as if he lived in a city under siege, and I forced him to eat olives, and his skin seemed to grow better even as I watched.

'Why are you starving yourself, master?' I asked.

'I fast until Greece is free,' he said.

'Then eat!' I hugged him. 'We have nigh on four hundred ships at Samos. All the cities of Ionia have united, and the Persians will never find a fleet to stand against us. No later than next spring, you'll see us sail up the river, and Ephesus will be free.'

He smiled then. 'Four hundred?' he asked. And ate olives at a furious rate.

I found olive paste and anchovies and fish sauce in the pantry, and made us a small dinner with bread and lots of *opson*, and I told him everything from the day that we helped Hipponax die until the start of this mission.

He shook his head. 'Your life is so full, and mine is so empty.'

'You teach the young,' I said.

'Not one of them is worth a tenth of you or Archilogos. I would trade ten years of my life for one bright spark to shine against the heavens.' He nodded. 'But I have had my great pupils, and plenty of them – and the last not the least. You are called Doru – the Spear of the Hellenes. I have heard this name.' He narrowed his eyes. 'And you think you have learned something about killing men?'

I shrugged. 'Nothing different from what you endeavoured to tell me ten years ago.'

'Sometimes the logos works one way to truth, and sometimes another,' he said. 'If we understood everything, we would be gods, not men.'

Too soon, I realized I had nothing left to say. He was not very interested in my forge and my farm, although in his presence, they suddenly gathered a kind of worthiness that they didn't have when I stood on the command deck of *Storm Cutter*.

We gazed at each other for a little while.

'You wish to see Briseis,' he said suddenly.

My heart beat faster. I expected him to say that she was away from town, resting from childbirth, dead.

'I often read to her,' he said. 'Nor should I have excepted her when I spoke of the bright sparks of intelligence I have brought to the logos – for of the three of you, the logos burns the brightest in her.'

I smiled to hear the most beautiful woman in the Greek world praised for her brain – but what he said was true.

'Come,' he said. 'We will go to her gate.'

In the near dark, Ephesus was inhabited mostly by slaves and men looking for prostitutes. No one paid us any attention as we walked together.

I followed him up to the gate of the house of my youth. This time, my heart slammed against my chest and I was unable to think, much less speak.

My master took me by the hand and led me to the gate as if I was a young student. I didn't know the slave on duty there, but he bowed deeply to my master and led him into the courtyard, where she lay on a long couch. A younger woman fanned her, and the smell of mint and jasmine filled the garden, and my head. Suddenly, it was as if no time had passed. My eyes met hers, and I remember giving a twitch, as did she, I think – such was the power of our attraction in those days.

She never spared the greatest philosopher of the age a glance.

'You came,' she said, after time had passed.

I trembled. 'You called to me,' I said. I was surprised at how calm my voice was.

'You didn't hurry,' she said.

'We are no longer young lovers, playing at the *Iliad*,' I said.

'We never were,' she returned, and her smile widened by some small fraction of one of Pythagoras's figures. 'We never *played*.'

I nodded. 'Why have you summoned me, Helen?' I asked.

She shrugged, and her voice changed, and she tossed her hair, like any other woman. 'Boredom, I suppose,' she said lightly. 'My husband needs captains. It is time you became a great man.'

I was not eighteen. She filled me, just lying on a couch. I could barely breathe. And yet, I was not eighteen. I took a deep breath, bit back my sharp response, turned on my heel and walked away.

You were never promised a happy story, my young friends. I'm afraid that we are coming to the part where you might prefer to stay home.

I headed out of the gate and back to my master's house. I shivered as if from cold, I was so angry – and so afraid. As I stood in my master's tiny courtyard, I raised my face to the stars.

'What have I done?' I asked.

They didn't respond.

My head was full of thoughts, like a bag of wool stuffed to the very brim – that I should go back and beg forgiveness, that I should send a note, throw rocks at her window … kill her.

Yes, that thought came to me, too. That I should kill her. And be free.

Instead, without much conscious thought, I packed up my leather bag, rolled my spare cloak tight and walked out into a quiet night in Ephesus. I had decided that if I could not have her, I might as well test myself or die. It is curious that we do our strangest thinking while we are under the influence of deep emotion. Suddenly I was not a trierarch or a lord. I was a young man bereft, angry, seeking death.

That is love, my friends. Beware of the Cyprian, beware. Ares in his bronze-clad rage has not the power.

I see consternation on your faces – I can only assume that none of you have ever been in love – you, thugater, I'd put a sword in you if I thought that you had, you minx! But listen to me. Love – the all-consuming fire that Sappho tells of, the dangerous game of Alcaeus, the summit of noble virtue and the depth of depravity described by Pythagoras – love is all. The gods fade, the stars grow pale, the sun has no heat to burn, nor ice to freeze, next to the power of love.

When she said that she had written to me from boredom, she struck me with a rod of humiliation. No lover can accept such a blow and remain the same.

I have had many years and many night watches, and the long hours before a hundred fights to think about love, and how each of us might have been, if we were not such proud and insolent animals.

I think – close your ears, girls – I think that men come to love though a mixture of lust and challenge, while women come to love through a different mix of lust and wonder at their own power – and desire to subdue another. As with Miltiades and Dionysius, and many others locked in a competition, there is more dross than gold in the ore, but what is refined in the fire is finer than either of the lovers could have made alone. Men come to love by challenge – the challenge of sex, the challenge of holding the loved one against all comers, the challenge of being the better man in the lover's eyes.

Briseis never ceased to challenge me. Her company never came free, because she valued herself above any mortal, and her favours were the reward for heroic action, heroic determination – heroic luck. The idea that she would summon me from boredom was a mortal insult to both of us.

So I shouldered my pack and went down the hill, past the sentries on the wall and out of the main gate. The moon was bright enough that I never stumbled. I was walking to Sardis. The Persian capital of Lydia – the heart of the enemy's power.

Did I say I wasn't eighteen any more? When Briseis is involved, honey, I'm always eighteen.

Or perhaps fifteen.

I walked all night, and all day the next day. I climbed the great pass alone, my head almost empty of thought from exhaustion, but I stopped and poured a libation for the men who died there fighting the Medes. At the last moment, speaking my prayer, I added the Medes who had fallen there – to my spear, and to others. My voice hung on the air, and I shivered involuntarily. The gods were listening.

I walked down the far side of the pass in a daze, and I didn't stop to eat or rest, and by the evening of the third day, I came to Sardis. Just as on my first visit, the gates were open. Unlike my first visit, I didn't kill anyone.

Sardis is a great city, but not a Greek city. There are Greeks there, and Persians, and Medes, and Lydians – a swarthy, handsome people, and the women are dark-haired, with large eyes and beautiful bodies, which they don't trouble to hide.

I was not of this world when I entered the gates. I must have looked like a madman, but Sardis had plenty of them. My Persian was still good, and I spoke it rather than Greek, and men made way for me. Most probably thought that I was one of the many prophets who afflict Phrygia, wandering and foretelling doom.

In my head, I was locked in a fearful fantasy, where the waking world of shops and handsome women merged with the chaos and death of the battle I had fought here. In the agora, I looked from booth to booth, trying to find the dead men I knew must be lying there.

I sound mad, but even as I was having these thoughts, I knew I needed rest, sleep, food. It occurred to me to hurry back to Heraclitus to tell him that I had found a place where the stream ran twice – that I could be in two times at once, merely by running a few hundred stades without rest or food.

My next memory is of sitting in a cool garden, eating lamb. It is a curious thing – one I have experienced all too often – that as soon as the rich, sweet food passed my lips, the curious half world of battle and gods vanished and I felt like a man again.

I was sitting across a broad cedar table from Cyrus, now captain of a hundred noble cavalrymen in the bodyguard of Datis.

I ate ravenously, and he watched me carefully – a healthy mixture of friendly concern and suspicion. We'd crossed swords often enough in the last years for him to know perfectly well where my sympathies led. On the other hand, I had saved his life and his master's, and that means more to a Persian than mere nationality.

He watched me eat, and he put me to bed, and the next day his slaves awakened me, and I ate again. I was young, bold and healthy – I recovered swiftly.

On that second day, he was waiting in the courtyard. 'Welcome to my house,' he said in Persian.

I knew the ritual, so I made a small sacrifice – barley cakes – to the sun, and ate salt on bread with him.

He nodded at my bag and gear. 'You are carrying a fortune,' he said. My gold and glass Aegyptian bottle was sitting before him on the table. He twirled his moustache. 'It pains me, but I must ask you how you come to be here.' He looked into my eyes. 'And why.'

Slaves brought me a hot drink. Persians drink all sorts of things hot, because mornings are often cold in their mountains, or so I've been told. This had the aroma of anise, and tasted of honey. I held his gaze, and I decided that having come all this way, I would behave as a hero and not as a spy.

'My lord,' I said, 'I will tell you everything, and to the utmost degree of honesty – like a Persian, and not like a Greek. But let me first say three things. And then you may decide if you need to know more.'

He nodded. 'Well spoken. Please, be my guest.' He waved at bread and honey, which he knew I loved, from the days when I was Doru the slave boy, and he and his friends fed me just to see how much I could eat. He raised a hand. 'I doubt not that you will tell me the truth. But lest you misunderstand – I know *exactly* who you are. You are a great warrior.' He smiled. Persians don't lie, and it was a genuine grin of admiration. 'I often dine for free or am given gifts of wine because I can tell stories of when I knew you as a boy. It is an honour to be your friend.'

I stood. Persians are very formal. 'It is an honour to be the friend of Cyrus, captain of the hundred that guards Artaphernes,' I said.

He blushed and rose, and I saw that his right arm was swathed in bandages. 'Wounded?' I asked.

'Yes,' he sighed. 'A petty skirmish over horses at Miletus.'

'Last autumn, at the edge of winter?' I asked.

He nodded.

'I was there!' I said.

He nodded. 'I know, young Doru. So – you will tell me three things. I must hear them.'

I sat back and warmed my hands with the ceramic cup full of hot tea.

'I serve Miltiades of Athens,' I said carefully.

Cyrus nodded.

'I love Briseis, daughter of Hipponax, wife of Artaphernes,' I said.

Cyrus started, and then slapped his knee. 'Of course you do!' he said. 'May Ahura Mazda blast my sight – I should have known.' Then he schooled his face. 'He is my lord, of course.'

'I am in Sardis seeking news of how Datis will fight us,' I said. 'But the bottle of scent is for Briseis, and the money is my own, and none of it is to buy treason.'

Cyrus drank tea, looking at the roses that grew up the wall of his courtyard in the morning sun. 'If I arrest you,' he said, 'you will be sent to Persepolis. The Great King has heard your name. You will be a noble prisoner and a hostage. In time, you might rise in court and be a satrap – you might command me.'

I shrugged.

'Or I might kill you. You do not deny that you are the enemy of my master?' He raised his eyebrow.

'No. Nor do I deny that I am here to learn your weaknesses. You see – I am a bad Greek.' I laughed.

He did not laugh. 'I never thought to say this – but a small lie on these matters would have let me sleep better.'

I shrugged. I had the advantage that I didn't care. I never loved the Ionian Alliance, friends. They were mostly East Greeks to me, soft-handed men who argued about firewood while the flames of their fire died. They had great men among them – Nearchos and Epaphroditos come to mind. But Briseis had hurt me, and I cared for nothing.

But – my role as a hero required me to speak.

'Instead of a lie, I'll give you a truth. I am here as a private man. I seek to give my gift to Briseis, and speak with her in Ephesus. I make no war on Sardis.' I frowned.

'Unlike the last time, you rebel!' He slapped his knees again. 'I was sword to sword with you in the marketplace!' He looked around. 'Does she love you, Doru?'

I shook my head. 'I don't know, Cyrus. I have loved her – since I was a boy. And she loved me.' I shook my head. 'Once, she loved me.'

'You have lain with her?' Cyrus asked. Persians are not shy about such things.

'Many times,' I assured him.

He nodded. 'She loves my master,' he said. He twirled his moustache again.

Now – I have to go off the tale again, to explain that among Persians, adultery, a mortal offence among Greeks, is something of a national aristocratic pastime, like lion-hunting. So my passion for his lord's wife made me all the more Persian, to Cyrus. I wasn't in a mood to calculate and manipulate – but I knew that this simple truth would render my mission for Miltiades almost incidental.

'Why?' I asked.

'He ruined her mother, of course.' Cyrus knew it as well as I. We had both been there. 'I would say – to a brother – that she tastes the forbidden because it is forbidden. That she loves power, but not Artaphernes.'

I might have rushed to her defence – except that his words struck me as truth.

'To lie with the mother and the daughter is a sin in Persia,' Cyrus went on. 'Many of us want him to leave her.'

I took a breath and let it go, and the balance changed.

'Let me go, and I will try to take her with me,' I said.

'Hmm.' He put his hand on the table. 'I am caught between what I want for my lord and what he wants. I will not be the agent of corrupting his wife. Despite my misgivings.' He contemplated me and combed his beard. 'I find I cannot order your death, although, to be honest, I have a feeling that would be best for the King of Kings.'

I remember shrugging. A foolish response, but then, what should a man do when his death is proposed?

'Swear to me that you will do nothing to harm my master, and that you will leave this city in the morning,' he said.

I put my hand in his. 'I swear that I will return to Ephesus tomorrow, and once there, my only purpose will be to see her and leave,' I said. If your wits are quick, you'll see how full of holes my oath was.

We clasped hands, and he finished his tea. 'I have business in the marketplace,' he said. 'Gather all the news you like. It will only discomfit you. You cannot fight the Great King. His power is beyond your imagination. I should send you to Persepolis as a prisoner – I would be doing you a favour. But I will let you see your doom – and then let you go to it. Perhaps you will save a few Greeks to be the Great King's subjects.' He pointed out the gate. 'Go – learn. And despair. And leave Briseis to her own end, is my advice.'

We embraced like old comrades. It is odd how we saw each other only in snatches, here and there – and how he had known me, not as a great hero, but as a slave boy – and yet we were ever friends, even when our swords were bloody to the wrist and we swung them at each other.

Never believe that Persians were lesser men. Their best were as good as our best – or better.

His permission – and it was that – to go and spy in Sardis chilled me, and I dressed and went out into the agora.

I passed from booth to booth, buying wine at one, a packet of herbs at another, listening to the gossip and the news.

I had been a slave, and I knew how to avoid being watched. Cyrus may have loved me, but he was a professional soldier, and before the sun was above the low houses, I knew he had put two men to watch me – Lydians, dark-haired men. One had a bad scar on his knee that gave him away even at a distance when he walked, and the other had the habit of crowding me too close – afraid he'd lose me.

I had learned about such things when I was a slave. Slaves follow each other, aiming at masters' secrets. Masters train slaves to follow other slaves, also searching secrets out. Slaves take free lovers and have to hide – or vice versa.

I noticed them before I completed my first tour of the shops and stalls of the agora, and I lost them by the simple expedient of walking into the front of a taverna on the corner of the agora and passing through the kitchens to exit at the back.

Then I walked up a steep street to the top, sat in a tiny wine shop and watched my back trail the way a lioness watches for hunters. I watched for an hour, and then I walked through an alley spattered with someone else's urine and walked down the hill on another narrow street until I came to the street of goldsmiths. I went into the second shop, kept by a Babylonian, and examined the wares. He had a speciality – tiny gold scroll tubes, for men who wore amulets of written magic. They were beautifully done. I bought one.

The owner had a Syriac accent, a huge white beard like a comic actor and more hand gestures than an Athenian. We haggled for a cup of tea and then a cup of wine. I was buying a tube of gold, not silver or bronze, and my custom was worth ten days' work, so I played at it as long as he wanted to, although our haggling was largely done in the first five exchanges.

He wrapped it in a scrap of fine Tyrian-dyed leather.

'Miltiades sent me,' I said after I counted my coins down.

'I should have charged you more,' he shot back. But he raised an eyebrow and winked. And put my coins in his coin box. 'I'll send for more wine. I thought the Greek had forgotten me.'

'When we lost Ephesus, we lost the ability to contact you,' I said.

He made a face. 'I have written some notes,' he said, and went upstairs into his house. I could hear him talking to his wife, and then moving around. Finally he returned.

'These are written in the Hebrew way,' he said, 'and no one – no one not a sage like me – could ever read them.' He smiled. 'Would you like a nice spell to go with your pretty amulet, soldier?'

'It's not for me,' I said.

'Beautiful woman?' he asked. 'You've been her lover for many years. And she loves you. And both of you too proud to surrender to the other. Eh?'

I stared at him, open-mouthed.

'Not for nothing am I called Abrahim the Wise, son. Besides, it's not exactly a rare story, is it?' He laughed wickedly. And began to make tiny dots on a piece of vellum.

He was making a pattern – a tiny pattern, meticulous and perfect. Of course, he was a goldsmith, and such men can always draw.

'The Persians?' I prompted him.

He peered at his work. 'Datis is forming his fleet at Tyre,' he said. 'He intends to have six hundred ships.'

I confess that a curse escaped me, despite my new-found piety.

'That's not the worst of it, son,' Abrahim continued. He glanced at his notes, and shook his head with his lips pursed. 'Datis has approached each of the islands – and all the leaders – with money. Gold darics. Sacks of them.' He looked at his work again. 'I saw the money caravan come through from Persepolis – not three weeks ago. Datis is determined to take Miletus and break the rebellion – even if he has to *buy* it.'

'What of Artaphernes?' I asked.

Abrahim shrugged. 'I am an old Jew of Babylon, and I live in Sardis,' he said. 'Don't ask me about Ephesus. I don't live in Ephesus. Datis comes here, and his money and his plans come on couriers from Persepolis. Artaphernes is a different animal. He strives to be great. Datis seeks only to win and curry favour.'

'Artaphernes' wife is my love,' I said. Whatever prompted me to say that, I'll never know.

'Briseis, daughter of Hipponax?' Abrahim asked. He looked up, and our eyes met, and it was as if I was looking into Heraclitus's eyes. Eyes that were a gate into the secrets of the logos. The man had seemed comic, even while bargaining. Now I felt as if I was in a

110

presence. His eyes stayed on mine. 'You, then, are Arimnestos. Ahh.' He nodded. 'Interesting. I am pleased to have met you.'

I shot an arrow at random. 'You know my master, Heraclitus,' I said.

He nodded. 'I do. Even among the *goyim*, there are great men.' He finished his work, and he sat still for a moment, and then he passed his hand over the tiny scroll, rolled it tight and put it in the tube. 'Like most young men, you are in a war between the man who acts and the man who thinks. Take my advice and think more.' He tucked the scroll tube into the red leather. 'Six hundred ships – ready for sea by the feast of Artemis in Ephesus. Datis will command them. Gold to every lord on every island – watch for treason. Understand?'

I nodded. 'Do I . . . owe you something?' I asked.

He laughed. 'I am a Jew, boy. The Persians broke my people, and I will help any man who is their foe.'

I clasped arms with him, and in his doorway, he called me back.

'I don't know you, boy,' he said. 'But I will try to give you advice, nonetheless. Go straight to your own people and never see her again. My scroll cannot protect you from – from what is between you.'

I smiled, embraced the old Jew and went back to the agora, where my shadows picked me up with obvious relief. I let them accompany me as I bought Philocrates a fine knife, and Idomeneus a bronze girdle, and my sister a pair of fine scissors – something the men of Sardis make to perfection. I bought myself a lacquered Persian bow – and then, on impulse, another for Teucer. I bought sheaves of arrows, and I bought a horse – a fine gelding, saddle, bridle and all. It is good to have money. Buying things makes you feel better when someone has just told you that the enemy has six hundred ships.

I bored my shadows to complacence, and then I walked back to Cyrus's house.

We ate together. Cyrus was quiet and so was I, but we were good companions, pledging each other's healths, and saying the prayers and libations together.

'You are as sombre as I am,' he said at the end of the meal.

'The rumour of the market says that your Datis has six hundred ships and a mule train of gold,' I said.

'What did you expect, little brother?' Cyrus asked, and he was sad – as if the victory of his master was an unhappy event. 'You cannot fight the Great King.'

I shrugged. 'Yes we can.' I thought of the beaches full of ships at

Samos, and the training. 'Ship to ship, we can take any number of Aegyptians and Phoenicians. Were you at Amathus?' I asked.

He shook his head. 'No,' he said. 'Artaphernes and I were campaigning in Phrygia.'

I nodded. 'I took four enemy ships that day, Cyrus. If Datis gathers six hundred ships, half of them will be unwilling allies – like the Cyprians. And after we beat him, the Persian Empire in Ionia will be at an end.'

Cyrus shook his head. 'It is a noble dream,' he said. 'And then all you Greeks will be free – free to be tyrants, free to kill each other, to rape and steal and lie. Free of the yoke of Persia, and good government, low taxes and peace.' He spoke in quick anger, the way a man speaks when his son or daughter is thoughtless at table.

Now I had to shake my head. Because I knew in my heart that he spoke the truth. The world of Ionia had never been richer – or more at peace – than when Persia ruled the waves.

'The freedom you prate of benefits the heroes,' Cyrus said. 'But the small farmers and the women and children? They would be happier with the King of Kings.' He drew his beard down to a point, twirled his moustache and grunted. 'We grow maudlin, little brother. I fear what will happen when we win. I think there will be a reckoning. I think this revolt scared my master, and even the Great King. Blood will flow. And the Greeks will know what an error they have made.'

I swirled the wine in my handleless cup and felt Persian. But I had one more arrow in my quiver, despite the way my head agreed with everything he said.

'Cyrus?' I asked, when he had been silent a long time. It was dark in the garden, and no slaves were coming.

'I am tired of war,' Cyrus said.

'Listen, big brother,' I said. I was pleased I had received this honorific from him – that I was part of his family.

He grunted, a few feet away in the dark.

'If you were Greek, and not Persian, how would you think then?' I asked.

He laughed. 'I would fight the Great King with every weapon and every lie at my disposal,' he said.

Persians do not lie.

We laughed together.

In the morning, I rode away after we embraced. I thought about him as I came to the pass, and I thought about him when I poured another libation for the dead of the fight there. I thought about Greece and Persia while I stood in the remnants of ruined grape vines at the top of the hill where the Athenians stopped the men of Caria at the Battle of Ephesus, where Eualcidas fell, the greatest warrior and best man of all the Greeks.

And, of course, I thought about Briseis. About her words, and her body, and how often the two are at odds.

It is the terrifying error of all boys to think that a woman's body cannot lie. That her words may lie, but her kisses are the truth. Chastity is a myth made by men to defend territory for men – women care little for it. Or rather, women like Briseis care little for chastity. Their territory is not lessened when they take a lover but expanded. They are, in fact, like men who are killers. They have learned the thing.

If you don't know what I mean, I shall not be the one to burden you.

Then I mounted my little horse and rode down the ridge to the river, took the ferry above the town and just after supper I came to Heraclitus's house.

He embraced me.

I didn't let him speak, beyond blessing me in the gateway, and told him that Abrahim the Jew of Sardis sent his greetings.

'Datis has all the gold of Persia and six hundred ships,' I said. 'I have to go to Miltiades. But I need to see Briseis. Will you take me to her again?'

He looked at me – a long time, I think. I don't really remember – or perhaps I don't really want to remember.

'Why?' he asked.

'I must see her,' I said.

Even sages make mistakes. 'Very well,' he said.

She sat in the dooryard where the porter would usually sit, her face hidden in the dark. Where her father had led me into his house. Where her mother had first toyed with me. Where Artaphernes had befriended me. In truth, if the toe *can* touch the same water in the stream twice, there were many echoes of the logos there.

'You left me,' she said. And then, in a matter-of-fact voice, 'And now you return.'

I shrugged. The silence deepened, and I realized that she couldn't see me shrug.

'I ran all the way to Sardis,' I said. 'You hurt me,' I added, and the honesty of that statement carried more conviction than all my pretend nobility and all the speeches I'd practised.

'Sometimes I hate you,' she said.

I remember that I protested.

'No – listen to me,' she said. 'You have all the life I crave. You are the hero – you sail the seas, you kill your enemies. When you feel powerless, you turn and leave. You run to Sardis.' She laughed, and it was a brittle sound in the dark. 'I cannot leave. I cannot come or go, kill or leave alive. It is greatly daring of me to come here, to my *own gate*, but I am a slut and a trull and a traitoress, and no one will think worse of me if I spend the night here, though they may think worse of poor Heraclitus.'

'Come with me,' I said.

'So that I can pine for you from your house? Perhaps I could talk of you with your sister while you make war on the Persians?'

Only then did I realize that she was crying, but when I went to her, her strong right arm pushed into my chest – hard – and she shook her head. Tears flew, and one landed on my cheek and hung there.

'Come and be a pirate queen, then,' I said.

She reached out and caught my hand.

At that contact, everything was healed – or rather, all our troubles were pushed away. For a few heartbeats.

'Datis has six hundred ships, or so I'm told,' I said.

'This is courtship?' she asked. 'He has what he needs to crush the rebellion. But my husband will win without him.'

Instead of answering her, I kissed her, being not entirely a fool.

She returned my kiss with all her usual passion. Our bodies never indulged in all the foolish pride of our minds. Our bodies united the way tin and copper make bronze.

But lovers must breathe, and when we separated, she pushed me away. 'Datis has more than six hundred ships,' she said, her voice a trifle breathy.

I put my hand on her right breast and traced the nipple. She caught my hand, licked it and pushed it back into my lap. 'Listen, Achilles. I am married now to a *man*. Not that posturing fart you killed. Artaphernes is my *choice*.'

I really didn't care. I imagined that she sought power through her marriages, but I was hardly in a mood to say so.

'My husband still seeks to reconcile the Greeks to his rule, but Datis wants them broken. Datis has been promised the satrapy to be made of Europe when the Greeks surrender. Datis has enough gold to buy every aristocrat in every city from Thebes to Athens. The tendrils of his power are felt among the ephors in Sparta. And he has bought every pirate on the Great Sea, from Cilicia to Aegypt and Libya.' She smiled into my eyes. 'I need to help my husband – see, I don't even lie. If Datis triumphs, my husband is the loser.'

Every time she said 'husband' was like a blow. A wound.

'Ah,' she said, and kissed me again. 'I never mean to hurt you like this.'

Then she pushed me away. She put a smooth ivory tube in my hand. 'For more than a year I have tried to contact you, you fool. Artaphernes loves you. He speaks of you. He *needs* you. Most of his captains are fools or simple men. With us, you could be the man you should be. A great man. A lord of men.' She put a hand behind my head. 'Why did you take so long to come to me?'

Then I felt defeated, and a fool. And my love and my hate were a deadly brew mixed together.

'You want me to stay here and serve your husband?'

'You thought I toyed with you?' she said, incredulous.

'No,' I confessed.

I remember it so well. If only I had walked away from her. If only I had never gone to see her.

'I thought you wanted to be rescued,' I said.

'You fool!' she muttered. 'You need saving. As a pirate – Achilles as a pirate? Come – come and be with my lord. And with me.'

'You spurned me, when I killed Aristagoras!' I said. 'And now you propose that I should share you with Artaphernes!' I shook my head, trying to clear it of the red rage. I had enough sense to see that if I killed Briseis, my life would end.

'I have children!' she said softly. 'I have dependants, women and slaves and family. My brother can't live without my protection. You expect me to leave all that, abandon my own, so that I could live as a farm wife in Boeotia?' She sat up. 'I have said it, Arimnestos – I love you. You, foolish child of Ares. But I will not be a farm wife or a pirate's trull. I have found a way for all of us to be happy. The Persians – Artaphernes is the best of men. And he loves you. And he is not young.' She smiled. 'I have enough honey for both of you,' she said.

'Yes,' I said. I had lived for two days as a Persian, and honesty was coming a little too easily to my lips. I could see it. Taste it. Like poison. 'You could,' I said, and my contempt was too obvious.

'Oh, how I could hate you,' she said. 'I should hate you, as you, by your last statement, have told me that you think I'm a faithless whore who lies with men for power – and yet you love me! Which of us is the greater fool?'

I stuck by honesty. 'I have wronged you,' I said. 'But I love you. And I don't want to lose you through pride. Our pride. Come away with me.'

She stood up. She was tall, and even barefoot her head was just below mine, and her lips were inches from mine, and she pressed close.

'I have offended you, but I love you, and I don't want to lose you through pride, either.' She smiled then, and standing, I could see her face in the torchlight from the garden. 'But I will not be second to you. You wish to be the hero of Greece? *So be it.*' She must have given a sign.

The blow to my head might have been from a rock, or a sword hilt.

I awoke with a pain in my head like a lance driven into one eye – the sort of pain boys get from drinking unwatered wine.

Too many blows to the head can add up, and this second felt as if it had fallen directly on the one received from the oars off Miletus. I couldn't see very well. I must have moaned.

'There he is,' Philocrates said. 'You all right, mate?'

They were all around me – my friends. Someone caught my hand, and I was gone again.

Recovery from wounds is dull story-telling – and not very heroic, when you find that you've been wounded by the woman you love. Not by any barb of Eros, either. Briseis didn't hit me herself – later I learned that it was Kylix – but it might as well have been her own hand, and she was never a weak woman.

'Ares and Aphrodite,' I cursed.

'Are both figments of the imaginations of men,' Philocrates blasphemed. 'We thought you were a corpse.' He grinned. 'A pair of slaves brought you to the beach, with that philosopher you prate about – bony thief of a man!' he laughed.

'Even in the dark, he was wise,' Idomeneus said, which was high praise from the Cretan, as he was not much for wisdom, as a rule.

'Fuck her,' I muttered.

'Heraclitus told us to run,' Philocrates said. 'We didn't linger, as you were covered in blood and he told us about the six hundred ships.'

I had been out-generaled by the Lady Briseis, knocked unconscious and sent back. And in my pack was the ivory scroll tube, in which she had meticulously detailed the ships that would serve Datis, the names of the men who she thought had already been bribed. So that I would use the knowledge to crush Datis and help her husband.

I had to laugh. This scene was never going to make my version of the *Iliad*, I thought. But I'm telling it to you, and I hope your busy lad from Halicarnassus puts it in his book. She played me like a kithara, between love and lust and hate and anger and duty, and I sailed to Miletus with the information she provided, because to withhold it to spite her would have been foolish.

How well she knew me.

I lay in the bottom of the fishing smack and tried not to look at the sun, and the pitching of the waves made me sick for the first and only time of my life, and we sailed along with perfect weather, all the way back to Samos and the rebel fleet.

We were four days sailing back, and my head was better by the time we landed on Samos. I put on clean clothes, then Idomeneus and I went directly to Miltiades. He was sitting under an awning with Aristides, playing at knucklebones.

'Datis has six hundred ships,' I said. 'They are forming at Tyre and they intend to crush us here, at Samos, in two weeks' time.' I looked around, ignoring the consternation on their faces. 'Datis has men in our camp, offering huge sums of gold to the commanders to desert, or even to serve the Persians,' I said.

Aristides nodded. 'I was offered ten talents of gold to take the Athenians and go home,' he said.

I was deflated. 'You already know?' I asked.

Miltiades laughed grimly. 'To think that Datis offered such a treasure to Aristides and not to me!' He shook his head. 'I think I'm offended.' He made his throw and rubbed his beard. 'Where has he got six hundred ships, eh?'

So I told them everything I'd heard from the old Jew and from Briseis.

They listened to me in silence, and then went back to their game.

'Should I tell Dionysius?' I asked.

Aristides nodded. 'You should,' he said. 'But I doubt he'll pay you much attention.'

'I suffered through his classes,' I said. 'He'll listen to me.'

So I walked across the beach, my fighting sandals filling with sand at every step. Dionysius had a tent made of a spare mainsail, an enormous thing raised on a boatsail mast with a great kantaros cup in Tyrian red decorating the middle.

There were armed guards at the door of the tent. Idomeneus spat with contempt, and we almost had a fight right there, but Leagus, Dionysius's helmsman, was coming out, and he separated the men and then faced me.

'Can I help you, Plataean?' he asked.

'I have news of the Great King's fleet,' I said. And immediately he ushered me into the tent. Idomeneus followed me after a parting shot at the guards.

'Act your age,' I spat at him. 'We're all Greeks here.'

Dionysius was sitting on a folding stool of iron, looking like any great lord. He was surrounded by lesser men – no Aristides or Miltiades here.

'So, Plataean. How went the mission on which I sent you?' he asked.

I saluted him – he liked that, and it cost me nothing. 'Lord, I went to Ephesus and contacted a spy paid by Miltiades. And another, a woman.' I didn't love him, and saw no reason to mention Briseis.

Dionysius smiled. 'Spies and women are both liars.'

That stung me. 'This spy does not lie.' But Briseis lied very easily, I thought.

'Spare me your romances,' the navarch said. 'Women are for making children, and have no other purpose except to ape the manners of men and manipulate the weak. Are you weak?'

I summoned up the image of Heraclitus in my head, and refused this sort of petty combat. 'My lord, I have intelligence on the fleet of Datis. Will you hear it?'

He waved his hand.

'Datis has six hundred ships at Tyre,' I said. 'He has the whole fleet of Cyprus – over a hundred hulls, as well as two hundred or more Phoenicians and as many Aegyptians. He has mercenaries from the Sicels and the Italiotes, and Cilicians in huge numbers.'

Dionysius nodded. 'That's worse than I expected. They cannot, surely, all be triremes.'

I shrugged. 'Lord, I did not see them. I merely report what the spies report.'

He rubbed his beard, all business now. 'The Cilicians, at least, haven't a trireme among them. They'll be in light hulls. And the Aegyptians – light hulls and biremes. But still a mighty fleet.'

'Both spies also report that Datis is sending men – the former tyrants and lickspittles – to buy some of the Ionians' contingents. Aristides of Athens received such an offer. I suspect other men—'

The navarch's face darkened with blood. 'Useless children, to fritter their freedom away on a few pieces of gold. Tell Aristides he's welcome to go and fight for his new master—'

'Lord, Aristides of Athens would sooner die than take a bribe on a law case, much less a matter as weighty as the freedom of the Greeks,' I said. I owed Aristides that much.

'Are you another of them? The schemers?' Dionysius came off his chair. 'How do I know these reports aren't planted by the enemy? Eh?'

In fact, even blinded by a mixture of love and hate, I had wondered if Briseis had sent me as a poisoned pill, to scare the Greeks with numbers and threats of Persian gold – except that Abrahim had said the same. I stood my ground. 'My lord – you sent me. Miltiades has been fighting the Persians since the war began – and you, pardon me, have not. For you to doubt me – to doubt him – is sheer folly.'

'Leave my tent and never return,' Dionysius said.

'You are in the grip of some ill daimon,' I said. 'We are all one fleet. Don't create divisions where none exist.'

'Take your ship and leave!' he ordered, screaming at me. 'Traitor!'

Leagus escorted me out of the door and down the beach. Then he took my arm. 'He's the best seaman I know,' Leagus said. 'But the power has unhinged him. I have no idea why. The mere sight of so many ships – it did something to him. I thought your words might sober him.'

I didn't know what to say. Men come to power in different ways and they react to it in different ways, as they do with wine and poppy juice and other drugs. But when I walked back to Miltiades, I was sombre and my head hurt. I threw myself down on one of the rugs he had laid over the sand.

'I thought you ought to see that for yourself,' Miltiades said.

'I tried to tell him about the bribes,' Aristides said. 'He ordered me killed – then exiled – on and on. He's lost his mind.'

Miltiades gave me a tired smile. 'It is odd – I should have had the command. But now a madman has it, and yet the fleet seems unable to take the command from him, and I can't seem to rise to the occasion.' Miltiades looked at me.

I sat up. 'Are you suggesting I should do something?' I asked.

Miltiades shrugged.

I looked at Aristides, and he would not meet my eye. Oh, everyone in Athens is so pious, until the moment when the need of the city outweighs all that petty morality. 'You two want me to kill Dionysius?' I asked.

Aristides looked resolutely away.

Miltiades shrugged again. 'I certainly can't do it.'

'Neither can I,' I said. 'It would be an offence against hospitality. And I have sworn an oath to Apollo.'

Aristides turned and met my eye. 'Good,' he said, and suddenly I knew that I'd misjudged him. I had passed some sort of test.

'Well,' Miltiades said, 'I guess we're with the gods.'

That was all right with me. I trusted Apollo to save the Greeks.

The next week saw more training. I had *Storm Cutter* in the water constantly, working on various manoeuvres. Most of the Lesbians did the same, and a few of the Samians, and all the Cretans. We may not have been the paragons that Dionysius wanted, but we were a hardened fleet, and the rowers were in condition.

Miltiades insisted that we learn some squadron manoeuvres, so we practised every day as a squadron, and Nearchos chose to throw in his lot with us. Nearchos was the boy I had trained to manhood, son of Achilles, Lord of Crete. He was no longer an arrogant, whiny puppy of seventeen, either. He was a man now, a hero of the sea-fight near Amathus in Cyprus, and he led five ships.

He was popular with the Athenians, and it was through him that I became friends with Phrynichus the poet. Phrynichus went about collecting stories every afternoon when men lay down for a nap, and after he had met Nearchos and heard his version of the deck-to-deck fighting at Amathus, the two of them sought me out.

I was lying on a carpet in Miltiades' tent, my head on a rolled chlamys, unable to sleep. To be honest, those days were as black for me as the days after Hipponax sent me from his house and tried to kill me. My head hurt, and pain is often part of low spirits. But I could not get the thought of her out of my head – as if her image and the pain were one thing.

'Arimnestos?' Nearchos asked.

I sprang to my feet, went out into the sun and we embraced. For two men encamped on the same beach, we hardly ever saw each other. He introduced the playwright, who asked me about the fight at Amathus, and I sat by the fire and told my story.

When I was done, Phrynichus asked me how many men I thought I had put down that day.

I shrugged. 'Ten?' I said. 'Twenty?' I must have frowned, because he smiled.

'I mean no offence,' he said. 'You have the reputation as a great killer of men. Perhaps the greatest in this fleet.'

What do you say to that? I thought that I probably was, but it would have been hubris to say as much. 'Sophanes of Athens is a fine warrior,' I said. 'And Epaphroditos of Lesbos is a killer, too.'

Phrynichus raised an eyebrow.

I leaned forward. He was a great poet, a man of honour. More-over, his words could make a man immortal – if you believe that word-fame lasts for ever, and I do. 'You have fought in a close battle?' I asked.

He rolled his hand. 'I've been in a few ship fights,' he said. 'I faced a man on a deck once. Never a big fight, in phalanx.'

I smiled. 'But you know how it is, then. When you ask me how many men I put down – how can I answer? If I cut a man's hand, does he fall? Is he finished? If I put my spear in his foot, he'll stay down for the whole fight, but I suspect he'll till his fields next season. Yes?'

He nodded.

'When I fight my best, I don't even know what's happening around me. In my last fight – off Miletus – I put a man down with a blow from my shield, and he was *behind* me.' I shook my head, because I wasn't putting this well. 'Listen, I'm not bragging. I just don't know. I fight by area, not by numbers. In a ship fight, I work to clear an area, and then I move.'

He smiled. 'You are a craftsman of war,' he said.

I met his grin. 'Perhaps.'

He leaned forward. 'May I serve with you in the battle? I'd like to see you in action.'

Look, short of Pindar or Simonides or Homer risen from the grave, he was the most famous poet of our day, and he was asking to watch me in the great battle where we were going to break Persia. What was I to say?

By an irony that I have long savoured, young Aeschylus and his brother were both in Cleisthenes' ship as marines – so that we had in one squadron the greatest living poet and the *next*. They had not yet competed head to head – but young Aeschylus could be seen haunting the same fires as Phrynichus, so that no sooner did I befriend the playwright than I met his young rival.

This is the thing that makes the Greeks strong, it seems to me. Aeschylus admired Phrynichus – so he sought to best him. Admiration begets emulation and competition. And in the same way, I was already a famous fighter, and men already sought to emulate me – and best me.

Never mind. I speak of Phrynichus.

Truth to tell, Simonides was a better poet. And Aeschylus wrote better plays. But Phrynichus made me immortal, and besides, he was a quicker man with a pun or a rhyme than either of the others – he could compose a drinking song on the spot. It must have been that same week that we were on the beaches of Samos, and we were all lying around a campfire – a huge fire – having a beachside symposium. There must have been a hundred men there – oarsmen and aristocrats mingled, as it used to be in those days. We had Samian girls waiting on us, paid for by Miltiades, and they were fine girls – not prostitutes, but farm girls, brisk and flirtatious, despite their mothers hovering nearby.

But one girl stood out. She was not a beauty, but she stood square and straight like a young ash. She had a beautiful body, muscled like an athlete, firm breasts, broad hips and a narrow waist. And she talked like a man, straight at you, if you asked for wine or some such. When she played at jumping the fire – showing her muscled legs and leaping high enough to fly away into the smoke-filled dark – all the men wanted her, even those who usually preferred men. She had that spark – that in Briseis is a raging fire. I felt it too, though I was only a week from my love, and in that week I hated all women with equal fervour.

The girl moved among us, and we all admired her, and then Phrynichus leaped to his feet and seized a kithara that one of the boys had been playing, and he sang us a song.

How I wish I could remember it!

He called her Artemis's daughter, of course, and he sang that her portion and her dowry was *time*, honour, the word-fame of man, and that her sons would conquer the world and be kings, and her daughters would sacrifice to the Muses. He sang of her in a parody of the elegies that men receive when they win games at Olympus or Nemea, and he praised her skill at jumping fires.

And he did all this while rhyming inside every line, so that his pentameters rolled like a marching army. We were spellbound.

The girl wept when it was done. 'What have I to live for that will compare to this?' she asked, and we all applauded her.

There were some good times.

I asked Phrynichus later if he had bedded her, and he looked at me as if I was a child and told me that grown men do not kiss and tell, which shows you that I still had a great deal to learn.

Another night, Phrynichus debated with Philocrates about the gods. Philocrates dared us to consider a world where there were no gods, and he suggested – through good argument and some sly inversion – that such a world would bear a remarkable resemblance to our own. Then Phrynichus rose and proposed that we consider a world where the gods did not believe in Philocrates. His satire was brilliant and so funny that I can't remember a word of it, except that I threw up from too much wine and laughing so hard.

Phrynichus drank when he wasn't using his head, and he and Philocrates and Idomeneus formed a drinking club whose members had to swear to be drunk every day as an offering to Dionysus. I tried to make fun of Philocrates for this display of piety, but he refused to be mocked – saying that Dionysus was the one god whose effects were palpable.

Just after the local feast of Hera, our navarch bestirred himself from his tent and ordered us to sea, to seize the island of Lade before the Persian fleet arrived. By now we received daily reports from merchant ships and outlying galleys – and the Lesbians had a dozen fast biremes and a pair of light sailing hemioliai on hand, and they did what scouting got done.

So on the morning after the feast of Hera, we rose, manned our ships – a scene of complete chaos, let me tell you – and sailed in a surprisingly orderly manner down the coast of Samos to Lade – the enemy squadron, led by Archilogos, slipping away ahead of us. We had so many ships that we filled the island. The Samians landed first, and they took all the good ground, so that by the time the Lesbians and Chians had landed, we, the extreme right of the line and the last in sailing order, were left with the rocks near the fort and nowhere else to camp.

I was leading Miltiades' ships and Nearchos's squadron, and I directed them to follow me to the beach opposite the island – the beach from which I'd launched my raid a year before. We were not sorry to be separated by half a stade of water from the excesses of Dionysius and the growing tensions of the camp.

Later, Aristides was listening to Phrynichus recite the *Iliad*, which always delighted him, and when he reached the scene where Diomedes takes the army forward and routs the Trojans, he turned to me and frowned.

'We need to get to grips with the Medes before the fleet collapses,' he said. 'The Samians have refused to train any more. They've mutinied, and the Lesbians are just as bad.'

That night, Epaphroditos and a few of his warriors swam over to us, drank wine and complained of how mad our navarch had become.

'We're not pirates,' Epaphroditos said. 'The man's notions of training are insane.'

Secretly, I suspected that all the Ionians could have used harder hands and stronger backs. But they were brave, and as far as I could see, this was one fight that would be settled through courage, not tactics.

'Besides,' he went on, 'I hear the Persians are on the way. We need a rest.'

I talked with him half the night, and Phrynichus listened to every word he said as if he were Hector returned.

Dionysius declared that we should have games to propitiate the gods in preparation for the contest against the Persians. It was the most popular decision he'd made since he ordered us to Lade. Men were bored, restless and yet listless. I felt that the Ionians were dangerously lazy. We were on the edge of victory, and they wanted to behave like men who had already won.

The prospect of games didn't excite me the way it had when I was younger. It makes me laugh now, to think that at twenty-three or twenty-four I imagined myself a hardened old man.

I had already triumphed in a set of military games, you'll recall, back on Chios when the revolt was young. Five years before. So I decided not to compete in every event, or to strive to win the whole competition. But events decided otherwise.

Next morning, Phrynichus said that he wanted to see Miletus before we fought. I had business there, so I collected a heavy bag and a letter for Teucer and we walked across the mudflats into the city, slipping past the Persian archers in the last gloom of morning to have a cup of wine with Istes. He depressed me by showing me the siege mound, now all but level with the height of the wall. 'Twenty days,' he said.

'Care to come with us?' I asked, and Istes shook his head.

'My place is here, with my brother,' he said. 'We will die here.'

'Cheer up!' I insisted. 'Apollo will not let us fail.' I could see the future so clearly that I was surprised other men worried so much. 'We will destroy their fleet, and then we will liberate all of Asia.'

Istes had lines around his eyes that were not there a year ago, and pouches from sleepless nights. He looked twenty years older than me. And he drank constantly.

I glanced at Phrynichus. 'This is the greatest swordsman in the Greek world,' I said.

Istes grinned. 'Someday, perhaps we can measure each other,' he said. I agreed – it would be good to face such a gifted man. That is the admiration by competition that makes Greece great. 'But I would rather stand beside you as we smite the Persians.'

'Flattery will get you anywhere, Plataean,' he said. 'You think we'll win this naval battle?'

'I do,' I said. We would win, I would take Briseis as my war bride and that would be that. My spear-won wealth would make a palace for her on my farm. That's what I had decided – to have her and punish her as well.

Feel free to laugh.

'I have to say that I've now fought the Persians every fucking day for a year,' Istes said. 'If you destroy every ship in their fleet – kill Datis, drown their navarchs – this war still won't be over. They're much, much tougher than that.' He yawned. 'But if you lose, Miletus falls – and the revolt is *fucked*.'

'You are tired,' I said.

'You know how it feels after a fight?' he asked me, one killer to another.

'Of course,' I allowed.

'Imagine fighting every day,' he said. 'Every fucking day. I've been at it a year, and I'm starting to go mad. My brother is worse – he was never the fighter I am, and fear is getting into his gut.'

Of course, you are familiar with the character of Istes in the play. Phrynichus knew his business. He was a great man, and he knew greatness when he saw it.

I left him to study his new hero, and I went out on the walls and found Teucer. He was at the top of a tower – a rickety thing of hides and wood and stone fill, just completed behind a section of wall that had been mined from beneath. The stonework of Miletus was so old and so good that the wall simply subsided without breaking. That's why we didn't use mortar in those days – mortar adds strength, but when a mortared wall is undermined, it collapses. Not so heavy stones fitted by master masons. Often, the old way is the better way – something for you children to remember.

They'd built a tower behind the subsided wall, and I had to climb a dreadful ladder to reach him, far above the battle. He had a big Persian bow, and he shot carefully at the slaves who were working to clear the rubble in the not-quite breach. He seldom missed, and very little work was happening. He had another man spotting for him, too, and they passed comments on individuals as they shot them.

'See red-scarf? He's got a death wish – oops! Wish come true.'

'White-belt? He's getting ready to step out to get that fascine – here he comes. You missed left. Now he's going to come around the other side of the wicker shield – ooh, nice. Dropped like a sack of barley.'

'Teucer?' I asked.

'Oh!' He put his bow down and embraced me. 'A pleasure to see you, my lord.'

I sat on my haunches after an enemy arrow ruffled my chlamys. 'Hot work here.'

Teucer laughed. 'This is my life, these days.'

'Care to ship out for the battle?' I asked as casually as I could manage.

He glanced at me, shot another arrow and exchanged a long look with his spotter. 'We can't,' he said, after a delay so long I thought I'd offended him.

The spotter was Kreusis, a younger archer who'd also served aboard my ship. His face was marked with soot and I hadn't recognized him at first. 'Sorry, lord. Histiaeus would cut our ears off. We're to hold the Windy Tower while you sailors fight their fleet. Our lord is afraid of an escalade during the sea-fight.'

I couldn't argue with that. It was the sort of thing I'd have tried myself.

I handed Teucer a bag of things from his friends on the *Storm Cutter* – a skin of wine, a sack of dried Athenian sausage and other delicacies – for a city under siege. He and Kreusis ate bread and sausage as I watched.

I also had a letter from his wife, who had wintered in Kallipolis and who I'd sent to Plataea when the weather broke with a pouch of money and a long letter.

He wept a little as he read it, then folded it away.

Finally, I gave him the fine Persian bow I'd bought for him at Sardis. He took it without acknowledgement. It was just a tool to him – a sign of how far gone he was in his head.

'We're going to die here,' he said. 'But I know now – thanks to you – that my wife and son will live. Means a lot to me. Wish I could sail with you – sail away.'

I told him to stop talking nonsense – that the Persians were as good as beaten. But I could tell he was beyond such things. I've been there: when the horizon is no longer the next week, or the next day even – it is merely the next instant. When you are there, you cannot see out.

We embraced again and I climbed down the tower, thinking dark thoughts.

Phrynichus was still talking to Istes. I hugged the swordsman. 'We'll win,' I said.

'You'd better,' he answered.

As Phrynichus and I walked back from the harbour, a couple of Persian archers had a go at us, racing along the rocks above us. That's terror – being shot at from long range with no chance of reply. We had to wade to get around the end of their lines and we couldn't move fast, and I cursed my arrogance in going by day. And not bringing a shield.

One of the Persians gave a great scream and plummeted from his rock into the sea. I walked over and retrieved his bow and arrows – soaked, but not ruined.

I saw Teucer waving from the wall. He'd shot the man at some incredible distance – Phrynichus has that shot in the play, of course.

Phrynichus shrugged – he was a cool man in the rage of Ares. 'It's a little like living in the *Iliad*,' he said.

'Imagine what a jumpy bunch they were, after ten years at Troy,' I said, and the poet nodded.

'I was thinking of Istes,' he said.

'Exactly,' I said.

Idomeneus claimed my new bow as soon as I reached the ship – dried it, restrung it and shot at everything that he could. He was an excellent bowman, as I've said before, and he'd decided that he needed a bow in the coming sea-fight, which was fine with me. After all, Archilogos's archers had unsettled me in the fight by the harbour.

He told us that the Persians were coming. 'They're camped just down the coast,' he said. 'Epaphroditos has seen them.'

Later that afternoon, Leagus, Dionysius's helmsman, came across in a skiff and went to Miltiades for permission to hold the games on our beach. We were delighted, and Miltiades and Aristides competed to build fires, lay out courses and prepare an altar and sacrifices.

The next day dawned grey, with weather threatening from the west. But the athletes came across in boats, and more than a few swam the half-stade in their exuberance, arrogance or poverty.

Miltiades acted as host, and he and Dionysius sat together in apparent camaraderie, made sacrifices with the priests and watched the competitions as if they were brothers. All of us were delighted by this display of propriety. We were further delighted when the men of Miletus sent a contingent to compete, led by Histiaeus and his brother Istes. They, too, sat under the great red awning that Miltiades had set up, and watched.

The competitions were, in order, the one-stade run, the two-stade run, the javelin throw for distance, the throw for accuracy, the discus, archery for accuracy, the run in armour – the *hoplitodromos*, the *pankration*, the fight in armour. I had intended to enter only the fight in armour, but as I lay on my bearskin by the awning where the judges watched, young Sophanes of Athens came up, naked and glistening with oil, and squatted next to me.

'You are the most famous man – as a fighter – in this host,' he said. He gave me a shy smile. We had not been friends since I killed the thug in Athens. 'I want to compete against you. These Ionians – most of them are hardly fit.'

'Wait until you run against my friend Epaphroditos,' I said. But his desire was genuine.

'I ...' He paused and looked around. 'I think that I blamed you

– that I had killed a man. It made me feel . . .' He stopped, blushed and looked at the ground between his feet.

I nodded. 'It made you feel greater and less than a man yourself, eh?'

'You slaughtered that thief like a lamb. And made me look like a boy.' He shrugged. 'I am a boy. But I want to win today, and I want to win against the best. The noblest. And I came to say that I wronged you over the killing. I didn't like what I had done – I made that part of you.'

'Nicely put,' I said. Goodness, he was earnest and polite and handsome and probably brave and morally good, to boot. He made me feel old at twenty-three. 'But I have spent a year coming to terms with killing. What I did that day was ill done. I don't regret the man I killed in the fight. But the man in the cellar – what Aristides says is true. That was murder. I have spent a year atoning to Lord Apollo, and all the gods, for my hubris.'

Sophanes grinned. 'Then you should run, lord. Competition is a sacrifice to the gods.'

What could I do? He was right. Besides, he made me feel like a slacker. So I pulled my chlamys over my head, and Idomeneus came up with my aryballos, oiled me and smacked me on the back.

'About time you got off your arse,' he growled. He was very tender of my reputation, which in a way was his, as well.

A word about exercise – though I normally try not to drone on about how much time I spent on my body every day – still do. When we were at sea, I rowed at least an hour a day with the oarsmen. The Pyrrhiche of Plataea included a set of exercises with an aspis, and I did that portion of the dance every day, lifting the shield over my head, and moving it back and forth across my body. On a full exercise day I would run eighteen to twenty stades and lift heavy stones in the way that Calchas taught me at the tomb of Leitos. In addition, I would practise against one of my marines with a wooden sword – some days, against all of them. My favourite sparring partner had become Philocrates. He was by no means the best of them, but he fought hard, and had long arms and was a dangerous opponent – with surprising inventiveness.

At any rate, I tell you this so that you won't think that I went soft between bouts of combat. None of us could afford to be soft in those days, when freedom from slavery depended on your ability to cut a rival down.

I made the final heat in the one-stade run, and again in the two-stade run, where I finished second, to my own delight. Sophanes won the one-stade, and finished behind me in the two-stade, which Epaphroditos won. I was surprised, and pleased, to see Stephanos's cousin Harpagos run well in both events. He was, by virtue of his position, a gentleman now, and he rose to it. Some men cannot. I shared a canteen with him and Epaphroditos after the second heat. We laughed together and told each other that we were still the men we had been five years before.

Stephanos placed well in the javelin throw for distance, and I lost the throw for accuracy by the width of a finger.

I think it was at this point that I recognized I might win. For those of you who have drunk the heady wine of victory, you know this moment – when you start to pull away from the pack.

The next contest was a surprise, as Philocrates – my Philocrates – won the discus throw with his first throw, a throw so far and so mighty that much bigger men simply shook their heads and declined to throw. They put the olive wreath on his head before the last men had thrown, and men said the gods had filled him, which made me laugh. But the victory made him a different man – open-faced and beaming with good will.

'I have no idea where that throw came from!' he said. 'I'm still not sure it was me.'

'Have you made your victor's offering?' I asked.

'No,' he said.

'Do not forget,' I said. 'Blaspheme in private if you like, but if you serve on my ship, you make public obeisance.'

When you are in command, you are always in command, children. Even when a man you call friend wins at the games. It pleased me to do well – but as commander, it pleased me more that many of my people were *also* doing well. I walked around and congratulated them.

The sun was still high in the sky, and the judges declared an hour's rest for all competitors. Then the archery started. The Lesbians had several fine archers, and the Samians had one, Asclepius, whose shots were so strong that I didn't think he could be beaten. Most men's arrows lofted into the target at fifty paces, but Asclepius's arrows flew straight as if shot from Apollo's bow. But as a group, the Cretans were the best.

I was out in the first round. I can shoot a bow, but not with archers like these.

Teucer was there, and he shot patiently and seriously. He just made the first cut and went on to the second round, the lowest-ranked man there. In the second round, he had to shoot against Asclepius. That was a bout to see – every arrow thudding home into the stretched hide at fifty paces, every shot inside the charcoal marking of the highest score. None of us had ever seen shooting like this. The judges sent both men to the third round with the issue undecided.

Idomeneus also went to the third round, and one Lesbian, an archer in service to Epaphroditos. The four of them poured libations and drank wine together, and then the target hides were moved to one hundred paces.

At that distance, even Asclepius had to loft his arrows. He shot first, and hit the charcoal every time. Idomeneus was next, and he placed two of his three arrows within the charcoal, but the third was caught by a flutter of breeze and sailed high over the target. We all sighed together, and Idomeneus bowed and was applauded by two thousand men – out of the competition, but with great honour. The Lesbian shot next, and only hit the charcoal once. He, too, received the applause of the whole army. Finally, Teucer stood to the line. He shot all three arrows so fast that a man who turned his head to speak to his neighbour might have missed the whole performance, and every shot went home in the charcoal.

Now there was open argument about how to carry on – whether to award both men, or to move the target. Miltiades rose to his feet and held up the baton of the judges.

'For the honour of Lord Apollo, we will have both of these men shoot again,' he said. 'Although we deem both worthy of holding the prize.'

There was much applause, and the hides were moved to one hundred and fifty paces.

At that range, a bull's hide is smaller than the nail on your little finger. A moment's inattention and your arrow drops short. At a hundred and fifty paces, a man with a Greek bow must aim it at the heavens to drop the arrow into the target.

It was Teucer's turn to shoot first. He used the Persian bow I had brought him, which pleased me. He shot one arrow, as directed, and it hit the charcoal.

We roared for him.

Asclepius took a long time with his shot. By his own admission, the Samian was an expert at close, flat shooting, and he didn't excel at the long shots. He waited patiently for the breeze to die. There was no rule against it.

I drank water.

Suddenly, without warning, Asclepius lifted his bow and shot. His arrow went high – very high – and came down at a steep angle into the target. Dionysius proclaimed it in the charcoal and we roared again. This was competition, dear to the gods. I remember slapping Phrynichus on the back and saying that now he had something to write about.

And then an arrow came from behind us. It lofted high over the spectators and the red awning where the judges sat, and it plummeted to earth like a stooping falcon to strike the target just a few feet from where Dionysius stood. He leaped in the air, and stumbled away.

Because I was near the awning, drinking water, I turned and saw the archer, who had shot from at least two hundred and fifty paces. In fact, I counted later two hundred seventy paces. His shot hit the charcoal. He raised his bow in triumph, gave a long war cry and ran.

He was a Persian. He must have slipped over the mudflats while we all watched the competition. He killed no Greek. He shot further, and better.

Miltiades awarded him the prize – an arrow fletched in gold.

We roared our approval – even Teucer and Asclepius, both of whom had shot like gods.

But later – much later – I saw Teucer pace off the distance. Night was falling, and he thought that no man watched him. He raised his bow and his shaft fell true, but a fist of breeze moved it, and later he told me that he missed the charcoal by the width of his hand.

We were elated by the shooting – the sort of heroism in which any Greek (and apparently, any Persian) might take joy.

I put on my armour with some trepidation. It wasn't really mine – it was a good bronze bell cuirass that Miltiades had given me, and while I liked it, it lacked the flexibility and lightness of the scale cuirass I had won in my first games – a cuirass that was hanging on its wooden form in my hall in Plataea with my shield and my war spears. A bronze cuirass never seems to fit just right over the hips. It flares there, so that the hips have full play in a long run, but that same flare makes a waist where much of the weight of the armour is borne, just over the hard muscles of the stomach, and that can make running uncomfortable.

Worse by far is running in ill-fitting greaves. They snap over the lower leg, covering a warrior from the ankle to the knee, and if they are too big they slip and bite your arches, and if they are too small, they pinch your ankles and leave welts that bleed – even in one stade. I'd spent all my spare time fitting and refitting those greaves – a plain pair in the Cretan style, worn over linen wraps.

It was a strong field – Epaphroditos, Sophanes, Stephanos, Aristides himself, Lord Pelagius's nephew Nestor, Nearchos of Crete and his younger brother, Neoptolemus, Sophanes' friend Glaucon, and Dionysius of Samos's son Hipparchus, a fine young man without his father's arrogance. He was next to me in the first heat, and I made the mistake of giving way at the first step – I never caught him. But I placed second, and went on to the next round.

The men I named had all gone on in their rounds. We were down to two eights, and the men running were the heroes of our army, the champions of the East Greeks and their allies. I was proud just to run with them. I drank water, pissed some of it away and lined up, the aspis on my arm as heavy as lead after just one race.

I was between Epaphroditos and Aristides, chatting with both, waiting for Miltiades to start us, when the cry went up.

The Persian fleet was sailing around the point. Their fleet was immense, and it came and came and came. They crossed the bay under sail and put in to the beaches at the foot of Mycale, and I stood on the shore and counted them.

Five hundred and fifty-three ships, first to last, biremes and hemioliai included. Just two hundred more ships than we had, including all of our lighter ships.

On the other hand, the Cyprians sailed like fools, and the Aegyptians were so wary that they edged away from us, though we didn't launch a single ship.

We took it as an omen, that the Persians had come while we competed. We watched them, and we laughed and called out to them to come and join us, and then, as if by common consent, we turned our backs on their display of imperial power and went back to our athletics.

I remember that walk away from the shore, because I hated the aspis I had on my arm, an awkward thing with a badly turned bowl and an ill-fitting bronze porpax. I still had the cheap wicker Boeotian I had purchased on the beach at Chios a year before, a far less pretty shield with a split-ash face and a plain leather porpax, but it weighed

133

nothing. In those days, there was no rule about competitions and shields, and besides, the Boeotian was, in fact, the shield I would carry to fight. I dropped my heavy aspis on my blanket roll, picked up my Boeotian and trotted to the start line.

Aristides looked at my shield with interest. 'Surely that big thing will impede your running,' he said.

I shrugged. 'It weighs less on my arm,' I said.

'I seem to remember that you beat me in this race four years ago,' he said.

I grinned. 'Luck, my lord. Good fortune.'

Aristides smiled. 'You are rare among men, Arimnestos. Most men would tell me that they were about to beat me again.'

I shrugged, watching Miltiades go to the start line. 'In a few heart-beats, we will *know*,' I said.

Epaphroditos laughed. 'Listening to you two is like an education in arete,' he said. 'Me, I'll just run my best. But for the record, Aristides, he may have beaten you in this race,' he grinned, and his teeth sparked, 'but I beat him, as I remember.'

We all laughed. I remember it well, the eight of us laughing. In all the Long War, there were a few moments like that, that sparkled like bronze in the sun. We weren't fighting for our lives. We weren't freezing cold or burning hot. No one was going to die. We were com-rades – captains, leaders, but men who stood together. Later, when all Greece was at the point of extinction, we never laughed like that.

There is a Spartan joke, that *eirene* – peace – is an ideal men discern from the observation that there are brief intervals between wars.

You laugh, children. Hmm.

I wish I could end this story right there – with eight of us lined up on the sand, ready to race. I remember it so well. Young Hipparchus, the Samian, was retying his sandals when Miltiades called us to order, and the poor boy fumbled the retie and ended up running with one sandal.

Miltiades held his cane even with the ground, and then swept it away like a sword cut, and we were off.

The race itself was an anticlimax of the worst sort, because Aristides and Epaphroditos became entangled within a few lengths of the starting line, and although neither fell, they never caught the rest of us – and they should probably have been first. Or perhaps not. But they were the two I had expected to have to outperform, and their removal gave me wings.

I passed Sophanes in the first five steps and ran easily, knees high, arms pumping, because my greaves fitted perfectly. In the race in armour, the armour is part of the contest, and my armour fitted.

Sophanes wasn't going to surrender meekly, however, and after fifteen paces, we were side by side, well in advance of the other runners. He tried to cut inside me at the turning post, and I shoved him with my big Boeotian shield, and he had to fall back a step.

Hipparchus, running with one sandal flapping, was still game, and he came on past the men who should have been the front-runners – because they were disheartened by their collision, I suspect. But his badly tied sandal finally fell away, tripping him, and he went down. He let out a cry as he fell, and I think Sophanes must have looked back, and that was the step he never retrieved. I ran to the finish and crossed first by the length of my leg.

Then I had a long rest while the other heats ran – three of them. The final eight had me and Sophanes of Athens, as well as my own man, the Aeolian Herakleides, Nearchos of Crete and some Chians I didn't know.

Nearchos came and put an arm around me. 'This is the life,' he said. 'Better than ploughing fields on Crete.'

'You've never ploughed a field in your life, lord,' I said, and they all laughed.

'He was my war tutor,' Nearchos told Sophanes.

'No wonder you are a hero now,' Sophanes said – the boy had a nice turn of phrase.

That was a race. No one fell, and no one clashed at the start line, where most mishaps happen. We all went off at full stride, and in that final race, no one had a loose sandal strap, a bad shield, a pebble.

We ran for the gods. I don't remember much of it – I was tired, and I was flying like a ship before the wind, without a thought in my head. But I remember that as we came to the turning post, all in a clump, Nearchos was first by a hand's breadth – but his paces were a little too long, and he landed his left foot well past the post and started his turn late. Quick as a shark takes bait, I turned inside him, my light shield *almost* catching the post as I scraped by, so that Sophanes, Nearchos and I were exactly together as we came out of the turn and ran for the spear Miltiades held out across the finish.

What can I say? We ran. *We flew.* We were in step, stride for stride, all the way home, and the army roared its approval at us, although I remember none of that. What I remember is how fast that spear grew, and how nothing mattered but reaching it. Nothing.

I won because my shield was a palm's breadth larger than theirs, and touched the spear first. Nothing else. Rather than arrogance, my victory made me feel humble, and I embraced both of them.

I'm not ashamed to say that I wept. As they say at Olympia, for a moment I had been with the gods. I think that all three of us had been.

The rest is a blur of exhaustion. Stephanos took me out in the second round of pankration, but Sophanes of Athens put him down in the third round before losing to Aeschylus the poet's brother in the finals. Athenians are good at games. They train harder than other men – even the Spartans.

I passed at boxing, and I watched a big Lesbian brute – Callimachus, no less, and never was a fighter better named – beat his way through other men like a plough through a field on its second pass, when all the big chunks are broken and the bad rocks already pulled. Aristides caught him again and again, but he was big enough to shake off the blows and continue, and he finally wore Aristides down and hit him hard, and Aristides raised his hand in surrender.

And then we were lighting the fires, and men were preparing for fighting in armour. I was tired, and I suspected that I had won the games. I was surprised at my own hesitation.

Is this how cowardice begins, I wondered, or how youth ends?

But I tied my corslet back on my torso, picked up my shield and went down the beach to the fires, with Idomeneus carrying my shield and my sword.

Aristides grinned sheepishly at me and shook his head. He was wearing a clean *chitoniskos*, and no armour.

'That brute almost killed me,' he said ruefully. He grinned at the 'brute' to take the sting out of his remark. 'I want to live to fight the Medes.'

I nodded. I felt the same way myself, but I also felt that as one of the best fighters, I would be seen to shirk if I balked at the armoured combat. Paramanos helped me into my armour and gave me a drink of wine.

'I think the gods have stolen your wits,' he said. 'Fighting your friends in the dark with sharp weapons. Grow up!' But he cuffed me on the back and wished me good fortune. 'Not much of a field, eh?'

There were only a couple of dozen men brave enough, or foolish enough, to fight with sharp weapons, in armour, at the edge of dark.

Many of them were Athenians and Milesians. 'The fewer the men, the greater the honour,' I said, but I remember giving him a sarcastic grin to go with the line from Pindar.

I faced Aeschylus's brother in the first round, and he hit hard, cutting pieces from the oak rim of my shield, but I ticked him in the pectoral under his sword arm on our third engagement, drawing blood from a place that showed when he overexposed his side in a long sweeping cut. The cut itself was under his armour, and I had to make him take the breastplate off to show it, and he was as surprised as Dionysius. I was awarded the victory, and the young man apologized for doubting my word.

I had a long rest, and my muscles started to stiffen before my second bout – which was against another Athenian.

Sophanes. Of course.

He was good – fast, light on his feet, careful. He wanted to dance.

I faced him with the opposite strategy. I stood my ground, barely reacting, offering nothing, allowing him to dance while I waited with bovine patience.

There isn't much to hit on a man wearing Greek armour and greaves and fighting behind an aspis or a Boeotian. I stood my ground, backing from his wilder rushes, and waited him out. After a number of engagements – some men were booing me, because I was so dull – my blade licked out and cut him on the bicep, and it was over.

'You fight like an old man,' Miltiades said to me.

'I plan to be one,' I said, which got a good response.

Most men felt I had won the games by that time, and my friends began to gather, dumping wine on my head, kissing me or throwing their arms around me. Epaphroditos and two of his men picked me up, carried me to the edge of the water and threw me in. Then a small crowd came and fished me out, and I cursed them for the effect on my armour.

The third round was just two of us. Too many bouts resulted in double hits, or real wounds, and knocked both men out of the competition. In our rules then, a double hit disqualified both men.

So it was me – and Istes.

He was reputed to be the greatest swordsman in Greece.

So was I.

It was still bright enough to fight, and we had fires lit on either side of us, and I think almost every man in the fleet was on that beach for our fight. If I had thought I had word-fame before that fight, I realized that every oikia in Greece would know me after this.

When we faced each other, we reached out our blades and touched them together. Istes grinned under his helmet, and I grinned back.

'Let's show them what excellence is,' he said.

What can I say? He was a great man.

Both of us must have decided the same thing – to dispense with the slow testing that most swordsmen employ in a bout. When Dionysius lowered his spear, we closed – instantly – and the crowd roared.

I threw three blows in as many heartbeats, and he fought back, a blur of motion, and our swords left sparks in the air. Then we circled apart, and neither of us was touched, and the crowd roared.

As if by consent, we closed again immediately, and this time I launched a combination – an overhead cut to draw his shield and then a punch with my shield rim and a back-cut to score on his thigh. I have no idea what he planned, but our shields struck – rim to rim, a jar like an earthquake up your arm – and my back-cut fouled with his overhead cut as I turned my body. I kicked out with my right foot as we both rotated on our hips and I caught him behind the knee – luck, I suspect – and he went down, rolling away. He rolled right over his aspis, something that, up until then, I had never seen a man do, and came to his feet a horse-length away.

If I had thought the crowd loud before, they were a force of nature now.

We saluted each other, and charged – shield to shield. Both of us cut high, and our blades rang together – back-cut, fore-cut. For the third time we fell back, and still neither of us bore a wound.

I had never faced anyone like him. He was as graceful as a dancer and as fast as me, with arms as long as mine.

Our next engagement was as cautious as the first three had been heroic, and we both tried counter-cuts at each other's wrists.

He was a bit faster. And he could do a wrist movement I had never seen – a roll of the blade that caused a direction change so fast I couldn't believe Calchas hadn't known it.

I gave ground at his next rush and tried a complex feint to get a cut at his shoulder – the same combination I'd used so successfully against Sophanes.

Instead, we had a chaotic muddle, as he was feinting into my feint. Both of us closed, our shield rims slipped inside each other and suddenly we were chest to chest.

I rotated on my hips to get away and saw my opening as I stepped back. I kicked with my left foot, straight to his hip, and he leaned out, went flat on his back – and the tip of his sword caught me on the sandal.

He was down, and I stepped over him – he'd gone down on his shield. He was mine – but he was grinning.

'Well fought, brother,' he said.

Then I felt the cold/hot of a cut – on my ankle, but my head resisted it for a heartbeat.

I'm proud to say that no man would ever have seen that wound. I wore Spartan shoes, as I always did to fight, and his blade, by some ill fate, had slid between the leather and the ankle bone to cut me. The wound was invisible, and darkness was falling. I'm proud, because although I felt the sly temptation to act the coward's part, I stepped back from Istes, the best swordsman I ever faced in a contest, and saluted him as he got to his feet. Then I put my sword and shield on the ground, unlaced my sandal and showed him the cut.

Perhaps some sighed for disappointment, but most approved. And Istes wrapped his arms around my shoulder and headbutted me, helmet to helmet – not in anger, but in elation.

He got the crown of olives. I got a cut on the foot. But we both felt like heroes.

The sun was a red ball on the horizon when all the winners sacrificed – even Philocrates – and I was declared winner of the games. I suspect Istes would have won if he had competed in two or three more contests, and I think Aristides would have won if he had had better fortune. Fortune is so much a part of a contest. But I won – my second games.

When I had sacrificed again, and put my crown on my head, I offered to take the archer's crown to the Persian camp.

People seemed to think that fitting.

I wore a chiton, because the Medes aren't big on nudity, and I wore my crown, and I ran across the no-man's-land with a torch.

The sentries were waiting. They were all Persians of the satrap's guard, led by Cyrus, and they had, apparently, watched the games all day. *They cheered me.*

I bowed to Cyrus.

'Are you the man who shot the arrow?' I asked.

Cyrus gave a dignified smile. 'Don't you think that would be the feat of a younger, more foolish man?' he said.

And then I saw that Artaphernes was there. And my heart almost stopped.

Artaphernes came forward, and I bowed, as I had been taught as a slave. I was never one of those Greeks who refused obeisance. Foolishness. I bowed to him, and he smiled at me.

'Young Doru,' he said. 'It is no surprise to any of us that you are the best of the Greeks. Why have you come here?'

'I come bearing the prize for archery, voted by acclamation of all the Greeks to the Persian archer who dared to wade to our shore and shoot – a magnificent shot. I am to say that had he remained, only honour would have come to him.' I handed the chaplet of olives and the arrow to the satrap of Lydia.

Artaphernes had tears in his eyes. 'Why are we at war?' he asked. 'Why are you Greeks not one with us, who love honour? Together, we could conquer the world.'

I shook my head. 'I have no answer, lord. Only a prize, and the good wishes of our army for the man who shot that arrow.'

He presented the prizes to Cyrus – as I had expected. And while the Persians cheered their man, Artaphernes stood next to me.

'Have you seen our fleet?' he asked.

'We will defeat it,' I said, with the daimon still strong on me.

'Oh, Doru,' he said. He took my hand and turned me to face him, despite the crowd of men around us and his guards. 'You saved my life and my honour once. Please allow me to save yours. You have no hope at all of winning this battle.'

'I honour you above all the men of the Parsae I have known,' I said. 'But we will defeat you tomorrow.'

He smiled. It was a wintry smile, the sort of smile a man gives a woman who has refused his hand in marriage.

He clasped my hand like an equal – a great honour for me, even among Greeks – and kissed my cheek.

'If you survive the battle,' he said into my ear, 'I would be proud to have you at my side.'

I started as if he had spat poison in my ear. 'If I capture you, I will treat you like a prince,' I responded. And he laughed.

He was the best of the Persians, and he was Briseis's husband. The world is never simple.

7

The next day, it rained, and the next as well, which was as well for all the Greeks, as many of us had small wounds, aches and pains that would not have served us well in the heat of battle.

The Samians began to behave badly. Many of their oarsmen refused to patrol, despite the Persian fleet being just twenty stades across the bay. Their odd behaviour enraged the Lesbians and the Chians. There were fist fights, accusations of cowardice.

We on the shore of Miletus were protected from all that, but not from the Persian army laying siege to Miletus. As if the unspoken truce of the games was over, the Persians attacked our sentries the very next dawn, shooting men on the wicker wall we'd woven to protect our ships, like the Achaeans at Troy. When it happened again the next day, I decided to do something about it.

On the third night, Idomeneus, Phrynichus, Philocrates and all our marines slept, if you care to call it that, out in the rain, on the rocks north of our camp. It was a miserable night, long and tedious, but we were rewarded when, after a lashing thunderstorm that hid the first paling of the sky, we heard the telltale clash of metal on stone that heralded the Persians moving up to their usual harassment position.

This morning's attackers were a dozen Lydian peasants with slings, and a hand of actual Persians, all officers come for the fun, talking quietly as they moved across the rocks, their magnificent bows already strung.

They walked to the same point on the rocks they had used the day before. Our northernmost sentry was fully visible, his dark cloak nicely outlined in the growing light, and all five Persian officers drew together and let fly.

I'm sure all their arrows hit the target, but I didn't see, as I was moving. And the 'sentry' was made of baskets, anyway.

I don't remember much of the first part of that fight, because there was so little struggle. The Lydians were just shepherds, and they surrendered.

Not the Persians. The Persians were a tougher proposition, five of them and four of us on a smooth piece of rock. It might have been part of the games. They came at us as soon as they saw us.

My first opponent was an older man with a heavy beard dyed bright red with henna. He had an axe at his belt and a short sword covered in beautiful goldwork that shone in the rising sun.

I remember wanting that sword.

I had a shield, my light Boeotian, and a spear – one of the short ones we used then, a man's spear, not one of these long things you use today.

Truth to tell, a man with an axe and a short sword has no chance against a man with a shield. But no one had told the old man, and he came for me fast and determined – like a man who knew his tools. I put my spear-point into his chest, and it glanced off – he had a coat of scales under his cloak – but I knocked him down with the force of my blow. He put a gaping cut in the face of my shield with his axe.

Two of the other Persians leaped at me, ignoring Idomeneus and Phrynichus. Both attacked me with a ferocity that belied the Persian reputation as careful fighters. They attacked like Thracians, all war cries and whirling cloaks. I took two wounds in as many heartbeats – nothing serious, but enough to drive me back.

But Phrynichus and Idomeneus were true men, and they were not going to let me die. Idomeneus speared the bigger Persian through the side. The man screamed, but he must already have been dead. The smaller man continued to rain blows on me while he baffled Phrynichus with his cloak. He was a canny fighter, and he used his cloak as a shield and a weapon, and Phrynichus stumbled back when he got a cloak weight in the head. But I had my feet under me, and I thrust hard with my spear, hitting the Persian in the head. His helmet gave under my spear-point – shoddy work, and no mistake – and he died like a sacrifice, his sinews loosing as if I'd cut them.

Philocrates was fighting the older man and another opponent, and they were both retreating across the rock face. Philocrates was everywhere – his spear was high and low, and he kept moving, facing one and then another, heedless of the bad footing. The two Persians wanted no more of the fight, I could tell, but backed steadily away, abandoning their comrades.

The fifth Persian shot Phrynichus with his bow. The shot was hurried, and the arrow struck the Athenian in the helmet. Unlike the Persian helmet, Phrynichus's good Corinthian held the point, but he fell, unconscious from the blow. The archer now put a second arrow to his bow and turned to Philocrates.

I threw my spear. The range was short, and in those days any spear you carried could be thrown.

I hit the archer and knocked him flat with the strength of the blow, but even as I threw, Philocrates missed his footing and fell on the rocks, and the younger Persian leaped to finish him.

I sprang forward, but Idomeneus was faster, throwing his spear. He missed his target, but the tumbling shaft caught the older man in the face. Blood spurted and the man fell to his knees.

The archer rolled over and cut at me with a heavy knife. He caught my shin and his blow was so hard he dented my greave and almost broke my leg. The pain was intense, and I fell, and then we were grappling on the ground. But I was covered in armour, and he had only the scale shirt that had saved him from my spear. We both had daggers after the first moments, and there was no thought of defence – we both stabbed wildly the way desperate men do.

I stabbed him five times before he stopped moving. He stabbed me just as often, but every blow caught on my cuirass, because the gods were with me and it was not my hour to die. Even unmanned by death, he tried to stab me again.

Persians. They can fight.

I got to my knees to find that Philocrates was also on his, and the younger Persian was hurrying the older Persian across the rocks and a dozen more Persians were on their way.

I retrieved my spear and stripped the corpse of the man I had killed with my dagger. His scale shirt was a model of perfection, small scales like the scales of a fish, washed in gold, with bronze and silver scales in patterns, edged in purple leather. I stripped him while watching the wary approach of the Persian relief column. They were calling their camp for more men, and a dozen Greeks were coming over the wicker walls to help us, too, but I didn't want to be rushed while plundering.

When I had the shirt, I laid the man out neatly, his hands crossed on his chest. I left him his rings. He had fought well, and saved his lord.

We were all cut up, and shaking – for an ambush, it had been a sharp fight. Idomeneus carried Phrynichus back to the walls. Philocrates was stripping the man I'd killed first. He, too, had a fine scale shirt, and his bow-case was covered in lapis and gold wirework.

I ran to the site of Philocrates's combat, and one of the oncoming Persians tried a long shot at me. The arrow skidded on the rocks, missing me by a horse-length or more.

As I had thought, the old man's sword was lying between two big rocks. As I reached for it, two arrows passed through my shield. One scratched my hand at the *antilabe*, and only the heavy leather of the strap kept me from taking a bad wound. The other went right through the shield face and hit my greave, but again the thin bronze held.

I got my hand on the sword hilt and stumbled back. My left leg would barely take my weight. I took an arrow to my helmet and two or three more hit the rocks around me. I paused, stepped up on to the biggest rock and waved my new sword at them, and then I ran like Achilles for our wall, dodging right and left as I passed through the rocks to make their archery a little more difficult.

Miltiades was waiting for me at the walls.

'You are a fool,' he said fondly.

I handed him the sword. 'First spoils, my lord,' I said. Then I hobbled down the wall to Paramanos, who was better than most physicians at bones and such, and showed him my leg. He had to cut the greave off my shin – the arrow had deformed it. Underneath, the shin was red and black, and it wept blood right through the skin.

Other men – Herakleides, I remember, and his brother – came and helped us out of our armour, and we were brought wine.

After a while I lay down under a sail and slept. I was exhausted, and my leg throbbed. I remember waking to eat a double helping of barley broth, and then sleeping again – two days' sleep in a single day. There's nothing like combat to drain a man.

When I awoke the next day, men had brought me a new pair of greaves. It is good to be a hero. Every man is your friend, and men you have never met will work hard to win your praise – or merely to perform some good act for you, as if you were one of the gods. Those greaves were a poor fit, but they were better than nothing, and some other Greek went bare-legged to combat that day.

Idomeneus cut sheepskin from my bedding to make the greaves fit against my legs, and he rewrapped my leg, which was clearly infected, or poisoned. I felt fine – elevated, even – and that can be a sign of fever.

What I remember best was my eagerness to try that fine scale shirt. It fitted me the way a shield cover fits a shield. It weighed nothing, and I felt like a god.

One of the smiths had pounded the dents out of my helmet and someone had repaired my poor battered Boeotian shield, which now had a small bronze plate riveted to the rawhide to cover where the arrows had punched through.

We were all armouring up, because the sun was rising in the east, across the bay. Where the Persian fleet was putting to sea.

I've seldom been with men so elated before a battle. What the four of us had done the day before was to show the Athenians, at least, that we could take the Persians man to man. The success of our venture – a palpable success, I'd add, with looted armour, a bow-case and a magnificent sword – had a powerful effect on every man on our beach, Athenians, Chians, even the mercenaries. The personal wealth of the Persians was legendary – but we'd just proven it.

I'll say this for Dionysius of Phocaea: his ship was the first off the beach, and he rowed up and down, coaxing us to greater efforts, telling every division, and even every ship, where to take their place in the line.

We formed in the bay with Lade behind us, and our line formed with the Samians on the left, with the Lesbians next. These two contingents made up more than half our line, one hundred and eighty triremes. Erythrae and Phocaea only contributed ten ships between them, but they were the best trained, and they were in the centre. Then came the Chians – a hundred ships under old Pelagius and his nephew, Neoptolemus, the finest of men and the proudest single force for size and beauty. On the right, we had the smaller contingents from Teos, Priene and Myos – about thirty ships altogether, perhaps the worst of our entire fleet. The smaller islands were hard-pressed to raise and crew a trireme. It was as if they had exhausted themselves by providing the thing, and had no energy left for training.

To the right of the mixed squadron were the Milesians, sixty-eight ships. On this day, Histiaeus came out of his city and led them in person. Some said that the men of Miletus had told him to go and not come back – his madness had worsened, and men feared him. But he left Istes in command of the Windy Tower.

And finally, to the right of the Milesians, there was Miltiades' contingent and the Cretans under Nearchos. They called us the Athenians, but unlike the force that Aristides had led at Sardis five years before, we were really pirates. None of my rowers was an Athenian citizen, although many of them had been born under Athena's gaze. More were Thracians, or Byzantines, or broken men from Boeotia and the Peloponnese. Even our marines were a polyglot bunch.

Nearchos's contingent was another fine one, with five well-built ships and highly trained crews. I had drummed it into the boy to take war seriously, and he did. He had spent a fortune on his oarsmen, and his ships were painted red, his helmet was painted red and he had a red shield with gold fittings.

A group of us – my friends and old comrades, and Miltiades' officers – met on the beach as if by common consent, to pour libations and pray and drink wine in the new dawn. It is nice to be the last squadron to form. There's plenty of time to make sure that all the rowers have their cushions, that all the thole pins are sound and secure, the hulls are smooth, every buckle is buckled and every lace fresh, new and strong. The vanguard must hurry out in the dark, leaving their canteens behind, or some other thing that irritates you all day in a big fight.

Paramanos got us together, going from group to group as we armed and inviting us to Miltiades' awning. When I arrived, I accepted the congratulations of every man on my feat of arms the day before.

'Nice *thorax*,' Aristides said. He took my hand. 'And a noble fight,' he added with a smile.

As Istes said, what would it be like to awaken one morning and find that you had forfeited all that adulation? And from such a man as Aristides?

That is what it is to be a hero. Unless you never deserved it, once you go up that ladder, you cannot come down.

At any rate, we were all there – all the best men of our contingent. Aristides made the sacrifices, and Cimon stood on one side of me, while Paramanos stood on the other, and Agios, Miltiades' personal helmsman and my former mentor, winked at me across the sacrificial fire.

They were all there, the friends of my first life, and some from my second – my pirates. Miltiades, and Phrynichus, and Nearchos whom I had trained, and his brother, and Idomeneus stood behind me with Phrynichus, and Philocrates took his share of the prayer without a ribald comment, and Herakleides the Aeolian, one of my first men, now commander of a trireme, and Stephanos. I smiled, because my men had done well.

We sang the paean of Apollo, and we made sacrifice, and then Miltiades handed round a great kylix of unwatered wine.

'Today, we are not pirates,' he said. 'Today, we fight for the freedom of the Greeks, although we are far from home and hearth.'

Let me tell you, Miltiades was always my model of a man – of greatness. He stood taller, acted taller, than other men. I still ape his manners – the way I swirl a cloak and the way I put my hand on the hilt of my sword are his. And when the sense of occasion was on him, he was not like a god. He *was* a god. Even Aristides was like a pale, priggish shadow next to the blazing sun of his glory.

We all drank, and when the kylix came back to Miltiades, he raised it on high. 'May we all be heroes,' he said, and poured the rest into the sand.

My ship was the last one in the water – the rightmost ship in the rightmost division. It meant that we had to row far to the east, well down the bay.

I must explain the way of it, or you young people will never understand what happened in the battle. First I'll draw the bay – a great shape like an empty sack, open on the west and with the bottom at the east. Up near the mouth of the sack – the lower side of the mouth, see? – is the island of Lade, and Miletus sticks into the mouth of the sack by the island, like a man pushing his thumb in. And the Persian camp, the siege, was south and west of the city, so that, as we formed our line, west to east, from the top of the sack to the bottom as it were, the city and the Persian camp were both behind us. We were, in effect trying to keep the Persian fleet from getting to the city and the camp.

Our line extended from the island all the way along the bay to well east of the Persian camp. Our line stretched for almost thirty stades.

There's an irony, too. We fought there again – at Mycale. But I'll tell that story when I get to it.

The Persians started forming earlier than we did and were still forming when my men rowed us the last few ship-lengths to form to the right of Stephanos in *Myrmidon*. So we rested on our oars and watched as the Aegyptian contingent formed opposite us, and then more Phoenicians beyond them.

Facing nothing.

Their line was, in fact, almost twice as long as ours. Part of that was because they left gaps between their divisions, and part was because aside from the Phoenicians, who were great sailors, and well trained, the rest of their ships had as little notion of keeping formation as the worst of ours. I could see the Cilicians, away at the Samian end of the line, and they were more like a cloud of gnats than a squadron.

For all that, I didn't like being outflanked by the Phoenicians. They'd split their best contingent, putting a hundred Phoenician ships at either end of their great crescent. They put their worst ships in the middle. Their plan was clear – to close rapidly on our flanks and crush us before we broke their centre.

We were still lying on our oars when Miltiades came out of the line under his boatsail. He was the leftmost ship in our squadron, hard by Nearchos. Together, we and the Cretans had sixteen ships – the best manned, and probably the best trained except for the Phocaeans.

Miltiades passed down the line and hailed each captain as he came up. When he got to me, he turned his ship under oars so that it came to rest on my right, usurping my place of honour.

'When we go forward, follow me,' Militades called. 'We're going to form a column, race downwind to the east, and try to sting the Phoenicians.' He laughed.

Fifteen of us against a hundred Phoenicians. 'Long odds,' I called back.

Whatever he replied was carried away by the rising wind, but I heard the word 'hero', and I waved.

Idomeneus had a mad grin on his face. 'This's what I came for,' he said.

I looked at the mass of Phoenician ships and smiled.

Like most pirates, most of my rowers were pretty well armed. Every man had a javelin at least, and many had a *pelte* or a buckler. A good number had better gear – a helmet, a leather hat, an aspis. On board the mighty *Ajax*, every man had a helmet and a spear, and some had swords. The older and more successful a pirate was, the better kit his rowers had, and that gave us a huge advantage in a boarding fight. On the Phoenicians, their rowers were slaves or captives or paid freedmen, but none of them had arms. Not that that ever seemed to cause them to row any worse, but if a boarding fight lasted more than a few minutes, our ships would always overwhelm theirs. In fact, one of our ships could put two hundred trained fighters against ten of theirs. That's why they preferred a fight of manoeuvre.

We'd also killed most of the best Phoenician crews at Amathus. They were shy now, and cautious of engagement.

But fifteen to a hundred was long odds at the best of times.

I pondered this, gathered my marines and my officers amidships on the fighting platform and told them what I knew. I pitched my voice to carry so that my oarsmen could hear everything I said.

'We're going to *sail* downwind on our boatsails, so lay everything on deck and stand ready,' I said to my sailing master. He was a black Libyan with a barbaric name like a noseful of snot, but we all called him 'Black' and he answered to it. I'd bought him on the beach at Lade and freed him on the spot – he'd been a helmsman way out west at Sicily, and I knew quality when I saw it, for all that he was new to my ship. Paramanos was black, and look how good he was.

'Then we're going to drop sails, turn back west and attack the tip of their pincer,' I said. 'I'm going to guess that Lord Miltiades will try to lure them into a luffing match upwind – their rowers against ours – until we hit the shore. If we do that, nothing matters except how far east and north of the battle we can lure the bloody Phoenicians. Don't get locked in a boarding fight if you can con your enemy into trying to outsail you. And friends – we in *Storm Cutter* can outsail anything they offer, can we not?'

They shouted back at me, and then I went forward to watch as Black had his sailors lay out the boatsail and Mal coached his rowers while Galas took the helm. I had promoted him to helmsman when I purchased Black. He watched Black with a critical eye.

I kept my eye on the Persians – though there probably wasn't a Persian among them, except for a dozen noble archers on twenty or so of their command ships. Somewhere was Datis himself. He'd have a deck full of them. But the rest of their fleet's people were vassals and slaves – and Cilician pirates, of course. Men just like us.

As I watched, there was a flash and a ripple all along the front of the Persians as their oars came out. It wasn't neat, or well drilled, but the mass of their great half moon began to move. It was a terrifying sight, truth to tell – they outnumbered us so badly, and their line filled your eye, almost horizon to horizon. They must have taken up fifty stades of ocean – more than five *hundred* ships. Until then, no one had ever seen such a fleet.

I refused to be terrified. Today was the day Apollo would smile on the Greeks, the day I would win Briseis, fulfil my destiny and go to glory. I had half a notion that I might die in the victory – it would suit all I had heard of fates that I die achieving my ambition, and my curse to Briseis.

Death held little fear for me.

I was still young then.

'Heads up, sailors!' I called from the bow. 'Attention to orders!'

Miltiades was turning out of the line, and he had a square torn from his big red awning flapping at his stern.

'Hoist the boatsail,' I called, and Black echoed it in his curious sing-song accent.

We turned with the steering oars, the rowing oars held clear of the water but ready to engage – all to save the rowers' strength. I looked back along our line, and I saw them come from line abreast pointed north to line ahead pointed east in fine style – one of the very manoeuvres that Dionysius had made us practise, in fact. Nearchos followed us, and eight of the Chians came out of their line and followed us – Neoptolemus and his contingent, I later learned. That made me grin – twenty-five ships were shorter odds, and now the Phoenicians couldn't just ignore us or we'd wreck them. I wondered what the Samians were doing to avoid envelopment at their end of the line, but fifty stades is a long way to see on a hazy morning.

We sailed due east with a strengthening breeze at our backs, and the water tore down our hulls, and we sang hymns and drinking songs. Miltiades sent an oarsman over the side, and he called out to each ship as it passed, ordering us to prepare to turn to port and form line ahead facing north when the red square flew again. I understood well enough, and I expect that all the other captains did, too – again, Dionysius's training paid off.

Opposite us, the Phoenicians and the Aegyptians didn't react to our manoeuvre, but carried straight forward under oars. The Aegyptians were in a mix of heavy ships and pentekonters, light ships that we Greeks would no longer put in the line of battle.

We got three stades to the east before they reacted, and by that time Miltiades' *Ajax* was even with the eastmost ships in the Phoenician division, so that we were actually threatening to outflank their fleet. For those of you who have never fought ship to ship, and I think that's every one of you, a rowing ship is most vulnerable to a ram in the flank, or the long side of the ship, where the bronze beak can roll you over or split the planks of your side and leave you to swim in the deep dark sea. Or sink in your armour and feed the fish.

We watched them with the avidity of men watching a sporting event. Late – very late – the tip of their crescent began to turn east to face us, but they were rowing and we were sailing, and although they were able to keep pace, their squadron began to string out over the sea, losing all hope of formation. We were strung out too, but the wind moves at the same speed for all, I suppose, and we still held our line. And they were rowing flat out to race against us.

Miltiades was the best fighting sailor I served under. Later, every man would praise Themistocles. He was a rabble-rouser and a politician, and he made Athens the greatest sea power in history, but Miltiades – like Dionysius of Phocaea – was a pirate and a seaman.

We raced two more stades to windward, and the breeze continued to grow behind us – the hand of the gods, we said to each other. Miltiades began to wave, and I sent a runner to signal Stephanos, astern of me. We were about to turn.

Miltiades stood on the helmsman's bench of *Ajax*, the red square bundled under one arm, his other arm hooked in the bent wood of the trireme's stern, watching the ships behind me. On mine, Black had the bow full of sailors standing about the boatsail mast, and Mal had the oars out and peaked, ready to stroke. Galas had a grin from ear to ear, the oars steady under his arms, ready to turn.

'Prepare for a hard turn to port,' I roared. 'On my command!'

By the gods, I thought, this is going to be glorious, win or lose. I had seldom gone so fast in a trireme – the wind directly astern had such power. I wondered if we could carry any of it through the turn.

I also noted that Miltiades was stiffening his ship by sending his marines and extra deck crew to the windward side, and I followed suit. Anything to get that railing down as we turned – or rather, anything to keep the leeward rail *out of the water*. I'd heard of a trireme rolling over in a turn, but I didn't want to be the first one to do it, either.

Heartbeats – my heart thudding against my chest, as if it would pulse right through the new Persian armour I wore. The hushed expectancy – the sound of the wind, and a gull screaming.

Miltiades let fly the red cloth, and I raised my fist.

'Hard to port,' I called.

Galas called his orders, and long training and good discipline told. Every port oar dipped together, and touched water – held. The starboard oars gave way. The ship heeled like a chariot on a turn – over, over farther – until my heart was in my throat and every man on deck had to hold the rail, and the port-side rowers had their oars so deep in the water they couldn't withdraw them. Somewhere amidships there was a scream as an oar broke and a man took the shaft in his guts.

And then we were around, and the sun was shining, and our ram was pointed at the Phoenicians, and we were racing like a spear thrown by Poseidon for the flank of the enemy line. Miltiades was around in style, and Stephanos was at my side like an eager dog – our line filled out even as I watched. The Cretans were no slower, and the Chians trailed away in some confusion, but that only served to make our line look longer.

As soon as the Phoenicians saw us turn, they began to turn to meet us, but they were fifty or so individual ships, not a squadron. And their rowers were tired.

The wind was so strong that it was pushing us even with our turn, even with our sails down. I began to eye the beach and the rocks at the foot of the bay – the east end – with a professional eye.

Then I ran amidships to the command platform.

'Diekplous,' I called to the helmsman. 'Oar-rake and right through. Then turn upwind – west.' Miltiades and I were facing four or five of the fastest Phoenician vessels, but they were the very eastmost. And if we oar-raked them, there was no point in lingering – they'd never come back to the battle. Right? Understand, lad? Because if we broke their oars, they couldn't row, and Poseidon would take them to the bottom of the bay and wreck them. Got it, my blushing beauty? I'll make a navarch of you yet, my dear.

Galas tapped his oars – a little to the west, and a little more, to compensate for that wind. Our rowers were pulling perfectly. My ship was half a length ahead of Miltiades when we engaged the first Phoenician. I can't be certain, but I think we were the first to engage that day.

Galas overcompensated for the wind, and we crossed the bow of our target fifty feet out – a deadly error had we been moving at the same speed, but we weren't. We were faster, and he leaned hard, having learned his lesson, and Mal called for extra effort from the port-side oars, and we heeled over again and slammed home into the Phoenician's cathead, shattering his row-gallery with the reinforced beam at the top of our ram. The whole starboard side of his ship seemed to explode as our beak ripped down the benches, and his seams opened and he was gone under the waves. That's what speed does for you in a fight.

'West!' I roared, elated. It was the cleanest sea kill I'd ever seen. Apollo was at my side and the liberation of Greece was at hand.

Miltiades' men were cheering as they rammed the second Phoenician and went straight at the third, rolling him over, two kills in the time it takes to tell the story. Stephanos's helmsman made the same error as Galas, overcompensating for the wind, and he missed his diekplous and swept past, but as luck would have it his bow caught the enemy ship's oars at the end of a sweep and broke them, killing as many oarsmen as our more spectacular strike.

Some ships missed their attacks altogether, and after our initial success, the Phoenicians rallied and struck back, but their rowers were tired and the only ship they killed was one of Nearchos's, rammed amidships with its beak stuck in its prey, as can happen when a ship strikes too hard.

At least ten of their ships died in that first strike. We had lost our god-sent speed now, but I had led the turn west, and other ships had fallen in with me. Miltiades was behind me, gathering up our stragglers, and the Chians were just engaging to the south – that is, on my left.

The bulk of the Phoenician squadron was ahead of me, and they were in confusion, because they couldn't choose whether to turn south and face the Chians or east and face me.

I was back in the bow, looking for their navarch. Somewhere in that huddle of ships was the command ship, and there lay the most glory, the most fame and a chance to kill the head of the Hydra.

But I couldn't make him out in the time I had. The ships closest to us had chosen to fight us as the most immediate threat, and we obliged, hurtling towards a well-manned ship at full speed. He had good rowers, and the collision threw me flat to the deck. We must have struck bow to bow, but his bow gave way – Tenedos worm, or dry rot – and his ship settled like a rock, even as his marines came over our bow like hungry wolves, and died, spitted on the massed spears of our marines.

I turned to Black, who stood behind my shield as if he was my hypaspist. Arrows had started to fly, and he was a target as much as me.

'If every Greek kills two Persians, we'll win,' I said happily.

He shrugged. 'The biggest fight I ever saw,' he said. He rubbed his jaw. 'But I've seen a few, sir. This luck can't last.'

Nor could it. By then, we were like an arrow in the guts of an animal. We'd wounded the Phoenicians, but we hadn't killed them.

My ship was scarcely moving and now my rowers were tiring. The first flush was over and there was *still* a sea of Phoenicians to fight.

'Boys need a rest, lord!' Mal shouted in my ear.

I caught Idomeneus's eye. 'We board,' I said. I ran back along the catwalk. 'Well rowed,' I called down into the thranites as I went past overhead. 'Rest in two minutes!' Down in the lower decks, they have little idea what is passing overhead – victory, defeat, death – hard to tell when all you see is the arse of the man above you and the length of his oar.

I got to the helmsman's station with a shower of arrows from a long ship ahead. I caught one on my shield.

'Lay me alongside that bastard,' I said. 'We'll board him and give our boys a rest.'

In fact, I was aiming at the northernmost ship in the Phoenician squadron – a ship at the 'back' of their now utterly confused pack. I hoped that by coming up the north side of this vessel, I'd get a few minutes' respite from the arrows of the rest.

He was having none of it, and he manoeuvred, and we manoeuvred, like two cats fighting in the dust – and we swept past each other at close range. There was a tall man in a Greek helm on the deck, and Idomeneus shot him in the throat – a wonderful shot, and he fell straight over the side.

Then we were past, and there was another Phoenician close behind – a heavy ship like ours.

He was apparently taken by surprise that we were so close, and our ram struck just aft of his bow, but he had his oars in and our momentum was too little and the angle too steep for a kill.

That was fine with me, and my rowers. We coasted down his side with a keening screech.

'Marines!' I called. 'Deck crew!'

Black had an axe in each hand – long-handled axes of the kind that horsemen carry. Axemen die like lambs in a sea-fight – no shield, no defence. I feared for him and my investment, but I needn't have worried.

As we slowed, I stepped up on the rail and took an arrow on my shield. I didn't wait for our grapples to go home. I leaped.

I had done this twenty times, yet I missed my footing and fell over the top bench. An enemy oarsmen kicked me, but his kick hit a lot of armour and I was getting up when the enemy marines came for me. I should have died, but an axe – a full-weight axe – flew right through the hide face of the first marine's shield and into his arm. Blood blew out through the shield, and I resolved on the spot never to go to war with the Libyans. Before then I had never seen a man throw an axe.

Black threw his second axe into the next man, and it hit poll first – not with the blade – but the poll hit the man in the temple and down he went.

Then I was up, and killing. I only remember Black and his axes – the rest is a blur – and then I was on their command deck with Idomeneus under my shield, shooting their officers at the distance a man could spit while I covered him and killed anyone who came for me. There were two Persian noblemen, and some Mede guards, and a noble Phoenician in scale armour from head to knee. He had a beard as long as his scale shirt, and Idomeneus shot him in his unarmoured face while the remnants of his marines tried to cover him – ineptly – with their shields.

The rowers were all Phoenicians, and they fought, as if to disprove everything I said earlier, but that was the navarch's ship, honey, and he had the best of everything, and Apollo had given him to my spear. So my own rowers had to arm and come over the rail. It was ugly and went on far too long. If I had to guess, I'd say that the only enemy rowers who lived through the slaughter were those who leaped the rail and swam. Maybe six, out of two hundred men.

That's the hard way to take a ship. And when the rowers fight – Poseidon, that's ugly. I have no idea how long it took, but it didn't get my rowers the rest I had intended against a nice effeminate enemy.

At Lade, there were no easy enemies.

There was cheering from the west. The haze over there was burning off, but not enough to give me a clue what was happening.

I went back aboard the *Storm Cutter* and found Galas in the bow with a handful of oarsmen. Water was coming in just forward of the first rowing bench. It wasn't coming fast, but it was coming in all along the seams.

To the north, a smaller Phoenician was angling out of their mob, looking for a fight. Our 'rest' was over. He spotted us and started towards us from about a stade away.

I looked back at the leak. It was a hard moment for me, in a day that was full of them.

'He's finished,' I said.

Storm Cutter's bow must have been damaged when he crushed the lighter Phoenician. My first ship. He was sinking under my feet. On a calm day, I'd have run him up a beach and saved him, rebuilt the bow, retimbered him – anything to save him. But in the middle of the greatest naval battle we'd ever seen, I had only one choice.

'Into the Phoenician,' I said.

By then, we'd wiped out their rowers, and men were hanging list-lessly by the benches, but Galas and Mal and Black got the sailors and the oarsmen to their places – bodies flung over the side, oars coming out through the ports.

We were too slow. The lighter Phoenician was coming at us from the north, already up to ramming speed and turning to get the best possible angle. But he was lining up on an abandoned, sinking ship. He had no way of knowing that we were all in his own command ship, or that it was already taken and the bodies gone.

It stank of blood and shit, but we had some life in us yet. We poled off with anything we could get our hands on – broken oars, spears, boat-pikes. Our first five strokes were so ragged that I was ready to despair, and Mal cracked his voice screaming, but the new ship was a spear-length longer, and half our oarsmen were in unfamiliar benches, a few on the wrong side altogether.

We had just enough way on us to row clear of the abandoned *Storm Cutter*. He served us one more time, taking one more victim with him into the deep. Wounded as he was, the Phoenician was over-eager and rammed home amidships at full speed. His ram cracked timbers and the water poured in, and *Storm Cutter* quickly filled and sank – still stuck to the Phoenician's ram. His rowers backed water like heroes, seeking to withdraw their ram, but their bow went down and down, as if Poseidon's mighty hand had them by the bronze.

They might yet have made it, but Nearchos of Crete shot from under our stern and hulled them neatly amidships while they were utterly defenceless, and they were dead men.

The cheering from the west was louder now.

We could feel it. The Phoenicians – their best – were shying off. Their navarch was dead, and no one was giving them orders, and the northernmost ships turned for the beach and ran.

We lay on our oars and panted, and some men laughed, and others wept. We had been close to death. I could feel the scythe on my cheek.

Behind us, while we did nothing, the handful of Chians under Neoptolemus harried the last Phoenicians to withdraw, and we had eighteen ships when Miltiades came past us and ordered us to form on his right. *Ajax* had a scar on her port-side timbers where a Phoenician ram had only just failed to get a kill, but otherwise he still looked like the mightiest ship on the Bay of Lade.

Just south of me, a pair of Chians carried the last Phoenician ship in our part of the battle, by boarding.

None of us, to be honest, could believe it. I suppose we expected that we'd get stuck in and the Lesbians would have to come and rescue us after they broke the Aegyptians, but we'd done it ourselves.

Miltiades harried us into line. The Phoenicians were re-forming on the Mycale shore in front of their camp. Forty ships or more – against eighteen – and we'd routed them.

I drank off a canteen of water and passed around another of wine.

As it came back to me, Black made a noise of disgust. He was looking over the sea to the west. He spat in the sea, drank from the wine and handed the canteen to Idomeneus.

'We're fucked,' he said.

I turned around. I can remember that moment as if it was today, this morning's breakfast beer. Until I turned, I was a hero in a victorious fleet, and we had just broken Persia's sea power, and I was going to be a prince in Boeotia with Briseis at my side.

The rising sun had finally burned off the haze.

We were alone.

Strictly speaking, we weren't alone, and I'll leap ahead and tell what happened, because from my deck it was hideously confusing. Just accept my word, children – we spent the rest of the day in an exhausted rage of fear and betrayal and confusion.

The Samians had changed sides.

Not all of them, of course. Some remained loyal to the rebellion, and more fled the treachery, although some men would say they were the worst cowards of all, taking no side. Of a hundred ships, eleven stayed with us and fought to the end. Those eleven tried to fight a hundred Phoenicians and every man aboard died trying, and the men of Samos still have a stele to them and their captains in the agora of their city.

But Aeaces, the former tyrant of Samos, had bought the aristocrats among them, and Dionysius of Samos (not to be confused with our mad navarch, Dionysius of Phocaea) changed sides, the bastard.

The treachery of the Samians left the Lesbians to the fates.

157

Epaphroditos chose to die, and he led his own men – the men of Methymna and Eresus – into the enemy, and they took many of the Cilicians down with them. But the Mytilenians chose another path, hoisted their sails and ran for it – twenty ships that we needed desperately.

In the centre, the Chians saw they were being deserted and did the noblest thing of all. They stayed together and resolved to cut their way out. They had no idea we had won on the right – who would have expected it of us? – so they hurled themselves against the mass of levies and mercenaries in the centre. That was the chaos that greeted us when the haze finally burned off, so that we couldn't see any of our ships at first because we didn't think to look for them *behind* the line of Aegyptians facing us.

Now, I also have to add that up to this point Datis, the Persian commander, thought that his own left – the Phoenicians we'd beaten – had been enveloped by a *larger* force. Friends like Cyrus told me later that that's what Datis had been told by the beaten remnants, because beaten men count every foe two or three times. So despite the defection of the Samians and the destruction of the Lesbians, Datis thought that the battle was still in the balance. He was holding back his reserve of Aegyptian triremes, waiting to see the rest of our fleet.

That's battle, on a giant scale. When hundreds of ships face each other, no one man can command them, or even guess what occurs. Datis won the Battle of Lade in the first hour, but the haze and the defeat of the eastern Phoenician squadrons made him cautious. Otherwise, he could have closed the gap and trapped us all in the sack. Miltiades would have died there, and Aristides, and Aeschylus. And many other good men.

As it is, I will cry when I tell who died. Just wait.

We rowed south, avoiding contact with the Aegyptian squadron. They had smaller ships than ours, and as I say, we could see no reason for their caution – all we could see was disaster.

We formed a circle, with our sterns together – a favourite ploy of the Athenians, like a phalanx formed in a box against cavalry. In this case, Miltiades did it so that we might shout from stern to stern.

Aristides spoke first. 'We must attack into their centre,' he said. 'The Milesians are still fighting, and many of the Chians.'

Paramanos shouted over him. 'Foolish bravery, my lord. Our few ships can't save one of them.'

'We can die with them,' Aristides retorted.

To be honest, that was my plan, as well. A defeat this great – the destruction of the whole fleet of the Greeks – would be the end of Greek independence. For ever. You who live now, you cannot imagine a time when Athens had *fifteen* ships on her best day, and eight of them were ours. Sparta had *none*.

Of course, I cared nothing for the East Greeks – except my friends. But the rebellion was all I had known, and the men of that rebellion were the friends of my youth, and besides – first and foremost – I knew that in that hour Briseis was lost to me.

I think I moaned aloud. No one heard me but the gods.

Nearchos shook his head. 'These are not my ships to squander, but those of Lord Achilles my father,' he said, with more maturity than I had. 'I will accept the dishonour – but I will withdraw. On my head be it.'

Miltiades balanced on the curving stern boards of his ship. He held up his hand for silence. 'Nearchos has the right of it,' he said. 'It is our duty, for the sake of all the Hellenes, to save what we can and live to fight again.'

Aristides cursed – something I had never heard him do. 'Fight again?' he said. 'With what?'

'Our wits, our ships and our swords,' Miltiades said.

In that hour, he rose to greatness. From that moment, he was no longer Miltiades, tyrant of the Chersonese. From that moment, he made himself the leader of the resistance, although many years would pass before men knew it.

'We must save as many of the Milesians and Chians as we can,' he said. 'Nearchos, go with honour. We were victorious. Tell your men – tell your sons. Had all men fought like you, we would have had the victory.' Then he turned to me. 'Arimnestos – we need to cut a hole in the net around the Chians.'

I had nothing left to give, but his words were like a summons and I stood straighter by the rail of my ship. 'Yes, lord,' I said.

'I think the Persians have ordered their captains to let any fleeing ship run,' he said. 'So we will "flee" to the centre, turn north and attack the Aegyptians.' He pointed at me. 'You lead – you have the heaviest ship. When you see my signal, turn north – just as we did this morning – line ahead to line abreast. Don't die like heroes. Gut a ship or two and make a hole. And then run. All I ask of every one of you is that you kill one more ship.'

Nearchos was weeping. 'I can't leave,' he said. 'I'll fight until you run.'

Miltiades smiled, the way he always did when he got the best of a deal. 'You must do as is best for you, son of Achilles,' he said.

Our rowers had rested for long enough for muscles to stiffen, but we had all swallowed cheese and garlic sausage, and we crept west under oars into the teeth of that west wind that had blown us to victory in the morning.

The Chians were oar to oar and bow to bow with the Aegyptians across the centre, and the Milesians were just a few stades from us, but deeper in, farther north, and now the Phoenicians we'd beaten had come off the beach – not to face us, but to finish the poor Milesians.

Our rowing was poorer than dirt, and I had no heart to curse my rowers. They had given their best, and for nothing.

But Poseidon took pity on us poor Greeks, or else that day's curses were all used up. In as much time as it takes a fast man to run the stade, the wind changed – right around. West to east. And a warm, damp wind hit us like the open hand of a beneficent god. In heartbeats we had our boatsails up on deck. Black took longer, and Miltiades passed us, and so did Aristides. They mocked us.

We were in a strange ship, and everything was stowed by strangers. As it happened, I thought it was a miracle that Black got the boatsail up at all. Then we were racing away west. Behind us, a rain squall appeared at the bottom of the bay and hit the Phoenicians. It was as if the gods were seeking to do all in their power to remedy the perfidious foolery of men.

I'll be honest – it had none of the breakneck enthusiasm of morning. We were tired to our sinews and we were no longer fighting for greatness. But like wild dogs, we were still dangerous.

And, lest I make the Aegyptians sound like an enemy to be trifled with, many men fight badly, late in a victory. I've done it myself. Why risk yourself when the day is won, eh? The Aegyptians were shocked when we turned on them, and timid. And why not? They were vassals of Persia, not friends, and their side was already victorious.

Had we known the future – had we been able to see the dark days at Artemisium and Thermopyle, when the Chians and the Lesbians stood against us, vassals of Persia, in those same ships – we would have left them to die. But who could calculate such a thing? Or abandon a friend?

And of course, they repaid us in their turn – on the beaches of Mycale. But that story is for another night, eh?

Where was I? Ahh – so we turned on the Aegyptians, eighteen ships, and our ships were bigger and our crews more dangerous, even so late in a long fight. They kept formation and many backed water, and we swept on, ignoring the timid, determined to relieve the Chians.

Miltiades was first to sink a ship – a small trireme that sank under his forefoot, caught in a bad turn. Herakleides the Aeolian was, by then, a master helmsman.

Paramanos quickly got the ship that tried to rescue that one, and then we were in among them like barracuda among baitfish.

Nearchos was the first to die. He was lost when the rain squall hit us, and he didn't see the Cilician who caught him aft with his ram. I hope he died quickly. His ship sank, and we saw it all.

Neoptolemus died driving his ship deeper and deeper into the Aegyptians, trying to save his uncle – who was already dead, mighty old Pelagius who would never again hold games on the beaches of Chios. He died with an arrow in his eye.

Another arrow killed Herakleides at the helm of Miltiades' *Ajax*, too. Miltiades took the helm himself. He killed men the way a man with a scythe reaps the ripe barley, but when his marines were all wounded, he chose to live, turned out of the maelstrom and ran. I saw him go and knew that it was time for me to go, too. Idomeneus was in the bow, killing with his bow, and the Aegyptians were hanging back, pelting us with javelins and looking for easier prey while we tried to break their oars, and in the distance, perhaps a stade away, I could see the Chians and the Milesians fighting their way to us – to the hope of rescue.

Two Aegyptians, bolder than the rest, came at me, and they knew their business. I was too cocky, and I thrust between them, looking for the double oar-rake, but they folded their wings like diving birds and they grappled us as we passed between after a shower of javelins that all but cleared my deck of sailors. They had marines – Aegyptian marines are first-rate troops, as good as our Greeks, man for man, with heavy linen armour, twenty or thirty layers of it quilted up, because linen is cheap in Aegypt. They wear bronze helmets, not like ours at all, and carry a heavy shield made of the hide of some river beast. Every man has a pair of wicked, barbed javelins and a huge iron sword, and they can use them. I've heard men say that the

Aegyptians are all cowards, but I've never heard a man who's fought them make such a foolish claim.

Just before they boarded, I saw Stephanos bring his ship into action. He was always one of the best helmsmen, and he was at his own oars. He caught the leeward Aegyptian at a stand, all her oars in, and he punched into the enemy's side like a shark closing its teeth on a corpse, and the Aegyptian's keel snapped. Stephanos gave me a wave and I returned it – the athlete's salute. Aye, I remember that moment, because Stephanos was like a god then.

But the other Aegyptian boarded us, undaunted by the death of their companion, and again like sharks, now that one had his teeth in us, the rest of them got bolder and came forward, and before we'd repelled the first rush, there were more ships coming in.

There was nothing we could do but fight. At sea and on land, there comes a moment in a fight when there are no longer either tactics or strategies. All you can do is fight. They grappled to our bow and to our stern and all down one side, and they came at us – maybe sixty marines against our eight or ten – I can't remember who was still standing – a vicious chaos of blood and swords.

Philocrates stood in the bow with Idomeneus, and they stopped a ship's worth of marines by themselves. I only caught glimpses – I didn't have the luxury of commanding any longer, and had to fight – but I saw Philocrates kill, and kill again, until the ship on the bow cut its grapples. But a chance-thrown javelin caught him in the head – stunned him – and he died there, under the great sword of an Aegyptian marine.

Phrynichus took an arrow in the arm, leading a dozen armed oarsmen against the second ship, but he got up on the rail, his blood flowing like water in a rainstorm, and he raised his poet's voice as if he was competing against Simonides or Aeschylus in the games:

'Sing me, Muses, the rage of Achilles!'

He sang, even as his blood flowed, and my sailors rose from their benches with glory in their hearts.

Galas and Mal – unarmoured – followed me with the remnants of the sailors from the deck crew, and we didn't wait for the onslaught of the third Aegyptian. As soon as his grapples came home, we were over the rails and into his benches, killing. We caught that ship by surprise – they must have thought us easy pickings, and fifteen men with axes made short work of the disorganized crew.

I cut their trierarch down with a single spear stroke where he stood at the foot of his mainmast amidships – the mast was still stepped, and Poseidon alone knows why – and I stood there breathing like a bellows gone mad. For those of you who have never fought in armour, children, you can only go a few hundred heartbeats – the best man in the world, Achilles himself, could do no more – before you have to rest. I loosened my chin strap, drank in sweet breaths of sea air and looked about me.

Idomeneus stood alone for as long as a woman takes to birth a child and held the bow, Philocrates's corpse between his wide-spread legs. Phrynichus was down, and his singing stilled, but his sailors had swamped the second Aegyptian. We'd swept the third like a desert wind.

But while we'd been fighting, three more had come for Stephanos. And rather than abandon us and leave us to die to save himself, he stood fast on our leeward side, and they boarded him. As I watched, his spearmen cleared the fighting deck on the boldest of the three, but the other two had extra marines and they poured men into the centre of *Trident*. Stephanos went into them with half a dozen of his marines, his spear flashing as if he was Ares incarnate, the red horsehair of his crest nodding high above the fight.

Six of them were trying to stop thirty or forty professional fighters. I roared my rallying cry, and Mal stood up from where he'd been looting a corpse, Galas tapped my breastplate to tell me he was at my shoulder and together with a few more sailors and a hand of oarsmen, we leaped back to our own ship, sprinted the length of the deck and leaped again to rescue Stephanos.

As my bare feet pounded along my own deck, I could see nothing, not even with my helmet cocked back on my head. I must have slowed to take fresh spears, because when I came on to Stephanos's deck, I had a pair in my hand.

I was first on to Stephanos's deck, coming in *behind* the enemy while they butchered Stephanos's unarmoured oarsmen. But as we arrived, another Aegyptian grappled Stephanos. At my back came Black and Galas and the deck crew. We met the new Aegyptians sword to sword and shield to shield. Mal died there, along with most of my sailors, unarmoured men facing the swords of Aegyptian marines. Further down the deck, it was even worse. I saw Stephanos fall, run through the thigh, and I saw his cousin, Harpagos, stand over him with a sailor's axe, and blood flew like ocean spray when he hit a man.

I was tired, and my cause was lost, and it was tempting to die – but Stephanos's loss filled me with an awful rage. And over that rage, or under it, I knew that godlike effort was required, or all my friends, all my men, would die. Those are the moments that define you, friends. Oh, thugater, you would have been proud of me that day. For it is not the sands of the palaestra that show heroism, nor the fields of the games. Nor the moment of a great victory. Any man worthy of his father's name should be able to stand his ground on a dry day with food in his belly and armour on his back, fresh and strong. But at the tail end of defeat, when the enemy close in like hyenas on the kill, when all is lost but honour, when you are covered in bruises and small wounds whose pain tears at you with every blow, when all your muscles ache and your breath comes in gasps like a pair of broken bellows in a forge – when your friends have fallen and no one will sing your praises – who are you *then*? Those are the moments in which you show the gods what your father made.

Galas went down when the marines of a fifth ship hit us. To be honest, friends, I have no idea how many ships were around us by then. Eight? Ten? My ship's deck was almost clear, but Stephanos's ship must have looked easier, and he had fifty enemy fighters crowding the deck – I remember that his hull was low in the water from the sheer weight of men on the decks, and the ship has wallowing, unbalanced, which made the fighting even harder. At the moment when I gave myself over to Ares, an Aegyptian officer had just stooped to take the gold amulet Mal always wore.

Who was I then?

This is who I was.

I went at them down the gangway amidships, crowded with men, and I remember with the clarity of youth. I had two spears and my Boeotian shield, and I ran at them – about three steps.

I remember because the first Aegyptian had a raven on his oval shield, leaning down to get the necklace, his eyes appalled that one lone madman was charging him. And Mal – dying – grabbed the man's shield with both hands and pulled it down.

That's a hero.

I put my spear into the Aegyptian's neck, just the tip, as delicately as a cat, and withdrew it, leaped high in the air above the pitching deck and *threw* over the falling corpse into the second man. Their shields are heavy hide, but my throw had Zeus behind it, and it penetrated his shield and his arm and I took my second spear and killed him, landing on his armoured chest as he tried to seize a breath and feeling his ribs give under my toes even as I rammed my spear underhand into the next man, stepped off the dying man, set my legs on the wood of the deck and pushed my shield.

The next man tried to step back but his mates wouldn't let him. I thrust my spear at his head and he ducked, stumbled, and I caught the rim of his heavy hide shield with my spearhead and *pulled* – then thrust into his undefended chest, and a flower of bright blood grew over his white linen cuirass and his soul flew out of his mouth. His corpse folded at my feet and I crouched down, almost kneeling on the deck, and punched my spear into the inside of the next man's thigh, the best stroke there is for a fighter, because there's an artery there and a simple cut will kill a man. His eyes widened at the fountain of blood, and he fell, fingers reaching for the wound, and I rose to my full height, braced against a sudden shift in the deck, and threw my remaining spear over his reaching arms at the next man, right over his shield, into the skull over his nose. I reached under my arm and plucked out my sword, and a flying axe took the sixth man where he was frozen, grey with fear as grim death reaped his comrades like ripe barley on an autumn day.

I could still see the crest on Harpagos's helmet and I roared like a beast – no war cry, but the bellow of Ares – and my foes were sick with terror, because I brought them death and they could not touch me. The next Aegyptian thrust at me with his spear, but his blow was hesitant, the fearful attack of the desperate man. What did Calchas say? Just this – when you face the killer of men, you lock shields and stand cautious. To run and to attack are both sides of the same coin – fear.

Black reached under my shield, caught the Aegyptian's shaft and pulled him off balance and my sword cut him down, a simple chop to the neck where his linen armour did not meet the cheekpieces of his helmet.

The thranites began to gather their spears and their courage and come up like the warriors grown from dragon's teeth in myth, so that the rowing benches sprouted fighters, and in ten heartbeats, it was the Aegyptians who were beset. We took heart, all of us, and we plucked their lives like grapes at harvest time, and the deck under my feet flowed with their blood. Thranites grabbed their ankles and knees and pulled them down, or thrust javelins up into their groins, and topside, my sword was waiting for any undefended flesh, and every time an Aegyptian set his feet, I would put my shield into his and push, and I never met a man of Aegypt with the power in his legs to stop my rush.

And they died.

The last man to face me was brave, and he died like a hero, covering the flight of his companions. He went shield to shield with me, and held me, and twice his big sword bit into my shield, the second blow cutting through the thick oak rim – but while his sword was stuck in my shield, I put my sword into his throat. He was a *man*. Thanks to Ares, his companions were not of his measure, or I'd have died there.

We had cleared the deck. And as I came to the rail, I cut a man's fingers off where he grasped it. I was a horse-length from the terrified men on one of the vessels grappled to *Trident*, and I leaped on to the rail.

'If you come to me, every one of you will *die*,' I roared.

The Aegyptians cut their grapples and poled off.

That, my thugater, is who I was in the hour of defeat.

Wine, here.

By the will of the gods, or the temerity of men, the Aegyptians let us go. My decks were red with blood, and empty – my deck crew was dead, almost to a man – I had no officers but Black, and my marines – both of them – sat in the scuppers, white with fatigue – and watched their hands shake.

All my best men were dead.

All of my friends were dead, too. Nearchos, Epaphroditos, Herakleides, Pelagius, Neoptolemus, Mal, Philocrates and two dozen others I had known for years. Phrynichus and Galas lay in their own blood on my deck.

We crawled away, like a wounded lion or a boar with the spear in him.

But for whatever reason, the Aegyptians just let us go.

And it was not for nothing. As we crept – oh, for the rowing of the morning – past the edge of the Aegyptian line, Chian ships began to come up behind us. First a few, and then more – a dozen. Two dozen. One of them was towing a prize, and I laughed, and then I saw a Lesbian ship I knew, and I hailed him. It was he who told me Epaphroditos was dead.

But we'd burst the bubble, and now the trapped rebels boiled out of the trap as fast as they could. I have no idea who survived, only that there were enough of them that the Aegyptians simply drew off and let us all go together. We might have had eighty ships, with a handful of Milesians mixed in. And Dionysius of Phocaea. Men tell me he had cut deepest into the enemy centre, all the way through, and put fire in an enemy ship on their beach before the battle collapsed around him.

He waved and rowed past, and his men were raising their boatsail. That wave was all the thanks we got, but it said enough.

Black crouched by my feet. I had the steering oars in my trembling hands, and he was the only officer left, except Idomeneus, who had rallied my rowers behind me as I fought aboard *Trident*. He, too, was a hero. He was covered in wounds, as was I, now that I stopped to assess. I had a bloody gash inside my right thigh that should have killed me – I'd never felt it. It must have missed the vital artery by the thickness of a thread, and I was able to see deep into my flesh.

'What now, boss?' Black asked.

I looked across the bay – ships turned turtle and ships afire, the smell of smoke, the ocean littered with dead men, swimming men and sharks.

'We should run for Chios,' I said. But Miltiades had lit a fire in me to save something.

Harpagos brought Stephanos's ship *Trident* alongside. He told me that Stephanos was dead. I groaned aloud – I had hoped he was merely wounded. It was the hardest blow of the day.

I got up on the rail – how my thighs hurt! – and called out to him. 'Miltiades is standing straight on for Samos,' I said, pointing to where Cimon, Aristides and Miltiades were raising their boatsails.

'I'm your man, not his,' Harpagos said. 'Stephanos never left you, lord. Nor will we!'

I was still grappling with the notion that solid, big, reliable Stephanos was dead. My best man – my first friend as a free man.

'I'm making for the camp,' I said. The decision came to me as if from Athena, grey-eyed at my side. 'I want my mainsail, and my rowers are done in.'

Black nodded, and Idomeneus shrugged, and Harpagos fell away and took station under my stern.

My rowers were done in, but I'll note that they landed like champions. We got our ship ashore despite the wind, and Harpagos landed *Trident* next to us in a camp almost devoid of life.

Black shook his head over a cup of wine. 'Boss, we'll just die here.'

I shrugged. 'Let's save something,' I said.

I don't remember saying anything else. I fell on my sleeping rug, and I didn't move until Idomeneus awoke me.

Fill my cup, thugater. And leave me.

8

The day after a battle is always horrible. A sea battle hides the worst – the stink and the visible horrors of the dead, and the screams of the wounded. Not many wounded in a sea-fight.

By wounded, I mean those with a spear in the guts or a cut so deep that only a physician can save them, or not save them, as the gods would have it. Because after a fight like Lade, every man has cuts, skinned knuckles, pulled muscles. Every man who has fought hand to hand on ships has small wounds – a deep cut on the arm, a burn, an arrow through the bicep. Some men have two. The fighters – the hoplites, the marines, the heroes – have all the little injuries that come with fighting in armour – the abrasions, the bruises where your armour turned a blow, the punctures where a scale was driven in through the leather. Add to that the sheer fatigue, no matter how high your conditioning, and you can see why a camp is silent after a battle. Tempers flare. Men curse each other.

I had never experienced so total a defeat as Lade. After the battle at Ephesus, I was busy rescuing a corpse and such heroic stuff. I missed the despair. Or perhaps I was too young.

Despair is a killer, children. I've seen it in women whose childbirth goes on too long, and I've seen it in sick men, but it is worst in a beaten army. Men kill themselves. The poets don't sing of it, but it happens too often. Men cut themselves or walk into the sea. Men die from wounds that ought to have healed.

Priests are busy, saving what they can. Good doctors make a difference. But on the day after a defeat, the men who matter are the leaders. Anyone can lead men after a victory. Only the best can lead after a defeat.

I awoke the day after Lade to the realization that Stephanos was dead. And Philocrates. And Nearchos. One by one, the weight of them came to my mind, so that it was as if their shades were gathering around me.

Philocrates was on my ship, wrapped in his chlamys, and Stephanos was wrapped in his *himation* on *Trident*. To a Greek, that's some consolation. We would honour them in death.

But not today.

I got up, poured myself a cup of wine and felt the pain of all my muscles and all my wounds, new and old. My head hurt. I said a prayer to my ancestor Heracles for strength – and I began to clean my armour, promising that if ever I came through this to my farm in Boeotia, I would build a shrine to Heracles and put his lion on the inside of my shield. Do you sheltered children know what armour looks like after a fight? Sprayed with blood, with all the fluids inside a man, with ordure – shit – and the leather full of sweat and fear. But I had no hypaspist to do it, and I needed to look like a hero.

When my armour was clean and bright, I began on my shield. The rim was broken where the brave Aegyptian had almost killed me, and the raven of Apollo seemed to me a mockery. Apollo had promised me victory. Apollo had allowed the Samians to betray us. Apollo had allowed treachery to triumph over virtue. *Fuck him.*

Let me say now, before I go on with the story, that we would have won Lade if the Samians hadn't cut and run. I know that's not the popular view. I know that today, Athenians suggest that the Ionians were an effeminate bunch incapable of defeating Persia without the spine of Sparta and Athens to hold them to the task – but that's all crap. The Phoenicians came to that battle wary of us, and the Aegyptians wanted no part of it and, in effect, only fought to defend themselves. If the Samians had held their place in the line, Epaphroditos would have routed the Aegyptians, and we would have won.

Why do I tell you this? Because my rage and bitterness were boundless. The cupidity, the foolishness, the greed of a few men had killed my friends and robbed me of my love.

The day after Lade, I wanted revenge.

Let me be clear, honey bee. I still do.

I washed in the sea – that hurt, believe me. Nothing like salt water on new wounds. Then I put on a clean wool chiton and boots, and my newly cleaned shirt of Persian scales. I put my sword belt on my shoulder.

Black came into my tent as I finished arming myself. 'So?' he asked.

'Gather the men.' I said no more, and he went.

Idomeneus took his cue from me, and he had a Tyrian cloak on his shoulder and my good bronze breastplate on his back when he came to me. Harpagos looked like a fisherman in a wool cap. I beckoned him to me, walked him into my tent and bade him dress like a trierarch.

'Part of leading is play-acting,' I said. 'You must dress the part. Today, we have to pull them up a hill the way an ox pulls a cart. Everything matters.'

He shrugged. 'Yes, lord,' he said.

I dressed him in a red wool himation and a plain linen chitoniskos with a leather stola. Idomeneus brought him a fine Cretan helmet from a dead Phoenician officer.

The helmet was covered in repoussé, a work of art.

'I've never owned anything so fine,' Harpagos said.

I shrugged. 'Enjoy it,' I said.

Idomeneus grinned. I frowned at him. 'You are the only man in this camp smiling,' I said.

'Good fighting yesterday,' he said. 'We lived. No reason to cry.'

That was Idomeneus – a man who lived at the edge of madness, I suspect.

Black wore a magnificent chiton when we emerged – purple with red and blue edge-stripes like waves, as nice a piece of cloth as I'd ever seen. And he had the sword I'd taken from the old Persian – not that I begrudged him it.

So we made a good show. The men were surly and quiet, but when they saw us, they understood immediately, and I saw men wipe their faces and look at the dirt on their hands. Good.

'We lost,' I said. There were about three hundred men on the beach, where the day before fifteen times that many had eaten breakfast and offered sacrifice. 'We lost, but life goes on. Lord Miltiades will not stop fighting. Neither will we, as long as there are fat Aegyptian merchants to take and gold to spend.'

All that got was a grumble.

'The Persians won't stir today,' I said, pointing across the bay. 'We hurt them badly, and they'll lick their wounds. But tomorrow, they'll come for us. So we'll have to be gone – away downwind to Chios, where we'll put Philocrates and Stephanos in the ground. And say the rites for all those who went down.'

That got a better reaction.

'But first ...' I said, and every head came up – every set of eyes locked on mine. 'But first, I mean to complete our crews in Miletus, and take off every man, woman and child we can save. Before the Persians storm it. Which will happen any hour.' I looked around, and the only sound was the wind making the empty tents flap like untended sails.

'We came here to save those people,' I said. 'We can still save some. Anyone with me?'

Not bad, thugater. Not bad at all. They were all with me, as it turned out.

We kept a good watch all day, so we knew when the Persians launched their assault on Miletus, just a few stades distant. They didn't take it by surprise, or anything like – but they knew that the town was nearly empty, and probably further lost to despair than we were on the beaches.

Most of the fleet of Miletus was lost in the fighting. The handful of ships who survived ran for Samos and Chios. Not a single ship ran for their own port – not even Histiaeus himself, who left Istes in 'command' of a city denuded of fighting men.

As I say – we kept watch. Twice we saw patrols set off from the beaches opposite, but neither came any closer than ten stades. My two ships were hidden by the bulk of the island. Who would have expected us to hide in plain sight?

At sunset, we launched. Most men had slept all day. Our muscles were stiff, but we ate every animal we found on the beach – cows, goats, all abandoned by the Greeks – and we'd stowed carefully the best of the loot from the rest of the campaign, our weapons and little else.

Once afloat, we lay on our oars in the channel between Lade and Miletus, our oars muffled and every man silent. The rocks hid us from the town and from the besiegers. But we could hear the fighting. The town was falling. There was no question of it.

I was in a curious race with time. I couldn't let my ships be seen against our shore when we moved – or the Phoenicians and the Aegyptians and the Cilicians would be on us like vultures. But if I waited too long, the town would fall.

Black waited with apparent impassivity, but Harpagos walked up and down the command deck of his trireme, and his bare feet were the loudest noise in the channel. Gulls moved and cried. The wind blew through a camp devoid of Greeks. In the distance, there was a murmur like summer thunder.

I remember the darkness of that hour, and the despair I hid. If I must remind you, the disaster of Lade lost me Briseis. For ever, as it seemed. The Persians have a phrase – they tell a condemned nobleman to 'go and hunt his death'. Well – I was on the edge of hunting my death, or perhaps past it – but I had my men in order, and I had fired them for this task, and I meant to do an honourable job before I hunted my death.

The sun was a line of crimson in the west, and our shore was dark as new pitch. 'Let's go,' I whispered.

'Give way, all,' Black said.

Every oar dipped, and we ghosted down the channel, followed by Harpagos. We made the turn, and there was the town.

Miletus was afire. The palace on the acropolis was burning, great gouts of fire leaping into the air like live daimons, and the summer thunder sound we'd heard was now the great-throated roar of a city being destroyed by fire and sword.

Miletus, the richest city in the Greek world.

We crept up the passage to the harbour, our oars carefully handled, our hulls tight against the mainland shore to avoid being seen. I began to curse. I could see soldiers in the streets of the lower town and people running and being killed, but there was no resistance.

'Apollo, render justice,' I said aloud. 'You *owe* me better than this.'

And just then, I heard the horn from the Windy Tower.

Of course, that citadel on the harbour was the last to fall – I should have guessed it from the first. I could see men on the walls – archers – and my heart leaped.

'Lay me under the sea wall by the tower,' I said to Black, pointing.

'Aye, lord,' he said.

We turned in the mouth of the harbour and I loved my men – every oarsman of them – as we raced for the tower.

I leaped to the jetty and Idomeneus followed me.

'Pole off,' I called, 'or we'll be swamped. Wait for my word.'

Black waved.

They were fighting hand to hand on the steps of the tower when I slipped in the postern with Idomeneus. The startled sentry took one look at us – and at the two great dark hulls behind us on the tower's jetty – and he fell to his knees. 'You—'

'We came for you,' I said. 'Take me to Istes, if he lives.'

We ran along the walls, all my wounds and all my fatigue forgotten, where men were leaning and pointing at the ships. It was worth it – all the waiting and the strain on muscles – to see those men, who had thought that they were dead, realize that they were going to live.

Istes was in the arch of the courtyard steps with a dozen other hoplites, holding the entrance. I watched him fight for a minute. In that time, three souls went to Hades on his blade, and as many fell back, wounded or simply too frightened to face him.

To fight that well – when you have *no hope* – is a great gift. Or a great curse.

In the Pyrrhiche, we practise replacing one another in combat. It is practised in every town, in every polis, in every gymnasium. No man can fight for ever.

'You switch with him,' I said to Idomeneus. 'I'll get this organized.'

Idomeneus flexed his shoulders and set his aspis and grinned. 'Aye, lord,'

'Don't go and get killed,' I said. 'I'm low on friends,' I added.

His mad grin flashed and he kissed me. 'I'll do my best, lord,' he said.

He stepped up behind Istes – none of the other men in the courtyard seemed to feel any need to give their lord a rest. Then, in between kills, he tapped twice – hard – on Istes' backplate.

Istes flashed a backwards look.

Idomeneus tapped a rhythm on his shield – and one, and two – Istes pivoted on his hips and slid diagonally to the right rear, and Idomeneus lunged forward, right foot first with a sweeping overhead cut that forced the Persian facing Istes to back a step, and then Idomeneus filled the spot and killed the Persian with a feint and a back cut, and the line was as solid as it had been a moment before.

Istes sank to a knee and breathed. Then his helmet came off, and he raised his head and saw me.

For a long moment, all he did was breathe and look at me.

'You came to die with us?' he asked.

'You're as mad as he is,' I said, pointing at Idomeneus. 'I came to rescue you, you soft-handed Asiatic.'

Then he embraced me. 'Oh gods, I thought we were all dead and no man would even sing of our end. There's no counting the fucking Persians. And there's Greeks with them – armoured men, fighting for their slave-masters.'

'I need you to get your men off the walls and into the ships,' I said.

'There are fifty women and children, as well,' he said. 'When the lower town fell, the smart ones ran here.'

'I have two ships,' I said. 'I will leave no one behind, even if it means I have to swim.'

Then he embraced me again and ran off through the courtyard, calling for his officers.

The hard part would be holding the stairs and the gate until the boats were loaded. The men on the stairs would be unlikely to live – and it is harder to get men to die when they know there is hope.

But Istes' men loved him. He told off ten to take the places of those fighting at that moment, who were the first to go to the boats – still dazed from combat and from their turn of fortune.

The next trick was to get the archers off the citadel walls without letting the Persians and Lydians know they were leaving.

I saw Teucer and waved. He came down off the walls. 'I heard you were here,' he said, a grin covering his face. 'It's true – you'll take us all off?'

I laughed. Despair had left me. Save a hundred lives and you'll find it hard to despair. Every Milesian going on board my ships gave heart to my rowers. Every woman with a babe in her arms was like new life for a wounded marine.

I tapped Idomeneus when I saw him flag. The Persians were relentless. They came in waves, determined to finish us. And they still didn't know we were leaving.

He hamstrung an archer with a thrust under his shield, pivoted as the man screamed and I was in his place before the man had fallen to the ground.

The Persian behind the falling man had a long spear with a heavy ball of silver on the end. I stabbed at him – three fast strokes, the same attack every time. The third time went past his defences and my spearhead went through his wrist, into his neck.

The man to my left fell – I have no idea what happened – and suddenly our line was gone.

I powered *forward* into the press, and my spear played on them like a stork taking frogs. I felt faster and stronger than other men, and I felt no fear. I was the saviour of Miletus that night, and the flames of the dying city framed my victims.

I cleared the stairs. What more can I say? I put down eight or ten men, and the rest fled. I took blows on my armour, and my opponents were not fully armed men, but it was still one of my best moments, and yet I remember little, save that I stood alone at the head of the stairs and breathed like a horse after a race, and behind me the line restored itself and the men began to call my name.

'Ar-im-nes-tos! Ar-im-nes-tos!' they called.

Down at the base of the steps, I heard officers calling, and men were forming. I picked up a heavy spear that lay discarded, hefted it and then I stepped out into the arrows of the Persians.

Two thudded into my shield, but I *knew* that the gods had made me immune. I stepped up and *threw* that spear into one of the Persian officers. He took it under his arm, and I stepped back and laughed. I took advantage of the lull to look at the citadel doors, but they were smashed, and nothing could close the gate but a line of men.

'Come to me,' I yelled at the Milesians, and they shuffled forward warily – I might be their saviour, but I was a stranger. 'Stand here.' I beckoned to the men in the courtyard. 'Close up – like a phalanx. No spaces. Listen to me. Their arrows can't reach you here. When we retreat, the left files retreat up the left wall stairs, and the right files up the right wall stairs. Understand?'

We still had a minute. I grabbed the rightmost and leftmost men. 'Follow me!' I called, and I took them in the gate. 'You go that way – single file, like forming or unforming the Pyrrhiche.'

He didn't understand, but another man did, and I pushed the first man into the third rank. 'Sorry, lad. I need a thinker. You – can you live long enough to get them up these stairs?'

The new phylarch shrugged.

'Here they come!' the men at the gate called.

I got back there with my two appointed phylarchs. We had time to take our places – me in the centre of the line, they at either end. We were seven men to a rank, three ranks deep.

'Listen up,' I said. 'We take their charge, and hold. On my word, we give ground to the edge of the courtyard – and then charge. Can you do it? No shirking – all together.'

And then they came at us. It was the bodyguard. Cyrus led from in front, and I knew him as soon as he came up the steps, and he knew me, as I heard it later, from my shouted commands.

These were the best of Artaphernes' men, picked swordsmen, nobles all, and men of discipline. They came into us together, and our line gave a step, and then we were fighting.

Cyrus didn't come against me – by luck or the will of the gods. He had a big wicker shield, and he pushed it into the man next to me.

I didn't await the onset of my man. I threw a spear – low – and took my man in the ankle, and down he went, and I went forward into the space, right past Cyrus. I had my second spear, and my shield was better than theirs. My second spear – like my old deer-killer – had a wicked tapered point like a needle, and I used it ruthlessly in the firelit dark, ramming it through wicker shields into their shield arms. I don't know how many men I wounded that way, but it was more than three, and then I stepped back into my place in the ranks, leaving a hollow behind me.

'Break!' I called, and we turned like a school of fish threatened by a dolphin and fled, just ten steps in the tunnel, and I turned. 'Stand!' I said, and the Milesians turned and stood like heroes. 'Charge!' I called, and we went at the startled Persians.

We had men down, and so did they, and the footing was treacherous, and on balance, it was foolish of me to charge like that, but foolish things are unexpected things, and we crashed into them and pushed them right off the platform of the steps, so that one of my file-leaders took an arrow in the side – we'd over-charged, and we were in the open.

'Back!' I called. We shuffled back as a storm of arrows fell on the portico. I tripped – a man grabbed at my leg, and I was looking into Cyrus's helmet. My sword point stopped a finger's width from his eye.

'Doru,' he said. He managed a smile, although I was about to slay him.

I stepped over him. 'Can you walk?' I asked, and he managed to get to one knee. Another wounded guardsman rose, holding his left arm – where I'd put a spear into it, no doubt.

'Let them go,' I told my men. *Apollo, witless lying god, witness my mercy.*

Six Persians shuffled away. They didn't meet our eyes. But they lived, and they had fought well. As my hero Eualcidas of Eretria told me once, everyone runs sometime.

I could hear argument in the darkness.

Istes came up beside me.

'We're out,' he said. 'All but ten archers up on the walls with all our remaining arrows.'

'No time like the present,' I said. 'By files, to the right and left, retire!'

Istes laughed. 'You Dorians have orders for everything,' he said.

We backed up the tunnel, and then they came at us.

Greeks. In armour.

They came fast, hard and silent, and the man who led them had a great scorpion on his shield. He put my right file-leader down and sent his shade away screaming at the first contact, and the line couldn't rally because the end men were retreating up the stairs.

Suddenly, our orderly flight was chaos.

Istes went forward into the fight, and all I could do was go with him. For ten heartbeats – maybe twice that – the two of us held ten armoured men.

Istes killed a man in that time. He was that good.

I didn't. I was facing three men, and one of them was the man with the scorpion on his shield. It was Archilogos.

It was bound to happen sometime.

I had sworn to save him and his family, before all the gods, at the shrine of Artemis. And he was one of the best fighters in the Greek world. We had the same training. We'd been in the same battles.

The gods send us these challenges to see what we're made of, I think.

The last thing I wanted Archilogos to know was that he was immune to my blade. I rammed my shield into his and made him stumble, and then I thrust at each of his two companions, fast as a cat, and then I jumped back.

Istes, as I said, killed his man.

He felt me back away, and he backed, and then we backed together.

Archilogos shouted for his men to get around me. 'They're abandoning the gate!' he roared.

As the leftmost man sprang forward, I threw my second spear and caught him in the outstretched leg, and down he went.

I was out of spears, but I felt the right-hand stairs to the wall under my right heel.

Archilogos came for me again, and I backed up a step and then another, and then he cut at my feet – remember, I had boots on, not greaves, because of my wounds. I got my shield in late – too late – and he got a piece of my leg, his blade slicing through my boot, through my bandages, to lay a line of icy fire across my calf.

But my shield rim caught his helmet as he leaned into the blow, and staggered him, and he fell.

Another man leaped into his place, and I backed another step and my heart fell to see the amount of blood I'd already lost. The step I abandoned glittered in the light of the doomed city.

I backed again, and the new man cut at my legs. I had no qualms about killing this Ephesian, and I parried his blow with my sword and turned my *xiphos* over his blade and cut his throat – a nasty move learned in close-quarter fighting. Not very sporting. But I thought I was dying.

Put yourself in my place. I had lost everything – friends, lover, ship. The rescue of the Milesians would make my name for ever, I thought. And if I died here – what more could I want? A sad end, but a great song. I could trust Phrynichus, if he survived his wound, to write of it.

When I took that wound, I thought I was done. It was too damned far to the ships, and I was losing blood like a dying man.

But nor am I a quitter. I killed the man with my xiphos and I got up another step.

Idomeneus leaned past me with a spear and put it through the next comer's faceplate, and I was up another step.

Teucer shot the next man, and he fell back, an arrow in his upper thigh, and he swept the steps clean for a hundred heartbeats. Then Idomeneus got a hand under my arm and I was up on the wall.

It is good to have companions.

'I'm finished, friends,' I said.

Idomeneus picked me up bodily.

'Like fuck you are,' he said.

Our wall was empty. Teucer was the last man behind us. He shot, ran to us, turned and shot again. No man of the Ephesians – even wearing full armour – wanted to be the first to put his head above the parapet.

'Can you stand?' Idomeneus asked. He could see something I couldn't.

'No,' I responded. The world was going dark on me.

He stood me up anyway. I sank to one knee.

Teucer cried, 'No!' and shot, right over my head.

The wall had a crenellated parapet on the city side, but on the courtyard side, just a low wall to keep foolish or drunken sentries from falling to their deaths on the flagstones benath. The stairs were recessed into the wall. We couldn't see the enemy on our steps, but I could see – even as the curtain came down over my eyes – the line of armoured men racing up the far steps, and Istes, alone on the wall, taking them. I have never seen anyone fight as well, unless perhaps it was Sophanes, but that was later, and Sophanes wasn't fighting in the last moments of a losing battle, doomed, against overwhelming odds. Istes threw them from the wall, he stabbed them, he baffled with his shield, his cloak, his sword, and they died.

But he was flagging. I could see it. And he'd sent his men away – they all said as much later.

In fact, Istes never intended to reach the ships. I saw him there, burning with godlike power on the wall, fighting so well that he seemed to glow with his own light. He had full bronze – cuirass, helmet, greaves, thigh guards, arm guards, shoulder cups, shield face – and his armour caught the fire of his city as it died, and rendered it a golden sun atop its last defended wall.

Teucer had three arrows left and he used them all for his lord – three more Ephesians sent to Hades.

Then Idomeneus was there, having put me down to run all the way around the wall to Istes. Idomeneus threw his spear over Istes' shoulder, and then tapped his shoulder – but Istes shook his head and went shield to shield with a big man. Behind that man was the Scorpion. Archilogos had shaken off my blow.

I dragged myself, one step at a time, paralleling Istes' retreat. Helmeted heads began to peek above our stairs. On the far wall, the man behind Archilogos fell with an arrow in his side.

Teucer cursed. 'That was my last arrow, lord.'

I managed a laugh. 'Might have been better if you hadn't told them,' I said.

There was a great black puddle under me. I got to my feet anyway.

On the opposite wall, Archilogos, my boyhood friend, faced Istes, the best sword in the world. Istes glowed gold.

'Miletus!' he roared.

Archilogos took his sword cut on his aspis and pushed forward with it, and Istes stumbled back and Archi cut up under the shield with his sword – once, twice, as fast as a hawk stooping – and Istes stumbled back, and I could see his shield arm was wounded.

Now Istes had fought all day. And he knew he would die.

But Archilogos showed himself to be a master. He gave the golden man no respite, and cut again – a heavy blow to the helmet.

He got Istes' shield in the face, though, and he went back, and Istes backed a step. Idomeneus tapped him again, and he said something. Later he told me that he begged Istes to live. Istes didn't reply, except to charge Archilogos. He had his arms out, and he ran like a man finishing a race, and he swept my childhood friend and slave-master off the wall in his arms, and they fell together to the courtyard, and as he fell he roared 'Miletus' one more time, and then he was gone, and his armour rang as he hit the flagstones.

Teucer had got me to the ropes over the wall by then. I must have been lighter by the weight of all my blood, but I remember stepping on a spear that one of the men had dropped to slide more easily to the ships.

'Go,' I said to Teucer.

He shook his head.

'Go, you fool,' I said.

He let go of my shoulder, grabbed the rope and slid off towards the deck of Black Raven.

I was the last man on the walls of Miletus – the last free Greek. I had no intention of leaving. The spear came to me as a sign, or so I thought. And Istes was dead. And Archilogos was dead.

So I had no reason not to be dead, too.

I had the strength to raise the spear over my head, and I set my shield, and waited for the rush. I could hear their feet on the walls, and I couldn't see very well, but I knew they were coming.

One Ephesian came out of the dark and his aspis hit my Boeotian, shield to shield, and mine broke like a child's toy. The blows from the Aegyptian must have weakened it.

But even blind with blood loss, I got my spear into his face, and he went down, cursing.

I stepped back and caught a breath. I was still alive.

I can only tell this as I saw it, honey. What I will say is what I saw.

Helen came to me on the wall – or Aphrodite, or perhaps Briseis. I like to think it was Briseis. Her hair was unbound, and her skin glowed like a goddess.

'This is not your fate, love,' she said. And she was gone.

That's what I saw.

So I threw the spear as hard as I could, right along the parapet. I stumbled backwards, my fingers reaching for the rope, almost blind. I found it even as a blow rang off the scale shirt on my back – a spear-thrust on the heavy yoke over the shoulders. I fell, my hands holding the rope, and my feet dropped free of the wall, and I slid down the rope. My palms burned, but I wouldn't let go.

I'm told I hit the mast quite hard. I was already pretty far gone, and I fell to the deck as if dead, all my sinews cut. But my armour did its job, and the wool stuffed in my helmet.

I remember the men crowding around me. I remember hands on my leg, and fire.

I have never run the stade since.

The women wept and keened, and men as well, as the oarsmen pulled us away into the dark. I lay cushioned in blood loss, far away and yet able to think clearly enough, and *Black Raven* unfolded his wings and swept us out to sea. The Phoenicians and the Cilicians and the Aegyptians never saw us, or thought we weren't worth their trouble, or simply let us go. We saved Teucer and a hundred other soldiers, five gentlemen of property, and another hundred women and children. Four thousand died and forty thousand were sold into slavery.

And that was just the start.

We made Chios in three days – three desperate days, when Harpagos, Idomeneus and Black did the work of keeping us alive while my body made the hard choices between life and death. I missed the moment when Idomeneus made a speech – he ordered the treasure thrown over the side, and he told them that the babes of the Milesians would be their treasure, and asked them to count the weight of the silver and tell him which was the most valuable, and they cheered as they threw it over. I missed that, although it is all part of the story.

The Milesians pitched in and rowed, and we shared what food we had, and everyone who had lived to flee the walls of Miletus lived to see the beaches of Chios.

The next thing I remember was Melaina weeping. There was a pyre for Stephanos, and another for Philocrates, and Phrynichus wept as he said their elegies. Alcaeus of Miletus – one of the gentlemen we'd rescued – organized funeral games.

Melaina cared for me, cleaning my wounds, bathing me, cleaning away the wastes of my body. My fever broke in the second week, and by the third week I could walk. Summer was almost over.

'The Persians will come,' I said. 'Come with me. I owe you – and your brother's shade – that much.'

She shrugged. 'I'll stay anyway,' she said. 'I'm a fisherman's daughter. I don't like the change. And my father is here, and my sisters, and all the children. Can you move the whole of Chios?'

Another week, while my body healed. Black was restless, eager to get to sea. Suddenly, there were Cilician pirates everywhere, and down the coast, a village burned.

Finally, I set a sailing date. The evenings were brisk, and the sun was lower in the sky.

We sat and drank wine until the sun set, wine that went straight to my head, and we ate a big tuna that Melaina's father caught. He came and clapped me on the shoulder. 'Stephanos loved you,' he said. 'You're a good man.'

That made me cry. I cried easily in those days.

It was harder to abandon Chios than it had been to leave Miletus, because unlike these cheerful fisherfolk, I knew what was coming to them. The light hand of Persia was about to be replaced by an iron fist. I watched the sun set, and I knew that it would be a long time before I saw it rise here, in the east.

Melaina came into my bed that last night, while I lay looking at the rafters. I didn't send her away, although our lovemaking had more grief to it than lust. But she left before dawn, and she was a proper daughter again on the beach when she poured a libation and washed Harpagos's shield in wine.

Then my keel was in the water, and I ceased to think of her, because we went to sail an ocean full of enemies.

We ran north, evading everything we saw, until we entered the Bosporus.

Kallipolis was still free. We beached, and I embraced Miltiades.

I'll make this brief. We wintered there. In the spring, Histiaeus – Istes' brother, who left him to die – came to us, asking that we follow him to make a pre-emptive attack on the coast of Phoenicia – to show that the East Greeks weren't beaten. It was a strategy that was a year too late.

'I'll stay and defend the Chersonese,' Miltiades said. 'It is mine. But I will lose no more men in Asia.'

Histiaeus was captured in Phrygia a month later, trying to forage for food for his oarsmen. Datis executed him for treason. It was a cheap death for a man who had led the Ionian Revolt. He should have died on the walls with his brother.

Less than a week later, Datis flooded the Chersonese with Scythian and Thracian mercenaries. He outspent Miltiades, ten to one, and in a week we lost four of our towns.

We expected it, though. The east was lost. We loaded our ships, taking every Greek man and woman – the survivors of Miletus, and Methymna and Teos, and all of Miltiades' men and their women. We filled ten triremes and as many Athenian grain ships, and we sailed away. The Scythians burned Kallipolis behind us, but we left it empty.

Datis landed an army on Lesbos, and he swept the island with a chain of men all the way across, looking for rebels. He crucified those he caught, and he took the best of the boys and all of the unmarried girls, and sold them as slaves or took them for the harem. Then he went to Chios and did the same.

There was no force in the world that could stop him. He harried the Aeolians, selling their children to brothels, and then he harried the Ionians, and humiliated them, island by island, until there was no longer the sigh of a girl or the worship of Aphrodite from Sardis to Delos. He broke the world of my youth. He destroyed it. I grew to manhood in the world of Alcaeus and Sappho. He destroyed Sappho's school and sold the students to satisfy the lusts of his soldiers.

You children know the world Athens made, and you think it good. I love Athens – but there was a fairer world once, a brighter place, with better poets and freer ways. Where Greeks and Persians could be friends with each other, with Aegyptians and Lydians.

Datis killed it, to break the spirit of the Greeks and reduce them to servitude. Truly, it was the rape of the islands that taught us Greeks what the Persians were capable of, and showed us why we would have to fight, or see our culture die.

Artaphernes resisted Datis, of course. But Datis was the Great

King's nephew and had won the great battle, and Artaphernes was considered soft on Greeks.

Datis raped the islands, and we sailed away and left them. I sailed *Black Raven* into Corinth and unloaded the refugees, While Black took him back to sea as a paid ship, for Athens, I brought them north, to Plataea.

Idomeneus was a bastard, for all I loved him, and when the treasure had gone over the side, none of it was mine or his – so I still had riches, and I spent them that summer. I settled forty families in the vale of Asopus, and when I was finished, the money of my piracy was gone, washed clean in rescuing them from poverty, or so I hoped.

And then I was just another farmer with a forge, for my gold was gone.

While I was spending money like a drunken sailor, I heard the rumours – that I was a murderer, that I was accursed of Apollo. All my father's friends spoke up for me, as well as all my own friends – Hermogenes and Epictetus the Younger, and Myron and his sons – but my absences, my riches and the constant murmurs of the sons of Simon, from Thebes, had their effect. Men pushed me away, in the little ways that men use when they are afraid. And to my shame, I responded with arrogance and let the distance grow.

It was a dark winter, with one beam of light. For when I was settling my Milesians, I met Antigonus of Thespiae, the young basileus of that town. He took ten of my families and made them citizens, and we became friends quickly – and as quickly, he courted my sister. He was a wealthy man, and he might have had any maiden in the valley of the Asopus, but he courted Pen, and in the spring he wed her, and men came to that wedding who had whispered about me, and my life was the better for it.

My mother stayed sober until the priest was gone, and I kissed her, and she cried. Then I folded my finery away and went back to the forge, and she went back to drinking, and men went back to whispering that the Corvaxae were all accursed.

There were other fights, that last year. But the Ionian Revolt died with Istes, as he fell, shouting 'Miletus'.

I suppose we thought that the Long War was over. And I had forgotten my slave girl. I tried to forget Briseis, and Melaina. I tried to forget all of it. I ignored my armour and my helmet and I worked on bronze kettles and drinking cups.

Until the archon came and asked me to return to teaching the Pyrrhiche.

My calf throbbed and burned, and my hips hurt when we danced, but they all admired my splendid Persian scale shirt and my rich red cloak, and Myron came and embraced me.

'Your new citizens have made us richer by a thousand gold darics,' he said.

'And fifty shields in the phalanx,' Hermogenes said.

The men of Plataea came to me, and clasped my arm. *Glad to have you back*, they said, but now I sensed the hesitation in their grips and the tendency of their eyes to wander when they spoke. Plataeans didn't just take off to fight in other people's wars. Or show up with a passel of foreigners.

But I was the devil they knew. And by then, thanks to the word-fame of my role at Lade, I was famous – so famous that it was hard for my neighbours to accept me as a man who danced and sweated and had trouble with his grape vines. Fame makes you different – ask any man who has won the laurel at Olympia or Nemea.

May none of you ever experience defeat, and the death of all your friends. Idomeneus remained, back at the tomb of the hero, but he was as mad as a wild dog. Black was fighting against Aegina for Athens. Hermogenes was like another man – a good man, but a farmer and a husband. All the rest of them were dead. Even Archilogos was dead. And I didn't dare allow my mind to think about Briseis. In some way, I let her be dead, as well.

But one of the saddest truths of men is that no grief lasts for ever.

My helmet was waiting, just where I had left it, on a leather bag on the great square bench that Pater had built. I had to hobble around the shop – my calf never healed, and as I said, I never ran well again – and I was angry all the time. Hermogenes forced me to work, and Tiraeus fired the forge, and after mending a few pots, my hands re-membered their duty.

I think it was a month after the Pyrrhiche, and perhaps three months after Pen's wedding, before I looked at the helmet. I was surprised by what a good helmet it was, how far along I had left it. It seemed like ten years – like a lifetime. There was the ding where I'd mis-struck when the boy came to me with news from Idomeneus. I blinked away tears. Then I took out the ding with careful, methodical planishing, which seemed more restful than dull.

When the bowl was as smooth as Briseis's breasts, I turned the helmet over and looked at the patterns I'd incised.

I had started the ravens on the cheekplates before I left. I did not love Lord Apollo any more. But the ravens seemed apt. If I ever stood in the phalanx again, I wanted to wear ravens.

Instead of going to work on the helmet, I took a piece of scrap, pounded it out flat and tapped the ravens to life on a practice piece. I made a dozen errors, but I worked through patiently, reheating as I went. It was two days before I was satisfied, and then I went back and put the ravens on the cheekplates in an afternoon. I had time left to go and help my slaves prop the grape vines. Then I went back, looked my work over carefully and polished it as the sun set behind the hills of home. I filled the ravens with lead on the inside, planished a little more.

Tiraeus kept an eye on me while he put a new bail on an old bronze bucket for the temple. And then he looked at my work.

'You've grown up,' he said. And then, his voice rough, he pointed at the back of the skullpiece. 'Little rough there.'

I picked up the hammer.

Ting-ting.

Ting-ting.

Part II
Marathon

Αἰσχύλον Εὐφορίωνος Ἀθηναῖον τόδε κεύθει
μνῆμα καταφθίμενον πυροφόροιο Γέλας·
ἀλκὴν δ᾽ εὐδόκιμον Μαραθώνιον ἄλσος ἂν εἴποι
καὶ βαθυχαιτήεις Μῆδος ἐπιστάμενος

Beneath this stone lies Aeschylus, son of Euphorion, the Athenian,
who perished in the wheat-bearing land of Gela;
of his noble prowess the grove of Marathon can speak,
and the long-haired Persian knows it well.

Epitaph on the Stele of Aeschylus the Playwright

9

It was late autumn, and the rains lashed the farm, and my slaves stayed in by the fire and made baskets for the next year's crop. I was in the forge, hammering out the face of a new aspis – I needed a shield.

The world was moving. I could feel it. The last cities of Lesbos were falling to the Persians, and in Athens, the *stasis* – the conflict – between the aristocrats and the *demos* was so bad that it had come to murder in the streets, or so men said, and Persian gold flowed like water to buy the best men. Closer to home, Thebes had begun agitating to take our city, or at least reduce our boundaries. And one voice carried clear from their agora to ours – Simon, son of Simon, loud in condemnation of our archon, Myron, and eager for my blood. Small traders bought us this news.

Empedocles the priest came out from Thebes in the last golden light of autumn, while the hillside of Cithaeron was a glow of red oak leaves. When he had given the blessing of Hephaestus to my forge and relit our fires after we swept the shop, he raised Tiraeus to the rank of master, as the man deserved. Then he looked at my helmet, running his thumb over the eyebrows and using calipers to pick out the measurements of the ravens on the cheekpieces.

'This is master work,' he said. He handed it to Tiraeus, and Tiraeus handed it to Bion. 'And you are the master in this shop, so it is right that you too should be raised.'

I think that the fires in my heart relit that day. I had not expected it, although in retrospect there were a thousand little signs that my friends had made plans for me to be raised to the rank of master. Other pieces were brought out by Tiraeus – things I'd forgotten, like a set of bronze pins I'd made for my sister's wedding guests – and Empedocles laughed with joy to see them, and that laughter went through me like lightning on a summer's day. I was, you know, for a time, the master warrior of all Hellas – but it never gave me the joy that making gave me.

Oh, there's a lie. Killing can be a joy. Or merely a job, or worse.

So, because two of us had been raised, we gave a special sacrifice at the Temple of Hera, where my sister, now a matron, had just been anointed as a priestess. She was two months pregnant, just starting to show, and she officiated with the dignity of her new status. And Antigonus of Thespiae saw nothing wrong with having a master smith as a brother-in-law, so he came with a train of aristocrats to my sacrifice, and Myron arrived with the best men of Plataea, and I saw the wine of a whole crop drained in a few hours – but I reckoned it wine well spent, because my heart was beating again.

The next day, I took ten more amphorae of wine up the hill to the tomb of the hero, and I gave a smaller feast for Idomeneus and his men, and many of our Milesians as well. We drank and we danced. Idomeneus had built a great bonfire, five trees' worth of wood, and we alternated between too hot and too cold, drank the wine and sang.

It was late in the evening, and the fire burned high, and the younger men and women were piling my straw into a great bale – the better to share other warmths.

I was twenty-seven, and I had never felt so old. But I was happy, pleasantly tired from dancing – the first good dancing since my leg was wounded. I was a master smith, and men came to my forge to talk about the affairs of the city. I might have been content.

Idomeneus came and leaned against me in the warm-chill of the fire's edge.

'What ever happened to that slave girl you took away to Athens?' he asked. 'Did you sell her?'

I had forgotten.

The gods sometimes work all together, and the next day, when my head rang like my forge from the wine, Hermes sent me a messenger from Athens, with payment for a load of finished bronze. He brought news that Miltiades had been arrested for wishing to restore the tyranny. And he brought a letter from Phrynichus, and a copy of his play, the famous *Fall of Miletus*. When I read it, I wept.

In the letter, Phrynichus explained that the play had been written to awaken the men of Athens to what the Persians were up to. He said that he had written it so that men might recognize Miltiades for his role in trying to save the East Greeks.

And he asked me to come to the opening of the play.

In Athens, they have a different form of theatre to what we have in Boeotia, and I think I should explain. Once, in my grandfather's time, I suppose, drama was about the same everywhere – much like a rhapsode singing the *Iliad*, except that the poet or a professional musician performed works of praise to the gods, or sometimes the story of a hero. In Athens, there was always a set of plays – at least three – and the best of the three received a prize in honour of the god Dionysus. Athens was certainly not the only city to give praise to the god of wine, nor to offer a prize for the finest poems in his honour, but Athens has a tendency to take things to extremes.

The tyrant Hippias was a great worshipper of Dionysus, and men say that he inaugurated the practice of using a chorus – a group of singers – to support the main line of the play. So the dramas became more like a team sport – the poet or singer and his team of chorus members competed. It was demanding, both physically and mentally, and that competition fired men to make it better, more complex, more vivid.

While I was a slave in Ephesus, someone brought in the inter-action between chorus and poet, so that men spoke and answered each other as if in a simple conversation in the agora. This may seem a small thing to you, children, but imagine a poor peasant from Attica, allowed to watch Heracles debate with the gods over his fate. Agamemnon begging his son to avenge him. Strong stuff. Sophists decry it as the end of men's piety, but I've always loved it.

Phrynichus had long led the way, winning prize after prize. But when he wrote *The Fall of Miletus*, he set drama on another course, because instead of writing about the gods and heroes, he wrote about an event that had *just happened* in the world of men. His play had many actors – not just a chorus, but a dozen more men each taking a separate role. There was Istes, fighting to the last on the wall – and Histiaeus, and Miltiades – and me.

I was not a citizen of Athens then, so I was not permitted to appear in the play. Besides, that might have seemed to some like hubris. But Phrynichus asked me to come to the judging of the play, to stand with him as his guest, and to stand by Miltiades.

The crops were in, and my slaves were, for the most part, decent men who could work for a month without me. Besides, Hermogenes would be there, and Tiraeus. I didn't stop to think. I took a horse, borrowed Idomeneus's young man, Styges, as my servant and rode over the mountain to Attica.

This time, I was much more careful in my approach to mighty Athens, and I rode clear around the city and arrived at Aristides' gate as the autumn sun set and men pulled their chlamyses closer against the wind and dark cold.

His wife came to the gate, summoned by servants. She surprised me by granting me the flash of her smile and a quick kiss on the cheek.

'Arimnestos of Plataea, you are ever a friend of this house,' she said. 'My husband is late coming in from the Agora. Please come in!'

I have always valued that woman. 'Despoina, this is Styges, acting as my hypaspist. He is no slave.'

She nodded to him. 'I'll see to his bed, then,' she said. 'You'll want to bathe.'

Not a question.

I was just clear of my bath, towelling down and wishing I had not put quite so much warm water on her floor, when Aristides came in through the curtain and embraced me, his wool cloak still carrying the cold of the outside. 'Arimnestos!' he said.

I had last seen him as his ship swept past mine, out of the pocket of death, at Lade. 'You lived,' I said with satisfaction.

'And you as well, my Plataean hero. By the gods, you fought like Heracles himself.' He embraced me again.

Other men had said as much, but other men were not the soft-spoken prig of justice, Aristides, and I valued those words – well, up to this very hour.

I followed him to a table set beside his wife's loom, and the three of us ate together. Later, it became the fashion to exclude women from many things, but not then. There was meat from a sacrifice, fresh tuna – a magnificent fish – good barley porridge, and rich wheat bread. In Plataea, it would have been a feast. In Athens, it was merely dinner with a rich man.

'How stands the case with Miltiades?' I asked after I had eaten my fill. Among Greeks, it is bad manners to ask hard questions during a meal. Truth to tell, it is bad manners in Persia, in Aegypt, in Sicily and in Rome, too.

Aristides wiped his fingers on a cloth – my sister would have kicked him, but customs differ from town to town – and pursed his lips. 'On the evidence, the jury can do nothing but convict him,' he said.

I could hear something in his voice. I raised an eyebrow. 'But?' I asked.

He shrugged. 'Men are seldom convicted on evidence,' he said. 'Miltiades' case has become a test of the reach of the Great King into our city. The case was brought with malice, by the Alcmaeonids, and I have reason to believe that the Great King paid for it to be done.'

I laughed. 'And the sad truth is that every one of us knows that Miltiades had every intention of seizing the city.'

Aristides frowned. 'I wish you would phrase things more accurately, Plataean. We know nothing of the kind. We know what he might have done had he defeated the Persians and Medes at Lade.' He shrugged.

I confess that I laughed. 'Aristides!' I said, as I understood. 'You are his advocate? You, his enemy?'

His wife laughed, and I slapped the table, and the Athenians' byword for justice and honour glared at us as if he was our pedagogue and we were errant children.

'It's not funny!' he snapped.

Try stopping a man from laughing with those words.

'Besides,' he said. 'I am hardly his enemy.'

'Of course not,' I said. I laughed again. I couldn't help myself, and his wife joined me.

'Why is it,' he asked, when we began to breathe again, 'that visitors here always mock me, and you, despoina, always abet them?'

I put a hand on his shoulder. 'If you will be *better* than other men, you must be patient with their mockery,' I said. 'Besides, we only tease you because we love you.'

'Why?' Aristides asked. Like most righteous men, he was impatient of teasing and had neither defence against it nor any idea why it was directed at him.

I shook my head and gave up. 'Forgive me, lord,' I said. 'Imagine I'm but a poor witless foreigner, and tell me how Miltiades might survive this charge.'

Aristides ignored my tone and nodded. 'Very well,' he said, taking me at my word. 'The question before the jury ought to be whether Miltiades sought to make himself tyrant or not. But the question that is actually facing the jury is simpler, and more complex – whether Athens ought to resist Persia or not. Had we won Lade, this trial would never have come about.'

I decided that I should not make the point that if we had won Lade, Miltiades would have landed here with fifty triremes and five thousand hoplites and made himself master in short order. Better not to say every thought that comes to one's mind.

'Men know that the Great King took Miletus. Thanks to Phrynichus, starting tomorrow, men will hear how close we came to defeating Datis – and how we were betrayed by the aristocrats of Samos. Do you know that the trierarchs there were stoned by a mob? Or that the eleven captains who stood with us are to have statues?'

'Someday I will find Dionysius of Samos in a dark alley,' I said.

'Too late,' Aristides said. 'His oarsmen killed him to erase the shame of their defection.'

'Good for them,' I said. It was, truly, the best news I'd heard all day. 'His shade will never go to Elysium!'

We poured libations to Zeus who watches over oaths, and to the furies who avenge men who are wronged.

'So,' Aristides continued, when the wine was pooling on the floor, 'to summarize, we seek to remind every juror – and indeed, every man – that we fought with the men of Miletus, and that, but for betrayal, we would have been victorious. And we seek to remind them that if the Great King rules here, our sons and daughters will service his soldiers like the virgins of Lesbos and Chios.'

That was close to a blatant lie – it was at least stretching the facts. The rape of the islands had been a horror – but it didn't represent the daily policy of the Great King. On the other hand, it had been terrible. I nodded.

'And if the men of this city see Persia as a threat, and see that we can stand against the Great King, then they will silence the Alcmaeonids and stand their ground, and Miltiades will be found innocent.' Aristides had risen to his feet. He was giving a speech.

I clapped. So did his wife.

He sat down and hung his head. 'But here in my own home, I'll say that I have very little hope,' he said. 'They tried to kill Sophanes today.'

I grinned. I didn't know that Sophanes was yet alive. 'I've seen that boy in action,' I said. 'Hired thugs will never get him.'

'Yesterday Themistocles was beaten,' he went on. 'He's rising to be the head of the Demos. I have no time for him – but he's with us against the Alcmaeonids and their supporters.' He shrugged. 'Men are afraid to speak openly.'

I rubbed my chin. 'Where is my suit against the Alcmaeonids for my slave girl and my horse?' I asked.

Aristides stopped as if he'd been struck. 'By Zeus Soter,' he said, 'I had forgotten. I must apologize – Miltiades is your proxenos, and he should have reminded me.' A proxenos is the man – usually a prominent man – who represents the affairs of your city in his own. Miltiades was the proxenos of Plataea in Athens.

I took a sip of wine. 'I mean to have that woman back,' I said. 'I'll turn to violence if I must. I swore an oath, which was recently brought to my attention. It lowers me to admit this – but I forgot her, too.'

'More than a year since we swore the suit,' Aristides said. 'You must *not* turn to violence, Arimnestos. This city is the symbol of the rule of law.'

'Hmm,' I said. Thugs were beating my friends. Miltiades was in fear of his life from his own people. And I felt alive for the first time in months.

By Aristides' shoulder, Jocasta raised an eyebrow – and moved one long finger across her throat.

I got her message as clearly as if she'd shouted it, and I smiled at her.

'What is there to grin at?' Aristides asked.

I shrugged. 'It's good to be here with you,' I said, with perfect honesty.

The next morning I went and visited Miltiades, who was being kept in one of the caves above the Agora. The men guarding him were mostly his friends.

'I'm safe here,' he said with a smile, after he hugged me. 'Unless Aristides gets himself a bodyguard, they'll kill him in the Agora. The rule of law is over. The Great King has bought the rich men, and they have bought the thugs. There'll be little justice after this.'

I could have said that there would have been little enough justice if he had made himself tyrant, but to Hades with that. Miltiades was my childhood hero, and my friend.

'I mean to take some action,' I said, glancing around.

'Legal action?' Miltiades asked. 'You are a foreigner.'

'You are my proxenos,' I said. 'And I have a lawsuit sworn against Cleitus of the Alcmaeonids.'

'So you do,' he said. He shrugged and raised both eyebrows. 'I fail to see why this is germane.'

I looked around. 'You trust all these men?' I asked.

'Of course,' Miltiades said, but his eyes said otherwise.

'Suffice it to say that if I move my case, you will have to act for me.' I bowed. Miltiades was no Aristides, and he did not know the law the way the Just Man did. 'And if there is no advantage to you, lord, I, at least, would reclaim the woman and the horse.'

Miltiades looked disgruntled – but he was too good a man to be despondent. 'I'll do my best,' he promised.

'I need to contact some witnesses,' I said. 'Paramanos? And Agios?'

'What have they to do with your damned horse?' he asked, and then realization began to dawn. He choked a moment, coughed and called to a boy who stood by, wearing the green and gold of Miltiades' father. 'Take Lord Arimnestos to Piraeus,' he said, 'and find the men he needs to see.'

'Aye, lord,' the boy said with a deep bow.

Aristides was a good man, the Just Man, but it was civil war in the streets, and by putting Miltiades, the fighter, in irons, the Alcmaeonids had muzzled their opposition.

I meant to have my slave girl back. And it seemed to me, after looking around for a few hours, that the fastest way through the tangle of Athenian politics would be to break some heads.

I have great respect for democracy, friends. But democracy needs a little help sometimes.

The first man I met with was Phrynichus. He was easy to find, in a good house high on the hill, hard by the Acropolis. I asked my way there, with one hand on my purse and a wary eye out for Alcmaeonid-paid brutes.

He was happy to see me. His fighting days were probably over – his two wounds had both been almost mortal, and he made it clear to me that he felt that the gods had sent him back to life to redress the balance of the loss at Lade. As he was the man who had sent the letter, I stayed a night with him, ate his food and tried to help out as much as possible, as I could tell that he was living small.

His wife Irene was kind, careful with money and smitten with a sadness that often comes to those who cannot have children – or perhaps poverty was wearing her down. I had a cure for poverty, and

I took her aside while her husband napped. She pulled a shawl over her head – she was not used to talking to men without a chaperone present.

I put a purse on the table. 'Your husband never received his share from our last voyage,' I said carefully. 'I don't like to speak of it – I know he was there for the principle of the thing, and not for filthy loot.'

Her eyes were carefully lowered, but now they came up and locked on mine. 'I understand,' she said steadily. 'You are clearly more of a gentleman than some of our other friends.'

I laughed. 'Don't believe it, lady. But that money is his, and perhaps I could buy some wine for dinner?'

She shook her head behind the shawl. 'I, for one, would appreciate some decent wine,' she allowed.

When Phrynichus was awake, he sat with me at the farm table that dominated the main room. 'Irene is happier today,' he said. 'What did you say to her?'

'I took the liberty of buying you some decent wine,' I said. I put a hand on his shoulder as his face darkened. 'Don't give me any shit, brother. You're poor as a frog without a swamp and you need a decent amphora to get you through the play.'

'If it ever goes on,' he said. 'Fuck me, Arimnestos. Cleitus and the Alcmaeonids paid to suppress it, and now they've threatened that if it goes on, I'll be beaten. Or Irene will be. They say they'll pay men to disrupt the performance, the way they broke up Miltiades' festival of return.'

I shook my head. 'Don't give an inch,' I said. 'I'm working on the problem of the Alcmaeonids.'

'What can you do?' he asked. 'I mean no offence, Arimnestos, but you're just a foreigner!'

'And you need a bodyguard,' I said. I knew where to find one.

That night, we ate good fish and drank good wine, and Irene lied like a good wife and said she'd found a big silver piece in the floor-boards. And in the morning, I made excuses and slipped away, feeling bad for having done so. Phrynichus needed me. But what he really needed was a success for his play.

My next stop was Cleon's. He was more sober than when last I'd found him.

'You're a thetes now?' I asked.

He shrugged. 'I drank the money I made with Aristides,' he said. 'After they died, I mean. And spent some on whores.' He looked around the main room of his house. It was clean, because it was empty.

'What trade do you work?' I asked.

He looked out of the door into the street. 'I was a pot-engraver,' he said. 'Hard to explain, really. I cut the scenes into the surface of pots before the painter painted them, on the most expensive items. But there's a whole new style of painting now, with no engraving, and I don't get much work, and what I do get – well, slaves earn as much as I do.' He shook his head. 'Before Yani died, I had a fishing boat – my pater's. That kept us on the right side of the ledger. But I sold it.'

'You don't have any land?' I asked.

'Not any more,' he allowed.

'Would you work for me?'

'Here? In Athens?' he asked.

I watched him for a moment, because I didn't need a drunk, but I did need to know that the man who'd stood at my shoulder in the fight at Ephesus was still in there. His hair was greying at the temples, his chiton was dirty and he had the weathered skin of a man who'd slept in alleys too many times.

'No,' I said. 'That is, I need you here for a few days. We'll break some heads. And then you'll have to leave, because the Alcmaeonids will eventually figure out who you are, and kill you.'

Cleon looked blank. 'And then?'

'And then you come with me to Plataea. And start again.' I walked over to him. 'Sell this house, go to Plataea and become a citizen. Stand at my shoulder. Be my friend.'

'On a farm?' he asked.

'If that's what you can do, yes.' I looked around the house. 'Anything to keep you here?'

'Not a fucking thing,' Cleon said. 'Who do we kill?'

Paramanos hugged me like a lost brother. I had last seen him covered with wounds from Lade and making a slow recovery when we fled Kallipolis, and we drank more wine than might have been wise.

It's a funny thing – Paramanos and I could have been great friends all along, I think, but for the fact that I used fear to cow him in the first moments of his service under me, and while he served me, I think he hated me. Relationships between men can be as complicated as those between women.

But Lade changed that, as you'll see. After Lade, those of us who survived it – we never forgot.

Black joined us, and Herk, my first tutor in the ways of the sea, and he and Cleon embraced, and we drank too much cheap wine, as I mentioned. Other men came around – oarsmen, sailors, hoplites.

'Miltiades needs us,' I said.

Agios, once Miltiades' helmsman, nodded, and Cleon shrugged, but Paramanos shook his head.

'I'm not a citizen here,' he said. 'And my status has been made abundantly clear. When I've had my fees paid, I'll be taking my money and going back to Cyrene.'

Black nodded.

I looked at him. 'You too?'

'Athens isn't my place,' he said.

'Herk, you're a citizen?' I asked.

'Oh, indeed,' he said. 'Born a thetes, but in the last allotment, I was a hippeis.' He shrugged. 'The men of property treat me like shit, for all that I'm a landowner now. You think I lived in Kallipolis as an exile? I hate Athens. The City of Aristocrats.' He looked around. 'You know what? For the commoners – the tyranny was better.'

Cleon barked his strange laugh, and I could see that the two of them got along very well.

I need to explain. For me, my loyalty to Plataea was absolute. To hear these three knock Athens – most especially Herk, who, by all accounts had made his fortune in her service – made me angry. Cleon I could understand. His city had let him down. But Herk?

'You're a thankless bunch,' I said. 'Miltiades made you rich in the service of Athens, and now he needs you, and you are running off to Cyrene?'

Paramanos stroked his beard. 'Yes.' He turned his head away. 'I've been threatened. My daughters have been threatened.'

Agios nodded, clearly unhappy.

'Gentlemen, sitting at this table are five bad men whose names make Syrian merchants shit themselves – and you are afraid of some threats from bum-boys in Piraeus?' I stood up. 'I'm going to take action. My actions are going to be carefully thought out, but I'm not going to use the law – except as bait. When I'm done, there won't be anyone to threaten your daughters. Join me. We all owe Miltiades.'

Paramanos made a curious face. 'Do we really owe Miltiades, friend?' He shrugged, but his eyes met mine squarely. 'Be honest –

Miltiades uses us, and now that he's down, he can't help us. Why should we help him? Listen – if it was you, or Herk, or Black or Cleon here – I'd carve my way through the bastards. But this is not my city, and not my fight.'

Black shrugged. 'I'm your helmsman,' he said. 'You bought me free. I do what you say.' He took a drink of wine. 'I got married,' he added, and moved as if he feared a reprisal.

'You got married?' I asked. 'What's she like?'

'Like any Athenian fishwife, but louder,' Paramanos said. 'You can meet her later. Tell me why I should help.'

I could marshal arguments – Heraclitus had taught me well – but I shook my head. 'No, brother. It's up to you. For all his little ways, Miltiades has been our friend. I think we owe him.' I looked around. 'Yes – he uses us. And by the gods, we know he wanted to be tyrant, and he'd have sold his own mother in a brothel to get it. But how often have we followed him to riches, eh?'

Paramanos shook his head. 'You know – we all know – that we'll do it. If only to find out what you have planned.'

'I need citizens,' I said. I wasn't going to stop to consider his sudden change of heart – I'd expected it. 'How many oarsmen on your ships are citizens? How many marines?'

'A dozen marines – many of them are *zeugitai*, members of the hoplite class. And I can round up fifty oarsmen who are thetes.' He looked at me. 'Why?'

'The muscle have to be citizens,' I said. 'And we have to have their families safe – on Salamis, for instance.'

My plan was simple – far simpler than Phrynichus and Aristides and their plans with complex choruses and speeches by actors. I explained what I had in mind, and then we mustered the oarsmen. It was winter – most of them were delighted to have a few days' work. Most of them were so poor when they were ashore that the prospect of moving their families to Salamis – the island off Athens, if you don't know it – sounded like a festival. I paid them enough to *make* it a festival.

Being lower-class men themselves, they knew where I could find other men – informants and the like. That was likely to prove the breaking point of my plan, and I had a simple solution to my need for information.

Money.

Twice I walked up the hills of Athens to Miltiades and asked him

202

for more money – ostensibly to plead my case. As he was my prox-enos, it was his duty to help me, and the first time he did so with a good grace. The second time, he was none too happy to loan me the value of a good farm in silver coin. But he did.

'What in the name of Tartarus do you need all this silver for, you Plataean pirate?'

'Buying jurors,' I said.

Crime eats money the way vultures eat a dead beast. Bribing a jury is an old and honourable tradition in democratic Athens, one that blatantly favours the rich, of course. Heh, democracy.

All forms of government favour the rich, honey.

I bought quite a few men. I divided the sailors and marines into teams, and I gave one to Cleon, and set them to watching Phrynichus. That was the most public team, and I was going to make Cleon vanish later. He had an additional set of duties, paying informers to look for my girl.

Agios led the scout team. They reconnoitred the Alcmaeonid estates.

The problem with paying out so much money is that it is impossible to keep it quiet.

It was near dark – every window had an oil lamp in it, and the more civic-minded brothel-owners had a big lamp out front, hanging from the *exhedra*, as well. I was climbing the hill in the alleys south of the Panathenaic Way to check on Phrynichus when they came at me – four men.

Two of them filled the street ahead of me. They had swords.

'That's him – the Plataean,' one called out.

'A friend sent us,' said the smaller of the two men ahead of us. 'We think maybe we should reason with you.' He laughed.

I could hear movement behind me, and I knew there were more of them. But the two in front of me were right on the edge – we were just shy of that moment when they would be keyed up enough to attack me. I've watched the process often enough – some men take for ever to be ready to fight, and others can fight at any moment.

I put a hand on my own sword – Athens was none to keen on men carrying weapons in the streets, but at dark, with a heavy cloak, no one would say anything about it. The smaller man laughed again. The odds were bad – one against four is insanity, unless you have no choice. The street I was in – an alley, really – was no wider than a man lying on his back full length, and I was at an elbow where someone's semi-legal building crowded the street and made it bend.

One of the men behind me stubbed his toe on a cobblestone and cursed. I heard the curse and felt the movement of his arms as he windmilled them to save himself – and I turned on the ball of my foot and punched the point of my sword into his side. I wasn't as clever as I'd wanted to be, and my blade skidded over his arms and the point caught in his ribs, and his fist connected with my face – not hard enough to stun me, but hard enough to rock me back.

Worst of all, as he fell away from me the point of my sword remained lodged in his ribs and the hilt was wrenched from my hand.

I pulled my cloak off by yanking it against the fine silver pin – which popped open and tinkled as it landed in the street, a nice find for the first child to look out of his door in the morning. The cloak weights slammed the smaller of the two men in front of me in the face – luck and training there – and made him duck back when he could have gutted me.

There's no conscious thought in a fight like that. There were no openings, no holds, no attacks that were going to get me free. I had no weapon. I kicked at the bigger of the men in front of me as I changed my stance, and then I leaped through the unshuttered window to my left, my back foot catching the oil lamp on the sill so that it landed behind me and exploded, lamp oil on my cloak and on the floor and fire spreading up my cloak.

But I had a wall between me and my attackers. I threw my burning cloak at them and turned to find three young men staring at me as if I was an apparition from the heavens – perhaps I was, with all the fire running along the floor behind me.

The fire – not a very big fire, I have to add – kept my attackers back for the space of three or four heartbeats, and by that time I was through the room curtain of wooden beads. This was not a brothel or a wine shop. It was a private house, and I passed through a room with four looms against the four walls, through another door as men shouted behind me and out into a courtyard. There were two slaves standing by the gate, and they looked as confused as men usually look in a crisis. I went past them – between them – without slowing, and I was in another street.

I ran up the hill. I could see the Pisistratids' palace on the Acropolis as a landmark. I remember offering my prayers to Heracles that I had so easily averted an ambush that should have killed me – really, if they hadn't stopped to talk to me, I'd already have started to rot, eh?

My prayers may have called the god to my aid, but they were otherwise premature. At the next corner I ran full tilt into the larger of the two men who'd confronted me in the alley. I bounced harder than he did, and he landed most of a blow with something in his left hand – a club, I suspect.

It caught me on the outside of my left bicep – hard – and numbed my arm. I stumbled back into a closed door and he recovered his balance, grinned in the feeble light and came to finish me.

But he paused to yell 'I've got him!' to his mates, and as he did that, the door under my numb hand opened and I fell through it, my legs pumping frantically to keep me upright, so that I carried the young man who'd opened the door right back into the room and knocked him flat.

He was quite small, pretty, and had make-up on his eyes – which were wide with sudden terror. I'd hurt him, no doubt.

There was a cloak hanging on a wooden stand at the edge of the bed – probably the boy's own, or forgotten by a client. I snatched it as the big man came through the door. I got it on my left arm, which was numb but not useless, and got my feet under me – this was moving so fast that the pain of the blow from his cudgel was just hitting me. The big man was coming in for the kill and I swirled the cloak, which seemed to fill the tiny room, and my right arm moved behind the cloak, lost in it, and my attacker flinched back.

It is a thing known to any trained man that men will flinch from a cloak or a stick, when neither can do them any real harm, even with a direct blow to the face. But my cloak and my fist were both feints, and my right-foot kick caught him in the knee before he could shift his weight off it, and I heard the joint pop. He roared and went down. The hand with the cudgel swept past me, and it was as if he'd decided to hand me his cudgel – despite the dark and the confusion, his left hand brushed against my right, and the club was in my hand.

There were men in the alley outside. By the sound of it, there were quite a few of them – not just the initial four.

My recent opponent was thrashing on the floor and roaring. As he made no move to harm me, I took a deep breath and hit him behind the ear with his own cudgel, and he went out.

The painted boy squeaked and ran through a doorway I'd missed. I followed him, eager to avoid the men on the street. We went straight into the building's central courtyard, which was full of men and boys on couches. My hip caught a table of pitchers of water and wine, and the whole thing fell with a crash. Then I was across the room, through a door that seemed to me the biggest and into the building's *andron*, with painted wall panels and a garishly painted ceiling – Zeus and Ganymede, as you might expect. Then I ran out of the main door under a pair of kissing satyrs and into a street that was brilliantly lit by cressets in the building I had just left – a prosperous brothel.

By the flickering light, I could see men coming for me from the downhill end of the street – a dozen, at least.

So I turned and ran, uphill. There is no fighting a dozen men at the edge of darkness.

I went one street and turned into an alley. I saw a big ceramic rain-cistern under a house gutter and leaped to it at full stride. I got a leg over the roof edge and I was up. I lay flat on the roof. I was unable to breathe, and my two wounds had burst into pain the way a flower opens with the dawn, and it was all I could do not to cry out.

I heard men run by – they were an arm's reach away – and meet with other men in the next street.

I looked around the roof. It was a low building, the sort of cheap private residence that filled the south slope of the hills before Pericles rebuilt the city. One storey, mud brick on a stone foundation with beams holding a roof that was also a place to cook, sleep in warm weather – make love, when privacy was required. The couple wrapped in blankets and furs had various naked limbs sticking out, and the man pulled the blankets closer, as if blankets would protect him.

I ran to the centre of the roof and looked. South was the high wall of the brothel and east was the wide Panathenaic Way, but north, uphill, the next roof beckoned. I had to keep moving – the men below were not fools.

I ran, leaped and my feet came down badly, punching straight through the seagrass of the roof so that my groin landed on the beam, and for a moment it was all I could do to curl my legs around the beam and moan. In the building underneath me, people screamed – and their screams were answered by running feet.

Sometimes the initial pain is worse than the resulting injury. I got a knee up on the beam and the blow to my groin wasn't as debilitating as I had feared. I sidestepped north as men gathered around the building, and north again, and this time I stepped over the roof barrier on to the next roof – slate, thank the gods! – and I ran across the firm surface. I could smell a fire that burned charcoal and I could smell hot metal, and I realized I was crossing the roof of a smithy – a big one.

There was an alley at the northern edge of the smithy, and I leaped it without pausing to reflect – and my arms just caught the edge of the higher roof – much higher, because the alley was like a giant step up. I hung there for long heartbeats, trying to gain control of my legs over the pain – and I swung my right leg over the roof edge and rolled.

My hips hurt and my groin hurt and my left shoulder screamed as if I'd been scalded with boiling water. This roof had an outdoor kitchen and a small shed where the owner stored his brazier and spare pots. I got myself into it – a counsel of desperation, let me tell you. If they found me there, I was dead – no more retreat. But I wasn't thinking well, and my instinct was the instinct of the wounded animal. I pulled the door closed and lay there, panting.

I listened to the men in the street as they searched the houses – broke in, beat people or threatened them. But actions have consequences, and the fates were not blind to my predicament. As they went from house to house, causing mayhem, men – and women – turned against them. Greeks don't take happily to the invasion of their homes, however poor.

I heard the smith roar with rage as his dinner crashed to the floor when the thugs overturned his table, He had weapons and the strength to use them, and he hit a thug so hard that the blow had that telltale sound of a broken melon – and then the wounded man started calling for his fellows.

The smith roared for the watch. His voice carried, and other voices – housewives, prostitutes and the patrons from the brothel – joined in.

Athens was a mighty city then – but not so big that the uproar of throaty thugs and fifty citizens didn't carry quickly.

The Scythian archers – the city police since the time of the tyrants – came just as a party of thugs were breaking into the house where I hid. I could follow their progress on the street by the sudden change in sound – the babble of citizens telling the Scythians what had happened.

My breathing was better, although the pain was still there. I lay still, my eye pressed to the door of the shed.

A man's head came up the ladder from the main room below. I didn't know him, but his ragged haircut and his expression told me he was one of my pursuers. He looked around the roof quickly, and then I heard him say that the roof was clear.

'Fucking Scythians!' came a voice from below, over the shouts of the householder, an older man with a shrill voice.

'Villains! Out of my house, you scum!'

I heard the man take a blow – a blow so sharp that his voice was cut off in mid-imprecation.

'We've got to get out of here!' a man said.

'Fuck that – this bastard is worth a hundred drachmas. Beat the Scythians and make them clear out. He's hiding – right here. Somewhere.' I knew the voice – my man from the alley.

'You fight the cops, you mad bugger.' The man who'd checked the roof was not having any of it. 'I'm off.'

'Coward,' the leader hissed, but by then, there were Scythians pounding on the door.

Then both of them came up the ladder and on to my roof. Beneath our feet, the Scythians were breaking in the door.

My two would-be attackers slowed briefly at the roof edge, then they dropped over the edge, heading south.

I just lay there, unable to do much to change my fortunes. I saw the Scythians check the roof – they spoke in their barbaric tongue, glanced around carefully, one man by the ladder with an arrow on his bow while another man poked around with his sword, but they didn't check the little shed.

I waited a long time after they vanished – I waited until the whole quarter was silent. Then I limped down the ladder, picked the householder up and put him on his bed, and sneaked out of the door.

I made it to Phrynichus's house under my own power. His poor wife was terrified at my appearance.

Phrynichus got me into bed – his own bed, as his apartment was too small for such luxuries as guest chambers. I lay there, trying to frame something polite to say – and then, finally, my *psyche* released its hold on my body, and I went away.

The next day, I limped about escorted by half a dozen oarsmen. I told all my people to lie low, and I made myself look afraid – and abashed – when Cleitus pushed past me in the Agora.

'Done meddling?' he asked with a smile. 'You don't look well, foreigner. Perhaps you should stop playing with fire and go home.'

'Yes, lord,' I breathed, exaggerating my injuries. In fact, my paid informants were bringing me titbits by the hour. All my plans and preparations took time, and I warned my people – the oarsmen, the informants and some paid thugs – that I wanted no violence until I said the word. And money – some Miltiades' and some mine – flowed like blood in a sea-fight.

Some of my new friends disliked being made to lie low. There were a few defections, but I was careful with my plans and no one – except Cleon, Paramanos and Herk – knew what I had planned. The informants were blind – each of them had a particular task – and given the scale of reward offered, I expected results, and got them.

Let me interject here. A man who's been free all his life might struggle at all this – but a man who's been a slave knows all about how and where to get information. How and where to buy violence. And how to plan revenge. Remember that the world of Athens ran on slaves, and slaves, at some level, dislike being slaves.

A week after my arrival in Athens, I knew where my girl was. She was working in a slave brothel by the Agora. I was tempted to grab her – but to do so would have given the game away. Shortly after my informers found her, the best pair – Thracians, former slaves who ran an 'inquiry service' – brought me the names of the men Cleitus had hired to beat Sophanes and Themistocles. I paid them a small fortune, and they left the city for a while – they guessed what I had in mind. Smart lads. Another informer – a woman, a prostitute with a quick mind – located my attacker, the smaller man in the alley, based only on my description. He was a big man in the lower-class neighbourhoods, a wine-shop owner and a money-lender. I paid the woman well and sent her to Salamis, too. My desire to send these people out of the city when they had served my needs was not altogether altruistic – I trusted none of them, and this way my prostitute could not counter-inform to Cleitus. Perhaps I wronged them – many were happy to help, just to strike a blow against the oppression of the aristocrats – but talk is cheap and informing can become a habit. So I sent them away, and Miltiades' money paid and paid.

I didn't share my plan with Aristides, or Miltiades, or even Phrynichus, although he was beginning to catch on, as was Cleon. Many Athenians are fine men, and their brilliance is legendary. Trust an Athenian to plead a court case or to write a play. But what all those brilliant men like Aristides and Miltiades had missed was that the Alcmaeonids weren't playing by the rules. They had taken Persian gold and used it to pay the mob – the same mob that should have been baying for their blue blood – to beat better men.

I had grown up in Ephesus, where the Persians intimidated the citizens, and where the citizens used force to intimidate each other. I had been a slave. I knew how the world worked, in a way that neither the Alcmaeonids nor the Just Man ever would.

When I was ready, I prompted Aristides to bring my civil suit, and he summoned Cleitus to appear in my case just one day after the Attic feast of Heracles, which seemed auspicious to me. The civil court met briefly, eager to be away to their feasts and holidays – many men went to the countryside for the feast of Heracles, of course, and some for the feasts of Dionysus. Across the Agora, a party of shipwrights were raising the theatre – a wooden stage and the big wooden building behind it called the *skene*, and the wooden benches where the best men sat. I was astounded at the speed with which they put it up – between the opening and closing of the law court, the workmen had the skene completed.

The law court was well briefed and Cleitus was caught by surprise. He turned bright red and shouted some foolishness. A date was set, and Aristides explained to the sitting members of the Boule that Miltiades would have to be released from prison to plead for me, because he was my proxenos.

That was the law.

Cleitus began to protest, and then thought better of it. Why wouldn't he? He held all the knucklebones, and all his foes were going to come to the same place on the same day – the feast of Dionysus.

I stood by the temporary theatre, watching, willing the thoughts into his head, begging Zeus Soter to help me to recover my oath and punish this man, and the king of the gods heard my prayer. I saw Cleitus lower his fist, turn away and smile. He was an intelligent man, as I had cause to know later – and he saw as well as I did that by bringing all his opponents together, he could hurt us the more easily, with his thugs and with the law. Then he agreed, as if making a magnanimous gesture, to allow my suit to be heard in the Agora on the day following the feast of Dionysus, in just four days.

The notion that we would all be vulnerable then ought to lull my opponent, I hoped. Because I planned to strike at the feast of Dionysus itself.

IO

Even back then, before we fought the Medes, the theatre of Athens was a famous thing, and much talked of throughout the Greek world. Technically, I wasn't welcome at the performances, as I was a foreigner, but again, before the performances were moved out of the Agora, everyone went – slaves and free men and citizens and even a few women – bolder spirits or prostitutes.

Athenian prostitutes aren't like the poor tribal girls in this town, thugater. Do I shock you, blushing maiden? What I mean is that in Athens, slave and free, man and woman, prostitutes have several protections before the law and, in an odd way, status. A few are even citizens. In those days, they strolled around the agora openly, made sacrifices – at least barley-cake sacrifices – at the public altars, and performed their services to the community behind the Royal Stoa. Not that I have any direct knowledge ...

It is also important to remember that theatre performances went on all day, not in the evening, and that one play followed another in fairly short order, interspersed with prayers and sacrifice at the public altars – don't forget that in those days, the drama was still a religious expression, and a symbol of civic piety. Men went soberly, as if to temple. When the satyr plays were introduced, to celebrate the god's love of revelry, that was different, although still pious. An initiate of Dionysus is still pious while puking, we used to say. And worse.

I stayed with Aristides the night before. He planned to make a tour of his farms before going to the Agora, so I rose early and walked through the deserted streets with Styges by my side. Both of us were heavily armed, and I had bandages on my left arm and all down my right leg where I'd cut it leaping from roof to roof.

We walked across the Agora, past the still-empty wooden theatre and the altars of the twelve gods, right around behind the Royal Stoa.

There, while girls and boys plied a brisk trade against the wall of the old building despite the early hour, I found Agios and Paramanos and Cleon.

'Ready?' I asked.

They all nodded. Cleon was sober. 'Have you got Phrynichus?' he asked.

'I have him. Styges goes straight from here to watch him. You make sure we don't have a surprise during the performance.'

We shook hands all around and they walked off down the hill. I stood alone, watching them go, surrounded by the urgent noises of men having a quick tumble or getting their flutes played on the day of the festival – many men thought it was good luck to couple on the wine god's day.

Then I gathered my wits and headed back to Aristides. I made it in time to eat a crust of bread in his kitchen with his wife and two of his boarhounds, and then I borrowed a horse and accompanied him around his farms, with Aeschylus the playwright at my left side and Sophanes on my right. Aristides mocked us for nursemaiding him. For my part, I had come to enjoy his company as a philosopher, and I was afraid that by the end of the day we would no longer be friends. But I had no intention of letting him be attacked when my own plan was so close to fruition.

We had just completed a tour of grain barns – Aristides was a wealthy man, for all his pretended humility – and we were riding down a road with steep property walls on either side when I saw a group of men on foot coming the other way – a dozen men, and many with cudgels.

'Back, my lord,' I said, turning my horse.

'Nonsense,' Aristides said. 'That's Themistocles. No friend of mine, but hardly an enemy.'

Which shows what a foreigner I was – he was one of the best-known orators in Athens, even then. And I'd never seen him.

Themistocles was another minor aristocrat, but by dint of constant public speaking and a good deal of political strategy, he had made himself the head of the Demos party – the popular party, or the party of the lower classes. In those days, such a role was considered a threat by all the other aristocrats. The path to tyranny usually lay through the control of the masses. Only the lower-class voters could form armed mobs big enough to force the middle class into accepting a tyranny.

I think I should say at this point how I think Athens worked then. Now, to be sure, nothing I'm going to say bears any resemblance to what Solon wanted for Athens, or even what the Pisistratid tyrants wanted. This is merely my observation on what actually happened.

There was Athens – the richest city in mainland Greece. Sparta may or may not be more powerful, but no one on earth would willingly buy a Spartan pot. Eh? The poor bastards don't even make their own armour.

All Athenians – or at least, all rich Athenians of good birth – seemed to be locked in a contest for power. An Athenian would put this differently, and prate about arete and service to the state. Hmm. Listen, children – most of them would have sold their mothers to become tyrant.

So, for those locked in the great games there were three roads to power – although each road had some side turnings and branches. A rich man might follow the path of arete, spending his money wisely on monuments at home and at Olympia or Delphi, competing in games and putting up teams of chariot horses, paying for triremes for the state, sponsoring religious festivals – all as part of a slow rise to public esteem. In this way, and by using public honours to promote his own followers, a man might build a gigantic faction that would allow him to leap to the tyranny. The Pisistratids had done it, making themselves tyrants. And the Alcmaeonids were on the same path, and Cleitus, in particular, exemplified the path of arete.

That said, I have to add that there was a deep division among the old aristocrats. On the one hand, there were the *eupatridae*, or well-born, descended from the gods and heroes, like the Pisistratids and the Philaids, Miltiades' family. On the other hand, there were the new men, the new families – all still aristocrats, but 'recently' ennobled by wealth and political position. The first of these families were the dreaded Alcmaeonids, whose famous ancestor, Alcmaeon, was enriched in Lydia by Croesus. There were other families of 'new men', and while at times the new men and the old families acted together – as aristocrats – to protect wealth and privilege, at other times they were at daggers drawn.

Then again, a man like Themistocles could choose a different path. He was born to comfort, and his father, Neocles, was reckoned rich enough, but he was not well-born by any means. However, by making himself the hero of the masses, the voice of the oppressed, the hand of justice to the lower classes, Themistocles harnessed the largely unvoiced power of the disenfranchised and the under-enfranchised, and turned them into a powerful force that could, on occasion, defeat the middle class and the upper class and demand power for their chosen orator. For all that the Pisistratids were wealthy aristocrats, they had always held the love of the demos – the people. And remember, odd as it sounds, in a well-run tyranny, the poor men had the most power.

Finally, a man such as Miltiades might find a third path. Miltiades and his father were members of one of the oldest and richest of the eupatridae families, but they rose to power and wealth through overseas adventures – piracy, in fact. Through military action, some-times in the name of Athens and sometimes in their own name, they accrued wealth by something like theft, and enriched other men who then became their followers and dependants, allowing them to attract a following in all three classes – and allowing them to build up a massive military force that neither of the other two systems ever created. If we had won at Lade, Miltiades might well have been tyrant of Athens. He'd have had the money, and the military power. That's the real reason Cleitus hated him.

Let me add that, however cynical I am, and was, about the striving of these men for power, I will testify before the gods that Aristides, for all his priggishness, never had any end in view other than the good of Athens. His party, if you can call it that, his faction existed only to support the rule of law and prevent any of the others from rising to tyranny. So let us say that there was a fourth faction – a faction of men who followed the path of arete with no end in view but the good of their city.

Naturally, that fourth party was the smallest.

So, I had fallen into the middle of the competition, and now I was sitting on my horse, blocking the narrow lane, as Themistocles and a dozen club-armed thugs surged towards us.

'*Chairete!*' Aristides called.

Themistocles was a handsome man, tall, well-built, with broad shoulders and long legs and a full beard like a fisherman. He had a sort of bluff, hail-fellow-well-met humour that made men like him. He stepped forward, but I'd have known him anyway, as he was a head taller than his followers and the best man among them. He looked like a good man in a fight.

'Aristides! A pleasure to meet an honest man, even if he is mounted on a horse!' His horse comment was meant to remind his own people that he, Themistocles, was walking, not riding.

Aristides nodded. 'I'm doing the rounds of my farms. Are you to be at the festival today?'

Themistocles leaned on his stick. 'Love of the gods and love of the people go hand in hand, Aristides.' He raised an eyebrow. 'I see we might make common cause, as we all seem to be sporting some token from the Alcmaeonids!' He pointed at the bump on his head and his black eye – to Aristides' injuries, and my bandages. Then he turned to me and, with an exaggerated manner, said, 'You must be the foreigner from Plataea, sir.'

Clearly he knew exactly who I was.

I slid from my mount and took his hand in the Athenian way. 'Arimnestos of Plataea at your service,' I said.

He nodded, glanced at Aristides, then back at me, and I thought he might let go of my hand. 'I have heard ... things about you.' He looked at one of his men. 'Recently.'

I smiled. 'Nothing that might disconcert you, I hope?'

Themistocles considered me, and then looked up at Aristides. He was finding, as men have found since the invention of the horse, that it is much easier to stare a man down than to stare him up. 'Your foreign flunky is making trouble among my people,' he said to Aristides.

Aristides shrugged. 'The Plataean is no man's flunky, Themistocles. And just as he is not *my* flunky, so they are not *your* people.'

'Don't be a stiff-necked prig,' Themistocles said, all the oil leaving his voice. He leaned closer. 'Your man has tried to buy my mob. We should be acting together these days, not making separate efforts. And the mob is mine, sir.'

Aristides looked at me, and I couldn't read what he was thinking. 'Is this true?' he asked.

I smiled. 'No,' I said.

'You lie,' Themistocles spat.

Aristides pushed his horse between us. 'Themistocles, I have warned you before that utterances of this sort will not win you friends.'

'Get your money out of town, foreigner,' Themistocles shot at me. 'No one buys mobs without my say-so.' That last was directed at Aristides, not me.

I stepped towards him and his people began to close around me. 'I am Arimnestos of Plataea,' I called out. 'And if one of you lays a hand on me, I'll start killing you.' I looked around at them, and they desisted. The man closest to me was a big man, but when his eyes met mine, he stepped back and gave me a smile.

I was the Arimnestos the man-killer.

Aristides looked pleased, which puzzled me.

'I mean no disrespect,' I said to Themistocles. I wanted no trouble with the demagogue. 'What I have paid for will only benefit you.'

He raised an eyebrow. 'Really?' he asked.

Aristides was watching me. I shrugged. 'I would not tell every man on this road,' I said. 'Nor have I bought a mob. I have bought information, and I paid well.'

'What kind of information?' Themistocles demanded.

'Information regarding my court case, of course,' I said.

This satisfied him immediately. 'Ah!' he said. 'A certain slave in the brothels, I gather?' he said, looking knowing and yet deeply concerned. The only sign of his hypocrisy was the speed of his direction changes.

'Exactly!' I proclaimed, as if stunned by his perspicacity.

He dropped me as if our business was done, then he and Aristides exchanged a commonplace or two and we passed through his retinue. When I glanced back, Themistocles was smiling at me. Aristides was not.

'What are you up to?' he asked.

'Nothing,' I said. I smiled at him. 'Nothing that would interest you, sir.'

He rubbed his beard. 'You've got Themistocles riled, and that's never a good thing.' He reined his horse. 'You know what you are doing? You're sure?'

I shrugged, because I wasn't at all sure that I knew what I was doing. 'I'm fighting back,' I said.

'Gods stand by us,' Aristides said.

When the sun was high, we left our horses at his stables and walked into the city together. Men were gathered everywhere, and I was reminded of Athens's power by seeing how many men she commanded. There must have been twelve thousand men of fighting age in the Agora for the performances, and that is a fair number of decently trained men – a greater total than Thebes and Sparta together, and therein lies the secret of Athens's strength. Manpower.

When Athenians gather, they talk. It seems to be the lifeblood of the city, and they talk of everything from the power of the gods to the roles of men, the rights of men, the place of taxes, the weather, the crops, the fish – and back to the gods. Standing with Aristides in the Agora, trying to guard him, I was dizzied by the power of the ideas expressed – piety and impiety, anger and logic, farming advice, military strategy – all in a matter of a few minutes.

We were all crushed together when the magistrates went to the public altar of Zeus near the Royal Stoa and made the opening sacrifices. Then the 'good men', the athletes, the Olympic victors, the poets, the priests and high aristocrats, processed to the wooden seats that had been arranged – pray, don't imagine anything elegant or splendid like modern Athens, honey. We're talking about wooden stands that creaked when too many fat men climbed the steps! But after some time, the crowd settled, and the poor metics and foreigners and lower-class citizens pushed in around the sides and in the space between the stage area and the stands.

Early on, I spotted Cleitus. He was wearing a magnificent embroidered himation over a long chiton of Persian work, and he was easy to pick out, as he was sitting in the first row of the stand.

A set of priests and priestesses came forward, purified the crowd and made sacrifices. Then we all sang a hymn to Dionysus together and the plays began.

I don't remember much about the first play – just that it was a typically reverent piece about the birth and nurture of the god. At least, according to an Athenian. We have our own ideas about Great Bacchus in Boeotia. But the second play was Phrynichus's.

I saw him as soon as the chorus came out. He was behind them, wearing a long white chiton like the one that the archon in Plataea wears, and he looked more scared than he had been when the Aegyptians were storming our deck at Lade.

I began to push through the crowd towards him. It was not easy – everyone had heard that *The Fall of Miletus* was a different kind of play, and men wanted to see the poet, to watch him as they watched his play. I had managed to get close to him when the chorus, dressed as skeletons in armour, linked arms and sang:

Hear me, Muses! What I tell,
Is wrought with horror, and yet heroes walked there, too!
And where our fair maidens once walked,
Fire has swept like the harrow,
Breaking the clods of dirt, and making the ground smooth.
Hear me, furies! And men of Athens!
We died on our walls, in our streets, in the breach,

Where the Great King's siege mound rose.
So that, where once our maidens for their young swains sighed,
Those same young men wore bronze, and for the
Want of Athens, there we died.

I've heard Aeschylus, and I've heard young Euripides. But for power, give me Phrynichus. And he was actually at the battle – well, Aeschylus and his brother were there, too. Aeschylus was also next to me as I came up to Phrynichus, pushing rudely through the crowd. He took my shoulder.

'Not now,' he said, pointing to Phrynichus, who was watching his chorus exactly as Agios watched his oarsmen in a sea-fight.

So I stopped and listened. I had been there, of course – and yet I was enraptured by his words. He laid the blame for the fall of the east on Athens. That was the point of his play – that the rape of Ionia was caused by the greed of Athens. Yes, he made Miltiades a hero – and that must have sat ill with some – but the greatest hero was Istes, and he towers over the play like Heracles come to earth.

It was frightening to listen to a man speak words I had spoken in council. And there was the man playing Miltiades – not that he was named, for in those days, that might have been considered impiety – and he stood forth and said:

Today, we are not pirates. Today, we fight for the freedom of the
Greeks, although we are far from home and hearth.

And men cheered. Cleitus looked around. He was angry – doubly angry, I think. His men should have made a disturbance by then, shouldn't they?

Hah! I'm keeping my plan from you children. It helps build the story, does it not? But not many men can say that in one day they bested Cleitus of the Alcmaeonids and Themistocles of Athens in a contest of wits. Let me tell it my own way.

The play was only halfway through when the first man in the crowd gave way to tears. And by the time Istes died (in the play, he asks 'Where is Athens?' as he falls to his death), men were weeping, some were pouring dust on their heads and the whole row of Alcmaeonids were looking uneasy under all that dignity and good breeding.

It was a mighty play.

And then there was my contribution.

Not long after Istes' death, when the angry crowd was to under-stand that the maidens of Miletus were being ravished offstage by the Persian archers, I saw a man come to Cleitus. His face was broad and puffy – or did I imagine that? And when he whispered into his master's ear, Cleitus flushed red and stood up.

We were separated by ten horse-lengths, but the gods meant him to know. I caught his eye. And I smiled.

Whatever the news was, it passed from man to man along the Alcmaeonid family seats. Several of them pointed at me.

Aeschylus watched them, and then Sophanes pushed up next to me.

'What have you done?' he asked.

'An act of piety and justice,' I said quietly.

I wasn't there to see it, but Cleon told the tale well. This is what happened.

In a south-side brothel owned by the Alcmaeonids, a group of oars-men swaggered in demanding wine – no uncommon thing during the feast of Dionysus. But when they had their wine, they demanded to see all the girls, and having chosen one, they beat the owner and his bruisers to death with their fists. Four men died. The girl they took away with them.

Oh, it's a nasty business, children.

Out by the tanneries, a small crowd descended on a taverna known to be owned by one of the gangs of toughs who 'organized' things in the town. They pulled four men out of the taverna and stabbed them to death. The four men were literally cut to ribbons.

Up on the hill by the Acropolis, another pair of bruisers were caught by a small mob and cudgelled to death. Sailors were blamed.

But the worst atrocity, in the eyes of the 'good men', was that someone – or some group of men – invaded one of the largest Alcmaeonid farms. In fact, it was Cleitus's home farm. His workers were badly beaten, and every horse in his barns was killed, throats cut with knives. Every horse.

Not everything I planned came off. I had wanted my own horse back, but the men who were sent to the farm misunderstood, and my nice mare died with all their stock. I hadn't meant so many men to die – ten is a big body count for a peaceable city – but when you make soup, the vegetables are best cut small.

I did what had to be done. I wanted the Alcmaeonids to be struck with terror. I didn't want them to consider fighting back.

I couldn't be certain what the consequences of my little gambit would be. And perhaps the consequences would have been less, if not for Phrynichus's play.

Cleitus had meant for the play to be cancelled, or if not cancelled, he'd planned a disturbance in the Agora that would have forced the magistrates to take action. That's what should have happened, but his bruisers were cooling corpses by then, their shades already far on the road to Hades. I'd paid another crowd of oarsmen and their friends to attend the play. I packed the crowd to get it cheering, but that was unnecessary, and I regret that I thought so little of Phrynichus. I didn't pay them to attack the Alcmaeonids. That happened all by itself.

The end of the play set off a convulsion of sorrow and regret. Phrynichus's words brought home to the mass of men what the fall of Miletus had meant – and what role they had played, or not played. Never once had he named the Alcmaeonids, or spoken harshly of the power of Persian gold – but when men dried their eyes after the last speech, a demand by a Persian general that all Greeks submit or share the fate of Miletus, the crowd turned on the Alcmaeonids like wild dogs.

They were pelted with filth, and their retainers were beaten. At first, men were restrained, both by the prestige of the aristocrats and by fear of their bruisers – but there were no bruisers in evidence.

Then some of the oarsmen grew bolder and pressed forward.

But the aristocrats weren't cowards – far from it. These were the leaders of Athens, and swords appeared, despite the law. Commoners were cut down.

The area behind the stands was now enveloped in the chaos of a formless fight. I pushed my way there, past men trying to join the fight and others attempting to flee it. I wanted Cleitus – I wanted to see his face.

Instead, I saw Themistocles. He was grinning from ear to ear, and yet he was struggling to restrain some thetes who had cudgels and were trying to finish off a fallen man.

Themistocles shook his head at me. 'You see what you've done?' he roared – not that he was displeased.

I pushed past him, looking for Cleitus. I took a blow on the shoulder and I wondered if the Alcmaeonids would be finished off right here in a massacre by the Royal Stoa, but the crowd wanted more and less than blood, and already the older aristocrats were clear of the crowd. And running. A sight that the demos never forgot.

Cleitus was holding the crowd back with a dozen armed men. The thetes feared his sword and his ability to use it.

I didn't. I pushed forward through the last edge of lower-class men, and I laughed at him.

As if by prompt on the stage, Paramanos appeared with my slave girl in tow. Her eyes widened when she saw me – until then, as I later heard, she'd assumed the worst. If there can be worse than working in a brothel in Athens.

I grabbed her hand and she came with me.

'I have back what is mine,' I called to Cleitus.

'You're a dead man,' he roared at me.

And then he ran, pursued by the sound of my laughter.

I gave her her freedom, as I had promised. It was a year or more late, and I paid her the best damages I could, hard silver for her lost year. She was never again the open-faced, friendly companion of our first weeks together. The gods had used her and cast her away, and I had forgotten her, who had sworn to save her. It's not a pretty story. How many men did she service in the Agora because I was heartsick?

But we made the Athenian aristocrats pay. No Alcmaeonid dared come into the streets for weeks thereafter, and my court case was won by the absence of my opponent, and the unanimity of the jury was a sign of the collapse of aristocratic power. Miltiades argued my case with a deep voice and an unworried countenance, because he knew he was going to win – both as my proxenos and in his own case. No jury in Athens would convict Miltiades of anything after Phrynichus's play. And the Alcmaeonid political machine died with their handlers. I'm afraid I taught the Athenians a terrible lesson, and they still fear the demos.

But I smile to think that Phrynichus and I saved Athenian democracy from the Alcmaeonids so that the man who wanted to be tyrant could save it from the Medes. The gods – who is so foolish as to not believe in the gods? – work in the strangest ways.

Aristides was distant for the next week, until my case was resolved. He was no fool, and he knew where the muscle had come from, and so did Themistocles. I went back to staying with Phrynichus, who was now deluged with money and offers of more from admirers as distant as Hieron of Syracuse.

Phrynichus knew I'd done something, but I never let on exactly what – and yet, by having Agios and Paramanos and Black and Cleon for dinner every night, Phrynichus became untouchable. We kept fifty oarsmen in the streets around his house at all hours, on Miltiades' money.

But on the day that Miltiades was released – the jury refused to hear the charges read, which had precedent in Athenian law, and seemed to satisfy everyone – I met him and Aristides together with Themistocles. We met as if by chance in a wine shop at the edge of the Agora, where well-to-do men used to cement business deals.

Themistocles didn't meet my eye. Miltiades, on the other hand, rose to his feet and embraced me.

'Money well spent,' he said. 'Pardon my doubts of you, friend. I will always be in your debt.' He gave me a broad wink. 'I don't think these other gentlemen liked their taste of your politics.'

Themistocles spat. 'I do not want to live in a state powered by blood,' he said.

'And yet you seek increased power for the lowest class,' Miltiades answered. 'What do you expect?'

Themistocles glared at me. 'I expect them to learn to be men of honour, and to stand in their places and vote – not cudgel each other like thieves.'

But Aristides shocked me. He took my hand and embraced me. 'I thought to hate you,' he said. 'I considered asking for a writ of banishment against you.'

Themistocles looked at him as if the gods had taken his wits. 'But you did not?'

Aristides shook his head and sat. 'Drink wine with us, Arimnestos,' he said. 'I invited Cleitus to join us, but he declined. I wanted all the factions.' He almost smirked. 'Perhaps their faction isn't worth having today.'

'They'll be back,' I said.

'So they will,' Aristides agreed. 'But no amount of Persian gold will buy them the mob now.'

'And for that, you forgive this foreigner who used violence to achieve his ends?' Themistocles asked.

Aristides shrugged. 'In former times, when a city had reached a point of stasis – civil war – the leading men would invite a foreigner, a lawmaker, to come and save them.' Aristides smiled. 'My wife told me that I was being a fool, and that I should see the Plataean as a man who came to Athens and restored order.'

I looked around at all of them. 'You see me as a killer of men,' I said. 'But I was trained by Heraclitus of Ephesus, and I know a little of how cities work. Athens has too many poor, and too few rich, for the rich to control the poor with fear and silver. Too many of Athens's poor are seamen and oarsmen. They're not cowards, as all of us around this table have cause to know. And they have no reason to love Persia.' I shrugged.

'I know all that,' Themistocles said. 'I don't need some eastern-trained foreigner to tell me.'

'You know it all,' Aristides said, 'but despite that, you did not act.' He turned to me and smiled. 'I prefer the rule of law, Plataean.'

'I am a man of property, too,' I said. 'Not as rich as you lot, but I have a good farm, a forge, horses. I, too, treasure the rule of law. But when one side controls the laws, the other side must appeal to another court.'

Aristides nodded. 'We all wish to ask you to leave the city now.'

I smiled. 'You are going to run me out of town after all?'

Aristides nodded. 'We have to. You killed ten men – and most citizens know how. You will be welcomed back soon enough.'

I rose to my feet. 'Gentlemen, I have fought for Athens, bled for Athens and now I have schemed for Athens. The depth of your thanks never ceases to amaze me.'

Aristides shook his head. 'Don't be like that, Arimnestos. If you were one of us, we would all now fear your power. Since you are an ally, we can ask you to leave, and trust you again in the future.' He said this as if it made sense, and in a way it did. But I was hurt, too. I had planned a brilliant campaign, and the only person who thanked me was Irene, wife of Phrynichus.

'What can we do for you, Arimnestos?' Miltiades asked.

I had the good grace to laugh. 'Nothing, unless it is to make sure that Phrynichus doesn't starve while you all plot the future of Athens.' And then I had a thought. 'Perhaps I will have something after all. I have in my hand a set of manumission papers for a slave girl. They've all been signed by a magistrate – how about if you all sign them?'

Her name, it appeared on the tablets, was Apollonasia – quite a mouthful for a twist-foot slave girl from Boeotia, but Apollo's daughter she certainly was. And all three of them – the three most famous men of their generation – put their stamps and their names across the magistrate's mark on her tablets.

It was the best gift I could give her. I went and fetched her, and introduced her – her eyes cast modestly down – and each swore that they would remember her.

She walked with us, out of the city. I stopped on the Acropolis hill to say farewell to Phrynichus, and I stopped in Piraeus to say farewell to Agios and Paramanos, and I stopped at Eleusis to say farewell to Eumenios, who I'd barely seen, because in Attica, eighty stades is reckoned a great distance. Cleon came with me, of course. And on our last night in Attica, at Oinoe, where my brother died, she came into my blankets, and kissed me.

'I'm going in the morning,' she said. 'I'll be a farmer's wife in Attica, and my sight tells me I will see you again. I was a vessel to lead you, and now I am free.'

I murmured something, because I was hard as rock and wanted to have her, and I didn't need any of her moon-gazing female nonsense just then, but she bit my shoulder hard to get my attention.

'You owe me,' she said. 'Give me a child of yours, or I'll curse you. Again.'

So I did.

In the morning, she was gone. I did hear of her again, and I know who she married and who our child grew to be, as you'll hear eventually, if you all keep sitting here.

But I'll say this of her in eulogy. She was a hero, as much as Eumeles of Euboea or Aristides. She was a vessel for the gods, and she stood her ground, and when they treated her like shit, she did not become shit. Eh?

I can never lose the notion that if I had gone back for her, the Greeks might have won at Lade. Foolishness. But I still carry the guilt for leaving her to bloody Cleitus for a year.

And he didn't send her to a brothel because he was *evil*, either. That's what you do with a club-footed chattel with good breasts, if she has no skills. Right?

I'm an old man and I have few regrets, but she is one. And when she lay with me that night and took my seed – I felt better. I won't say otherwise. Much better.

When I awoke in the first light, she was gone, but sitting on my leather bag, where her dark head had lain just hours before, was a great black raven. It cawed once, and the beat of its wings frightened me, and then it rose into the sky with a cry.

I lay still with my heart beating hard, and my body felt lighter. Indeed, when I rose from my blankets, my hip and lower leg hurt less – much less. I've never run the stade since Lade, but from that moment I got something back. Something more than mere muscle and tissue.

II

My third return to Plataea was the easiest. Perhaps my fellow towns-men were becoming accustomed to my travels, or perhaps Simon, son of Simon, had just lost his supporters in Thebes and had no money with which to blacken my name. In any event, I went back over Cithaeron in winter, froze my arse in the high pass and made a sacrifice on the family altar nonetheless, and came down to green Plataea in time for spring harvest.

The truth is that Plataeans can be ignorant hicks, and it's possible that the winter was so cold that they never noticed I was gone.

Either way, I was there for the first harvest, the barley harvest, and my spirits were high – whatever the raven gave me, it was strong. I settled Cleon on a small farm in Cithaeron's shadow, and he seemed happy enough. I ploughed my fallow land with Hermogenes, and won his grudging praise for my unstinting work. I made new props for grape vines and I pruned everything I could get a sickle to. I gath-ered all my male slaves and on the spot freed the two Thracians who had been with me since my first return, and then told the rest exactly how they could work their way to freedom.

When the spring farm work was done, I threw myself into the forge, making pots and pitchers and cups and temple vases with Tiraeus and Bion. For twenty days, my forge was never silent. Even Hermogenes worked the forge, and that was rare, because despite his skills, he'd become a farmer first and foremost.

At the feast of Demeter, we danced the Pyrrhiche and I eyed the new crop of boys-become-men with the wary amusement that men have for boys. They preened and slunk away by turns, and lost their heads whenever a pretty girl walked by. Despite which, by the end of the festival, I had a notion of who was worthy and who was worth-less, and where they might stand in the phalanx.

I had not taken naturally to being the *strategos* of the town – or perhaps I had. My father was briefly the polemarch before his death – the war archon. And no man had been formally appointed to either role since his death. The Plataeans had not stood in battle a single day since the Week of Battles. Indeed, in all the town, there were only six of us who had faced iron in the storm of Ares since then.

There was me. There was Idomeneus, who was accepted as a citizen despite his alienness, because he was the priest of the hero. There was Ajax, a Plataean who had served with the Medes against us in the Chersonese, and of whom we nonetheless thought highly. There was Styges, who had followed us to Lade. Hermogenes had served me for two years in the Chersonese, and had fine armour and a steady hand. Lysius of Plataea was another local man – he'd served for four years under Miltiades before buying a good farm along the Asopus. That was it, in my generation.

The fifty Milesian families brought us a wealth of war experience. Teucer was the best archer our town had ever seen, and I used him to organize the men who carried bows – in those days, honey, archers still walked with the phalanx. And Alcaeus, who was the chief lord of the survivors, was as good a man in spear-fighting as Idomeneus, and owned full panoply, with thigh guards and arm armour and even foot armour shaped like his own feet, so that when he was fully kitted, he looked like a bronze statue.

The Milesians added real fighting power. And that allowed them – as Ionians and foreigners – to gain acceptance more rapidly than they might otherwise have done.

And finally, there was Cleon, who took one of Simon's former farms, a Corvaxae property that I granted him, just over the hill from mine, running hard by Epictetus's vineyards. He was never fond of war, but he'd stood in the front ranks several times. Plataea was delighted to have him, and Myron got up a collection to buy him an aspis and a helmet, as he had sold his.

In those days, a small city like Plataea knew that its warriors were its lifeblood, and we danced together as often as the feast cycle allowed. Young men hunted together on Cithaeron, and some – a few – came to the forge and learned spear-fighting, or went up the hill to Idomeneus or down the Asopus to Lysius. We all taught the same things – how to use your shield and your spear-shaft to keep the enemy's iron from your body, and only later how to plunge the iron home yourself.

As the bronze-smith, I had a fair idea who had armour and how good it was. As a group, Plataeans were well-to-do, thanks to the money Athens paid us for grain. And those famous three victories in a week had put good helmets and greaves in almost every farm. They might not fit every generation, but they were there, and when a new generation appeared, there was some trading and some trips to the bronze-smith. The men were as ready for war as dancing the war dance and wearing armour to exercise could make them.

That summer, I started the custom of taking a large group of young men up on to Cithaeron, camping, living hard and hunting. We are not aristocrats in Plataea, but what the Spartans say is true – it is only through hunting that men grow accustomed to war. Well, actually, life as a slave can make an adequate substitute, but I wouldn't recommend it as a training programme.

When the barley and the wheat were in the ground, when I'd sent two wagons of finished bronze away to Athens and another to Corinth, and before my grapes began to ripen, I told the men, young and old, who had gathered on a pleasant summer evening in the yard of my forge that I would lead a hunt on the mountain.

There were only two dozen of us, that first year. We walked up the long road on Cithaeron's flank, and I thought of my old tutor, Calchas, and how much he had taught me. I took the boys – I can't call them anything else – to Idomeneus, and he added in a dozen young men of his own, boys who had been sent to him to learn the ways of war. We stayed the night there and had a bonfire, and the boys listened open-mouthed as we told them war stories.

Cleon came along. He didn't say a word, and he drank too much – but he knew how to hold a spear.

And the next day we began to teach them to hunt deer.

Some of those boys had never thrown a real javelin. Now, boys are boys, and no boy in Plataea – at least, no citizen's son – was so poor that he hadn't made himself a straight stick with a sharp tip. But we Plataeans lack the organization of the Spartans or the Cretans or even the Athenians, where every citizen gets some training.

I wish I could tell you that I had the foresight to see what was coming – but I didn't. I felt, instead, that I owed something to my home city. By training boys, I could pay it back. So I led them up Cithaeron, killed some deer and tried not to laugh as I watched them stumble about, cut each other with axes, mis-throw their javelins and tell lies.

Boys. Was I ever so young?

Still, it was all a great success, although I had to keep Idomeneus off some of the prettier boys with a stick, and I truly wondered what kind of Cretan vices he was teaching the boys who were sent to him – but I was not his keeper. Together we led them up the mountain, and two weeks later when we came back down, they were leaner and faster and better men in every way – or at least, most were. And not just the boys. Cleon was much more himself. But in every herd there are a few animals doomed to die, and man is no different.

After the first time, men came and asked for their sons to be taken, and even some of the older men – such as Peneleos, son of Epictetus, who had no war training and wanted to catch up – came to me, and my life filled up. I worked, and in between bouts of work, I trained the young.

In early autumn, when the grapes began to ripen and I was watching the weather and all the farmers around me to see who would plough and plant barley, my sister arrived with gifts and a new baby, and we hugged her. She went and saw Mater, who mostly lived alone in a wine haze with a couple of slaves who knew their business. Then she came back, took a bite of dinner and shook her head.

'You need a wife,' she said.

I all but spat out my food.

'I've found you a fine one,' she went on. 'You need someone to run this house and take care of Mater. When's the last time you ate a decent meal?'

I looked at the food on my fine bronze plate. 'What's wrong with this?' I asked.

'Any peasant in the vale of Asopus eats better than this,' she said. 'Bread and cheese?'

'My own barley and my own cheese!' I said.

Penelope looked at me steadily. 'Listen, Hesiod,' she said, and giggled, and I had to laugh with her. Hesiod was a fine farmer and a brutal misogynist, and while I loved his words, I didn't agree with all of them. I knew what Pen meant.

'I don't need a wife,' I said.

'Which slave warms your bed?' she asked. 'Alete? Is it you?'

Alete was an old Thracian woman who helped with Mater. She grinned toothlessly. 'Nah, mistress,' she said. She laughed.

Pen looked around. 'Seriously – who is it?'

I shrugged. 'You are embarrassing me, sister. I have no bed-warmer in this house. It makes for bad feeling.'

'I'll tell you what makes for bad feeling,' Pen shot back. 'Surly men without wives, in dirty houses with dull food.' She looked at me. 'Unless that Cretan has trained you to like boys?'

I could feel the telltale signs of defeat. 'But I don't need a wife,' I said feebly.

'My lord's sister Leda went to school – a school for girls – at Corinth.' Pen was remorseless, like Persian archery. 'You get to choose her hair colour and I'll take care of the rest.'

'Black,' I said, almost unbidden. Black like Briseis, I thought. *I cannot marry – I love Briseis.*

But I knew Briseis was lost to me for ever, and I was lonely, in the brief heartbeats where I allowed myself to think about anything but work and training.

Later that autumn, when Atlas's fair daughters the Pleiades set, when all the grapes were in and those that went for wine were trodden and we had a week while we waited to see how good the wheat might be, I took almost a hundred men up the mountain. The harvest was already looking to be fabulous – perhaps legendary. And we needed a break from labour. Besides, deer meat kept many hearths fed that summer while we waited to see if the new year would do better than last year's evil rains, and the Milesians were poor – they had started with nothing, and every deer we killed kept their eyes shining. And in those days, honey, most Greeks lived and died on barley – and barley, as Hesiod says, goes into the ground when the Pleiades set and comes up when they rise – a winter crop. The Milesians needed food to get them through the winter.

This time we swept the slopes of the mountain with something like efficiency, and Idomeneus cursed and said we'd ruin the hunting. I promised that the next hunt would go up behind Eleutherai, a longer expedition and better training – and a new stock of deer. We killed seventy animals and carried the meat home, and while we were up on the mountain, the older men discussed politics and war.

The Persians were coming closer. The Great King had sworn to burn Athens, or so men said, and Eretria in Euboea too. The rumour was that Thebes was willing to swear fealty to the Great King for aid against Athens.

'We'll have to fight,' Peneleos said.

Everyone looked at me. And I was old and wise.

'Bullshit,' I said. 'The Persians are mighty, and their armies are huge and they own more triremes than all of the Greeks ever did – but do you know how *far* Sardis is from Athens?' So much for my wisdom. My only concern was closer to home. 'If the Thebans get involved,' I said, 'then we could find ourselves in a fight.'

'My pater says one Plataean is worth ten Thebans,' said young Diocles, son of Eumenides. Eumenides had stood his ground when my brother died at Oinoe.

'Your pater should know better,' I said. 'When the Thebans come, they'll have ten men for every one of ours. And our knees will rattle together like dry leaves in a wind.'

'We can stand against them in battle or stay in our walls,' Idomeneus said. 'What I would fear is raids – greedy men, well led, coming for cattle and slaves.'

'That's a scary thought,' Peneleos said. 'That's war the way bandits make war on honest men.'

Hermogenes was eating deer meat, and he belched. 'That's how war is made, out there in the world,' he said.

'Aye,' Cleon said.

'We should have an alarm, and a select group that could come out at a moment's notice and run down thieves,' Idomeneus said. 'Better yet, four or five alarms, all a little different, for the quarters of the territory around us, so that the moment we hear the alarm, we know where to run.'

We all agreed that the Cretan had a fine idea, and when next the assembly met after the feasts and contests of Heracles, I moved that we create a select militia and that the alarms be built, and it was carried. So those who took part in my deer hunts on the hillside became the Plataeans' *epilektoi*, the picked men, and we built the alarm fires and set signals after the wheat harvest, which old men said was the richest in twenty years, and some said the richest they'd ever seen. At the feast of Hera every one of us made sacrifice, so that smoke rose without cease to the heavens, and Hera smiled on us. The Milesians filled their cottages and their new barns, and sold the surplus over the mountains in Attica as we did, and their sons came up the mountain with me, and some began to buy my armour.

Cleon somehow managed to have a poor harvest in a year of plenty. I went to visit him, taking a wagon to fetch his surplus, and he brought me just ten medimnoi of grain.

'What in Pluton's name?' I swore. 'Did you sleep all day?'

Cleon looked at the ground. 'I'm not cut out to be a farmer,' he said.

'What will you eat this winter?' I asked.

He made a face. 'Your handouts?' he asked, and his voice was bitter.

Despite Cleon's failure, it was a good year. After my second plough-ing and before the turning of the year, when the days finally begin to get longer and the rains let up a little, I travelled over the mountains into Attica to meet my prospective bride, a girl of fourteen years called Euphoria, whose father was a wealthy cavalry-class man from the hills north of Athens. She had been Leda's schoolmate at Corinth, and she could read and sing and weave, and when I arrived ... well, she's worth a better story than that. So perhaps I should tell you how I met Euphoria.

12

She didn't have black hair. She was as blonde as the sun, and her hair was like a banner for men's attentions. Men crowded around Euphoria like vultures on a battlefield, like ravens on a new corn crop, like seagulls on a fishing boat with a fine catch, and she may have loved the attention she received, but she appeared to be immune, as some men are to the arrows of Apollo. She was showered in presents from the time she was old enough to walk, and some men called her Helen. Her father was Aleitus, a famous hunter, and her mother, Atlanta, had won every woman's foot race in Greece and was that rarest of creatures, a female athlete. Euphoria had the body of a grown woman when she was fourteen, with deep breasts and wide hips – and she had hair of gold. Have I mentioned that?

My sister filled me in on these details as we sat at the big farm table in the main kitchen of our house at the edge of winter. The hearth smoked, and the smoke rose through the rafters in beams of sunshine, like the arms of the gods reaching to earth. Still makes you cough, though.

Pen raised her hand and ordered more small beer with a crook of her finger. Life as the wife of an aristocrat agreed with her.

Her husband, Antigonus, was a good man. He doted on her and yet made good company for me, and several of his friends slept in the andron and would accompany us over the mountains. Pen told me that I needed some aristocratic friends. But the very idea of marrying into the aristocracy of Attica made my stomach roil, and the thought of marrying a famous beauty put me off my food.

'You are a famous man,' my sister said. 'You need to marry well.'

'I am the bronze-smith of Plataea,' I said. 'What will her father say if I take Tiraeus and Hermogenes?'

Pen stuck her tongue out at me. 'If he's as well bred as people say, he'll welcome them, and you. But why try his patience? And why don't you have any presentable friends?' She rolled her eyes at her husband's sister, Leda, who smiled knowingly and batted her eyelashes at all the male guests indiscriminately, despite being married to some lordling at Thebes.

'Miltiades? Aristides?' I laughed. 'Perhaps Idomeneus? Have you met Cleon?'

Mater made one of her rare appearances. She dropped on to a stool by Leda and barked her laugh. 'Idomeneus is very well bred,' she said, 'for a wolf.' She looked around at all of us. 'If you take Idomeneus, make sure he doesn't kill anyone. Penelope, motherhood agrees with you more than it ever agreed with me.' She beamed a mixture of wine and affection at us. 'I am *so pleased* to see both of my children returning to the class that your father abandoned.' She turned to me. 'Cleon is a stray dog, not a wolf. You'd do better to put him down – he'll bite your hand in the end.'

I went straight out to the forge and began to pound a lump of bronze with a hammer. I pounded it into sheet – a slave's job, but one that allowed me to hit something very hard, again and again, until I was calm and Mater was back in her rooms, drunk and silent.

But the next morning she was back again. 'Why don't you ask Miltiades to meet you?' she asked. 'He can stand as your mentor. He's a man of property, and as I have cause to remember, he has beautiful manners.'

'He's killed more men than Idomeneus,' I spat.

'Why must you behave like a beast, my love?' Mater asked, putting her hand on my face, so that I could smell the wine on her breath.

I steeled myself and gave no reply, except to go back to the forge and make sheet out of bronze stock – again.

My aristocratic guests were surprisingly tolerant of my affection for my forge. Idomeneus took them hunting, and on the third day of their visit I joined them, and we flushed a boar up behind Eleutherai in driving rain. Antigonus was there, and Alcaeus, the leading man of the former Milesians, as well as Teucer, who had a farm hard by my own purchased from waste land that Epictetus had been saving for his sons, Idomeneus, of course, and Ajax and Styges. My guests were Lykon, a very young man with pale skin like a girl and longer lashes than was quite right, and Philip, Antigonus's guest-friend from Thrace.

Philip was an excellent hunter, and in fact had been included by Penelope because his skills might impress the prospective father-in-law. Lykon was recklessly brave – the sort of courage that you have to show when you look like a pretty girl and have a high-pitched voice. I liked Lykon immediately – he was not afraid to wash our wooden bowls around the campfire, and now, faced with a boar, he simply lowered his spear-point and went at it.

Lykon was between the boar and me. We were in open woods, high on Cithaeron. The ground was broken and rocky and rose steeply behind the boar, and it was littered deeply with oak leaves that muffled sound and made movement treacherous. It was cold enough to numb your hand on your spear, and raining.

The hounds were as surprised as the rest of us. We'd been on the trail of a deer – a deer that Philip had wounded and we all wanted to bring home. The boar was no part of our hunt, but now our young-est man was facing it, and it was not small.

The boar put its head down and charged. Teucer leaped up on a stump and shot – no aiming, no pause to think – and his heavy war arrow punched the animal in the side and deflected it. It skidded to a stop and Teucer shot it again, then Lykon tried to get the point of his spear into it – but from inexperience, he didn't know that you never spear a pig in the face. The spear-point caught on the beast's snout, which is full of muscle and gristle, and glanced off its tusks – and the creature barged under his point, into his legs, and down he went.

Teucer put a third arrow into it as it tried to savage Lykon.

Philip and I reached it at the same instant. It backed a step and I put my point deep in the chest, under the chin, a low thrust as good as any I made in battle, and Philip, may the gods bless him, leaped high and plunged his point right down between the animal's shoulder blades. Then another arrow thudded home – I was so close that I saw dust fly from the beast's hide as it hit despite the rain – and Antigonus and Idomeneus were both there, adding the weight of their spears, and the thing was dead.

Lykon lay still, and for a long moment I thought his slim back was broken.

His right leg was ripped from knee to groin, a long but thankfully shallow gash that missed his privates by the breadth of a finger. And where he'd curled up to cover himself, the boar's snout had broken his nose and its tusk had slashed across his face.

He looked up at me, his face a mask of blood and tears. 'Sorry,' he said. 'I fucked that up.'

We laughed. Lykon was a man after that. The facial scar was a gift from the gods. No man would ever have taken him seriously without it. As it was . . .

Well, you'll hear, in time.

Lykon was the son of an important man from Corinth, a magistrate and shipowner, and Pen was very fond of him – all of us were. So we voted, like Greeks, to wait for his leg to heal before setting out. That meant two weeks of guesting three aristocrats, and the consequent drain on my pantries and staff.

I tried to think of it that way – the peasant way – but the truth is, they were fine men and I had a fine time. We hunted some days, and Idomeneus and Ajax came and stayed – for the first time, I'll add – and there was wine and talk in the andron every night.

In the second week, Cleon turned up. He had been to the house before, and Hermogenes liked him. So he came into the courtyard and Styges brought him wine.

The first I knew of it was the sound of raised voices outside my forge. I pushed out through the hide curtains and there was Cleon, red in the face, and my brother-in-law was being held by Philip.

'What are you doing?' I asked.

'This is what you brought me to Plataea to do?' Cleon asked. 'To be your servant?'

Lykon sprang forward despite his wound. 'Antigonus meant no offence,' the boy said. 'How could we know you are a free man?'

In truth, Cleon looked as if he had slept with dogs – his wool chiton was badly soiled and had wine stains all around the hem and down the front. He had no leg wraps under his sandals, and no chlamys or himation. He looked like a slave.

Antigonus had treated him like one, and Cleon had punched him.

Antigonus was a gentleman. He apologized, and admitted that he had committed hubris.

But Cleon's lips trembled and he walked out of my gate. 'I came . . .' he said, and then he spat. 'Never mind. I won't come again.'

He stalked off down the hill. I called his name, but then I let him go. You can only do so much for a man.

Mater was surprisingly sober. I'm not dull-witted – I know why. For once, Pen and I were living the life Mater had wanted, and she stayed sober enough to be part of it, although it might have been truer to the gruesome drunkard's creed if she'd managed to be roaring drunk and ruin the whole thing for everyone – the element of self-loathing in the drunkard is the ugliest part of the whole thing.

But she didn't. She and Pen sang with Leda and the better slaves joined in, and she did loom work in the andron while the men argued.

Mostly, we talked about the Persians. Antigonus and Lykon and Philip were equally awestruck that we'd served in the east. Philip saw the Great King as a force for good, a great aristocrat who would make the world a better place – but he liked a good war story. Lykon took the opposite tack – his father owned ships and had no time for Persia.

We debated when, and if, the Great King would come for Athens. Idomeneus and I insisted that we could have won Lade, and Philip maintained that the Great King could never be defeated.

We drank a great deal of wine. Pen mocked us from her loom, and Mater proclaimed that it was high time I stopped wandering the world like Odysseus and got myself a wife and some sons and daughters.

What I didn't know was that Mater had sent a messenger over the mountains, to Athens.

During his recovery, Lykon couldn't hunt, so he hobbled around the farm, asking hundreds of questions, and I returned one evening, cold through, with a deer across my horse and Philip's laughter floating up the hill from the crossroads where he was drinking with Peneleos.

Ting ting.

Ting ting.

I went into the forge, expecting to find Tiraeus, and there he was, sure enough, guiding Lykon through making a cup.

I laughed. 'I'm not sure what your father would think,' I said.

He laughed. 'Pater worries that I'll sleep with older men,' he said. 'He'd never object to a little work.'

Lykon's time in my shop put the seal of aristocratic approval on my smithing. I see that now. By the time Lykon was ready to go over the mountain, I had shown all of them how to start a helmet, and I had my brother-in-law's deep-bowled Corinthian roughed out, so that the skull stood proud to the cheekplates and the elegance of the shape had begun to show.

At any rate, we were fast friends by the time we rode up past the shrine, two by two – Antigonus with Pen, Idomeneus with Lykon, Teucer with Philip, Alcaeus with me, and a passel of slaves behind us on donkeys with hampers of food and some gifts. It was cold, and our breath rose to the heavens with the breath of the animals, as if we had fires burning inside us.

We had a snowstorm the second day, and we chose to stay an extra night back at the shrine. The two women who lived there asked me about Apollonasia, and when I told them that she was free and had a dowry of forty drachmas, they laughed and offered to follow me over the mountain. I didn't tell them the price the poor girl had had to pay for her dowry. I don't brag of my failures. But it served to remind me, when I was feeling cocky, of what failure was like.

I left the rest of them, rode to the summit despite the snow and made sacrifice there, surrounded by an endless field of white, with a clear view over all of the earth as far as I could see – out to sea to the south, and over all Boeotia to the north, so that the smoke of hearths in Thebes was a smudge that I could see far over the dance floor of Ares.

And all I could see in the rim of the world was war.

And then we rode down into Attica.

Aleitus had a tower. It was a fine building, of carefully cut stone in the Lesbian manner, and I liked it immediately, although the rooms smelled of smoke all the time. I had money – I thought that I might build myself a tower. Our house had had one once – a small thing. But the one Euphoria's father had was another thing entirely. It was elegant and strong.

He met us in his courtyard and I liked him, too, although he wasn't sure of me. He wasn't a big man, but well-muscled, grey-haired but with plenty of life left in his face, and he was surrounded by dogs – big boarhounds of a kind we don't have in Boeotia. The dogs barked and barked at so many strangers.

The blonde woman-girl who dashed into the courtyard and stood locked in an embrace with Leda had to be my intended bride, and I found that my tongue was stuck to the roof of my mouth.

She was beautiful, the way Briseis was beautiful. I looked at her, and I became aware that Pen was laughing at me.

Her father clapped me on the shoulder. 'Happens to all the suitors,' he said. 'Don't spend too much time with her – she'll eat your brain and leave you a drooling idiot. I've seen it happen again and again.' He laughed – the way a strong man laughs when he is wounded.

The young woman in question glanced at me, smiled and went back to her friend. So much for *my* vanity.

Still, that's why we have rules of hospitality and customs – to pass the time when our brains are fuddled by sex. I managed to get down from my horse and introduce my friends and my sister, and then we were in his hall and my slaves were laying out a selection of my gifts.

One of the many rewards for a life of piracy was that I had some beautiful things to give as gifts. Aleitus received a gold and coral necklace from Aegypt, and a gold cup that had come off the captain's table of some Phoenician merchantman, with a long body and a swan's head. That was for Euphoria.

My Tyrian dyed wool passed without comment, and a pair of bronze water pitchers – my own work, let me add – were virtually ignored. But I'd made a pair of boar spears to match the ones I'd seen at Aristides' house, with long staves and sharp bronze butt-spikes and heavy heads, and Aleitus passed over some much richer gifts to pounce on them.

'Now, these are a sight for sore eyes, lad!' he pronounced.

No one had called me lad in quite some time. It made me laugh.

Still, the company was good, and Euphoria sang and showed us her weaving, which I have to admit was superb. In fact, I'd never seen such fine work from a girl her age.

'I love to weave,' she said, and it was the first serious, grown-up thing I heard her say. 'Do you know anything about weaving?'

I thought about a number of answers – I had, after all, watched my mother and sister weave all my life. 'No,' I said.

'Is it true that you are a master smith?' she asked.

'It is true,' I said.

Her eyes went back to her loom. 'Are your hands always dirty?' she asked.

'Often,' I allowed.

She nodded. 'Then if we wed, you must be careful not to touch my wool,' she said. Her eyes flitted across mine. 'I should like to marry a man who could make something,' she added. 'But Pater says you are low, so I shall not get my hopes up.' She wore an enigmatic half-smile as she said this, and I was too much a fool to realize that this girl-woman was playing me like a lyre.

Low, is it? I thought. But I wiped the rage from my face.

We hunted rabbits the first day, and I knew from the start that I was being tested. It was wonderful. I felt as if I was living in the epics, and here I was competing for Atlanta, or Helen, or Penelope.

The wound on my leg didn't bother me as it had, but I still had trouble keeping up with Lykon and Philip, and it was all I could do to run the rabbits down. Philip killed four and Lykon two – but Lykon, without a word, began to edge them my way in the last hours, and I managed to kill two with my club before the sun set.

'I would have expected a man as famous as you to be faster,' Aleitus said. It was not quite a sneer – indeed, by the standards of a rabbit hunt, any man who killed was allowed to wear a garland – but his barb went home. Fleetness of foot is one of the most important aspects of war-training, as the Poet recognizes when he calls Achilles 'swift footed'.

I swallowed my anger and nodded. 'I was swifter,' I said, 'when I was younger.'

Aleitus laughed. 'Not yet old enough to know when an excuse is hollow,' he said.

I almost rode away that day. But my friends calmed me.

The second day we got a dose of winter rains, and we stayed indoors, listened to the women sing and swapped stories. I told some of the stories I'm telling now, and my host's doubts were plain on his face, and some of his friends – local gentlemen – sneered.

Let me pause here to say something about them. They were hippeis and richer – rich farmers, aristocrats, mostly of the eupatridae – and most of them shunned Athens the way other men shun impiety. They never went into the city – the city I had already come to love. They had their own countryside temples, and sometimes they went to the assembly to vote, but they were the 'country' party, and they loathed the oarsmen and the metics and the tradesmen, and wanted Athens to be Sparta – a land of aristocratic farmers. To them, I was a combination of alien things – a smith, a foreigner. But they were, taken together, good men.

When the weather cleared in the afternoon, we went out into the fields below his tower to throw javelins. I have my moments with the javelin, but I've never practised as much as I ought, and while Apollo and Zeus have sent me some good throws, none came to me that day. My first was so bad that men laughed. One of the 'local gentlemen' was heard to say that my reputation as a killer of men must be one of those 'provincial tales' that would not stand up to scrutiny.

Idomeneus grinned from ear to ear and came to stand by me. We shared the same thought – to kill the fool. But my brother-in-law, Antigonus, who by that time I loved like a brother, kicked me – *hard* – in the shin. I whirled on him, looking for blood. He stood his ground. 'They want to provoke you,' he hissed. 'Do you want the girl or not?'

Antigonus was the right man to be my brother-in-law, that's for certain. I took a deep breath and walked away. It was a close thing – if one of them had laughed again, there would have been blood.

The third day, we hunted deer in the hills north of the city. More of the local gentlemen came along, and it turned out that we were hunting in teams – in a competition.

I had all my travelling companions in my team. We didn't know the ground and we didn't know the habits of the local deer, and neither my prospective father-in-law nor any of his friends showed the slightest compunction in abandoning us to our ignorance. We were left on a mountain road. In the distance, we could see the sea by the shrine of Heracles, over towards Marathon. The countryside was beautiful in the weak winter sun.

I waited until my competition was out of sight.

'Right,' I said. 'Philip, you are the best hunter. My guess is that we should go downhill to the water.'

Philip glowed with pride at being singled out among so many warriors. 'Water – yes,' he said. Then he shrugged. 'But I smell rotting apples, and if there's one thing deer love in winter, it's an old apple orchard.'

We broke up then, going six different ways to locate the apple orchard like scouts for an army. It was down the hill, almost ten stades away – Philip had the nose of a hound. But we found it.

Philip came up to me. I was still mounted.

'There are deer lying in the orchard,' he said. 'At least six, and perhaps more. You and Idomeneus are the best spears – yes?'

I nodded. 'And Teucer,' I said.

Philip grinned – he valued the archer. 'Of course. The rest of us will push the deer into you, if you'll make the crawl.'

He got me to a tall rock that rose like a temple column and helped me climb it. From the top, we could see the apple trees, hoary old things with all their leaves down, and I could see the brown-grey smears that were deer lying in the high, dead grass.

Then passed an anxious hour, as Idomeneus and Teucer and I crawled around the orchard to get downwind of the beasts. Twice, we heard the local party blowing horns in triumph, and on one occasion we could see one of the bucks raise his head to look for the sound.

Philip and the beaters started too early – or perhaps we were too slow pushing our spears through the wet, cold grass. Either way, we were a hundred paces from where we wanted to be when Philip blew his horn and the deer began to scramble to their feet.

I leaped up, cursed and began to run.

Teucer didn't. He rose to one knee and started to shoot.

He saved us from failure. We would never have reached those deer – my best throw with my best spear fell short – but Teucer knocked six down with eight arrows, incredible work at that range through scattered trees and high grass.

But then teamwork came into it, because none of his arrows killed, and we ran at the wounded animals, me calling out orders, the other men spreading out from two sides.

I was running hard, cursing my leg, and I saw my mis-thrown spear sticking in the ground and managed to grab the haft without slowing. The biggest buck was vanishing from view into a thicket of dogwood and thorns. I plunged after it and it turned – a big stag, as tall at the shoulder as a small horse.

I threw my good spear and the beast shied and took a blow meant for the head on the shoulder, but he fell, and I was on him with my other spear. I thrust home twice, and the animal shuddered, and his eyes filmed over, and he lay still.

I felt more for that stag than I do for many men I kill. He was a magnificent animal, trapped, with no chance at all – the dogs had been released by then and they were hard by us.

So I knelt, closed the stag's eyes and said a prayer to Artemis, then I pulled my throwing spear clear of his shoulder and followed the sound of the dogs.

By the time I caught the pack, all six animals were dead. We were a good group, and every man followed the nearest target without much shouting and did his duty.

Then came the work. We had six dead deer, and we treed them in the apple orchard, split and gutted them, then began to clean them. We were far from water, and despite the chill of the morning, we stripped naked to save our clothes. And we were pious men, and Lykon and Philip, who both revered Artemis, led us in a hymn we didn't know, and we burned the first fruits of the beasts – their hearts and livers – on a rock that had certainly served as an altar before. By the time the last carcass was ready to be moved, we were covered in blood and ordure, and we walked down the road like a Dionysian revel gone hideously awry. We bathed in a stream, and laughed, and threw icy water at each other.

But when we were dressed, I arranged to put the carcasses on donkeys, and I paid a pair of farm boys to bring them along by the high road and not the farm road, and then my whole party returned to the tower, apparently empty-handed.

Aleitus and his friends were drinking in the courtyard, and they laughed at our discomfiture, and made ribald comments about what we could have been doing in the woods, ten men alone, that we were wet and had no deer and were so clean.

Euphoria came down the stone steps from the tower to the courtyard with a tray of wine cups, and conversation stilled. She had that effect, with her slanting eyes and her long, straight nose.

'If you caught no deer,' she said to me quietly, as she handed me a cup, 'why do you have blood under your nails?'

I smiled into her eyes. 'You are observant,' I said.

'You play dangerous games,' she answered.

And truly, when our deer arrived, the local men were silent, and their eyes were not friendly. We had killed six to their two. Now let me tell you children, lest you wonder, that in those days, a kill of two deer for a party of ten men was a fine catch – and six deer was a ridiculous bag, almost an affront to Artemis. Bordering on hubris.

I cared nothing for those men. If men will seek to compete, they must take the consequences. I do not push myself on others – but ever they will strive against me, and the result is always the same. I mean no boasting, by the gods!

Aleitus looked at the row of carcasses and he turned to me, and his face was red. 'Do you not fear that you affront Artemis, with so many kills?'

I shook my head. 'No, lord. I made immediate sacrifice of the first fruits of every animal, and I prayed as soon as my spear went home in the stag, who is, you must allow, a magnificent animal.' I walked over to him. 'Am I mistaken, lord? Or was it your intention that we should *compete* at hunting?' And I laughed in his face.

He was angry. But he mastered his anger, like a man of breeding, and merely raised an eyebrow. 'The slaves will eat well,' he said. 'If I'd known of your prowess, I'd have invited more guests.'

243

There was a laugh from the gate – a laugh I knew well. 'Did you set Arimnestos a challenge?' Miltiades said.

He slid off his horse, magnificent in a cloth-of-gold chlamys over a purple chiton worn double-belted for riding. His horse had a gold harness, and there were four men with him, each armed with a boar spear and riding matching black horses.

Miltiades defied convention by embracing me before embracing the host. Then he turned to Aleitus. 'He used to drive me wild,' Miltiades said. 'Any task he's set, he excels – or breaks the tools. And when challenged, he is a dangerous animal, our Plataean.'

Miltiades' charisma filled the courtyard. I was a famous man in those days – but Miltiades was the sort of man who bestrode the earth, and other men crowded around to see him. And he had come to be part of *my* hunting party.

'Let me see this girl I've heard so much about,' Miltiades demanded. 'Where is she?'

Aleitus rubbed his eyes. 'Lord Miltiades?' he said.

'I'm sorry, Aleitus. I was invited to join this young scapegrace's hunting party, and I'm late. Am I still welcome? I think our grandfathers were guest-friends. And I must say, I've brought you some fair gifts.' He boomed with laughter.

Aleitus looked as if the gods from Olympus had just arrived. 'Lord, it is an *honour* to have you to guest. I had no idea our grandfathers were guest-friends, but I would be delighted – that is, I'm very pleased. Come and drink this cup with me.'

Aleitus was just beginning to recover when Miltiades slapped me on the back and laughed. 'And that prig Aristides is on his way as well,' he said.

I thought my prospective father-in-law might faint.

Mater had invited them in my name, and her instincts, wine-sodden as they might have been, were keen. For a party of Boeotians to ride rough-shod over the local countryside, slaughtering deer and making local men feel small, would, no doubt, have ended badly for someone. But it was hard for any bad feeling to survive when Miltiades was in a hospitable mood, and Aristides was the exemplar of arete, and between the two of them they created an atmosphere that the rest of us could only strive to emulate. In fact, they made me feel young.

That week was, I think, my reward for the rescue of Miltiades.

Great lords of Athens don't usually have a week to waste hunting. On the other hand, I can imagine what Mater wrote:

If you want to cement your alliance with Plataea and my son, go hunting with him and get him his Attic bride.

Say what you will about Mater – and I do, believe me – she understood how aristocrats think and work. Marriage is not pleasure – it is alliance and bargain, and great men use their daughters the way peasants use a prize foal. As I will, thugater. Bah – I'll find you a pretty one. This fellow from Halicarnassus . . .

To be honest, when I arrived, I had the feeling that my suit would be rejected at the first decent interval, and after the young lady called me 'low' I wanted no more part of the game save to humiliate my host. But the arrival of my famous friends altered the balance. What had appeared manly revenge the previous night now felt petty and mean-spirited, and over wine that night, I rose and apologized to all the men – mine and my hosts – for playing such a foolish joke.

'I suffer from pride,' I said to my host. 'It is a fatal error in a man who is but a bronze-smith, to seek always to compete in every game.'

Aleitus showed his mettle then. He rose, took my cup from my lips and drank from it. 'You speak like a hero,' he said. 'I sought to belittle you. Men told me you were low-born, and brought only dirty hands to my table.' He glanced at Aristides, who returned a hard smile. 'I will be more careful who I listen to in future.'

'Cleitus, of course,' Aristides said later that night. 'Anything you put your hand to in Attica, he will try to destroy. He has sworn your death, and your ruin.'

I shrugged.

The rest of the week passed very pleasantly. We ate a great deal of deer meat, and we failed to find a boar, to my host's deep annoyance, and I invited him to come and hunt with us on the flanks of Cithaeron.

But it was the evenings that live in my memory. Hunting becomes a blur – to be honest, if it hadn't been for the killing of six deer, I doubt I'd remember anything about that. Killing deer is seldom memorable the way killing men is memorable. Deer don't fight back.

At any rate, it was during that week that I lay on a couch with Miltiades, and Aristides, and drank good wine, and learned that Datis had a fleet, and was raising an army, and that his target, the target ordered by his king, was Athens.

245

13

It was bound to happen. I may have been foolish enough to imagine that Darius would forget Athens, or that his reach wasn't long enough to punish the one Greek state powerful enough to contest with him – but I was wrong. Darius never forgot Athens, and as the dead of Lade rotted on the sea floor and the timbers of broken ships washed ashore to become firewood, as a year passed, and another, and Artaphernes sought to heal the wounds Datis had caused and return his satrapy to peace and prosperity, so Datis, ever eager for power and the praise of his uncle, raised ships and soldiers for a new expedition. His intention was to do to Athens what he perceived Athens had done to Sardis – to sack the Acropolis and burn her temples.

For whatever reason, Datis bragged of his intentions. So when ships docked at Ephesus and Tyre, and on the blackened quay where men were rebuilding Miletus, they saw the evidence of the gathering of a mighty fleet, and they heard tell of a regiment of Sakai, the bronze-clad heavy archers from the steppes of Colchis, and two regiments of Medes, marching all the way from Persepolis to bolster the Lydians and Carians in Datis's army.

I will digress here to say that I have always thought that Datis planned to take Sardis for himself, and then to knock Darius from his throne and make himself King of Kings. Such has always been the Persian way – the war among the strong makes the winner stronger still. Not unlike the Greek way, come to think of it. Very like the competition to be first man in Athens, if you ask me.

Miltiades told me of the Sakai and the Medes while lying at my side, eating figs. 'Paramanos brought me that titbit,' he said, 'from a messenger who came over the passes from our friend the Jew of Sardis.'

I admit that even there, in the safety of Attica, far from Sardis, I felt a frisson of fear. 'So Datis is really coming,' I asked. And I thought of Artaphernes – and Briseis.

As if my thought could be translated into concrete reality, Miltiades put a small ivory tube in my hand. 'Another friend sent me this,' he said. 'Datis really is coming.'

I opened the tube and took out a scroll, and my heart hammered in my chest. For the first time in days I forgot Euphoria, her father, my farm and my forge. In my hand was a slip of paper in Briseis's handwriting.

Datis sails after the great feast of Artemis. 660 ships, 12,000 men.
Tell Doru that I live and so does my brother.
Tell him that our Heraclitus took his life after Lade.

I couldn't breathe. 'I thought her brother was dead too,' Miltiades said. 'Now he commands ships in the Great King's fleet. He is becoming a great man, among the Greeks who serve Persia.'

I barely paid him a thought. 'Heraclitus is dead,' I said. I wept.

But in my head, I rejoiced, because Briseis was not dead, and she had written to me.

'He is.' Miltiades rolled on his back, drank wine from the kylix that was circulating and flipped the lees across the room, where they rang on the rim of one of my bronze water urns. He cared little for Heraclitus, or any philosophy. 'If they come,' he asked carefully, 'can Athens count on Plataea?'

Suddenly, his addition to my hunting party was put in perspective. But he had, at least, waited two days to ask his question.

A hush fell over our part of the party, and I could see Aristides, who lay with Sophanes, lean towards me, the better to hear me.

I laughed grimly. 'Unlike Athens,' I said, 'Plataea is a democracy. We would have to vote to stand with you against the Medes.' Then, seeing their faces, I shook my head. 'You know we will stand with you. Plataea exists because Athens stands ready to march on Thebes. We are not ingrates.'

Aristides rolled off his couch and clapped my shoulder. 'I told you he was a man of honour,' he said. Perhaps not his best-thought-out compliment.

Miltiades looked serious. 'This won't be about honour,' he said. 'This will be about survival.' He looked at me seriously. 'Forget

Briseis, boy. She is not for you. Marry this girl, have strong sons and help me save Greece. That is your fate.'

Just for a moment, I hated him. Then I caught sight of Euphoria at her loom. She was chatting with Lykon – but she flashed me a smile.

In telling of politics, I threaten to forget Euphoria, which is unfair to her. She adorned some dinners, and played the kithara for us, and she and Pen and Leda sang together. I still remember them, their heads together, singing the Paean of Apollo in a way that haunted me, their high voices like the Muses themselves, and I mean no hubris, one voice brushing lightly on another in the heart of the music.

And there was a small feast – I think it was a local peasant feast, for Pan, who is a peasant god from the old days and almost unknown here. In normal times, I don't think the household would have been allowed a feast, but with so many important guests – and more came in, including Themistocles, of all men!

He took my hand and embraced me. 'Well met, Plataean,' he said.

I considered a sharp reply – but again, the dignity of my elders restrained me. So I returned his embrace and we were reconciled.

Aleitus gathered his people and took us all on a cold picnic to the shrine of Pan in the hills, fifteen stades away.

The festival was a small thing, and had never seen so many rich, famous men. But Miltiades refused to allow the 'big men' to wreck it. This is where his touch was gold. He threw himself into dances and drank harsh new red wine with shepherds and farmers, and Aristides and Themistocles had no choice but to join him. I think they were better for it.

We sacrificed a bull to Pan, the richest sacrifice any man there could remember, and we added a hundred voices to the hymns. As darkness fell we gathered wood for a bonfire that was the largest I think I ever saw, because after a week of *agon*, manly competition, even gathering firewood was something at which every man sought to excel. The farmers and peasants laughed to be waited on by Euphoria and Penelope and Leda and half a dozen other gentlewomen.

When the dancing started, it was clear that on this hilltop the women danced with the men, and Aleitus allowed it, and so our maidens and matrons joined the ring of women, and we saw them dance – a rare sight in those days and rarer today. I remember spinning Euphoria in the middle of the circle when it was my turn, and her face grinning up into mine. And when the men and women went off into the dark, I envied them. I tried to kiss her at the edge of the fire, and she laughed and slipped under my arm and vanished. A few moments later, she was with Pen and Leda, giggling. Pen waved at me – and I could not take offence. Aristocrats' daughters do not lose their virginity on the cold grass.

Briseis would have, though.

While I was thinking on Euphoria and Briseis – their similarities and differences – Miltiades came up and put a hand on my shoulder. 'Marry her quick, before she sees how old and ugly you are,' he said.

I tried to smile, but I couldn't. She was talking to Lykon, who was, I fear, both younger and prettier than me. But even as my heart began to grow warm, Lykon pointed at me across the fire – and when his gaze met mine, he smiled.

I smiled back. Hard to be jealous of a boy so open-hearted as to plead your suit for you. Which I still think he might have been doing.

'Cleitus has gone into exile,' Miltiades said.

'That sounds good,' I said. My thoughts were elsewhere.

'Not for you, Plataean. He swore at the Temple of Athena to have your head. I have witnesses. He went into voluntary exile to have a freer hand in arranging his revenge and my downfall. He's hiring mercenaries from all over Greece – masterless men and wandering warriors.'

I laughed. I could deal with Cleitus much more easily than I could deal with Euphoria. The firelight played on her golden hair and turned it orange, and now she and Pen and Leda were dancing together, a woman's dance that moved the hips and shoulders. Euphoria swayed her hips in a way that suggested there was fire in her, and I had to look away. My eyes met Miltiades'.

He shook his head in mock disbelief. 'You've got it bad, Doru.'

I shrugged. I didn't see any point in denying it, as my eyes had already gone back to her.

Lykon was watching her, too.

'Cleitus means to kill you,' Miltiades said.

I shrugged again. 'He's welcome to try.'

'Your arrogance borders on hubris, lad.' Miltiades put an arm around my shoulder. 'I think one of the reasons I've always loved you is that you remind me so much of me,' he said, with a little self-mockery. He held out a skin of resinated wine, and I took a healthy pull. 'He won't come at you for single combat. He'll come with a hundred men.'

Just then, watching Lykon devour Euphoria with his eyes, and watching her shy return of his attentions, I would happily have fought all hundred as a demonstration sport, as men sometimes fought duels at the Olympics. 'Into Plataea?' I asked, thinking about it. 'What, from Thebes?'

'Or from the sea,' Miltiades answered. 'It's only forty stades.'

I nodded, sobered. And as I considered how to defend myself from that whoreson Cleitus, Euphoria linked arms with the other girls and, hands high, they began to sway – all their hips shot out together, like married women in the Dionysian dances, and they dissolved into giggles – and then across the fire, her eyes locked with mine.

She didn't look away, and I could have stared at her for ever just then. One lock of her bright gold hair was loose, and it trailed away on the wind of the fire, and her face was the face of a goddess. A golden-haired goddess.

Aristides and Sophanes pushed forward through the throng to stand with Miltiades and me.

'Now, this is a party!' Sophanes shouted. He was just twenty, I think, and he'd fought well on the Lade campaign, of course. He was newly married and in love with all the world. 'I wish my wife was here,' he added. 'I'd carry her off into the dark like a satyr.'

'And she'd tell you that she was too cold for love,' Miltiades said.

'Not my wife,' Sophanes said. 'I keep her warm.'

Aristides put his hand on my arm and looked at Miltiades. 'You warned him?' he said.

'I did,' the big man answered. 'And he laughed it off. Love has obscured his fine sense of danger.'

Aristides shook his head. 'If the Medes come in the spring,' he said, 'you and your Plataeans will matter very much to us. This is more than friendship. Watch yourself.'

Euphoria had disappeared into the darkness.

'If Cleitus comes at me in Plataea, I'll make a drinking cup of his skull,' I said.

Aristides choked on his wine.

'That's my boy,' Miltiades said.

★

Euphoria never burned my heart like Briseis – but suddenly she was in it. So on the last day, I went to her father, bowed and asked for her hand.

Behind me stood Miltiades and Aristides, Alcaeus, Antigonus, Philip and Themistocles and a dozen other gentlemen.

He looked around at them before he met my eye. 'I suspect it would be political death for me to refuse you,' he said. And he smiled, and I thought that, despite our first brushes, we might grow to be friends. 'But I swore to Artemis when her mother was dying that I would allow her a choice in the matter of her husband. Shall I send for her?'

Suddenly, I found myself nervous – I who had cleared the deck of a Phoenician trireme by myself. My heart beat the way it does just before I enter a fight, and I wanted to get away.

Euphoria came down to the courtyard surrounded by the other girls. Pen led her down the steps and Leda was hard at her heels. But they weren't giggling or playing. They were solemn, and Pen wouldn't meet my eye.

It was the dirty hands that did it, I realized. She didn't want a low-born smith who would soil her weaving. She wanted someone like Aristides, who could stand in the front rank when required, but otherwise kept his hands clean.

It was rather like a lost battle. Once I saw how doomed my case was, my calm returned and I determined – because I liked her very well – to bear her refusal with a good grace.

She walked up to me, eyes downcast, her blonde hair piled artlessly on her head and neck. Her simple wool chiton was woven from wool that probably came from their own sheep, and it showed off her figure – her slim, slightly rounded waist and her wide hips and straight back. Few women have dignity at fourteen. Euphoria had it. She came up close to me, and only then did I realize how much shorter than me she was – by a head or more. She gave the impression of height with her dignity and carriage.

I expected her eyes to flick to Lykon, but they did not. They stayed firmly fixed on the ground in front of her.

'Lovely maiden,' I said. I managed a smile. 'You would make me the happiest of men if you would consent to be my bride. Yet,' I added, to soften the blow, 'I live in far-off Boeotia, on a farm, and I hammer bronze for my bread, and no one will understand better than me if you choose to stay closer to hearth and home.'

Then she raised her eyes – a pale blue, like good steel. And she smiled, a sort of half-smile as if she was about to laugh – at herself. 'My loom will be as comfortable by your forge as it would be in any house in Attica, I expect,' she said.

Pen was grinning.

I didn't understand, and in my confusion, I tried to think of something noble or witty to say, to turn aside my disappointment. I've been told twenty times by friends that I had never looked like such a fool in all my life, and that what I said was 'Huh?'

She laughed aloud, a real laugh, such as maidens usually hide, so that her belly moved and her breasts rose and fell under the bindings of her chiton.

'Yes!' Pen said to me, poking me in the side. 'She said yes!'

She said yes?

It took me a long time to understand. Not until I had digested her agreement did I understand how important it had become to me that she had said yes. In the time it takes Zeus to throw a bolt to earth, at the whim of a maiden, my life changed.

14

We set the wedding for late winter, and I rode back over the mountains with my companions. We celebrated the feast of Artemis at Plataea, and they rode away to their homes.

It is one of the saddest comments on men, honey, that war and death make for a long story, but a winter of contentment and happiness can pass in a single breath. Our barns were full, our byres were full and all that winter we hunted on Cithaeron, we danced the Pyrrhiche and we discussed strategies against Persia. Women sat at their looms and wove and put in their own comments. We stored food, we worked on our leather. My forge roared every day as I made helmets – a few good ones, and more of the new-style open-faced bowls, which men now call 'Boeotians'. We called them dog-caps. If not for Cleon, the winter would have been perfect – and forgettable.

I spent my spare time learning to engrave. Tiraeus knew something of it, and had a set of gravers among the tools he'd brought with him from when he was a tinker. I bought more tools, fine steel from Corinth.

But a few weeks before I was due to return to Attica, I found Cleon lying out in the freezing rain, drunk and asleep. At first I thought he was dead. I took him home, cleaned him and sobered him, and then he wept.

The next day, he was drunk again. I waited him out and sobered him up.

Tiraeus was in the shop. 'You're wasting your time,' he said. 'He's a drunk. Let him go.'

'He saved my life once.' I went back to trying to scratch marks accurately on smooth bronze.

By now I was a better engraver than Tiraeus, and I began to put borders on everything I made, acanthus leaves, olive leaves, laurels, waves, whatever I fancied. I was planning to make a fine table setting for my new wife.

Instead, I kept having to sober Cleon. He cost me a day's ploughing, as I had to leave the turning of the wet, cold earth to other men so that I could sit inside with him. But after another day of it, and with due apologies to Hermogenes and Tiraeus and Styges, who, in effect, lived with me, I sent all the wine away to my warehouse in the town. All of it. We had nothing to drink on the hill but water.

Cleon still managed to find wine, however. He was drunk again the next day, drunk and desperately sorry, so that he followed me around the farm begging me to forgive him and kill him. I'm ashamed to say I punched him and left him where he fell.

On his fifth day in my house he tried to fall on one of my swords. He wedged the sword into the cracks in a floorboard, but he was drunk and botched it, so that when he fell, his weight *mostly* knocked the blade flat. He ripped himself open over the ribs, and all the slaves had to help move him and clean him.

That night, Mater came downstairs. She came down to where I was sitting with him in the andron. I had no thoughts in my head – I was just going through the motions of friendship, because in just five days I had come to loathe him and his weakness.

But Mater came down, and she sat by him. 'Leave him to me,' she said.

So I did.

I have no idea what she said – as one drunk to another.

But the next week, just a few days before I left for Attica, he came out to the forge, sober and in a clean chiton. He sat on the hearth for a while and watched me. I was trying to engrave a pattern of animals – I wanted to put my stag on the bowl I was finishing, and I had botched it so badly that I was angrily polishing the lines off again.

'May I show you how to draw a stag?' Cleon asked. He was so hesitant it would have broken your heart, honey.

I was none too tender with him. 'Try,' I said. 'Be my guest.'

I don't know what I expected – when drunk, men claim all sorts of skills, and I still didn't know whether he had had a skinful or not, although he looked pale enough.

He took the metal to the rawhide window for light, and he took my black wax and began to draw.

In three lines, I could see the stag. Before he had the antlers done, he wiped the whole right off the bronze and started again, but this time his hand was surer, and the lines went down as if he were copy-ing them from something he could see – and perhaps he could, inside his head.

I was delighted. I was delighted in many different ways – as a crafts-man, as a friend, as a man trying to reclaim a drunk from Hades.

And when I took the graver in my fist, he snatched it from me. 'I do clay, mostly,' he said, 'but I know how to grave metal.'

I held up one of my borders. 'As do I,' I said.

He frowned. 'You are scratching,' he said. 'You need to cut the metal.' He picked up my heaviest graver and began to push it across the surface of my bowl. 'Like this. Careful strokes. Deeper where you want a heavier line.'

At first his hands were tentative and slow, and he left tiny errors on the lines – still deeper and better cut than mine, but wavering. But then he drank some warm milk, and his hand steadied, and before the afternoon was over, Tiraeus had slapped him on the back and the three of us polished the finished bowl together and set it in the glow of the fire to admire our shared work.

'Can you stay sober?' I asked him.

He looked at me. 'I doubt it,' he said. 'How much engraving do you have for me?'

Tiraeus laughed. But I knew he was telling the truth.

I remember the ride over the mountains. We'd already started the first ploughing, and as Hesiod says, 'The boneless one is gnawing on his foot'.

It was the ugly time when the days grow longer, but only so that more rain can fall, and still nothing comes from the earth, and men think winter may never break. There was snow everywhere on the mountain, and yet our horses made short work of the ride, and we came down into the plains of Attica without losing a toe from frost-bite.

Aristides was there first, with Jocasta, an unexpected ally in this marriage business, and she and Pen were immediate friends. Miltiades came with his wife, a vapid Thracian princess I'd met often enough before. Even the Alcmaeonids were represented in the person of Kineas, an elder, a member of the Areopagitica and a powerful man. He was pleasant and dignified. It was a very public wedding, and the little Temple of Aphrodite where we were bound together was filled to the outer row of pillars with guests.

I remember little of the ceremony except my own sense of importance, which makes me laugh now. I was delighted that so many famous men had come, and yet I was decent enough to be equally delighted to see Paramanos and Agios and Harpagos, whose ship was in Piraeus and who had kept his cargo waiting to come up and kiss my bride. With them were a dozen oarsmen and marines who had the wherewithal to travel into the hills above Marathon to see me wed.

Euphoria was so beautiful on her wedding day that I couldn't think of much else, to tell the truth. I remember the look in her eyes when I lifted the veil, and I remember how she rested her hip against mine in the chariot as we rode from her father's house to the house we had borrowed to be 'mine'. Her women bathed her – winter is an unkind time for weddings, I have to tell you – and men sang songs about the size of my member and the depth of her cunny – oh, you blush, my dear. You've never heard wedding songs?

And when I undressed her, she devoured me. Who knew that under her humour and her nimble fingers and equally nimble head lurked a woman of flesh and blood? We coupled – well, all night. Her body was like a feast, and all I could do was eat.

But I'll keep the rest of those memories for myself. I will only brag, like other bridegrooms I have known, that I kept her warm, and she craved my warmth often enough to make my sister blush. Like you, blushing girl – but not so often nor so red. Look, friends – she's gone off again! You could heat a room with her warmth!

We rode back over the passes into Boeotia and started our new lives.

And for the rest, I remember little enough. Except that we were happy, and healthy, and in love.

It didn't last. Nothing worth having ever does. But it was the happiest time of my young life.

15

Spring in Boeotia. The feast of Persephone, the dancing maidens, the birth of ewes and kids, the rain, the mud, the first green, and then the burst of flowers from the ground as if the earth is impatient for new life – which she is. And soon enough, the barley harvest, which was as rich and fecund as the autumn wheat harvest had been.

Euphoria was pregnant. She filled our old house with herself, and as soon as the jasmine blossomed we had sprigs of it in every room. There were flower-wreaths on every door, and a dozen new women, her women, and her father's gift to me, with as many boarhounds – and they wove and chattered and cooked and laughed and barked.

Mater bloomed as well. I heard her singing with Euphoria on the second day she was in my house, and I shook my head, waiting for my new wife to discover what a horror my mother really was. But Mater did not fail.

Was it Cleon? Was Cleon a mirror to her? Or was it having a daughter-in-law of her own class that brought her downstairs and into our lives?

I grumbled. I won't lie. I had little love for Mater, and when she was sitting at my table, night after night, she was like a blight on my crops.

Euphoria was not afraid of me. She never was – a rarity in those days, when men feared my wrath. Ah – you still fear it, do you, young man? Very wise. My hand is not yet a willow branch. But in those days . . .

Nonetheless, when I was rude to my mother, Euphoria would look at me across the room. 'May I have a word with you in private, my dear?' she would ask. And when we had a door between us and the rest of the world, she would say, 'I am mistress in this house, and I insist that my husband have the manners of a gentleman. Rude to your mother? How boorish is that?'

I remember it well, my honey. Her tongue was as sharp as my sword, and she was seldom wrong. And I was so besotted with her that I seldom troubled her with a reply. Indeed, I felt that I was the luckiest man in the world that such a creature had agreed to be my wife. I sometimes wondered if I was one of those monsters in our myths who keeps the maiden until slain by a hero – was I the hero or the Minotaur?

And we did fight. It will sound odd, when you consider her birth and mine, but I found her stinginess offensive. She disliked spending our winter stores on guests, on Cleon, on Idomeneus. She would keep yesterday's barley in a pan by the hearth to feed to local men who appeared through the spring mud to talk about politics, and she tasted all the wine in my cellar, then divided the amphorae into those for guests and those for the house.

'We are not poor!' I remember shouting at her.

'And I will keep us that way!' she shouted back.

On another evening, when Idomeneus made a remark about the age of the lamb he was eating, I winced – there was some screaming. I remember asking, 'Are you the daughter of some shepherd? No – Attic shepherds are generous. A slave, perhaps?'

'Slave?' she roared, turning on me. 'This from a man with his arms black to the elbows?'

Now this hurt, as I washed and washed each night before I went into the house, because I didn't want to seem like the blackened smith to my glorious, aristocratic wife.

I cocked back my hand to hit her. Most men hit their wives, and with various amounts of reason – some because they are weak fools who have to be stronger than someone, and others because their women hit them first. But let us be honest – men are, by and large, bigger than women, and far stronger, and my pater taught me that any man who uses force on a woman, to get her into bed or merely win her agreement in argument, is contemptible.

You heard me. If you think otherwise, let's hear it.

Despite which, married for a month, I found myself with a hand in the air. And I wasn't going to give her a swat – I was going to knock her teeth out. Trust me – I know what I intended. Rage consumed me. Black hands, indeed.

You have to love someone to be that angry, I think.

She didn't flinch.

I stormed out of the house rather than hit her. I got a horse and rode over to see Peneleos, and had a cup of wine with him and his sister and his wife. They told me, in short, that I was a fool and I needed to go back and apologize – excellent advice – and I rode back to find Euphoria's door shut and barred, and I had to listen to the sound of her weeping. I called, and she shouted something.

Peneleos had told me not to worry if we weren't reconciled before bed. But I couldn't sleep, and it was a long, long night. I lacked the courage to go to her door again, and when I went to the pantry to get a cup of beer in the night, the two kitchen slaves – both hers – flattened themselves against the wall in terror of me.

When the sun rose, I went out into the courtyard and sang a hymn to Helios, hoping that she would come down, and then I went and lit the forge. Tiraeus came in, munching a crust of stale bread. He had no idea that there had been a quarrel.

'You look like goat crap,' he said, after we had worked for an hour.

'Bad night,' I said.

'Bah – newly-weds!' he said. 'She's pregnant. You can stop fucking now.' His grin took the sting from the words.

'No,' I said. 'We had a fight.'

He shrugged. 'Never been married,' he said. 'But it does seem to me that most people fight. You and me, for instance.'

That was true enough, and Tiraeus and I were, in some ways, closer than any other two men I knew, except maybe me and Hermogenes. When we shared a project, we were inseparable. Craft made us closer than brothers. And still we could disagree on everything and anything, and when a helmet or a cup was in that dangerous stage just short of completion, it would all boil over into anger and disappointment and outrage. We were so used to it that we'd get the edges on a helmet trimmed and shake hands and say, 'Tomorrow, we fight.' And we'd laugh – but the next day, as we raised the last lines on the skull, the fight would start.

All of which is by way of saying that, as usual, Tiraeus had a point.

'So, what did she do?' he asked.

'Served Idomeneus some three-day-old stew.' Put that way, it just didn't sound as bad.

'I see. Death sentence for that, I agree. And what did you say?' Tiraeus punctuated his remarks with taps on the bowl he was planishing.

'I . . . called her a slave. Pretty much.' I cringed at the thought.

'Ahh.' Tiraeus picked up his bowl, stared at the area he was planishing and shook his head. 'Well, that doesn't sound so bad.' He looked

259

at me. 'You call me the son of a whore all the time.' His smile told me differently, and I understood – both that he felt I had behaved badly, and that he resented my epithets when I was angry.

And while I took this in, the door opened and there was Euphoria with a cup in her hands – warm wine and spices. 'Husband?' she asked from the door. She had never been in the forge before.

'Wife?' I asked in reply, and I caught the handle of the cup and pulled her gently in. 'Welcome to the forge.'

'Empedocles would have a fit,' Tiraeus said. He got up from his stool and came over. 'I'll just step outside for a piss, eh?'

I put a hand to stop him. 'Wife, I have behaved badly, and I used a phrase which no free person should ever use to another. I wish to apologize in front of my fellow master smith. And I understand that I am guilty of doing the same to him – when in anger.'

'You do have a temper,' Tiraeus said.

Euphoria looked at me for a moment. There were questions in her eyes, and those questions were, in some ways, more painful than shouted arguments and closed doors. 'Apology accepted,' she said. 'I've brought you wine, and there's breakfast for both of you in the andron.'

The breakfast was an apology of its own – eggs and good bread and spiced wine for me and Tiraeus and for Hermogenes when he came in from the vines. And that day I learned what was best about Euphoria – the thing that made me the luckiest of men. When she accepted my apology – why, then, the argument was *over*. I have known women – Briseis, I must confess – who hold a grudge for ever. But Euphoria, however angry she might have been, dismissed her anger as the sun burns through a morning fog, so that once the anger had passed, it never needed to be recalled.

Beautiful breasts and a lovely waist and a face like a statue are all very well – but an even temper and a sense of fairness will last longer. Ask any married man. Or woman, for that matter.

That was the spring of contentment. We argued – twice, I think, and I'll tell the story of the second time in a moment – but we also ate and danced and made love and went into Plataea for market days – together. And because Euphoria was such a lovely, pleasant girl, everyone wanted to meet her, and suddenly I was a man with friends, acquaintances, invitations.

Penelope visited twice – it was only thirty stades from her home to mine, and once the roads were dry she could come on a whim. As the days grew longer and hotter, and the season prepared to turn again, she was pregnant, too, and delighted to be so, and she told me with a giggle that she thought that the bonfire of Pan had had a salutary effect, and her husband rolled his eyes.

They were served our best food and drink, I noticed. And then dismissed, because there are fights not worth having.

We hosted Myron to dinner before midsummer's eve – he hadn't eaten in my house since my father was alive. His wife had arranged it with Euphoria, although neither was present for the dinner. Instead, most of the men who came were older men. Peneleos was there, and he was my age, as was his older brother Epictetus; and Bion was there because he was my right hand and welcome any time. But the other men were older – Draco seemed older than the hills, and Diocles was only a little younger than Mater, and Hilarion, once the life of the party and a poor farmer, was now a cheerful and wealthy man.

They were my neighbours. We also invited Idomeneus down from Cithaeron, and Alcaeus of Miletus, who had status in Plataea by virtue of being the lord, in effect if not in fact, of fifty good spearmen who were now citizens.

We had a good sacrifice up the hill. I remember that I watched the skies for a day, praying for good weather, and I remember that we still had to squelch our way across the best barley field because we'd had rain, but our little altar was high and dry on the hilltop. Myron made the sacrifice, and he mentioned my father in his prayer. And then we gave the fat and the bones to the god, and squelched our way back down to the house with the slaves carrying the skin and all the meat, and we had quite a dinner – a whole sheep. The slaves shared in it. I had quite a few slaves by then – with my wife's I had twenty. Too many, and they were starting to breed more.

We had a proper symposium, too, with good talk about civic duty and the difference between men's laws and god's laws. It was all very pleasant, and then we began to talk of Persia.

Myron held up his hand and we all stopped talking. 'I want to discuss a matter of business,' he said. He had quite a presence by then. I could remember him as a young farmer, but by that time he was an orator and a man of immense dignity.

'Arimnestos, I intend to put it to the vote after the first feast of Heracles that you be the polemarch of the city. Polemarch and strategos, both.'

'What's a strategos?' Hilarion asked.

That was a fair question. In those days, many towns had a pole-march, but only Athens and Sparta had strategoi. They were officers – real officers, the way we had officers when we served Miltiades. Every strategos had responsibility for a body of men when the phalanx formed, and this made the phalanx more flexible in combat. The old polemarchs were often politicians and sometimes soldiers, but they *formed* the phalanx – that is, they knew where each man should stand in the array. And they fought in the place of honour – the right end of the front rank. Usually, they died there. But they didn't normally issue any orders – beyond getting every man to the battlefield, and into his place in the line.

On that evening, Plataea had perhaps two thousand hoplites – armoured warriors. We'd grown in the last ten years, and the Milesians had brought us new fighters, and we were richer. Bion and Hermogenes, for instance – both men had been slaves, and yet now they were prosperous farmers with full armour. Wealth – individual wealth – translated directly into fighting power in those days. In my father's time, we'd fielded fifteen hundred hoplites only by freeing slaves and putting them – virtually unarmed – into the rear ranks.

So, our military power was greater. And Myron proposed formalizing my control of it. I nodded. 'Of course,' I said.

'This is no empty honour,' Myron said. 'There is a Persian fleet on the seas. News has reached me that the Medes intend to sack Naxos, and then they will come to Attica. Athens will expect us to stand with them.'

It was still chilly in the evenings. We had a brazier in the middle of the room, but the men were still huddled in their himations, and I remember that I could see my breath when I spoke.

'This spring?' Bion asked.

'This summer, at least,' Myron answered. 'Are we ready, Arimnestos?'

I rolled off my couch and cursed the cold floor. 'We are as ready as a city at peace can be,' I answered. 'We dance the Pyrrhiche at least twice as often as we used to do. I take the younger men up the mountain as often as I can – and I will make it more often this spring. Short of war itself, the hunt and the dance are our best methods of training.'

Hilarion shrugged and pulled his cloak over his feet. 'Why do we need to fight the Persians?' he asked. 'I know you all think me slow-witted – but what has the Great King ever done to me?'

'Not a thing,' I answered. 'He is a good ruler and a great man, or so I hear. But, Hilarion, when is the last time you fought in the phalanx?'

'You know as well as me – the fight at the bridge, where we helped Athens against the men of Euboea.' He grinned. 'I didn't really fight, either. I did some pushing from the fifth rank, I think.'

'We've had fifteen years of peace because Athens has stood between us and Thebes.' I paused to spit, and every man present joined me.

Diocles nodded. 'True enough,' he said.

'We're about to pay for those years of peace,' Myron said. 'The price will be high. And if the rest of Boeotia submits to the Great King, we will be alone. Our city will be wide open when we march away.'

Myron's words brought the reality home to every man in the room.

'By Ares!' Peneleos said. 'Is it so bad? Is this certain?'

Myron looked at me – as I was his principal source of information.

'Peneleos, when there are dark clouds in the north, do you expect rain?' I asked.

He nodded and raised an eyebrow. 'I expect it, but it does not always come. Sometimes the rain goes to Thespiae or Hisiae.'

'Exactly,' I agreed. 'The Great King may never take Naxos. He may forget Athens, or the men of Athens may make a peace with him. A storm might come up and wreck his fleet – it's happened before. But the dark clouds are right there, friends, and we would be foolish not to be prepared.'

'I plan to ask the assembly for money to repair the walls and raise two new bastions – all stone – to cover the gate,' Myron said. 'I will ask that every free man send a slave to work, so that the repairs are done immediately, as soon as the planting is in. And I will be asking for the richest men to contribute to the towers. I will pay for one of them myself.' He looked around.

Bion gave me a slight nod of the head.

'I will pay for one third of the second tower,' I said, 'with the help of Bion and Alcaeus.'

Idomeneus surprised us. 'I will pay for one third,' he said. 'From my own funds,' he added.

Diocles and Hilarion and Draco muttered among themselves, and

Epictetus and Peneleos, sharing a couch, leaned in, and in the end the five of them agreed to share the cost of a third of the tower.

As the men gathered to walk home, I found myself with Peneleos and Epictetus.

'I have a hard time seeing myself as a leading man,' Peneleos said. 'I'm a second son. I am *not* that old.'

I laughed. 'You're older than me,' I said. 'And I'm about to be polemarch.'

Bion shook his head. 'Plataea lost a generation in the three battles,' he said. 'And in the fights with Thebes before that. Think of your fathers and brothers – all dead.'

That was a sobering thought, but a true one. Myron had been my father's friend. My father should have been here to be polemarch, and Diocles' father should have been here, and Epictetus's father, and my brother, and Hilarion's older brother – on and on.

'We're a city of young men,' Hilarion quipped.

'If we have to fight the Medes, we'll be a city of widows,' Bion answered him.

The assembly was dull enough, and I remember none of it – not even my formal elevation to polemarch and strategos after the feast of Heracles, thirty days after the summer solstice. I was allowed, as polemarch, to choose the other two strategoi myself. We'd decided to have three, one for each of the towns that made up Plataea before the alliance with Athens turned us into a real city.

Right away, my new rank plunged me into politics. I wanted Idomeneus and Alcaeus – or at least Lysius – as officers. I wanted the strategoi to be men who had been under the hand of Ares, who knew the sound of spears and shields. But all of us – even Lysius and Ajax – lived in one district, over by Hisiae. So I wasted good workdays going to meetings to talk with the local men in the other two districts. I knew them all – there were only three thousand citizens back then, and we all knew each other pretty well. I kept hoping to find some retired mercenary, some man who had served under Miltiades or even with the Medes.

Now that I think of it, in those districts closest to the river they had most of the good farmland, and I suspect their sons didn't need to go to sea to win a few silver coins. Ours did, over by the mountain.

There were good *young* men from those districts. Bellerophon, son of Epistocles, who lived as close to Thebes as a man could and not be a Theban, was a fine young man with full armour who had been to every deer hunt from the first, got spear-fighting lessons from Lysius and also spent all his spare hours with Idomeneus. He was from the Asopus district. But he was seventeen years old, and no bearded man would take an order from him.

'Try his pater,' Myron said, when I asked his advice. 'He's a wealthy man, and a decent one. If the son's such a good warrior, the pater won't be a sluggard,' he added.

Hmm. Well, you'll see how that worked out.

The northern district was the hardest. The men over there were almost Thespian, and they had their own ways, and a few of them complained that in the event of a fight, they'd march with Thespiae and not Plataea. Before the great wars came, men were freer with their citizenship.

But that very freedom saved me in the end. My brother-in-law, Antigonus, owned farms in Plataea. His free men were liable for service as *psiloi* or *peltastai*, and it occurred to me that, if Myron would accept it, he would make a first-rate strategos.

So he was granted citizenship. In fact, Myron discovered that his family had always been allowed to be citizens – a very convenient discovery, let me tell you – and I appointed him as strategos. This proved to be a fortuitous choice. Antigonus brought us another fifty hoplites of his own – all men of Thespiae, but people didn't care so much then, as I say – and he had riches which he used to improve the armour of his district, and of course he had most of that armour made at my forge.

My forge grew that spring. Tiraeus and I shared the same shed, of course, and Bion had, since my pater's time, had his own anvils and his own fire just up the hill, by his house. But when the money came over the mountain that spring – money from Athens, I mean, for worked bronze we'd sent in the autumn – and when Antigonus placed a huge order for armour and helmets, then Tiraeus wanted to build his own shed.

'I need a pair of slaves,' he said. 'So do you. We do too much of the donkey work. And we need some boys – fee boys, who want to grow to be smiths. We could triple our output.'

I already had Styges, who had gradually made himself into my apprentice. But I found two more for me, and Hermogenes found a couple for his father, and suddenly my forge was crowded.

We put up a shed for Tiraeus, and as soon as it was done,

Empedocles came out from Thebes and blessed his fire. We had a sacrifice and Empedocles initiated all of our new boys, slaves and free together, because the god cares nothing for such stuff.

'You know the Medes are coming, eh?' he asked me. It was easy to forget that he was a Theban, but sometimes it came back.

'Even in little Plataea, the news has come,' I answered.

'Don't get your back up. The godless Athenians are in for it. Thebes is safe – we're not fools.' He sat back and drank wine.

'We are.' I handed him an altar plate I'd made as my sacrifice to the god. On the face, Cleon and I had engraved a scene of the smith god returning to Olympus after being cast forth, led by Dionysus.

'When did you learn to do such fine work?' he asked.

'The older man you raised to the first degree?' I said. 'He's an engraver.'

Empedocles whistled. 'You have quite an operation here,' he said. 'Why not put it all in one building? Like the potters in Corinth? You have water, charcoal, three master-smiths and an engraver. And a reputation, at least as far away as Thebes. They may spit when they mention you, but they'll all hurry to buy your bronze.'

'I have never sent a shipment of my bronze to Thebes,' I said.

'Men sell it from Athens,' he said. 'You are quite well known in Thebes, my boy. Simon son of Simon keeps your name in the ears of many men – although not to your favour. And ...' He paused, drank from his cup, and looked up at me. 'And there are men in Thebes who plan to kill you.'

I shrugged. 'Let them come, then.'

'Don't be a fool, boy. Someone – someone with a great deal of money – has hired a whole band of cut-throats.' He shivered.

'If they come from Thebes to here, it would be war,' I said. 'I don't think Thebes wants war with Athens.'

Empedocles shook his head. 'Simon is loud in proclaiming that Athens would not care if you were killed,' he said.

Now it was my turn to shake my head. 'Old news, priest. I am the polemarch of Plataea, and my death would burn Thebes the way a hot forge burns charcoal.'

'They made you polemarch?' the priest said. 'You have come far, my boy.'

'I have, too,' I agreed. 'If you find Simon, tell him to go away and never come back – and I, for my part, will not hunt him down and kill him. Let the bad blood be over. But tell your archon – for me, and for my archon – that if men of Thebes come here, or even hired men, coming from Thebes, then we will fight, and Athens will stand with us.'

'Not if Athens has been destroyed,' the old priest said. 'I'm sorry, lad, but what they plan is to get you this summer, while Athens can do nothing to help you. Even now, the Athenians debate in their assembly – they debate sending Miltiades and Aristides away as exiles, and making submission. Perhaps you should join them in exile – just for a while.'

I told Myron everything Empedocles told me, and he dismissed it all with a wave of his hand. 'I'm sure Simon would like to kill you,' he said. 'But Thebes is in an awkward place right now, and they do not need a war with Athens.'

'Empedocles makes a good point, though,' I allowed. 'Once the Persians are at sea – and by all accounts, they are – Athens can hardly send their hoplites over the passes into Boeotia to help us.'

'The Thebans would be fools to trade short-term advantage for the punishment Athens will dish out later,' Myron said.

'Not if they can count on the Medes to defeat Athens,' I said. 'Look, they have a workable strategy, or so it appears to me. And I see other hands in this, Myron. If we're tied up here – why, then there are no hoplites to march to the aid of Athens.'

'I think you have delusions of grandeur, young man,' Myron said. 'I agree – it's more of a threat than I saw when first I heard of it, but this is not the way cities behave. We are not children in the agora. I will send a messenger to Athens, and another to Thebes. But that will be the end of it.'

I thought he might be right. I only knew pirates and easterners. Here, in sober, steady Boeotia, even the Thebans were probably better men.

'Perhaps I should muster all our men, just so that the Thebans can see how ready we are.' I was hesitant to ask this, as a general muster cost our city a little money – and the foundations of the new towers were just going down. But the seed was in the ground, and most farmers had a holiday – or as much holiday as a man can get between ploughing his fallow ground, shoring his grapes and watching the pests eat his olives.

'That is a fine idea,' Myron said. 'One week from today. The Theban heralds will be here by then.'

I don't remember a thing about that week apart from the glow of the forge and the rush to finish as many bits of harness and armour as I could manage. I had thirty repairs sitting around my house – helmets, breastplates, spearheads. I worked night and day, and so did Tiraeus and Bion. And across the stream, in the city, my compatriot, Heron the Smith, worked iron and steel as fast as I worked bronze.

But the muster was glorious. I could remember what our men looked like when we went off to Oinoe to help Athens – dun cloaks, no swords, men without shields hiding in the rear ranks, and only a dozen men in full bronze.

Now we had a front rank of almost one hundred and twenty-five men, and every one of them had a bronze panoply – breast- and backplate or scale armour, or at least a leather *spolas*, and an aspis – a few old men with Boeotian shields – greaves on every man, and good helmets, most crested Corinthians. I was pleased to look down my front rank and see how many of those helmets were my own manufacture – almost twenty. And behind them were ranks of men with good shields and good helmets, even if most of them were dog-caps of bronze. Every man in the front rank had a good spear and a sword, and most of the second-rankers, and some of the third- and fourth-rankers, as well.

The Milesians were the best equipped, with armour all the way back to the fifth rank. My brother-in-law's men were the next best, and they would get better all autumn as I hammered out their bronze. My neighbours looked almost as good – Bion was armoured like Ares, as was Hermogenes, and Tiraeus, Idomeneus and Styges – all of us in full panoply, with thigh guards and arm guards, too.

Fifteen years of peace may rob a town of the fine cutting edge of war practice, but it does give a town the riches to spend on armour.

I had asked every man to have his wife make him a red cloak. I didn't expect them to be dyed Tyrian red, like the Spartans, although a few rich men did. Most were brick red, from madder, and striped in white or black, as is our way in Plataea. But most men had done it – even those who had no armour – and with those cloaks and our new dog-caps of bronze in every rank, we made a fine show in the agora, and many women stopped to watch and older men clapped to see us.

Myron wore his armour, but he watched. I intended to put him in the fourth rank, dead centre in the phalanx – because he was too important to risk, even though he was a decent fighter and a brave man and owned good armour. He stood at the edge, swapped jokes with men, and finally came up and slapped me on my scaled back.

'Very good, Arimnestos.' He pointed at the three Theban heralds, who stood silently off to the side, watching as our men laughed, joked and shone.

Then I called out the epilektoi – most of them eighteen or nineteen years old, although not all, by any means. And while the phalanx sang the Paean of Apollo, we danced our Pyrrhiche.

It is one thing to dance for the war god when musicians play and men sing. It is another to dance in the full light of day, when a thousand men beat the time with their spear-butts and sing from inside their helmets, and the song rebounds from the bronze and rises like a pure offering to the war god and the Lord of the Silver Bow.

Idomeneus and I had changed our dance many times by then. It had been a simple dance that allowed men to learn their place in the ranks and not much more. Our new dance exchanged ranks, taught spear-thrusts and parries, and had men duck to the ground, leap in the air over a thrust, even fight to the rear. My young men danced with unbated weapons, and more than once a sharp spear ripped a furrow across a new-painted shield – but the rhythm went on, and as we sang of the deep-breasted nymphs who served Apollo, we stomped with our left feet and pivoted together, ducked, clashed our spears and exchanged ranks again.

When the hymn was finished, we stood silently for some heart-beats, and then all the women and old men and boys raised a howl of joy to the heavens.

Myron went over to the heralds and handed them a scroll.

'Tell your masters that we seek no quarrel with mighty Thebes,' he said. 'But if Thebes seeks a quarrel with us . . .' He did nothing grand or dramatic, merely flicked his glance down our ranks and over the new towers, one half-built and the other with its foundations complete. He looked back at the heralds. 'If Thebes seeks some quarrel, she may find us a tougher vine to hack away than ever she imagined.'

My wife loved that I was polemarch, and when I donned my armour for the muster, she embraced me, sharp scales and all. She had come to terms with her husband the smith, but her husband the polemarch was perhaps the figure she had expected in her maiden dreams.

She wove me a new cloak with her own hands, a fine red one dyed scarlet with some rare dye from the east, and with her own hands she dyed a new crest for my new helmet, so that mere days after I finished the helmet, the horsehair and the cloak appeared on my worktable in my forge. That chlamys was as thick as a fleece and as warm as a mother's embrace. It hangs just there, and moths have troubled it, but any woman among you can see how well woven it is.

The day I found it, I put it on and wore it for her, and then I carried her up to her room and we made love on it. I wore it proudly when I mustered the phalanx before the Theban heralds, and I wore it whenever I wore my armour, for many years after.

I came straight back to the farm after the muster, with all the epilektoi at my heels. I kissed Euphoria, patted her belly, which now had the smallest, sweetest swelling, and gathered a pair of my shop boys to carry my gear. Then in full armour, my picked men and I ran and walked by turns all the way up the mountain to the shrine of the hero. There, Idomeneus and Ajax said the words, and we sacrificed a couple of big steers and ate like kings, and then we lay in our cloaks like real soldiers and woke with the first light to run along the flank of Cithaeron to Eleutherai.

By noon on the second day, I had them all tired and surly, with the cockiness of the muster sweated out of them, and by the fourth day of the hunt even the Milesians were flagging, and my veterans were watching them with a certain callous satisfaction.

I was tired too – try wearing armour for five days! It chafes on your ribs, rubs your hips, weighs on your shoulders. Your helmet becomes a ring of fire on your head, and greaves – greaves become your enemy, not your ally. But the only way to become accustomed to armour is to wear it. There is no other way. I made my picked men run in it, cut firewood in it, gather brush in it, skin deer in it.

My name was taken in vain – often.

'Curse me now,' I said. 'When you fight the Medes, you'll praise me.'

The sixth day I let them rest. The complaining increased – this is the way with men, slave or free, soldier or priest. Real carping requires breath and time.

The seventh day was supposed to be the last, and we had games. Or rather, we were supposed to have games. The sun was up in the sky, and we had made the sacrifices, and Idomeneus was staring at the guts of a rabbit he had sacrificed. He had the oddest look on his face.

'I've never seen a liver like this,' he said.

I looked – not that I'd know one liver from another – and past him I saw two things to give me unease.

Over towards Eleutherai, I could see a pair of men on horses, riding the hill road, flat out.

And down in the valley in the direction of my farm, I saw a column of smoke rising.

In Boeotia, fires happen. Woods catch fire in the dry of summer, and men start fires to open up new farmland or simply to get a better view. Men burn off their fields. Houses catch fire when lamps are left unattended.

So I had no need to panic, except that the juxtaposition of the riders and the fire worried me. It was a big fire. And Idomeneus was not happy with the animal he had just sacrificed.

Bion came up next to me. 'That's our place,' he said, and my stomach flipped.

'How can you be sure?' I asked.

'I'm sure,' he said. 'Did you bank your forge fire?'

'By Hephaestus,' I said, 'of course I did.' You are always a feckless young man, to people older than you.

'Hmm,' he said.

Idomeneus killed a lamb, slit it open and cursed. 'I don't really know much about divination,' he said from the growing pool of blood at our feet. He was kneeling in the dead lamb's entrails. 'But something is wrong. Dead wrong.'

So I ordered the epilektoi to muster, instead of preparing for the games. They cursed at being so early into their armour, but by then they were cursing anything I ordered. Even the young feel pain, or so we old men joked. Our muscles had had years to harden, and theirs were still soft.

About the time the first files were falling in, another column of smoke leaped to the heavens.

'That's our beacon fire!' Tiraeus shouted.

It was true. It was lit in the right place, and it let out smoke in a thick column and then stopped – and then started again. I watched two repeats.

It was the will of the gods that we were already assembled – and that we had armour, and that we were so high up that we could read the signal clearly and see, too, the very moment it burned into life.

But fear reached icy fingers down my throat. If it was Simon, then he had struck at my home and I was not there.

But Euphoria was. Lovely, pregnant Euphoria.

I didn't scream. I was a good soldier, and a man who had seen a few fights, but I drank a cup of wine to steady my nerves and told myself the truth – that if she was dead, raped or stolen, I was forty stades distant and there was *nothing* I could do for her.

This is what it is to be a veteran, honey bee. You see too clearly. I counted her dead, or brutalized, and went on with my business. Because war is serious, and I was the commander, and my rage was not yet to be unleashed.

So I finished my wine, ate an apple and didn't fret while the last ranks fell in. Outside, I didn't fret. In my gut, I lost a year of my life.

We had started down the road to Eleutherai by the time the riders came up the hill. They knew where to find us – my Thracian freedmen.

'Lord,' the lead rider said. 'Men came – a hundred or more. Your mater says we are to tell you that the farm is closed to them, and safe. But they came from Thebes, and they will go home the same way, on the old road.'

'Where is my wife?' I asked.

The older of the two shrugged. 'Your mater ordered us,' he said. 'I know no more.'

While we spoke, another beacon sent its smoke to the heavens.

'Mater is right,' I said. 'They're running back down the old road to Thebes.' I turned to my boys. 'Ares has sent us a serious contest,' I shouted. 'Are you ready?'

They shouted – a roar that echoed off the rock walls of the mountain. Later, men said that they heard it out on the farms and thought that Cithaeron had come awake.

I put myself at the head of the first file. 'Let's run,' I said, and we were off.

I sent out the two Thracians as scouts – they had horses and they were good riders. In my head, I did my best to estimate what might happen. The Thebans – if they were Thebans – had a thirty-stade head start. On the other hand, they must have marched all night. They must have been tired.

My boys had had a day of rest.

Most of my boys had never seen a spear thrust in earnest.

I had a long run down the mountain to think about it, and my thoughts were dark. I wanted to run home first. I wanted to *know*. I wanted to know why it was Mater who had sent these men, and not my wife.

But my farm was in the wrong direction now. From Eleutherai, I would lead my men north and east – the farm was due west.

We passed through Eleutherai like a summer storm. Eleutherai is, technically, in Attica. I told the basileus to send word to Athens – but that help, if it came at all, would be ten days away.

I led my boys out of Eleutherai, down the mountain, down the pass and along the rocky road to Thebes.

As we entered our own territory, we met Lysius and a dozen of his neighbours, all armed, and Teucer, coming across the fields with some light-armed men – and as soon as they met with me and my mounted scouts, they ran off ahead of us. Teucer caused me to writhe with frustration and fear – he'd seen the fire at my farm, and the beacon, but he hadn't gone up the hill to investigate. He knew nothing.

Lysius and his men fell in with us – they'd met the Thracians on the road. And a dozen stades further on, we met another party, small farmers and Milesian settlers under Alcaeus, so that I had almost two hundred men behind me as we ran across Asopus at mid-morning. I gave them all a break. Swift as I had to be, these men had run almost forty stades, most of them in armour. If we were going to fight, we needed a rest.

The two Thracians were brilliant, covering the ground in front of us and raising the farmers, and I wished I had cavalry like the Lydians and the Medes had. But I didn't. I rested the men an hour, and then we were off again, cutting across the fields of the eastern township to try and gain a few stades on the men we were pursuing.

It was noon when we found the first body – a man in a dog-cap with a pair of spear wounds in his body. His name was Milos, and he was a farmer from along the Asopus.

We moved his body off the road and ran on. After a stade, there were three dead men all together – all Asopus-side farmers.

'The men of the Asopus district must have made a stand here,' Bion said as he panted. 'Listen, boy – I'm finished. I can't run another step. I'll stay and bury these men, and send on anyone who can follow.'

Bion wasn't the only man who was finished. I told off ten men, so that there would be no shame – and told them to guard the bodies. The rest of us went on at a slow jog.

My Thracians found the next bodies – all strangers. Two of them had arrows in them – Teucer's arrows. And at the road junction, where the old road to Thebes and the new crossed, there were a dozen more strangers, some wounded and some dead, and two of our men to tell us that our Plataeans were harrying the column as it retreated, and that there were more than a hundred enemies, and perhaps two hundred.

We were close. But I knew we were not going to catch them. We were just ten stades from Theban territory.

Every man in the column knew it, too.

But we said our prayers to Ares and ran on. My slaves had dropped out by then, and I had my shield on my arm and my helmet on top of my head, and most of me hurt as much as if I had already fought. My legs burned, and my left arm felt like a bar of iron sagging from my shoulder, and even my shield strap was an unbearable burden. If I felt like that, what were my boys feeling like?

But we were close.

At the top of the next hill, I was jogging so slowly that walking might have been faster. But when I came over the hill, I could see them – a dozen armoured stragglers in a dense shield wall, trying to avoid a steady rain of arrows.

We were close. My heels grew wings and I ran on.

Behind me, my boys began to shout. I looked back, and men were stripping their greaves off and casting them aside to run faster. Some stopped and threw up, others stripped off their breastplates – and then they ran on.

The dozen stragglers broke when they saw us coming, and the fleetest two made it, but the rest died in a shower of arrows and javelins, and then Teucer was next to me, and other men I knew – about twenty, all light-armed men that Teucer had rallied. I wanted to embrace him, but I didn't have time.

We ran down the last hill, and I could see the dark mass of them, crossing the stream that made the border between my city and Thebes. There were quite a few of them. And most were already in Theban territory.

I knew immediately what I had to do – what Myron would say if he was here. I ordered the boys to halt.

'Form up,' I shouted. 'Get in your ranks. Form up, form at normal order.'

The ground down to the stream was a single hayfield, and on the far side, another the same. Not for nothing do foreigners call Boeotia the Dance Floor of Ares. Flat ground, perfect for war.

Men and boys came down the road. They were strung out over several stades, and while my little phalanx formed, the enemy scrambled up the banks of the stream to safety on Theban territory. In my heart, I wanted to run down and kill them all – myself, if I had to.

There was more at stake, though. More even than my own revenge, although the image of Euphoria's death – rape, torment, horror – came before me every time I paused or thought about anything but the task at hand.

My child. She was carrying my child. If this raid came from Simon, how he would enjoy slaying my unborn child.

The mind is a dark place, friends.

I held the line in my head, though. I gathered my men, formed them in ranks and then, and only then, did I take them down the hill.

The enemy now stood in neat ranks on the far side of the stream. They weren't even trying to make more ground.

They were good fighters. I could see by how quiet they were, how little shifting there was in their ranks. Of course they were tired, and they had lost men – and lost their bodies, as well, which humiliates any soldier.

When we were half a stade away, they began to shout insults at us.

We halted. I walked forward with Teucer. He already had his orders.

There he was – Simon, son of Simon. He wore plain armour and a big crest, and he came out of the ranks to meet me like a long-lost brother.

'Look who it is,' he laughed. 'The polemarch of Plataea. Better stay on your own side of the river, little cousin, or big, bad Thebes will eat your pissant city the way a lion eats a foal.'

'Nicely put,' I shouted at him. 'You brand yourself a whoreson of Thebes, traitor.' I spat. 'You are, in fact, your father's son.'

'Laugh while you can, Plataean,' he shouted back. 'I left your wife dead in your dooryard and burned your fucking house, and there is *nothing* you can do but cry like a boy. And next time, I'll get *you* – and all the men who stand between me and what is mine.'

In that hour, my fate dangled in the wind – along with the battle we were about to fight, and perhaps the fate of Athens, too. With the words 'dead in your dooryard', I think that most of my sense of reason left me. Not that I hadn't expected it, after the sacrifices went foul and the riders appeared and the column of smoke.

I never promised you a happy story, thugater.

Simon taunted me again – something about what he'd done to her body, and how ugly she was. I started forward at him. Had I reached him, he and his two hundred friends would have cut me down, and then what might have happened?

Teucer didn't flinch, or ask permission. He shot my cousin down, right there, in cold blood. His arrow flew true, and Simon died with a look of complete disbelief on his hateful face and an arrow coming out of the top of his chest, just above his breastplate. And that changed everything. Suddenly, the hired men knew that their paymaster was dead – and I was alive.

My boys charged without a word from me. We sang no Paean, and we were not in any proper formation, but we went over that stream, up the bank, into trained men.

I remember none of it. Oh, that's a lie – I remember going up the bank, almost losing my footing, the jar of a spear on my aspis and another ringing off my beautiful new helmet. And then I was into them, killing.

After a while, we pushed them off the stream bank, and then they must have known that they'd had it. I remember Teucer at my back, shooting men in the face or foot when they troubled me. Apollo guided his hand, and he was like death.

They were hired men, and their employer was already dead. After a while they broke. I suppose I killed my share of them, but there were far more alive than down when they broke. It is always the way. Men only die when they turn their backs to run.

Our light-armed men were not tired; most of them hadn't got en-gaged, except perhaps to lob a few javelins on the unshielded flank. My rage communicated itself to them – and they followed the hired men.

Anyone can kill a man who turns his back.

I followed on wings of rage and revenge, so that when I surfaced from my flood tide of blood, I was far down the road to Thebes. I had no spear, just a sword – my shield was cast aside. Beside me was Idomeneus, and at my back was Teucer, and around us were thirty freedmen and slaves, all busy stripping the corpses.

We were ten stades into Theban territory. My body would scarcely obey me – I couldn't have raised my sword arm to defend my poor Euphoria.

I looked down the road to Thebes, and it was empty.

Idomeneus laughed aloud.

'We fucking killed them *all!*' he said.

I've heard since that over two dozen survived. So we didn't, in fact, kill them all.

But close enough.

I don't remember much after that, except that I made my way back to the stream, and men tried to talk to me, and I ignored them. I stripped my armour and left it on the ground with my helmet and my weapons, and I ran – naked – back up the road. I was exhausted, but I ran anyway.

I remember nothing, except that I made the run all the way. Perhaps I walked. Perhaps I lay down and slept. But I doubt it.

The column of smoke from the burning barn rose over all of Plataea, mingling high up with the smoke of three signal fires. I ran across fields, ripping my legs on briar and my feet on the small, hard, spiky nuts that litter our fields at high summer. Not that I noticed.

I ran until I could not see, until my breath came like fire into a bellows, and sweat flew from me. I had run thirty stades in armour, fought a battle, and now I was running another thirty stades. My right arm was all blood to the elbow, sticky and brown, and there were wounds on my thighs and ankles and a deep cut on my left bicep – no idea how it came there – and still I ran.

Did I think that I could save her if I ran far enough?

Perhaps I wanted to burst my heart.

I remember seeing that I had run all the way to the fork at the foot of the hill, and what I remember best was the strange temptation I had to keep going – over the stream and up to the hero's tomb. And perhaps away over the mountain to Attica, and over the sea to Aegypt. To keep going and never go home, and never *know*.

Perhaps I lost my wits.

But I turned my feet, lengthened my stride and ran up the dusty lane, sharp gravel under my hard feet.

Halfway up the hill, the road turns just a little, and you can see straight to the gate in the wall that surrounds my house.

The house itself was burning. Although it was stone and mortar, and solidly built, they'd fired the floorboards and the roof beams, and the stone was cracking and falling, and the whole thing had become a chimney, carrying my riches to the skies in an intended sacrifice.

I didn't give it more than a glance.

My great wooden gate, for which my father had forged the straps and hinges and cut the oak, was broken and twisted. On the ground was a heavy beam from one of the sheds – Tiraeus's shed, as it later proved. They'd used it to break the gate.

Around the gateway, women lamented. They keened, high wails like the cries of bloody-handed furies tearing to the heavens, demanding revenge. Well – they had their revenge, but as usual, it brought no child born of woman back to life.

I pushed through them. The gateway was packed with corpses, some of them black with fire.

My farm had not fallen lightly, and my people had not died alone.

Bion lay across the threshold, his spear broken in his hand, his body ripped asunder.

Cleon lay by him, throat ripped and with ten great wounds in his body and a broken axe clutched in his hands.

They lay across the woman they had died defending, and even she had a sword in her hand, and the edge of the blade was bloody. She had not gone down easily. She had not been raped. She was dead before such thoughts could occur to any man, however evil.

She was not pregnant, and as I stood there, I realized that her hair was not blonde.

It was not Euphoria. It was Mater. Mater had died in the gateway, sword in hand.

My mind couldn't accept it – couldn't take in the loss of the three of them in one blow. In truth, all my being had been aimed at Euphoria, and I had forgotten how many people I loved were in this farm.

Mater.

I lifted Bion off her legs and laid him down with dignity, although his intestines trailed behind him as I dragged him across the yard.

I lifted Cleon too, and now I was weeping, because he had died like a great man, and there were dead enemies at his feet.

And Mater – how I had hated her for so many years. Yet here she was, sword in hand, like any hero you might name. Ares, she died well. And sober.

I rolled her corpse over, and she had that smile on her face – that smile she wore when she saw that I could say the verses of Theognis, or when I brought Euphoria under the roof, or when she met Miltiades.

That she wore that look with a spear in her guts made her seem very great to me.

But when I went to lift her, two other hands reached beneath her shoulders – bloody hands, but smaller.

Euphoria's hair was wild, her chiton was unpinned at one shoulder, so that one breast showed on the right, and there was blood on her feet. She took Mater's shoulders and lifted, and we laid her down with the other heroes who fell defending the dooryard.

'She locked me in the basement,' Euphoria said. She wasn't crying. 'She said it was my duty to live.'

Tiraeus and Styges had held the door to the forge. The hired warriors had given up after they lost two men, then went and fired the house and ran off. So Styges had let my wife out of the basement before the house collapsed into it.

And more, Mater had saved so much – wall hangings, gold and silver – all thrown into the forge building. Bion and Cleon held the gate while she did it, and then she joined them, and they all died together. Or that's how Styges told it, who had stood in the door of the forge and held it.

Euphoria held me, crooning. She was strong, and I was suddenly unmanned. It was everything – Bion's death, Cleon's, Mater's – and Euphoria being alive. And fatigue, I suppose.

Styges asked me if we had fought. I must have told them something, because the women stopped screaming for vengeance. And then Euphoria brought me wine – neat – and I drank a cup, and passed out like a drunkard.

When I came to, it was night and I could scarcely move. My thighs hurt so much that I had trouble rolling over. I was lying on gravel in my forge yard, and I had a blanket of my wife's weaving over me, and she was snuggled to my side, her head against my shoulder.

'I thought you were dead,' I said.

She shook her head and her arm embraced me, a good, long squeeze.

In the morning, my legs still ached as if I was an old man. My shoulders and arms weren't much better, and one of the cuts on my thigh was deeper than I had thought and wept pus.

The bastards had raped any female slave they caught and killed three of my male slaves. So my yard had the mourning of defeat, along with the dreadful fear of my slave girls that they were pregnant. I went to the stream and washed myself, with a prayer to the stream itself for the filth I was putting in her, and then I went back up the hill carrying water, and Euphoria began to wash the women clean, which is the only kindness you can do for a raped woman.

I got Styges and Tiraeus, who both had small wounds, to bind mine, and then I helped with theirs, and then we began to take stock.

We hadn't lost an animal – the byres were up the hill, and the bastards never made it past the yard. They'd burned the one barn they reached, which was full of barley and hay. It was a loss, but it only held the ready stores for the house and the animals. The house was gone, though. A house that my great-grandfather built of stone and mortar – the best house in all of south Plataea. The home of the Corvaxae, great and small.

Simon burned it, destroying the work of his own family, and he killed his own step-mother in the courtyard. May the furies rip his liver for ever. May every shade in Hades treat him with the contempt of a matricide and a traitor.

I was standing in the yard, looking at the wreck of the house – rubble and not much more – when men came through the gate. Teucer and Hermogenes, Idomeneus and Alcaeus and all the men of the epilektoi.

I walked over to Hermogenes and put my arms around him. 'Bion died in the yard,' I said.

I took him by the hand to where his father was laid out. The women had already bathed his body with the water I brought them, and anointed him with oil, and put coins on his eyes. Hermogenes fell to his knees, wept and poured sand over his head.

Other, smaller steadings had also been hit. On the way back to Thebes, the hired men had lost their discipline – if they ever had any – and they'd killed and raped whatever they could catch. So I was not alone in my mourning.

But Teucer took me aside. 'Are you blind with rage?' he asked.

I shook my head. 'Euphoria is alive, and the unborn baby,' I said. 'I have my wits about me today.'

Teucer led me outside the old house wall. 'This man was with them,' he said. 'I took him alive. He is my slave now.'

Fair enough. A hired man was nobody's – not a citizen anywhere.

Capture meant enslavement. I had played by those rules – I knew the game.

'I won't kill him,' I said.

The man met my eye for a moment as I approached him. Then he looked at the ground.

'You fought for my cousin Simon?' I asked.

'Simon?' The man spat. 'Cleitus paid us. Simon came along for the ride, the incompetent fuck.'

You think he should have held his tongue, friends? But why? He was our slave, and he knew what he had to do if he wanted to live. We needed no threats. Nor would I have done any differently, had I stood in his shoes.

I nodded. I looked at Teucer.

'Ask him why they came,' Teucer prompted.

'Okay, I'm game. Why did you come?' I asked.

'We were fucking paid to kill you, mate.' The man shrugged. 'Nothing personal.'

Teucer kicked him so hard he fell to the ground. 'Lord – Arimnestos is called "lord".'

The man got himself upright. 'We were paid to kill you, lord,' he managed. 'Could have just told me.'

'Can I buy him from you?' I asked Teucer.

'You will kill him?' Teucer said.

I shrugged. 'Perhaps.'

'Buy me a good working man, then. This one will be a lazy fuck.' Teucer put the man's rope in my hand. 'All yours. Now ask him what signalled them to start.'

I looked at the captive. He was squatting in the dust, but his eyes still had the glint of – pride, or resentment, or just stubbornness. I liked him a little for that. He was beaten, but not defeated.

He nodded. 'We was told to wait until we saw fires at Chalcis,' he said. 'Runner came in yesterday morning.'

Teucer nodded. 'See?' he asked.

I did see. If there was smoke rising over Chalcis – why then, the Persians must be in Euboea.

If the Persians were in Euboea, then the attack on Attica was close – two or three weeks away, at most.

If the Persians were about to attack Attica, then Athens would be paralysed, and it was safe for Simon to attack Plataea.

Secrets inside secrets, like the boxes which nest inside other boxes, smaller and smaller, until there's a tiny nut or a silver bell in the centre of seven or eight of them. Someone had plotted this very carefully – as I had suspected.

'Want to be free?' I said.

'You bet,' he said.

'Hmm. We'll see. That corpse is my mother. That one is a man who saved my life fighting. That's my best friend's father. Those women? My slaves.' I looked at him, and he grew pale.

'I—' he sputtered.

'Do as you're told,' I said. 'I know you're a hoplite. Somewhere, you are probably a gentleman.' I looked around. 'Right now, you're a slave, and if you fuck up, someone will kill you. Now – truth now – did you rape?'

He shook his head. 'No,' he said. And as I said – it was obvious he had been a gentleman. I believed him.

'Good. Then go and start helping.'

I sent Styges and one of my forge boys running for Myron, and I asked him to order the muster of the whole phalanx on my say-so.

Myron arrived on a mule, without ordering the muster. 'Why?' he asked, as soon as he had his leg over the beast's back. 'You slaughtered Thebans on their own ground. We're in for it now.'

I shook my head. 'Bold front, archon. I don't think that we did wrong – ask any man here, whose wife is lying with her throat slit. That's my *mother* over there.'

He spat. 'Fucking Thebans. Very well. What do you suggest, pole-march?'

I had the advantage that all the epilektoi were together, so that my officers – that is, my real officers – were there to advise me.

We'd had two hours to plan, and we'd hammered it out while we waited for Myron and cleared the rubble of the house. A hundred men – even a hundred tired men – can accomplish a great deal in a short time. My burned barn was now a dark smudge on the ground and my ruined house was a pile of fire-blackened stone out beyond the house wall. The burned beams had been stacked and three pyres of scrap wood from all the surrounding farms built on the hilltop. All that in a few hours.

By now I was much calmer. I'd had time to breathe, and no one let me do any work – nor did Idomeneus do any, as he was a lord now and a priest. Alcaeus was the same, so the three of us watched other men lift stones while we debated the campaign.

And when Myron asked, we were ready.

'How are the towers?' I asked.

'The west tower is done, and the east will be complete tomorrow or the next day, if the wind continues to blow dry.' He shrugged. 'They'll be done before Thebes can march.'

That confirmed what we'd hoped. 'Then this is our plan,' I said. 'First, we free all the slaves who built the towers.'

'Zeus Soter!' the archon said. 'That's the whole year's profits gone.'

I nodded. 'Not just for you, lord. But listen. We lost ten men yesterday – we'll lose ten times that in the next month, and that is *if we win*. We need those men as citizens. Yes?'

He shook his head. 'Perhaps later—'

I disagreed. 'We need them now. Because we want to put them in the armour of the dead hired men, install Lysius as their officer and leave them with another fifty picked men to guard the walls. In fact, we don't want them to sit within the walls. We want them to march down to the ford and camp, with light-armed men prowling around. If you dare—' I looked around, 'I'd send Teucer tonight to burn some barns in Thebes.'

Myron shook his head. 'You are talking about kicking a hornets' nest,' he said.

Idomeneus raised a long, plucked eyebrow. 'Ever faced down a bull in a meadow, archon?' he asked.

Myron nodded slowly. 'I have, too. You think that as long as we look tough, they'll back down.'

Alcaeus laughed. 'Not really, lord. The truth is, they have twelve thousand hoplites and we do not. But a show of aggression – especially after the tanning we gave those hired men – might slow them up for a week or two.' He shrugged. 'Lysius can always pull inside the walls later, when he sees the dust cloud coming.'

Myron gave a grim smile. 'All this planning suggests that you won't be here – with the phalanx.'

'That's right,' I said. 'According to our prisoners, Euboea was burning yesterday. Chalcis is being served up to the Persians. By the time we march, Euboea will have fallen.'

Alcaeus nodded. 'And Datis has the heart of the sailing season at his back,' he said. 'He'll move straight on to Athens.'

'And Athens will fall without my phalanx?' Myron asked softly.

I laughed. 'A thousand hoplites?' I made a face. 'Athens can find twelve thousand, and perhaps fifteen. They don't need the weight of our spears.' Secretly, I suspected that they *did* need the weight of our spears. 'But Athens has factions, Myron – factions the like of which you can't imagine. If we appear – to honour our agreements, and without being asked – we will strengthen Miltiades' hand. Enormously.'

He looked at me, and I looked at him.

'Archon,' I said, 'please. If Athens falls, or Medizes, Plataea is doomed. Thebes will eat us the way a gull eats a snail. Our only hope of preservation is to act – aggressively – for Athens.'

Myron looked out from our hilltop. Men were still carrying brush for the pyres to burn the bodies, and below, other men – my neighbours – were breaking up the biggest chunks of rubble with iron tools.

'When I was a much younger man,' he said, after a while, 'I stood in your forge yard with your father and a few other men, and we agreed to make an alliance with Athens to preserve our city from the yoke of Thebes.' He turned, and met my eye. 'I think the decision for today was made that day. I was wrong to slow the muster. I will see to it, and you will take my citizens over the mountain and do what you can.' He stood straight, as if ten years had fallen from his shoulders. 'May Zeus and Ares and Grey-Eyed Athena stand by you, for if you lose the phalanx, even in victory, why then our city will fall.'

When he went back to his mule, Alcaeus looked at me. 'Plataea is lucky to have so many great men in so small a city. Would that Miletus had done as well.'

'We may yet fail,' I said.

He shrugged. 'Of course. But not for the lack of trying.'

'Let's go and kill some Medes,' Idomeneus said, and he grinned.

We burned Mater, Bion and Cleon on the hilltop that afternoon, with wine and sacrifices and a priestess of Hera from the temple. And when they were ash, and the fires were great smoking columns not unlike the pillars of smoke that the raiders had left behind, the priestess came to me and proposed that I pay for a statue of Mater in the temple.

'She was a great woman,' the priestess said. She was a matron with iron at her temples and a vast reserve of dignity. 'Young women need examples of how to live – and die.'

I all but spat at her. 'She was drunk every day of her wedded life,' I said.

The priestess stepped back. 'Speak no ill of the dead!' she commanded. 'Is that the way you will speak of her? Or as the hero who fell defending your home?'

I gave her the money. There's a new statue that bears no resemblance to her – the Persians broke the one a local man made, smashing it to gravel with hammers. But in Plataea, the new temple honours Mater as an avatar of Hera. Take from that what you will.

While I mourned, the phalanx mustered.

A thousand men may not sound like many, but every man needs a slave and a donkey or a mule to carry his kit, to cook for him and keep him in fighting trim. And a thousand mules with two thousand men is a long column to lead over mountain tracks. It takes time for men to put their houses in order, and time to gather enough food for thirty days, and time for the slave to kiss his own wife. Time to make sure you have your second-best cloak as well as your war cloak, time to make sure that someone packed you some garlic sausage and some fresh onions from the garden.

My packing was done – my mule was still picketed high above Eleutherai, and my friends had rescued my kit from where I left it by Asopus. My good Persian shirt of scale was on Lysius's back, and my old helmet with the raven crest was on his head to puzzle the Thebans – and he did it no dishonour.

Euphoria fussed about, finding me oil with lavender in it, and retrieving – as if by a miracle – my father's heavy walking stick from the collapsed cellar of the house, charred a little but still strong as iron. And when she had seen me cared for, she took me by the hand and led me to our spring, up by the vineyard, and then she bathed with me, in the deep hole by the spring. There were men all about us on the hill, but none came near, and the olive grove hid us. There's no modesty when you bathe in an open sink of rock, and pregnancy or none, we made love. And then we washed again, and she put on the robe Mater had saved – a beautiful thing of red-purple, with gold embroidery. And I helped her put up her hair in a net of linen.

In the dooryard where Mater had fallen, she poured the libations on my shield and wiped it with a new linen towel, and then she did the same to my sword and my spear, and finally, defying convention, to my helmet.

I longed to crush her to me, but I did not. We were Greeks, not barbarians. Our women send us to war with dry eyes, and we left as if going to the fields and not to face death.

There was still smoke rising to the heavens from the funeral pyres when we marched. As we climbed the hills towards Cithaeron, we were joined by the main body from the agora of the city itself. In the distance, as we climbed, we could see smoke rising over Theban territory, and there were wolfish smiles as we went. The epilektoi marched first, up the same road they'd marched just ten days before on their way to the late-summer hunt.

They weren't boys any more. When they had torn into the hired men, they took losses – ten killed outright, another dozen dying of wounds. In a community as small as ours, the loss of twenty young men was a knife wound in the gut. Everyone was the friend, the lover, the wife, the sister or brother of one of the dead.

But they had killed, and won, and that changed them most of all. When we walked up the trails to the tomb of the hero, every man in my front rank knew that he was worthy of the blood of his fathers. He knew that he had been proven in fire, and like bronze, hardened by the working.

I could make you an argument that the hired men did us a favour by attacking us, but I'd be full of shit. There is no 'good war'.

We stopped at the shrine, as Plataeans have since the Trojan War, and we poured libations. Some men shouted for me to sacrifice my new slave on the tomb. His name was Gelon, and he was a Greek from Sicily. He heard them call for his blood and he stood there with my shield on his shoulder, watching me.

I looked at Idomeneus. It was his choice, really. He shook his head.

'No,' he said. 'We have shed enough blood, and the hero craves no more.'

He sacrificed a ram we'd brought for the purpose, looked at its entrails and shook his head.

'This isn't going to be good,' he said.

I spat. 'I didn't need entrails to tell me that,' I said.

We slept in our cloaks, and in the morning, after Teucer and the light-armed men rejoined from their raid into Thebes, we marched away over the mountains.

16

It was hot on the plains of Boeotia, and cold in the passes above Cithaeron. But when we came down off the passes, the sweltering sea-heat nearly choked us, and the humidity was such that a man could sweat through his chiton before he had it over his head.

I intended to keep to the high roads as long as possible. I didn't want to give away my march. This sounds odd, in light of what transpired, but I was very conscious of the passage of days, and it seemed all too possible, to me, that we would arrive to find Athens surrendered, or beaten – in which case I needed to get away unmolested by the Persian cavalry. I was very aware – as Myron wanted me to be – that I held the future of Plataea under my hand.

So we were wary, and stayed to the north of Attica as the shadows lengthened and the summer ended. We turned east as we came down the main pass, and marched for two days across uncultivated land, skirting Oinoe. Men saw us, but they did not come forward to speak to us, and I had a handful of my light-armed mounted on horses to keep me informed of the terrain, and we made good time.

A week into our march, and we were in Attica proper – an Attica bereft of citizen men. Doors were locked against us, and there were only slaves and women, and few enough of them, too. It was as if a dread disease had swept the land and killed them. There was even wheat left in some fields. One night when we camped, my men reaped a whole field with their swords and left three silver coins on the doorstep of the empty house in payment, and we baked bread the next night after grinding it in an empty grist mill and baking it in ovens we found cold.

A day's march from Athens, and we could see the Acropolis as clear as day on the horizon. It was not on fire, and I assumed that if Athens had surrendered or made peace, all these folk would have come flooding back down the roads to their farms. So I left my brother-in-law in charge, took my new slave and rode hard for Athens as the sun rose.

The gates were still open.

The streets were packed with people – all the farmers from the farms I'd just marched past, I expect. Most of them didn't pay me a glance as I rode by, because the only men who would have been interested in me were in the Agora, voting. Any man still on the streets was a slave, a freedman or a foreigner.

If I had thought that the Agora was full for Phrynichus's play, I was shocked to see how packed it was that late-summer day. I had to dismount and leave my horse with Gelon. Then I shouldered my way forward – I'm not a small man, but neither am I a giant, and no one wanted to make way for me. It took me an hour – five speeches – to make my way from the Tholos to the centre of the Agora, where the speakers stood.

For most of that time, I could see Miltiades.

He stood virtually alone. The men who stood by him were unknown to me, except Aristides and Sophanes, both of whom stood so proudly that they looked like men fighting in a desperate last stand.

When I was close enough, I could hear a man argue from the *bema* – the speaker's platform – that there was no need for Athens to march to the aid of Eretria, that Euboea was an ancient enemy of Athens (true enough, friends) and the Great King was welcome to lay them low. And more such stuff. In that hour, as I bulled my away across the Agora and felt every wound on my body, I heard every cringing excuse to avoid war, every noble sentiment against it, speeches of cowardice and speeches of sublime nobility.

When I was almost close enough to touch Miltiades, a man ascended the bema who looked like one of Themistocles' men. He stood with his head bowed for a moment, and then he raised it.

'What more can we do?' he asked. 'Miltiades asks that we form the phalanx and march to defend the coast – even to save Chalcis. But I ask – why must we fight alone? We have walls. And Sparta is *not* coming. Thebes has made their own peace. We are alone, men of Athens. Are we the protectors of Greece? Sparta craves that title – let them act the part.'

He got quite a cheer, too.

While men were cheering – it is easy to cheer for other men to do the hard work while you sit home, I find – Miltiades raised his head. He was plainly dressed, for him, in a dark chlamys over a plain white chiton with one stripe. The gold pin at his shoulder was his only concession to rank. He raised his head and his eyes met mine – and lit up the way my eyes lit when they crossed with Euphoria's.

He waited until he could clasp my hand. And then he pulled me sharply, so that he towed me as one ship will tow another after a storm. He didn't bother to mount the bema. He simply raised my hand, the way a judge in games raises the hand of a victor.

'You lie,' he roared. 'Plataea is here!'

Chaos.

Men shouted – one thing, and then another. I saw my father-in-law in the crowd, and I saw Aristides, and I saw Cleitus. I had thought him an exile until then. Our eyes met, and the hate flowed like wine.

I was still locked in that when the archon basileus pushed to my side.

'Do you have an army?' he asked.

'A thousand hoplites,' I said. 'Which is every man we have.'

He embraced me. He, an aristocrat, who had no love for me or mine, but he embraced me, and then he pointed to the bema. 'You have my permission to speak,' he said.

So, although I was a foreigner, I mounted the speaker's platform. The crowd was not quiet, but I didn't care. I raised my hand.

'I have brought the full muster of Plataea,' I shouted. 'And left Thebes afraid. Plataea stands with Athens!'

And by the time I came down from the platform, they were already voting Aristides and Miltiades as strategoi, and sending the phalanx out to fight.

As every schoolboy knows, the assembly voted ten strategoi. Aristides and Miltiades were but two of them, and Cleitus of the Alcmaeonids a third. And even when they began to muster the phalanx, half of the generals were still dead set against war – or at least, offensive war. The very next thing they did was to vote for a runner to be sent to Sparta to beg for help – that's how it sounded to me, anyway. And why not? The Spartans, for all my sneers, were the best soldiers in Greece – perhaps in the world.

I stood with Miltiades as he hurried men to get their kit. Many men of the phalanx were already prepared – had been so for days. Men of the other party were unprepared, or at least most were, so assured were they that the phalanx would not march.

The polemarch of Athens was Callimachus of Aphidna. He was an older man with a fine reputation, both as a warrior and as a politician. I have heard men say that he hesitated, that he only marched when Miltiades threatened to take his men and sail away – Miltiades, after all, had his own army from the Chersonese, almost a thousand hoplites with more military experience than the rest of Athens put together. Not so. Let us be fair. He was hesitant – extremely hesitant – to march. Remember, this was before the Persian fleet had even been sighted. The Persians were just a rumour of terror up the coast – although on a clear day, you could see the fires in Euboea rising to the heavens.

He was hesitant for a reason. I tasted this hesitancy myself.

It is one thing to march in the phalanx. It is another to go in the front rank – and yet another to be a killer of men, a hero, a man who can change a battle. But *all of them* – the killer, the front-ranker, the rear-ranker – have more in common than any of them share with the polemarch and the strategos. On their shoulders rests the burden – fight, or don't fight. March or don't march. Choose correctly, and your name will live for ever. *For ever.* Choose badly, or get cursed by the gods, and your city is lost, your friends killed, your elders butchered, your women raped and sold as slaves.

Understand?

If you aren't hesitant about fighting, then you are a fucking idiot.

And those men who voted against the fight? They had to go and stand shoulder to shoulder with the men who voted for the fight, and each had to depend on the other. The city was divided about evenly, I'd say, half for glory, half for caution.

Callimachus was right to hesitate.

I watched the chaotic preparations – the same mess as our Plataean preparations but magnified ten times – and shook my head.

'Why such a hurry?' I asked. 'Tomorrow morning will be as good as this evening – and surely you won't march before dark?'

Miltiades pursed his lips. 'If you hadn't come just when you did, god-sent, I would not have carried this debate,' he said.

Slaves came up with his kit, and his hypaspist, a Thracian I'd seen with him before, shouldered his shield and flashed me a blond smile.

Miltiades smiled himself when he saw his panoply. 'If I can get them clear of the city before night falls,' he said, 'I have a chance. If we're here in the morning, we'll never march.' He shrugged. 'I could be wrong, but I don't think so. I have a feel for these things.'

Aristides came, surrounded by men I knew – Sophanes, of course, but also Agios and Phrynichus and a dozen oarsmen I recognized, all dressed as hoplites. Their kit was as good as our front-rankers. Athens has money, and money buys armour.

'I suggested that we free a thousand slaves and put them in the ranks,' Aristides said. 'And these fools declined, saying that it would be too hard to choose what tribes they would go to.' He shook his head. 'Some of them even wanted to decline the service of the armed metics.'

I stood there while the sun sank, and I had nothing to do but think. After a few minutes, or even an hour, I turned to Aristides. 'Plataea will take your freedmen,' I said. 'Put them in my rear ranks. Then your proud citizens have nothing to complain about.'

He gave me a thin-lipped smile. 'Tomorrow,' Aristides said. 'Today, we march out of the city. Miltiades is right. Today, or never.'

The shadows were long enough to make a short man tall when Miltiades took his tribe out of the gate. It was a purely symbolic march – Miltiades was to Athens as I was to little Plataea, and his men were ready. Many carried their own gear, poor men who knew no other trade but fighting, and they had been assembled and ready since the last vote.

Aristides marched next, with the men of the Antiochis. By the time Miltiades' men cleared the sacred gate, Aristides' men were ready to march, even though his tribe, by ill-chance, contained many of those most determinedly against the war.

The other strategoi were less ready, but Aristides had set the example by marching despite having a third of his *taxis* missing, and so the other *taxeis* of the tribes marched away as soon as their turns came. I stood and waited – after all, I had a horse – and what I saw heartened me. Men continued to come to the square behind the sacred gate, kiss their wives, pour a quick libation and run down the road, with a slave or a servant and a donkey hurrying after them, so that there was a constant flow of stragglers and sluggards behind the march of the army. The strategoi had left almost half the army behind. It could have been a disaster, but the men of Athens – even those against the war – did their duty.

When I mounted my horse, darkness was falling.

'Have we won, do you think?' Gelon asked me. I laughed to hear him say 'we'.

'We haven't won,' I said. 'We haven't lost. We've marched, and if Miltiades is to be believed, that means we're still in the game.'

'You could free me now,' Gelon said. 'No one around to kill me.'

I nodded. 'I could, but I won't. You fight in the phalanx – and fight well. If you live, I'll free you.'

'Free me first,' he said. 'I'm fucked if I'm going to fight as a slave. No one will want me anyway. Who ever heard of a slave hoplite?'

That was true. 'I tell you what, Gelon. If the Athenians free their slaves, I'll put you in with them.'

'As a slave?' he asked, daring.

'As a free man, you whoreson. Now get your arse moving down the road.' Gelon made me laugh, in a dark way. I was coming to like him. He bore slavery with a kind of amused contempt that made it impossible for me to punish him while he showed his resistance every minute. I respected that. I also thought that another man – Idomeneus, for instance – would have beaten him to a pulp.

The sun was setting, and although we didn't know it yet, Chalcis had just been stormed. One of the richest cities in Greece – an ancient rival of Athens, at sea and on land, the city that colonized Sicily and southern Italy and even the coast of Asia – had fallen by treachery to the Great King. Datis ordered the warriors massacred and the women and children sold into slavery, just as he had at Miletus and Lesbos.

His tame Greeks turned away from the slaughter, but the Sakai and the Medes and the Persians butchered the men and the elderly and set fire to the city – every house and every temple. The column of smoke rose to the heavens like a sacrificial fire, and could be seen from the Acropolis, as Datis intended.

Datis sent his cavalry across the bridge to sow terror the way a farmer sows barley.

The women were loaded into his troop ships, weeping at their state – women who had been wives, who had known love, who had sat at their looms proud of their family names.

And the ships, crewed by Phoenicians and Ionian Greeks, got their sterns in the water, unfolded the mighty wings of their oars and turned their ram-prows south, with a gentle wind at their backs and a protected sea. It was too late for Poseidon to intervene. The Great King's fleet was at sea, the oars pulled to the lamentations of five thousand new slaves.

Their rams were pointed at Attica. And even as we marched out of Athens and made our first camp in the hills north of the city, even as men groused or had second thoughts, Datis's scouts were riding through the long grass by the beach, at Marathon.

17

Last night, while we were drinking, the young scribe from Halicarnassus asked me why Athens didn't meet Datis at sea. It's a damn good question, given the size of Athens's fleet today.

The truth is, in the time of Marathon, there was no Athenian fleet. I realize that this sounds impossible, but the fact is that the tyrants and the oligarchs shared a healthy fear of the demos, and the fleet gives the demos power, because the power of the fleet is its rowers, not its hoplites – the thetes who pulled the oars. So noblemen owned warships – Tartarus, friends, I owned a warship at the time of Marathon! Aristides owned one, Sophanes' family owned one, and Miltiades owned ten at the height of his power. That was the Athenian fleet, the accumulation of the ships of the rich – not unlike the way they formed a phalanx, come to think of it. And all the ships Athens could muster might have made fifty hulls. Before Lade, fifty hulls had been accounted a mighty fleet. But the world was changed by the Great King's decision to spend Greece into defeat. His six hundred triremes – give or take a hundred – won him Lade, though it strained his empire to maintain them, and they emptied the ocean of trained rowers.

But Athens had nothing to offer against his six hundred. Our hulls were all on the beach at Piraeus, all those that weren't ferrying refugees across to Salamis or around the coast to the Peloponnese.

The first night we camped in the precinct of a temple of Heracles perched high on the ridge above Athena's city. My Plataeans were still forty stades away to the north, and I saw no reason to bring them along yet, as we had no word of the enemy and the Athenian camp was in enough disorder as it was.

Greek armies are usually only as good as the time and distance they are from home. The first night, with the army close enough to home to sleep there if they wanted, with none of the discipline or shared experience that an army builds with every camp and every smoky meal, they are just a mob of men with little in common except their duty to the city.

Many of them have no notion how to live rough, or how to eat without their wives and slaves to cook. The aristocrats have no problems – the aristocrat's life as a gentleman farmer and hunter is perfectly suited to training campaigners. But the potters and the tanners and the small farmers – all strong men – may never have eaten a meal under the wheel of the heavens in their lives.

Gelon and I bedded down with Miltiades' men, who had none of these problems and little but contempt for their fellow Athenians. These were the men he'd led at Lade and a dozen other fights, and they were confident in themselves and in their lord.

Aristides' men were a different matter. Let me just say that since Cleisthenes' reforms – fairly recent when we marched to Marathon – all of the 'tribes' of Athens were artificial constructs. Cleisthenes had sought to break up the power bases of the great aristocrats (like Miltiades) by ensuring that every tribe was composed in equal parts of men of the city (the potters and tanners, let's say), men of the farms (up-country men, small farmers and aristocrats, too) and men of the sea (fishermen, coastal men and oarsmen). It was a brilliant law – it gave every Athenian a shared identity with men from the parts of Attica that most individuals had never visited.

Another thing that he did – another brilliant thing – was to heroize everyone's ancestors. In Athens, the principal difference between an aristocrat and a commoner was not money – freedmen and merchants often had lots of money, and no one thought of them as aristocrats, believe me! No, the biggest difference was ancestors. An aristocrat was a man descended from a god or from a hero. Miltiades was descended from Ajax of Salamis, and through him back to Zeus. Aristides was descended, like me, from Heracles.

My friend Agios was descended from parents who were citizens, but they had no memory of anything before their own parents. Cleon's father was a fisherman, but his mother had been a whore.

But when Cleisthenes passed his reforms – this happened while I was a slave in Ephesus – he gave every tribe a heroic ancestor, and declared – by law – that everyone in the tribe could count that ancestor in their descent. I've heard men – never Athenians, but other

Greeks – say that Cleisthenes brought democracy to Athens. Crap. Cleisthenes was a far, far more brilliant man than that. I never met him, but like most middle-class men, I revere his memory as the man who built the Athens we loved.

What he did was to make every man an aristocrat.

In one stroke of law, every oarsman and every whore's son had as much reason to serve his city as Aristides and Miltiades and Cleitus. To live well, with arete, and to die with honour. I'm not saying that it worked – any better than any other political idea. But to me, it is a glorious idea, and it made the Athens that stood against the Great King.

The main consequence was that the precinct of Heracles was filled with men who would never, ever have been in a phalanx fifteen years before. When my father died serving alongside Athens in Euboea, their phalanx had about six thousand men, and while the front ranks were superb, the rear ranks were poor men with spears, no shields, no armour and no hope of standing for even a heartbeat against a real warrior. That was the way.

But the new Athens had a phalanx with twice as many spears – almost twelve thousand. And from what I could see, almost *all* of them had the white leather spolades for which Athens was famous. The city owned the tanning trade back then, and their white leather was prized from Naucratis to the Troad. They all seemed to have helmets, too.

See, what Cleisthenes did was to create a city where a man who made pots and worked a plot of land just big enough to yield two hundred medimnoi of grain – about a tenth of what my farm yielded in a good year – would spend his surplus cash – a *very* small amount, friends – on armour and weapons. Like an aristocrat.

Thugater, you are laughing at me. Am I too passionate? Listen, honey – I may be tyrant here, but in my heart I'm a Boeotian farmer. I don't want the aristocrats to rule; I want every man to stand up for himself, take his place in the line, farm his plot, eat his own figs and his own cheese – raise his hand in the assembly and curse when he wants. When I'm honest, I realize that I joined the ranks of the aristos pretty early. It may be that, as my mother said, our family was always with them. But I never wanted power over other men, except in war.

Now you're all laughing at me. I think I should keep my story for another day. Perhaps I'll go and sulk in my tent. Perhaps I'll take blushing girl here for company.

Hah! More wine. That was worth the interruption. Look at that colour!

Now, where was I?

In the morning, I mounted my horse and Gelon got on my mule and we rode away north to find my brother-in-law and the Plataeans. The Athenians turned east after they passed the great ridge and headed for the sea.

I reached my men before noon, and found that they were fed, well slept and ready to march.

Antigonus shrugged. 'I enjoyed being polemarch,' he said. 'Go back to the Athenians. I'll take it from here.' He grinned and slapped my back, but when we had the army moving, he came up beside me in the dust. 'Don't ever do that to me again,' he said quietly. 'When you didn't come back last night, all I could see was panic and horror. The Persians had you, the fucking Athenians had arrested you – what was I to do?'

'Just as you did,' I said, and slapped him on the back in turn.

I had brought a pair of guides from Miltiades, both local men from the Athenian phalanx who knew all the trails and small roads that led east from our position. So we made good time, although the way was never straight and at one point we actually crossed some poor farmer's wheat field – two thousand men and as many animals crushing his precious crop. But it was the only way to join two paths. Attica had some of the worst roads in the world then.

I rode ahead with Gelon and Lykon and Philip the Thracian, both serving as volunteers as their cities had no part in this war, and we found a camp – three hayfields, all fallow or recently cut, with stone walls all around, on a low ridge with a stream at the bottom. It's one of the best positions I've ever found, and I went back to it on another occasion. We slept secure. I had sentries every night already – a lesson learned from my first campaigns.

We rose with dawn – all that hunting on Cithaeron had good effect – ate hard bread and drank a little wine, then moved. Before noon we were up with the tail of the Athenian force, which was moving down through the olive groves that crowned the ridges around Aleitus's farm and tower. I knew the trails here – again, from hunting – and my guides were off their own ground. So I took us a little north, over the same ridge where Aleitus's party had killed two deer, and down through the old orchards where mine had killed six.

296

Aristides was first that day – the tribes have a strict rotation in everything, from order of march to place in the battle line – and he was the strategos in charge, because the Athenians rotated the command. He was choosing his camp when I rode up with my little party.

He smiled when he saw me. I didn't smile – any pleasure was wiped from my heart when I saw that he was with Cleitus.

Aristides raised a hand. 'Stop,' he said.

I had my hunting spear in my fist.

'We are here to fight the Medes, not each other,' Aristides said.

'Look,' I said. 'You found a horse!' I snorted. 'I thought I heard that something had happened to them.'

Cleitus had his sword in his hand. 'How's your mother?' he asked.

Aristides hit him – hard – in the temple with his fist. Aristides was a good athlete and a fine boxer, and Cleitus fell from his horse.

But when I rode over to him, Aristides caught my spear hand in a grip of iron.

'In this army,' he said, 'there are other men who hate each other – political foes, personal enemies, men with lawsuits. We have tribes with rivalries, and men with conflicting interests in money – men who have absconded with wives and daughters, men who committed crimes. And worst of all, as both of you know, we have men who have taken money from the Great King and who will use their power to break us the way they broke the East Greeks at Lade – through defection and treachery.'

Cleitus got to his feet and put a hand to his head. 'You have a heavy hand, sir.'

Aristides nodded. 'We are in the precinct of Heracles – ancestor to all three of us. You will both come with me to the altar and swear – to the gods – to keep the peace and fight together like brothers. You are *leaders*. If you fight each other – we are *finished*.'

'He killed my *mother*,' I said. 'And his actions served the Great King. He's taking the Great King's money. He planned to kill me to keep the Plataeans out of this.'

Cleitus looked at me with the kind of contempt I hadn't seen in a man's eyes since I was a slave. 'You live in a world of delusion, peasant. I would *never* do anything to serve the Great King. I am an Athenian. I will crush you like the insect that you are – for hubris. For treating my family as if we were at your level. Killed your mother?' He laughed. 'It should have been you – and it is no care of mine if some raddled Boeotian whore got in the way.' He turned to Aristides.

'I swore to kill him and all his family. He has insulted me and mine.'

Aristides crossed his arms. 'Cleitus – most men in this army think your family are traitors.' Cleitus whirled around in angry denunciation, but Aristides cut him off with a raised hand. 'If you refuse to swear my oath, Cleitus, I will send you from the army, and I will cease defending you to the demos.' More quietly, he said, 'This is not the agora, nor the palaestra. He insulted your family? You insulted his? By all the gods, we are talking about the existence of our city! Are you a playground bully or a man of honour?'

I had lowered my spear-point. Aristides always had that effect on me. His moral advantage was almost as great as Heraclitus's – he lived the words he spoke. But I was still angry.

'Aristides,' I said, 'I honour you more than most men, but he killed my friends and fellow townsmen – and my mother. He killed them for vanity. His so-called revenge? He brought it on himself, by trying to treat me the way he treats the demos – as lesser men.'

'You killed his horses – fifty horses. The value of ten farms. You killed them.' Aristides stood in front of me, imperturbable. 'You killed them to humiliate the Alcmaeonids. Not to save Miltiades – but for your sense of your own honour. Deny it if you can.'

'He murdered my people!' Cleitus said. 'Family retainers!'

'Thugs,' I said. 'Aristides, this is foolishness. You, of all men, know why I did what I did.'

'I do,' Aristides said. 'You did what you did to achieve what you perceived as justice. As did Cleitus.'

'He killed my mother!' I yelled.

'My family is *in exile*,' Cleitus said. 'My uncle died – he *died* – far from our city. Thanks to you, the dogs of this city bay for our blood and the little men – tradesmen, men whose grandfathers were *slaves* – treat us with contempt. For that, I would kill you and every man and every woman with a drop of your blood in his veins.'

'So both of you can wallow in selfishness, pride, self-deceit – and Athens can be burned by the Medes.' Aristides raised an eyebrow. 'Come with me – both of you.'

Such was his authority that we followed him. He led us over the brow of the hill on which the precinct of the shrine of Heracles stood. Suddenly, in the blaze of the late-summer son, we were looking down the hill to the plain, the fields and olive groves of one of Attica's richest areas, all the way to the beach at Marathon.

And from the curve of the beach, as far north as the eye could see, were ships. Hundreds of ships – ships as thick on the sea as ants around an anthill when the plough rips it asunder. Many of them were already stern-in to the beach, over by the marsh at the north end of the bay. They were unloading men, and tents – or so I guessed.

Closer to us, in the open ground at the foot of the hill, there were a dozen Sakai cavalrymen. They were looking up the hill at us. They had gold on their arms, in their hats, on their saddles, and every one of them had a heavy bow at his waist and a pair of long spears in his fist.

'There they are. The Persians, the Medes, the Sakai – the armoured fist of the Great King, here to chastise Athens for her sins. Now – choose. Stand here, in the sight of the enemy, and fight each other to the death – and on your heads be the future that you squander. Or both of you can swear my oath. Fight side by side. Show the army – every man of whom knows your story, and your hate, believe me – that war with Persia is bigger than family, bigger than revenge. And when the Persians are gone, you may kill each other, for all I care.'

Silence, and the wind sighing over the golden wheat fields down by the sea.

I nodded. 'I will swear,' I said. What else could I say? Aristides was the Just Man. What he asked was just.

Nor was Cleitus – for all that I still burn with hate for him – less a man than I. 'I will swear,' he said. 'Because you are right. I will go farther – because I am a better man than this Boeotian pig. I paid men to fight against you, Plataean. But I am sorry that your mother died. For that – alone – you have my apology.'

I might have muttered an apology for the death of his uncle – even if I did, his was the nobler gesture, but then, his was the greater crime.

This is so often the way with men. The gesture is the thing that we remember – the grand apology, the noble death. Did my mother's noble death wipe clean a lifetime of woe? Did Cleon's? Is a great apology the equal of a great crime?

I don't know, and Heraclitus was no longer alive to tell me.

We stood on either side of the low-saddled altar of Heracles, clasped arms like comrades and swore to stand together against the Persians, to support each other and be brothers and comrades. We followed Aristides, word for word, until he finished.

'Until the Persians are defeated,' Cleitus added.

'Until the Persians are defeated,' I repeated, meeting his eyes.

'You are both idiots,' Aristides said.

I'd like to say that a spirit of cooperation swept the army after I swore not to kill Cleitus, but I'm not sure anyone noticed. This is the problem with acts of moral courage and ethical purity. Had I struck him down with my hunting spear, I'm sure there might have been consequences, but having stayed my hand, there was no observable change. Heraclitus and Aristides both told me that the only reward for a correct action is the knowledge of having acted well – fair enough, but I suspect that you have to be Aristides or Heraclitus to feel that such knowledge is enough reward for the sacrifice of something so deeply satisfying as revenge.

At any rate, we made camp in the precinct of Heracles. From the summit, we could see the Persians unloading their ships.

I brought the Plataeans to the north of the Athenians – the left end of our line of camp, and the spot closest to the enemy. We took the rocky end of the temple precinct, almost like a small acropolis.

It wasn't much ground, but it would be easy to defend, and it had a big stand of cypress trees in the centre – good shade. As I considered it, I saw a man turn aside to relieve himself in the woods, and I caught him. 'No man relieves himself inside the camp,' I said.

Even with the hunting, they'd never been on campaign. Most of my men had no idea how fast disease can stalk a camp. So as soon as we'd stopped, I gathered the warriors in a great circle and stood on a pile of shields so that they could all hear me.

'All men will sleep here, on the rock,' I said. 'The cypress trees will give us shade and some shelter, but no man is to cut one, or build a fire under them, for fear of offence to the god. Nor is any man to relieve himself inside the precinct. I will mark a boundary for such things below. Nor will any man use the stream to wash himself, his animal or his clothes, except where I mark it – so that the stream herself will not feel defiled. And so no man's shit will float down into our cook pots,' I said, and they laughed, and my point was made.

The Plataean strategoi chose their ground, and then we went down the ancient ramp behind the high ground and chose a low bog for men to use, and had slaves dig trenches across it and lay logs. And we chose a place for the slaves to draw water and wash clothes.

'Water is going to be a problem,' Antigonus said.

'I don't understand why we have to have all these rules,' Epistocles said. He shook his head. 'If I have to go in the night, do you really think I'm going to walk all this way?'

'Yes,' I said.

'Well, you can guess again,' he said, with a foolish little laugh.

'Epistocles, you are an officer, and men will take their lead from you. If men start pissing in our camp, it will soon become unliveable. This is the most defensible terrain for ten stades. Don't piss on it.' I grinned at him, but only in the way I grin when I'm prepared to use my fists to make a man see sense, and he backed away.

'You seem to think you can give orders like a king,' he said.

'This is war,' I said. 'Some men it makes kings, and others it makes slaves.'

'What's that?' he said.

'Never mind,' I said, and we went off to find space for two thousand men to sleep.

We spent two days making camp and watching the Persians make theirs. They had to land all those men, and some of us wondered why we didn't just rush them when they had about a third of their men ashore – it was discussed, but we did nothing.

In fact, there was something awe-inspiring about the size of the Persian force and their fleet. They also had almost a thousand cavalry – deadly horse-archers, Persians and Sakai – who had been further north, filtering down from Eretria in pursuit of the last force in the field there, an army of Athenian settlers and Euboeans who had retreated in good order from the initial defeats but gradually died under the arrows of the Sakai. We had had no idea that they still existed until a runner came in on the third morning – a man with an arrow in his bicep who collapsed as soon as he entered the army's agora.

When Athens had defeated Euboea in my father's time, they had determined to hold the place thereafter, and they sent four thousand settlers, lower-class Athenians, to become colonists and to hold the best farms. There was no love lost between the settlers and the locals, but when the Persians came, they made a good force. They fought three small actions with the Persians, trying to break out, and finally they got fishing boats and shuttled across the straits, right under the noses of the enemy – but then the cavalry fell on them. Those men had been fighting – and running – for two weeks.

It was Miltiades' day to command, and he summoned us all as soon as he heard what the messenger had to say.

'One day's march north, there are two thousand men – good men, and they're dying under the arrows of the Sakai.' He looked around. 'I propose we take our archers and our picked men, and go and relieve them.'

Callimachus shook his head. 'You cannot split the army,' he said. 'And you cannot defeat their cavalry. That's why we camped here – remember, fire-breather? So that their arrows could not easily reach us.'

Miltiades shook his head. 'With picked men, if we move fast and take archers of our own – we can beat them. Or at least scatter them, the way dogs can drive lions off their prey.'

Aristides nodded. 'We have to try. To leave those men to their deaths – no one would ever speak well of us again.'

Miltiades looked around. 'Well?'

'I have a hundred Plataeans who can run the whole distance,' I said. 'And twenty archers to run with them.'

Miltiades smiled. But before he could speak, the polemarch shook his head.

'If we must do this, then every man should go – in the dark. We can feel our way with guides, and be across the ridge before the Medes know we've gone. We'll catch their cavalry napping.' He looked around, the weight of the responsibility heavy on him. I think he would rather that the Euboeans had died at home.

But he was right. Miltiades wanted a heroic raid, but if we were all together, and we moved fast, we'd accomplish the mission with much less risk.

Everyone chose Callimachus's method over Miltiades'.

We rose in the dark, hours before the morning star would rise, and we slipped away behind our temple precinct hill, leaving three thousand chosen men to hold the camp behind us. By the time the sun was up, our leading men – my Plataeans – were less than ten stades from the hilltop where our Euboean-Athenians were making their stand.

I wanted to run down the road with my epilektoi, but I knew that the only way to do this was with massed bodies of impenetrable spears. I hadn't fought cavalry since the fight on the plains by Ephesus, but what I had learned there seemed pertinent – stay together and wait for the horsemen to flinch.

By mid-morning, we were spotting Sakai scouts, and Teucer brought one down with a well-aimed arrow. The next time we saw a party of them form, Teucer had a dozen of his light-armed men together, and they lofted arrows with a little breeze behind them.

The Sakai rode out from under their little arrow shower, but their counter-shots fell well short, and after that, it was like a deadly game of rovers. Our archers could out-range theirs, and that meant that they couldn't come in on us, and twice Teucer's little band took one of the Sakai off his horse, or left the horse dead, and they gave us room.

The Athenians had a city archer corps, all dressed like Scythians. They were mostly poor men, but very proud, and they shot well enough. There were two hundred of them, and they were all together just behind my Plataeans, so that the one time an enterprising Mede worked around my flank in some hedgerows, he emerged into a veritable hail of arrows and ran off leaving two of his men in the wheat.

Casualties like that – ones and twos – don't seem important when I tell a story as big as Marathon. But in skirmishes – in harassment – a dozen dead men can be as important as a lost battle. Our arrows were hitting them, and they weren't reaching us.

So just before noon, their captain, whoever he was, decided that enough was enough and sent his best men to stop me.

I wish I could say that I saw what was coming – but it was more luck than anything that we weren't caught naked.

As usual, I have to digress. Hoplites – heavy warriors – don't wander the countryside all dressed up for war. It is hot in Greece, and the aspis is heavy, as is your thorax and your helmet and your spear. Once a man has the aspis on his shoulder and a spear in his hand, his speed is cut on the march.

Perhaps it is just that Greeks are lazy. I have, in fact, spent all day marching with an aspis on my shoulder. But in the old days, we seldom did it. Instead, we carried our weapons, and our servants – sometimes free hypaspists, sometimes slaves – carried our helmets and shields.

After the cavalry tried to work around our rear, I halted the column and ordered the Plataeans to arm. That actually increased my vulnerability for a while. Imagine two thousand men on the road, just two or three abreast, in no particular order. Then imagine that every second man is busy finding his shield-bearer and getting his aspis on his arm, his helmet on his head. Some men had their body-armour on and others did not. Some men had additional pieces of armour – thigh armour and arm guards, such as I wore. All of these were carried by servants.

In my case, I wore my scale cuirass all day, but the rest of my gear was in a wicker basket on Gelon's back. I even considered changing my shoes – I had 'Spartan' shoes on my feet, and I considered, given the difficult fields on either side of the road, changing to boots.

Some men were sitting in the road, changing sandals. Others were stripping naked to change into a heavier chiton to wear under armour.

Got the picture? Chaos. I hate to think how long we were on that road without a single spear pointing at the enemy. I aged.

It is different at sea. At sea, you do not engage until you are ready. But on land – especially facing cavalry or light troops – they can hit you whenever they desire it. I was the leader, and I had fucked up. I could feel it. And now – too late – I was trying to retrieve my error. It was a lesson, if you like.

As soon as I had a party of men armed, I filled the road with them, regardless of their place in the phalanx. And as soon as the bulk of my men were armed, I started them filing off the road to the left, where I could see the shields of our Euboean refugees flashing among the rocks on the hillside.

Our guide, the wounded runner, pointed and gestured, and my eyes were on him when the Persian cavalry came for us. We had about a third of our men formed when they galloped around the corner of the field from behind a grove of olives. They already had arrows on their bows. Their leader was out in front on a big bay horse, and as he came around the corner he gave a whoop, leaned over and shot.

That arrow went into my shield and the head emerged on my side, a finger's width, just over my wrist where my hand entered the antilabe.

'Form close!' I called, and I was scared – shocked silly. I had just enough nerve to tip my helmet from the back of my head over my face. Every man pressed into the centre of the front rank as the shields overlapped.

Where had they come from?

I cursed my failing in not forming up earlier, and I wondered how the rest of my column was doing, and I nearly shat myself in fear. These were not Lydians with spears. These were noble Persians, well led, with discipline and murderous bow-fire, and my men were unprepared.

The first hail of arrows hit our shields. A man screamed as an arrow went into his knee above the greave – his scream might have been my scream.

They came past us, close enough for us to see the markings on their horses and the embroidery on their barbarian trousers and to feel the earth moved by four hundred hooves.

The next storm of arrows broke over us like a big wave on a beach. I felt my shield lifted, moved, rocked as if hail was falling on me, and something screamed off my helmet and I blinked away the pain. My vision was limited to the eye slit in my Corinthian, and sweat was pouring down my body. But I saw it now – the Persian commander had sprung an ambush from behind the olive grove, and I was lucky that I'd paused to form my men or we'd already be dead. Luck. Tyche. And he had made two mistakes. He sprang his trap a little early, before my left flank was out in the field, away from the rocky wall that his horses didn't want to cross. And he went for us – the formed men – when he could have fallen like a smith's hammer on my unformed men on the road.

Instead, we were trapped against the field edge with a rubble pile from an old barn on one flank and the road full of slaves and Athenians on the other – but we'd stood our ground. It sounds easy enough. You try it.

Even as his first arrows rattled against us and men fell, he learned his third error, although I was as surprised as I imagine he was.

We had archers in our ranks.

As the Persians swept past us, Teucer and his archers rose from within our ranks, or knelt under the rims of our shields, and shot. Indeed, Teucer was leaning his weight against my hips as he shot, arrow after arrow. He had no horse between his thighs, no reins to manage, and his quiver hung comfortably under his left arm, where I carry my sword in battle, and he drew and shot and drew and shot, three arrows for every one by the Persians, and his had Apollo's hand behind them.

When an arrow hits a man in the phalanx, he screams and falls, and his armour makes a mournful clatter as he goes down – but his mates close over him, alive or dead. It is but one step to the front to fill the hole.

When a horseman takes an arrow – better yet, when a *horse* takes an arrow – it can be a disaster for a dozen other men. One horse can fall over another, and a few casualties, by ill-luck or the will of the war god, can stop a charge dead, or cause the animals to flow around their target the way small boys divert a stream on a summer's day.

We had fewer than three hundred men formed, but all of Teucer's archers were in our ranks – perhaps thirty men, and some javelins – and they shot at least one Persian for every one of us who fell. I suspect that, man for man, the Persians were the finer archers – but the best archer on a horse, shooting at armoured men behind big shields, is going to lose the contest to the poorer man with his feet firm on the ground, shooting at the enormous target of a man on a horse.

And Teucer was the best archer I've ever known. He was safe under my shield rim, and his arrows did not miss. He made chaos of their files, and they broke and rode away, and their red-bearded officer lay, redder now, with one of Teucer's black-fletched arrows in his throat.

We spearmen played no role, except to stand and not run, and to be a living wall of wood and bronze for Teucer's archers. We didn't bloody our spears that day. The archers won that engagement for us, and gained status with us as a consequence.

The Persian commander watched his best cavalry break around us, leaving a dozen of his noblemen face down in the hayfields, and he gathered the rest of his cavalry and rode away, no doubt reckoning, like a professional, that the terrain was against him and he had no reason to take a risk.

He was wrong. There's more to battle than counting the odds and chances and watching the ranges of the enemy weapons. The Athenians and Plataeans were Greeks – men of the phalanx, where fights are decided not by spear-fighting but by the will of the mass. To every Plataean – and to every Athenian coming late to the fight – it appeared that we were the better men, and the Persians were afraid. Not true, of course, but on such foolishness is victory made.

We watched their dust cloud go, and a few fools shouted that we should follow them, but the Persians wanted us out in the open and we were happy in among the olive groves and low ridges where they couldn't easily ride around our flanks. We let them go.

In half an hour, Miltiades passed through my position. I chose to stay formed and watch the Persians, lest they fall on the rest of the column, or at least, that was my decision on the spot. Miltiades went up the hill and fetched out the Euboeans. I'll be honest – I was shaken. To my mind, Teucer and his archers had just saved me from a string of foolish errors. Command is different. It is not the same as serving in the front rank. I had been thinking of the wrong things, at the wrong time, and I knew how close my whole force – every Plataean – had come to dying at the hands of a hundred Persians.

The rescued Euboeans were in poor shape. They had no archers – few Greeks did, in those days, except old-fashioned cities like Plataea, and we wouldn't have had half as many without the Milesians – and the Persian cavalry had been able to get close, every day, whenever they wanted. A few of the Euboeans had the spirit to abuse the corpses of the dead Persians as they came down – one man told me that this was the closest he'd come to hitting one since the first day – but the rest simply stumbled off the steep rocks of their hill and begged us for water in the croaking of frogs, for they were parched and weary and had given up hope.

Then we all turned on our heels and marched back to our camp. And the Persian cavalry rode away. I lost three men dead – all young epilektoi in the front rank. Lykon took an arrow in the greave – it held, but he couldn't walk for a day from the pain. My wounded were mostly gashes to the head and neck – sometimes arrows went deep in the phalanx and got in among the men with no helmets, skidding from head to head. Two men with arrows in their thighs had to be carried, and that was hot, miserable work.

As soon as our scouts said that the Persian cavalry was gone, most men peeled off their armour and gave it to slaves to carry, but I wouldn't allow my epilektoi out of theirs – I was deeply shaken by the speed with which the Persian cavalry had appeared from behind the olive grove. No one grumbled this time. But it was a long walk back to camp, looking over our shoulders all the way, and blessing every hill, every stream, every rocky field that covered us.

Greece is treacherous ground for horses. Praise the gods.

The rescue of the Euboeans may have been full of arete, and it may have pleased the gods, but it cost us in several ways and it had disastrous consequences.

First, the Euboeans were spent. Of almost two thousand men who came down off that hill, fewer than two hundred stayed with the army. The rest simply went home. This is another part of being Greek that needs explaining. Even the Athenian-Euboeans felt that they had done their duty, and more. They had faced weeks of danger and survived, and they went to Athens or returned to their farms without anyone's permission – and no one suggested otherwise. The actual Euboeans, about a hundred of them, remained, mostly because their city was gone and their wives were enslaved and they had no further reason to live. They were a silent lot.

Second, the Euboeans saw the Persians as invincible. It is no fault of their own, but when men have been harried and driven for weeks, beaten and beaten again, they magnify the danger and the power of the foe to increase their own sense of worth. I am an old man of war, and I have seen it many times. When they sat in our camp and told their story to crowds of Athenians – many of whom had been against this fight from the first – they spread fear like a palpable thing. They didn't mean to do it, but they did. The day after we rescued them, our army was ready to fall apart.

Third, all the Persian cavalry had been sent to dog the Euboeans. Datis, like any good commander, had sent his best troops to prevent the Euboeans from linking up with us. Now that we'd 'gained' them, the Persian cavalry – mostly Sakai, to be honest – were no longer distracted.

The morning after we 'rescued' the Euboeans, I combed my hair on the summit of the precinct of Heracles, sitting on a rock. When I had combed it out, Gelon braided it quickly – two thick braids which he wrapped around the crown of my head as padding for my helmet. He did it better than any of my other servants or hypaspist had done – tighter and faster, too. I remember that we had just seen a raven off in the left of the sky – a poor omen – and we were wondering aloud *why* the gods bothered to send a bad omen.

Down at the base of the hill, a big group of Athenians – mostly poor men with no armour – were cutting brush for bedding. They were in a long field, and at the far end was a stand of brush and ferns, and twenty or so men were cutting the brush and gathering bags of fern. They sang as they worked, and I remember being content – even happy – as I listened to them.

The Sakai fell on them like the Eagle of Zeus falling from the heavens on a rabbit. They came on horses, and they leaped the stone walls at either end of the field, cutting the men off from the camp as easily as if they were children caught stealing apples in an orchard. One brave man tried to run, and three of them chased him down, laughing. They were so close that we could see them laugh. The leader took a rope off his quiver, whirled it around his head like a performer and tossed it neatly over the runner. Then he turned his horse and dragged the man, screaming, over the rough ground.

At my side, Teucer drew his bow. It was a long shot, even for my master archer, but he drew the feathers all the way to his mouth and loosed, and the arrow seemed to linger in the air for ever – flying and falling. The Sakai man was riding parallel to our hill and he didn't see the arrow, and it fell into him as if Apollo guided it. He tumbled from his horse and screamed.

I hoped the man caught in the rope would rise and run. But he didn't move. I think he was already dead.

The other Sakai let up a thin cry, and as one, they turned and butchered the Greeks they had caught. They killed them all – twenty men lost in a few heartbeats. They ripped skin from their victims' heads and their backs the way men skin a rabbit, and they rode across our front, flourishing their ghastly prizes and screaming their thin war cries. Then they rode away.

A day later, our servants were afraid even to get water from the stream.

The meetings of the strategoi were demoralizing, too. We met every morning and every evening – and some days more often. If two strategoi began to talk and a third saw them together, he would wander over, and before you knew it, all eleven would be there.

They seemed to love to talk, and they would discuss the most trivial things as seriously as they discussed – endlessly – the strategic options of the campaign. Firewood? Worth an hour of discussion. A general pool of sentries? Worth an hour of discussion. A new type of sandal for fighting? An hour.

By the fourth day, I was ready to scream. Because what we *needed* to discuss was the war. The Persians. The enemy. But like the proverbial corpse at a symposium, we never seemed to discuss the options fully. I had come to the conclusion that the polemarch liked all the talk because each day of talk made him feel useful, while postponing the moment of decision for yet another day.

It was on the fourth day that Aristides exploded.

'If the Medes could be destroyed with talk, we would certainly triumph!' he shouted. It came from nowhere, and his orator's voice carried across the summit of the camp, and all the strategoi fell silent. Gods, half the camp fell silent.

The Athenian polemarch glared at him. 'It is not your turn to speak,' he said.

Aristides, the Just Man, stood his ground. 'This is all drivel,' he

309

said. 'If no one else will say it, I will. The Persians are peeling our army apart. There is dissension and fear. Our numbers are even – they have a few more men, perhaps. We must attack them and defeat them before our men follow the Euboeans home.'

Cleitus – the unlikeliest ally – agreed. 'We must do something about their cavalry,' he said. 'Our men fear the horses like nothing else.'

'Why don't we simply return to Athens and show them the strength of our walls?' Leontus asked. He was the most brazen of the anti-war strategoi, a handsome man who had the reputation of being a servant of the Alcmaeonids. 'I hear so much about how we should fight a battle. Are you fools?' He grinned. 'Datis has a few *thousand* men more than we have, and a force of cavalry we can never hope to match. If we pack and march away in the night, he'll burn some olive groves and go home. He hasn't the *time* to lay siege to Athens.'

He looked around. Many of the strategoi agreed with him. I had to admit that he had a point – and I loathed him, politically.

'Miltiades brought us here to save the Euboeans,' he went on. 'And look what we saved! A few beaten men. The assembly never meant for us to *fight Persia*. Let's gather the army and have a vote. I'll wager gold against silver that they vote to go home and defend the walls. And who can blame them?'

But arrogant men often over-reach. I've done it a few times myself, and I know. He carried on when he ought to have been silent.

'You think you have an army? We have nothing. There aren't enough *gentlemen* to fight any one of their regiments, and the rest of these men are chaff – useless mouths. The Plataeans will vanish at the first onset – bumpkins, a political stunt by Miltiades to make the rest of you credulous fools feel as if we have allies. The *best* men of Euboea didn't stop the Medes for ten days. And their own lower orders sold the town to the enemy.'

Leontus might have carried the hour if he'd shut up before he offended every man standing there.

Aristides gave me the slightest of smiles and nodded his head. He was encouraging me to speak. In fact, he was egging me on.

'Are you bought and paid for?' I asked.

Leontus whirled, face red.

'You lie,' I added. I wasn't angry, but I put on a good angry face. I knew what politics required. If I humiliated Leontus – immediately and publicly – his suggestions would wither and die on the vine. 'My men stood and faced the Persian cavalry. You lie when you say we will run. But since the Persians have bought you, you are paid to say such things.'

I walked over to him – deadly Arimnestos, killer of men.

Leontus was not, in fact, a coward. 'This is insane,' he said. 'I only say what—'

'How much gold have the Medes paid you?' I roared.

He flinched. He only flinched from my bellow, but the men in the circle thought that he looked guilty, and there was a murmur.

'We are going to be massacred!' he shouted, and left the meeting in a swirl of his cloak.

That helped morale, I can tell you.

The next day, the fifth day since the Persians landed, I sent my servants down to the stream in the morning to draw water, with all of Teucer's men concealed in the rough ground at the foot of the hill.

But the Sakai had not been the eyes and ears of the Persian Empire for nothing. A dozen horsemen came up, looked at the Plataean servants in the stream and rode away. They smelled a rat.

Such is war.

At the other end of the line, Miltiades tried a similar stunt, sending a forage party far out into the fields near the beach to gather hay and cut standing wheat, and laying an ambush with his old soldiers, but the Mede cavalry looked it over and rode away.

In the centre, emboldened by our success, the city men of two tribes went down the hill with sickles to gather wheat. Most men had eaten all the food they had brought, and fear of the Persian cavalry was keeping supplies from reaching us.

The Sakai fell on them in full view of the army, killed or wounded fifty and dragged twenty of them off into slavery. In an Athenian tribe of a thousand men, the loss of fifty was considerable.

At the next meeting, Miltiades finally spoke. Many men disliked him and feared his pretensions – he made little secret of his intention to make himself tyrant. Generally, he did best for the cause of the war by saying little. But that evening, he had had enough.

'War is not a game for children,' he said bitterly. He had their attention, right enough. 'Demostocles, your men went down the hill like fools.'

'We only did what you did!' Demostocles shouted.

Aristides shook his head. 'You don't have a clue, do you? You don't understand, because you've *never made war*.' He crossed his arms. 'This is not a day of battle with Aegina. This is not a war of Greeks with Greeks. The Plataeans and Miltiades' men laid ambushes and had reinforcements ready. We call this "covering" our foragers. And the Sakai and the Medes and the Persians – they have made war, too. They saw little things – a broken bush, a line of footprints in tall grass – and they knew that the men were covered. And let them be. But in the centre, you took no precautions—'

'Leontus is right!' Demostocles said. 'They are better men than us, and we will all be killed. I am not afraid of your Plataean thug, Miltiades! No one can accuse me of taking Persian gold! They are better at this skulking manner of war than we are. I want to demand a vote – right now – to go back to the city.'

Aristides' voice was calm – and strong. 'You are *afraid*. And like a schoolboy caught in a lie, you don't wish to admit that you made an error. So, better that we abandon the campaign and retreat to the city than face the Medes, eh? Or is it that you'd rather abandon the campaign than admit that you need to ask the rest of us *how to make war*?'

'Vote,' Demostocles demanded. 'And fuck you, you pompous prig. I was killing men with my spear when you were shitting green.'

'Too bad,' I said. 'If you'd learned anything about war, you'd be a better strategos.' I held up my hand to silence him. 'Listen – I'm not pissing on you. When we went after the Euboeans, I almost lost my whole phalanx. Why? Because I had no idea how fast the cavalry could come at me. Our servants still had our shields – Ares, it could have been a disaster.' I shrugged. 'And I've been at war since I was seventeen. Fighting the Persians is *not* like any other war. We have to roll with the punches and learn from mistakes, the way a good pankrationist does when he fights a bigger man. Eh?'

It was always rewarding to say something sensible and have men like Aristides give me *that look*, the look that indicated that in the main they thought me a mindless brute.

Demostocles looked stunned that I'd admitted to failing. It took the wind out of his sails and left him speechless. Concession and apology can be like that.

'We need a concerted foraging strategy,' I said. 'Every taxis cannot go on its own. And I think we need to contest the plain with them – even if it costs us. We need to go down there and show them who owns those fields, man to man. If we let their cavalry ride where they please, eventually they will beat us. Or that's how it seems to me.'

The polemarch gave me a long look, as if up until then he'd thought me a fool. Perhaps he had. I was, after all, Arimnestos the killer of men, not Arimnestos the tactician.

Miltiades came forward again. 'I have a plan,' he said. 'I think we need to attack their cavalry, and put it out of the war.'

Many voices spoke up then, and not all of them were strategoi. The problem of the Greeks is that we all like to talk, and all the famous men came to the meetings of the strategoi, whether they held rank or not. Themistocles was a strategos but Sophanes was not, and he attended anyway. Cimon, Miltiades' eldest, held no rank, and he was always there, and seemed to feel freer to speak than his father – on and on. So we had closer to a hundred men than eleven.

The many voices shouted Miltiades down. Leontus began urging a vote on returning to Athens. Of the hundred men standing there by the altar, the vast majority were with Leontus. What I couldn't tell was how many of the strategoi were with Leontus and Demostocles.

But the voices calling for the vote were loudest.

Callimachus stepped forward and blew the horn at his hip, and the Athenians grew quieter.

'We will vote on the idea of returning to the city,' he said.

Uproar.

'We will vote in the morning,' he said. 'This meeting is adjourned.'

Miltiades followed him as he walked away to his tent. A dozen other men went to follow them, and Aristides and I tried to stop them by forcing them to face us and debate the whole issue – we kept them there several minutes, and Miltiades was gone.

Somewhere in there, I caught Aristides' eye. He gave a small shake of his head.

He thought we'd had it.

So did I.

I went straight back to my camp and found my brother-in-law and Idomeneus, and I took them off into our little stand of cypress trees.

'If the army breaks up, we need to plan our own retreat,' I said.

'Ares' dick!' Idomeneus said. 'You must be joking, lord. Or is it Lade again?'

I shook my head. 'Aristides thinks they'll vote to retreat to Athens in the morning, and there will be immediate desertions. He paints a bleak picture, lads.' I shrugged. 'We're a long way from home. And if there is a traitor—'

Idomeneus shook his head. 'We're all right,' he said. 'Keep the archers safe, head for the hills and walk the high ground all the way home. Could take a while, but we'll live.'

'What do we eat, drink?' I asked. His strategy was the one I liked, too – but it was fraught with danger.

'Steal what we can – hunt when we can.' Idomeneus shook his head. 'It will suck, that's for sure, lord. But the boys will get it done.'

Antigonus looked at the speaker's bema in the middle of the encampment. 'If what you say is really true,' he said, 'we should be gone in the morning.'

'Then men will say we deserted,' I said.

Antigonus shrugged. 'Will we care? If these bastards run for Athens, the Persians will eat them, and someone in the city will sell it out just the way the Euboeans were sold. And the Ionians.'

'And it won't be a thetes,' Idomeneus added. 'I heard that bastard at your little meeting, lord. Chalcis was betrayed by an aristocrat.'

I nodded. 'I heard that, too. Doesn't matter, though. Antigonus, what's your point?'

He frowned and looked at the ground. 'It's not a very glorious thought,' he admitted, 'but if Athens is going down, we don't need to give a shit about what they think of us – our duty is to get our people home alive.'

It made sense. He was a good man, my brother-in-law.

'If we cut and run before the Athenians break up,' Idomeneus said with his terrible, callous practicality, 'their cavalry will waste a day or two killing Athenians and we'll never see them. Lord, it could save many men.' Then he reverted to form. 'Seems a horrible waste, though.' He grinned.

'Waste?' I asked.

'This should be the most glorious battle of our time,' Idomeneus said. 'If these fuckheads waste it, I'll go and fight for Persia. I'll never forgive them.'

'Get the boys ready to march – without getting them ready to march. Tell them we might try a raid on *their* foragers tomorrow and they'll be a day in the field.' I was keeping my options open.

I went and walked through the camp – the whole camp.

It was like the camps of the East Greeks before Lade.

314

Worse, in a way, because at every fire, men urged others to go home. To cut and run. I thought they were cowards, and then I realized that, in effect, I'd just done the same.

Why can't Greeks get along? Why can't they maintain a common goal?

We lost Lade when the Samians sailed away and abandoned us – for the greed of a few men.

I saw Marathon going the same way, and I wanted to weep.

It was almost dark when Paramanos found me.

'You move too fast,' he said. 'Miltiades wants you.'

That was like the old days. I knew what he would want. He'd want the Plataeans to join with his men – the professionals – in covering the retreat of the army. I'd already thought it through. I was about to tell my own lord – a man to whom I owed a great deal – to sod off. I wasn't losing any Plataeans to save Athens.

That's how bad things were that night.

Miltiades had a tent. Few men did in those days. Greece is kind to soldiers, and it seldom rains. But Miltiades had fought everywhere, and he had a magnificent tent – another reason for men to hate him. If they needed a reason, of course.

I went in, and a slave handed me a big cup of wine.

Miltiades was wearing a simple dark chiton and had boots on.

'I need you and twenty of your best men,' he said.

That caught me by surprise. 'What for?' I asked.

'We're going to raid the Persian camp,' he said. 'It's the only hope we have. I convinced Callimachus to put off the vote until tomorrow night. He fears treason in the city just as much as I do. He's not a fool. He's just cautious.' Miltiades drank some wine. 'Listen – Phidippides the herald just came in from the mountains. The Spartans haven't marched yet. It'll be five days – at least – before we can expect them. *But they are coming.*'

Aristides came in through the beaded door. He was wearing plain leather armour. 'They want us to die,' he said.

Miltiades shrugged. 'They're pious men, our Lacedaemonian friends. They have a festival.' He shrugged. 'To be honest, I doubt I'd hurry to save Sparta from the Medes, either. But when Phidippides' news is known, the last heart will go out of the army. Five days is too long. We have to strike.'

'I'm ready,' Aristides said.

'Arimnestos hasn't heard the plan,' Miltiades said. He glanced at me. 'Will you do it?'

'Do what?' I asked.

'We need a demonstration in front of the Persians – by men who can fight or run in the dark.' He shrugged. 'I can give you *all* the Athenian archers to go with you. I wouldn't sacrifice you,' he said, as if reading my mind.

'Where will you be?' I asked, but I was already smiling, because, by all the gods, I saw the whole plan as neatly as if it was stitched into leather. 'The horses!'

'Told you he was smarter than he looked,' Miltiades said.

'If we pull this off, the army will stay,' Aristides said.

'And if we fuck it up, we'll be dead,' Miltiades said. He shrugged. 'I can't take any more officers' meetings.'

'I'll drink to that,' I said. 'I can get a hundred men.'

'Then take a hundred,' Miltiades said. 'The more you take, the more noise you'll make. What can you do, though?'

I remember making a face. I remember laughing. 'Have you noted that, while we sit here doing nothing, the Persians sit there doing nothing?' I said.

They both nodded.

I raised my cup and poured a libation. 'Ares – Zeus's least favoured child. If they fear us at all – and they must – then they have to fear a night attack.' I grinned. 'So let's feed them one. I'll go for their ships.'

Ever been out for a walk at night?

Ever been out for a walk outside the city?

As joyously as we prepared to make our raid, the truth was that none of us had ever been in a night attack. There's a reason why men don't make night attacks on land.

At sea, it's different. At sea, there's always a little light – and not much to bump into, if you steer badly. But on land?

I roused my epilektoi as soon as I got back, but just preparing them to march took me too much time. By the time I'd led them to the base of the hill and out into the fields, the moon was high and we were late.

The Athenian archers were supposed to meet us opposite their camp – which turned out to be far too vague a direction on a dark night. I looked for them for as long as my heart could take it. Miltiades was long gone, heading up into the hills to get around the marsh and the Persian camp, and I needed to make noise to keep the enemy focused on me. I was taking too long. Everything was taking too long.

I gave up on the Athenian archers when I saw how far the moon had moved across the sky.

'Where the fuck are they?' I hissed at Teucer when I got back to my own men. The archer shrugged.

So we set off across the fields in the middle watch of the night, an hour late for our plan and moving too fast. We made a great deal of noise.

The hedgerows, which seemed to run straight by day, were like the maze of the Minotaur by night. I'd follow one for a distance and then realize that I had gone close to the sea rather than closer to the enemy – and time was passing. I could all but hear Clotho's shears trimming the wick of Miltiades' life.

When the Pleiades were high in the sky, I took my bearings like a sailor, found the north star and realized that, again, I was leading the long file of my men away from our camp and towards the sea – and *not* closer to the enemy encampment.

Resolutely I put my right shoulder to the sound of the sea – close now – and searched the next wall for a gate. I crossed, the rest of the men stumbling behind me and making enough noise for an army, which I guess was the idea, and found myself walking across a hay-field in the full light of the moon – towards the sea.

Of course, the beach curves – radically, in come places – and I'd simply missed my mark. Again.

My heart was pounding, my anxiety had reached a lethal intensity, my helmet burned my head and I was sweating through my armour – and we still weren't within long bowshot of the enemy.

Idomeneus came up beside me. 'You thinking we should go on the beach?' he asked.

'No,' I said. Because there was no cover at all on the beach. We'd be seen two stades away, even at night.

Of course, even as I thought that, I realized that being seen two stades away might be a fine thing.

'Actually, yes,' I said. 'We're going along the beach.'

Idomeneus laughed. 'Good – I was worried you were lost.'

I chuckled – I remember the falsity of my laugh, how it caught in my throat. When you are the fearless leader, it is important to appear fearless – and knowledgeable. I thought of all the stupid things

I'd seen other leaders do. Now I knew why they did it. Somehow, command on land was not like command at sea – too many choices, perhaps. Maybe it's just that your men can simply walk away if they lose trust in you.

Down to the beach.

As soon as we reached the beach, I could see the enemy camp – the ships, drawn up as thickly as fleas on a dog, and the fires inland from the beach all the way past the marsh to the hills. We seemed incredibly close, although in reality we were five long stades from the ships – but because of the curve of the beach, we were looking at the ships across the water, and they were *close*.

As soon as we were down the dune, I hissed the order to form front by files. We were strung out, but the boys were fast and probably as eager to get formed up – to feel the comfort of the next man's shield – as I was to get them formed.

Still no alarm. So we moved forward. Sand filled my sandals, and I had to remind myself that the beach was, despite the labour, easier on me, and easier on the lads, than tying to cross the farms of the Marathon plain.

After two stades, we seemed to be level with the first Persian ships – and still there was no alarm. I tried to reassure myself that if Miltiades were attacking, I'd hear something from him – the hills were visible as a loom of dark against the paler darkness of the sky to the north and west.

Another stade, and the ships were so close that it seemed we could swim to them. We were just two stades – less, I think – from the ships that were beached when a man on one of the anchored ships, a Greek, called out, asking who we were.

'Men!' I responded, but in Persian.

'What?' he asked, his voice echoing over the water.

'Men!' I called back again, this time in Greek.

And that satisfied him.

By such threads do empires hang.

Now we were running – stumbling more like – through the dark. I had a new notion – that I'd put fire into some of their ships. I'd done it before, at Lade, and it had done the trick, and there were plenty of fires near the ships.

Less than a stade – no alarm.

How the gods must have laughed.

We came to the first fires – a line of blazes long since burned down

to coals – and my men broke ranks and began to slaughter the oarsmen at the fires without my orders. The whole situation slipped away
from me in those moments – one second, I had a column of trained
warriors running through the dark, and the next, there were screams
and all my men had gone.

Or that's how it seemed to me.

To my mind, killing the oarsmen was a complete waste of time, but
as a diversion, it did well enough. The problem was that there were
about a hundred of us, and almost sixty thousand oarsmen. With the
best will in the world, my men couldn't make a dent in them. And
then they began to fight back.

It was chaos on the beach, and Tartarus, too – arrows falling from
the sky as the Medes who had camped just to the north shot into
the confusion, and the thousands of oarsmen, unable to believe there
were so few of us, fell on each other – Phoenicians against Cilicians,
Greeks against Aegyptians.

I pulled Idomeneus out of the fighting and dragged him clear the
way you pull a dog out of a fight.

'Order the rally!' I remember shouting at him. He had a horn and
I did not.

He looked at me with dull, lust-filled eyes. 'I was fighting,' he said
reproachfully.

'Order the rally!' I said again.

He lifted the horn and sounded three long blasts.

All along the beach, men heard it. Some understood and some
were lost in the fog of combat.

I put my spear in the gut of a man with no shield – I had to assume
in the dark that anyone without a shield was one of theirs – and ran
back a few paces.

'Plataea! On me!' I roared, again and again.

Men came to me in dribs and drabs, some bringing their little swirl
of combat with them, some alone.

It took for ever. Everything takes for ever in the dark. Idomeneus
sounded the horn again, and again later, and still I had fewer than
half of my men – my picked, best armoured men. I could not afford
to leave them on the beach.

The trouble – my fault – was that I had not set a rally point or
explained to them what I wanted *after* we hit the enemy. I had to
trust that they would know the signal from the hunting expeditions.

In the end, most did, but men died because I didn't know enough to plan the recall as part of the attack. Another lesson learned at bloody Marathon.

Every time we blew the rally, we ran back down the beach, a little farther from the ships. By the time I had eighty men – perhaps a few more – we were a stade from the enemy. We should have been clear.

We weren't. We had taken too long – far too long. And the sun was coming up in the east – still only a line of grey-pink out over the ocean towards Euboea, but it was going to rise like the hand of doom. We were just eighty men, caught a long way from our camp.

I cursed and killed a man. By then we were fighting Medes – real soldiers. They weren't swarming us, but their braver souls started to come in close while others shot at us from a distance. The light was still bad, their bowstrings were damp and Teucer and his lads were shooting back, so we were relatively unscathed, but I could see better with every passing minute, and that meant that they could, too.

I was in the centre of my own line. Nothing for it – we needed a miracle.

'Ready to charge!' I called out.

There was that reassuring sound as every man closed a little to the centre and the shields tapped together. Perhaps you've heard it in drill – it is a sound that always gives you heart, that rattle. It means your friends are still together – still in good order, still with enough heart to fight.

I took a deep breath. We were fighting Medes – they couldn't understand me.

'When I say charge,' I bellowed, as loud as my throat and lungs could manage, 'you go fifty paces forward, turn and run as if the hound Cerberus was at your heels. Hear me, Plataeans!'

There was a cry – something like a war cry, something like a sigh.

'Charge!' I called, and we went at them.

The Medes were ready for it. They broke as soon as they saw us come, and only our boldest and fastest caught any of them. I certainly didn't – the Mede I had my eye on vanished into the near-dark of the bushes up the beach.

Idomeneus, bless him, sounded a single blast as I hit my forty-seventh stride, and we turned together, like a figure in the Pyrrhiche – which it is – and ran. We were off down that beach like frightened boys chased by an angry parent, and every man understood that we had to break contact now, or die when the sun rose.

But Persians have good soldiers, too. Somewhere in the scrub was an officer who knew his business, and within seconds of us running, they were chasing us and arrows began to fall. Then it was every man for himself. Some of my boys cut inland, across country. A few ditched their shields. Most didn't – when archers are shooting you, the last thing you want to give up is your shield.

I stuck to the beach, and most of the Medes followed, worse luck. Had they stayed a little longer, run away from our false charge a little further, we might have made a clean exit, but we were not so lucky.

After a few minutes of running, I looked back and they were gaining. After all, they had light body armour, which most of them were not wearing anyway, as they'd been awakened by our attack. They had neither helmets nor greaves.

They were cautious, but they were getting the measure of us.

An arrow hit the middle of the back of the yoke of my armour. Thanks to Ares' hand, it turned on the two layers of bronze, but the power knocked me flat. As I rose, another arrow hit the same place, then another glanced off my shield, heavy arrows, and another rang on my helmet, and I thought – *Fuck, this is it.*

I got my feet under me and turned.

One of the Medes fell to the beach, his life leaking out between his fingers as he grabbed at the shaft embedded in his guts.

Teucer was right at my shoulder, shooting calmly. One, two – and men fell.

'Turn a little left,' he said.

I did, and two arrows hit the face of my shield, and he shot back – zip, pause, zip.

With every shot, a Mede fell.

Another arrow into my shield, but now the Medes were scrambling for cover – Teucer dropped four right there, coughing their lungs out in the sand.

'Run,' I said. I gave him three steps while I stayed – another arrow off the top of my helmet – and then I turned and ran.

My breath was coming like a horse's after a gallop – I sucked in air the way a drunkard sucks wine and my legs burned as if I had run ten stades. The wound Archilogos had given me in the fall of Miletus had a curious numbness to it against the pain of all my other muscles, and sweat rolled down my forehead and into my eyes.

The light was growing. I was running down a beach that was well enough lit for target practice, and I was going more and more slowly.

Ares, it makes me want to spit sand to remember it: fleeing like a coward, and knowing – *knowing* – that in a few moments I would be dead anyway. When it is your last – when all is lost – it doesn't matter whether you were a demonstration or a deception or a last stand, friends. No one worth a shit wants to die with his back to the foe.

So I turned.

An arrow meant for my back screamed off the face of my shield.

I meant to take one with me, but I was out of everything, the daimon had no more to give me, and I – the great fighter of the Plataeans – slumped down behind my shield. I got smaller and smaller as the arrows thudded in.

But I could breathe, and I did. I panted like a dog, and I couldn't think of anything, and arrows fell on my shield like hail on a good crop – twice, arrowheads blew right through the face of my aspis.

Oh, children, that hour was dark. When I had my breath back, I knew it was just a matter of how I chose to die. I could make it last, down under the rim of my aspis, until they got a man into the brush to my left who could shoot me in the hip or the arse. No laughing matter. I could try to turn again, but to Hades with that. My legs were gone. It seemed to me that the best course was to attack them. It would get the whole thing over with the quickest, and if anyone watched me – if there was a single bard left in Greece to sing after this debacle – at least men would say that Arimnestos died with his face to the foe.

I took a dozen more breaths, rationing them, taking the air in deep. Then I allowed myself five more – the margin of life and death. Five breaths.

Arrows continued to slam into the face of my shield

On the edge of the fifth, I rose to my feet. I sneaked a last glance down the beach behind me – and my heart leaped with joy. It was empty. My men had got away.

In some situations, nothing would be grimmer than to die alone, but in this one, it filled me with power. Being alone made me feel less a failure. More a hero.

I leaned forward, into the arrow storm, summoned up power in my legs I didn't think I had and charged.

Anyone asleep?

Hah! You flinched, thugater. You think perhaps I died there, eh?

Pour me a little more wine, lad.

Yes, I charged. As soon as I got my face over the rim of my aspis,

I could see that they were well bunched up, about fifty strides away – that's why so few arrows missed, I can tell you.

I remembered running with Eualcidas, at the fight in the pass. Here, like there, my feet crunched on gravel. I kept my shield up, and the arrows fell on it like snow on a mountain.

And then they stopped.

There were screams – screams of pain and screams of terror. I lowered my aspis a finger's breadth and peered forward, though the pre-dawn murk, the sweat, the slits of my helmet.

The Medes were falling – a dozen of them were down and the rest were scattering. When I reached them – alive, of course, you daft woman – not a man was alive, and they looked like porcupines for the arrows in them.

I turned away from rosy-fingered dawn and the pale sea. There were men coming out of the bush – a hundred men, with bows.

The Athenian archers had found me.

I laughed.

I mean, what in Hades can you do but laugh?

When you write this, I suppose you'll leave out all the little men – the archers and peltastai. And when I say 'little', I mean small in the eyes of the great. But they were good men, as you'll see. The psiloi. The 'stripped' men who wear no armour. This is the story of the little men, and you can ignore what happened next if you wish. But it had more effect on the battle than most of the heavily armed men and the gentry would ever want to admit.

The archers were elated – they'd saved a famous hero and laid waste to the Medes, and I knew that as long as those men lived in their little houses and their shacks on the flank of the Acropolis, they'd tell and retell that story in their wine shops, at the edge of the Agora, in the bread stalls.

Several of them – the boldest – sprinted down the beach and tore a souvenir loose from the huddle of corpses. The first man to pass me shot me a grin.

'You alive, boss?' he asked as he ran by.

I had fallen to one knee. I gave him a smile, got to my feet and wandered after him.

In the distance, the Medes began to rally. Did I mention that they were first-rate soldiers? Just lost half their numbers in an ambush,

and they were coming back. I hate any man who says the Medes and
Persians were cowards.

The Medes on the sand were wearing gold and silver – professional
soldiers wearing their pay. The Athenian archers were poor men and
my friend, the first who passed me, whooped when he reached the
bodies. But he was a public-spirited man, and he held something aloft
that flashed in the new sun and he shouted 'Gold!' and the rest of the
archers came pouring out of the scrub at the edge of the beach, some
men jumping down the bluffs and sand dunes.

They stripped those corpses like men who knew their way around
a corpse. I cast no aspersions, but by the time I caught up with them,
there was nothing left but skin, gristle and bone.

'Better look to your bows, lads,' I said, pointing down the beach.
I stepped forward and fielded an arrow that might have hit a man,
scooping it on the face of my shield, and the muscles in my shield
arm protested hard.

'Lad, my arse,' an older man said, but he grinned. He had thick
arms and heavy shoulders – an oarsman, I suspected. 'You're that
Plataean, then, eh?'

'I am,' I said. Then I put some iron in my voice. 'Bows!' I shouted.

Most men jump when I say jump. The archers did.

'Who's the master archer, then?' I asked.

After most of them had loosed a couple of arrows – with no effect
beyond driving the Medes back up the beach – the older man turned
to me again. 'With the other half of the boys – they went for the
centre of the camp. We couldn't find you. And I kept getting lost – so
I made for the beach.' He gave a lopsided grin. 'I'm a sailor – or was.
Beaches make sense to me.'

I had to laugh. 'We need to get out of here,' I said.

'That's sense, too. We've had our lick at the Persians.' He looked
around. 'And we've got whatever they brought.' He called to the
men by the bodies, 'Got all the bows? All their quivers? Arrows?'

To me, he said, 'All their kit is better than ours – better bows, by
far.'

'I know,' I said.

'Give me a Persian bow anytime,' he said, flourishing his own.

'These aren't Persians,' I said. I pointed at the low felt hats and
boots. 'They're Medes, a subject people of the Persians – similar, but
not the same. They wear less armour. Sakai are different again – bigger beards, more leather and better bows.'

'Ain't you the sophist, though.' The former sailor held out his arm. 'Leonestes of Piraeus.' Arrows began to drop all around us.

'Let's run,' I said.

We did. After a few hundred strides, they had to carry me – I was mortified, to say the least. One young sprig took my aspis and another peeled off my helmet.

We left the beach when it began to angle away from our camp and we ran inland. It was easier in daylight – I could see the line of hills and mountains at the far edge of the plain and the rising ground that marked the shrine and sanctuary of Heracles.

As soon as we left the beach, we lost the Medes. I think they'd finally reached the end of their enthusiasm. My Plataeans must have put down twenty of them – perhaps as many as fifty. It's never good when armoured men face unarmoured. And then the ambush by the archers probably dropped at least another thirty. Fifty dead is more like a bad day's battle than a couple of skirmishes before breakfast.

The Medes retired to lick their wounds. We carried on across the hayfields and wheat fields and fallow barley fields, jumping stone walls and avoiding hedgerows. We were about halfway to the sanctuary of Heracles when I felt the ground moving. I needed to stop – my lungs were white-hot with pain. Other men must have felt the same – as soon as my group stopped, all of them did.

The feeling that the earth was trembling increased. I looked around – and saw the dust.

'Cavalry!' I panted. 'Into the brush!'

To our right was a fallow field with low stone walls and patches of jasmine and other low bushes. It was also full of rocks.

We piled in, in no particular order.

'Get to the wall. This one! You – stand there! Bows up!' That was me – the orders flowed out of me as if I was channelling the power of Ares.

Leonestes joined me. 'Form a line – get your arse to that wall, boy! Bows up – you heard the man! Get a shaft on the string, you whoreson.'

The cavalry was almost on us. But as is so often the case on a real battlefield, they hadn't seen us. They had other prey.

'The first volley will win or lose this,' I said. My voice was calm. I remember how all the fear of the night raid had been replaced by my usual steady confidence. Why? Because in the dark I had no idea what I was doing, did I? Out here, it was just a ship-fight on land.

Men on the flank of the galloping cavalry saw us, of course – but far too late to make any change of direction for the mass. But if Miltiades had raided the horses, he hadn't had much effect, I remember thinking to myself.

I glanced at Leonestes, because he was taking so long to give the order that I wondered if he was waiting for me to give it.

He winked. Turned his head to the enemy – raised his bow.

'Loose!' he roared. 'Fast as you can, boys!'

The next shafts rose while the first flight were in the air. Rose and fell, and a third volley came up, far more ragged than the first two. Some of the Athenian archers were little more than guttersnipes with bows, while others had fine weapons and plenty of training – probably archers from ships.

So among a hundred archers, there were maybe twenty real killers, another fifty halfway decent archers and thirty kids and make-weights.

Same in the phalanx, really.

The arrows fell on the cavalry and they evaporated. I remember that when I was a child snow fell on the farm – and then the weather changed and the sun came out, hot as hot, and the snow went straight to the heavens without melting. The cavalry went like that: a brief interval of thrashing horse terror, all hooves and blood, and some arrows coming back at me – a man took one and died just an arm's length from me – and then they were gone, out of our range, and rallying.

That fast.

They slipped from their horses, adjusted their quivers – and came at us. A couple of dozen began riding for our right flank – the flank closest to the sea. They did this so fast that I think they must have practised it. For the first time, I understood the fear the men of Euboea had for the Persians. These were real Persians – high caps, scale shirts, beautiful enamelled bows.

I ran across the ground to the men we'd just killed – the horses were still screaming. Six. Our brilliant little improvised ambush had put down only six men.

I picked up two bows, scooped the big Persian quivers off their horses while arrows decorated the ground around me and ran back towards the thin line of Athenians.

I got a fine bow – wood so brown that it seemed purple, or perhaps that was dye, and horn on the inside face of the bow, with sinew in between. There was goldwork on the man's quiver, and a line of gold at the nocks on the bow.

'Anyone who doesn't have a Persian bow, get back,' Leonestes shouted. 'Way the fuck back, boys. A hundred paces.'

The dismounted Persians in front of us – about fifty of them – walked confidently forward. Even as I watched, they stopped. Most of them planted arrows in the ground for easy shooting.

The cavalry reaching around our right flank was making heavy going of it – they'd found the tangle of walls and hedgerows. Some of the younger Athenians began to drop shafts on them, as if it was sport. It's always easier to be a hero when the enemy can't shoot back, I find.

The Persians to our front weren't in any hurry. The cavalry gave up on our right flank – a poor, hasty decision and just the kind of thing that happens in war. They got low on their horses' necks and rode across our front, and one of our archers with a Persian bow emptied a saddle as they crossed us – heading for our left flank, closer to the hills and the camp.

In war, people make mistakes, just as they do in peace. A few minutes ago, these self-same Persians had been chasing someone across our right flank. We'd put a stop to that – and in the to and fro of combat, our Persian adversaries had forgotten their original foes.

The cavalry rode hard to get around our left, and then suddenly they were fleeing, and they had empty saddles – and there were men behind them throwing spears, and other men with armour running at them.

This transformed our fight – one moment, the Persians were exchanging slow, careful shafts with our best archers, and the next, they were running to get their mounts before our friends on the left captured the lot. It was close, but the Persians won the race and rode away.

They rode about a stade, pulled up and were hit by an invisible hand that plucked a couple of them from their saddles and made all the horses scream – slingers. Only a dozen of them, as I later learned – but that was the final straw for the Persians, and they raced for their camp.

That's the part of the fighting that I saw. I stayed out there, with the archers, for an hour or more, and men came past us – little men, as I say – dozens of them, with javelins and bows and slings, and a few with nothing but a sack of rocks.

No one will ever fully explain that morning. Word went out that

Miltiades was in trouble, I guess. Or Themistocles asked them to go out and support the archers. Who knows? It wasn't part of any master plan, that much I know. However it came about, a couple of thousand Greek freedmen and light-armed men – men too poor to have a panoply and fight in the phalanx, but citizens too proud to abandon Greece – flooded the fields and hedgerows and stone walls. I estimate that, with the Athenian archers added in, they might have killed three hundred of the enemy. Nothing, you might say.

Nor was there any glory to it. When you are naked and have no weapon but a bag of rocks, you don't go walking out in the open. No – you crawl along hedgerows and share the stone walls with the foxes and the tortoises, too.

But the Persians and their allies simply didn't have a horde of light-armed men to keep our light-armed men at bay, and they couldn't afford the steady casualties it would have taken to clear the field. And our little men made those fields a nightmare.

As the morning wore on, our light-armed began to take losses. If they were too bold, in their little groups, the enemy would cut them off and slaughter them. All told, I would bet that if the gods made a count, then the barbarians actually killed more Greeks than we killed barbarians that day.

But again – as I keep saying – war is not about numbers. War is about feelings, emotions, fatigue, joy, terror.

I got up the hill to our camp and was thronged by men who had to clasp my hand or slap my back.

'We lost you!' Idomeneus was *weeping*. 'Oh, lord, I am ashamed.'

I shook my head. Who would not be delighted by this display of loyalty?

Teucer had it the worst. 'I was right at your shoulder, lord,' he said, clearly unhappy. 'And then I found that I was by another scaled shirt – and it was Idomeneus. I had lost you in the dark.'

'All dirt comes out in a good wash,' I said. 'How many did we lose?'

Idomeneus shook his head. 'Too many, lord. Almost twenty. And your brother-in-law, and Ajax, and Epistocles, and Peneleos.'

Ares, that hurt. Not Epistocles – his loss was Plataea's gain. But the rest – Pen would kill me for losing her husband, and Peneleos . . .

'Maybe they'll come in,' Teucer said. 'You did.'

I lay down, my spirits low. It always happens after a fight, but this was worse. I hadn't done anything except get my men lost – I had scarcely bloodied my spear. But I'd lost twenty of my best – irreplaceable men with heavy armour and fighting skills. Ajax was as good a spearman as I was – or he had been.

I was lying in the shade, feeling bad, when Miltiades came.

'You're alive, then,' he said. 'Praise the gods.'

That made me smile, because Miltiades so seldom invoked the gods – not in that voice.

'I'm alive,' I said. 'And unwounded. But I lost a lot of men.'

He still had his shield on his shoulder – you can reach a point of exhaustion where you simply forget to strip kit off. In fact, I was lying in my scale corslet. I clambered to my feet to embrace him. He was looking beyond me, back towards my camp.

'I never got near their horses,' he said, in disgust. 'We waited for your diversion, and when it came, we struck whatever was nearest.' He gave me a grim smile. 'I missed their horse lines in the dark, and we were in among the Sakai. We killed a few, I suppose.'

I had never seen Miltiades so down.

'And Aristides?' I asked. I was suddenly struck with fear. *What if Aristides was dead?*

'He made it to the horse lines,' Miltiades said bitterly. 'But accomplished nothing, and lost twenty hoplites getting away. He may have killed twenty of their horses.'

'But he lives?'

Miltiades nodded heavily. 'He lives.' He shrugged. 'It is chaos out in that field. Half the hoplites will have lost their shield-bearers before this debacle is over. Better if we'd fought a field battle.' He stared at the ground. 'How did it go so wrong?'

I had my canteen, and I poured him a cup of water, and he dropped his shield and sat heavily. He had a gash on his leg – he wasn't wearing greaves. I washed his leg myself, and when Gelon came up I sent him for an old chiton I could rip to shreds for wrapping.

I didn't want him to see that Miltiades was weeping.

You can see, from the hindsight of forty years, that all was not lost – but trust me, thugater, while Miltiades sat on his aspis and wept, I felt like joining him. We had lost many good men – and to our minds, schooled in the war of the phalanx, we had accomplished nothing.

We had not robbed the Persians of their cavalry, and we had not put heart into the phalanx with a bloodless victory.

But while Miltiades wept, the light-armed started coming in from the fields – and the barbarians did nothing to stop them. Indeed, had I gone to the edge of the field, I'd have seen something that five thousand other Greeks saw – a stupid act of bravado that changed everything.

One of the groups of psiloi had crawled quite close to the Persian camp and found no one to fight, so they grew bored. Before they could crawl back, one boy leaped up on a stone wall – in full view of both armies – and bared his behind at the Persians, sitting on their horses by their camp. He made lewd gestures, and waved, and fanned his buttocks.

The Persian cavalry sat tight.

Everyone saw this exchange – everyone but Miltiades and me, of course. And in those moments, our light-armed felt their power. The barbarians felt their power. Every thrown rock made our boys bolder and every empty saddle made the Persians more afraid.

Before I limped back to camp – with my aspis on my shoulder and my helmet on the back of my head – we owned the fields of Marathon from the mountains to the sea, although I didn't know it yet. And not because of our gentry and our hoplites.

It is funny, is it not? We went to rescue the Euboeans, and in succeeding, we almost wrecked our army. And then, to retrieve that error, we mounted the raid on the Persian camp. We all got lost in the dark, and accomplished nothing – but as a consequence of our intention, the 'little' men came to our rescue, and flooded the plain with stones and arrows, and the barbarians felt defeated.

Best of all, the elated little men came up the hill to the camp and bragged of their stone-throwing victories to their masters, the hoplites.

Shame is a powerful tonic with Greeks. So is competition and emulation. And no gentleman wants to face the idea that his servant may be the better man. Eh?

That was the day of the little men. Before it dawned, we were on the edge of defeat. After it, we had enough votes to stand our ground. And that, in many cases, was the margin.

Listen, then. This is the part you came for. The Battle of Marathon. But remember that we only stood our ground because the little men won it for us.

Wine for all of them, boys.

★

The first sign of change came while Miltiades was drying his eyes and restoring his demeanour. I had bound his leg and he was using a scrap of my old chiton to wash his face.

My brother-in-law walked up as if his appearance were nothing extraordinary. I wrapped him in an embrace that he still remembers, I'd wager.

He looked sheepish. 'We got lost,' he said.

That made me laugh. And laughter helps, too.

I think that was the turning point. Antigonus came in with seven of our missing men – not a wound on them. They'd gone to ground at the break of day, but as our psiloi gradually drove the barbarians off the fields, his little party got bolder and managed to move from field to field. They'd even kept their shields.

Ajax came in without his aspis and with a serious wound in his thigh, carried by a trio of Athenian freedmen who asked for payment.

'Stands to reason, don'it, lord? We gave up lootin' to carry your frien', eh?'

I could barely understand the man, but I gave him a silver owl and another to each of his friends, and then I got Miltiades to send his doctor. The arrowhead was still lodged deep in Ajax's thigh. The doctor brought a selection of what appeared to be arrowhead moulds – long, hollow shafts with a hollow for the head of an arrow at the end. They split in half. He used them with ruthless efficiency – rammed the tool into the wound, got the little mould around the arrowhead, so that the barb of the arrow was neatly surrounded with smooth, safe metal, and pulled the shaft free. There was a great deal of blood, but Ajax stopped screaming as soon as the shaft came clear, and he managed a watery smile.

'Ares' *cock*,' he grunted. 'I think I'm fucked.' His eyes rolled, and he panted, shaking with the exhaustion that only the panic of pain can cause.

'Don't be a whiner,' the doctor quipped and shook his head. 'Don't try and run the stade for a few days,' he added, and smiled. Then he poured raw honey – a lot of it – straight on the wound, and wrapped it so tight I saw his arms bulge with the effort.

Miltiades watched, fascinated – all forms of making and craft fascinated him. By then, more and more of the psiloi were coming up the hill, and the camp had started to buzz.

I heard laughter, and the unmistakable sound of a man bragging. And then more laughter.

I looked at Miltiades. 'They don't sound beaten,' I said.

Perhaps it was the rest and the wine, but Miltiades, a man fifteen years older than me, leaped to his feet. He looked *alive*.

He went out from the stand of trees, and the next I looked, he was standing in the middle of a group of the Athenian archers, with Themistocles, and they were laughing. Leonestes saw me and beckoned, and I went over.

'Just telling our tale,' Leonestes said. 'How we rescued you. How you charged the Persians—'

'Medes—'

'Barbarians – all by yourself. Like a loon.' He grinned.

Miltiades raised an eyebrow. Then he stepped up on the dry stone of the sanctuary wall and peered out over the plain towards the Persian camp. 'They aren't stirring,' he said. 'I can see a line of mounted men, right close to their camp. Nothing else.'

I think that's when the light dawned on all of us.

'I think they're scared,' I said.

'They're a long way from home,' Antigonus added with a nod at their ships.

Miltiades agreed. 'It's hard to put yourself in the enemy's place, isn't it?' he said.

Themistocles fingered his beard. 'Have we won, do you think?' he asked.

'Won?' Miltiades asked. 'Don't be silly. But we've pushed them off the ground, and our supplies can reach us. And maybe we've made them feel what we feel. But won?' He looked at the cavalry far across the plain. 'We won't win until we put a spear into every one of them, Themistocles. These are Persians.'

Themistocles was looking at their fleet. 'We should never have let them land,' he said. 'But that's for another day. What's the plan now?'

Miltiades laughed. He seemed ten years younger than he had a few minutes before. 'First, we win the vote,' he said. 'Then, we fight.'

By mid-afternoon, the vote was a foregone conclusion. The hoplites were shamed by their servants. There's no other way to put it. Every gentleman needed to wet his spear, and that was that.

There were more than three thousand men, by my reckoning, around the altar that evening as we gathered for the vote of the strategoi. They shouted for the vote and they demanded that the army make a stand.

Leontus tried his best. First he demanded that I be excluded from the vote, as I was a foreigner. The polemarch allowed that. I thought that Miltiades would explode – but then the massed hoplites and not a few of their servants started to chant.

Fight, fight, fight!

Miltiades relaxed.

But when it came to the vote, the result was a shock – five strategoi for fighting, and five for marching back to Athens.

The massed hoplites began to chant again – *fight, fight, fight!*

Someone threw a rock that hit Leontus. Athenians can be bastards. Other men threw rotten figs and eggs, too.

Callimachus raised his arms, and even the loudest hoplites fell silent.

'Don't be children,' he said, in his powerful voice. They didn't make him polemarch for nothing. Grown men – spear-fighters – flinched at the admonition in his voice. 'This is the life of Athens we discuss here. These are the men you appointed as strategoi. Act like citizens.'

So they did. And I was afraid that Callimachus, so calm and so in command, was going to carry us right back to the city.

Callimachus ordered the strategoi to vote again, but the result was another tie. War and politics make for strange alliances. Cleitus of the Alcmaeonids voted with Aristides the Just and Themistocles the democrat and Miltiades the would-be tyrant. The fifth vote for battle was Sosigenes, a well-known orator.

The dissenters were just as disparate, and the split belied any notion that men had been bought by barbarian gold, despite all the muttering after the battle. Men were voting from actual conviction, and that is when politics grows most heated and most dangerous.

I happened to be next to Callimachus after the second vote.

'By Zeus, lord of judges,' he said. 'I should never have allowed that smooth-tongued bastard to exclude you, Plataean.'

'No,' I said. 'I'd have fixed this.'

He gave me a hard smile, and then Miltiades came across the circle of strategoi and stepped up on his aspis. 'Of course,' he said, 'the polemarch is also a strategos. He must have the deciding vote.'

Miltiades' comment brought new silence.

Callimachus muttered one word. I heard him say it. He said 'Bastard' quite clearly.

Callimachus looked around the circle, and the silence of the army was thick enough to make cloth. 'Should I ask for another vote?' he asked the strategoi. All of them shook their heads.

Miltiades opened his mouth to speak, but Callimachus glared him into silence.

Callimachus had a pebble in his hand. He tossed it back and forth, for as long as it takes a man to eat a slice of bread. 'We do not just stand here for Athens,' he said, looking around, and men in the front rows repeated what he said. He spoke slowly, like the orator he was. 'Nor do we stand only for Athens and Plataea,' he added, with a nod to me. 'What we say here, what we do here, win or lose, is for all the Hellenes. If we return to Athens and submit earth and water to the Great King ...' He looked around again. The silence after his words were repeated was absolute.

He tossed the pebble at Miltiades' feet. 'Fight,' he said.

The hoplites erupted in cheers, like men watching a race at a games. The cheers were audible everywhere – even in the barbarian camp.

Immediately after the vote, the dissenters gathered around Miltiades, and Leontus took his hand. 'We'll be there in the line,' he said. 'We want to win.'

'Not the way we wanted it,' said another, Euphones of Oinoe. 'But we'll stand our ground.'

Then the dissenters walked off. I think they were wrong, but by the gods, they did their part on the day, and that's how a vote is supposed to work. That's what made Athens great – not just the men who voted for the fight, but those who voted against and fought anyway.

Then all the men who had backed him gathered around, and you would think they'd just voted a new festival – they were beaming with happiness, and hundreds of men came from the surrounding dark to pump their hands and clap their backs.

'So,' Aristides said, when the mass of well-wishers had gone to their rest. 'Fight tomorrow?'

'Too many front-rankers fought today,' Miltiades said.

'Or ran,' I said, with a wink, and the other strategoi laughed.

Miltiades agreed. 'Took exercise, at any rate,' he quipped. I thought he looked a foot taller. 'Tomorrow, Themistocles, I want the little men back in the fields, sniping at the barbarians. But tomorrow, I'll have five hundred Athenians – fifty men of every tribe – at the base of the hill, formed close. To give the psiloi cover if they have to run.'

'To show we're still warriors, more like,' I added.

That got me a look.

Aristides nodded. 'Tomorrow's my command day. You have a plan? You should be in command.'

Themistocles agreed. 'I have the next day,' he said.

'And I the next,' the polemarch added. 'You may have my day, as well.'

Miltiades grunted. 'Watch yourselves,' he said. 'Too many days and I could be addicted, like a drunkard to wine or a lotus-eater.' He looked out over the darkening plain. 'But I will fight on my own day, so men may not say that I acted from hubris. Let the barbarians stew.'

'They may march,' I said.

He shrugged. 'If they march, we fight, whatever day it is,' he said. 'But the more I look at this – now that my eyes are opened – the better it appears for us. Look – they have a fine camp, and good protection from wind and weather. But where can they go from Marathon? All roads go through us. If our little men bleed them every day – and I speak frankly, gentlemen – what care we if we lose psiloi? But every dead Mede is one less for the day.'

No one disagreed. It was true.

The next day, the psiloi went down the hill in a wave. They were better organized than on the first day, and Themistocles played a role in that. And he led the hoplites out on to the plain – more than five hundred, or so I thought.

The barbarians countered with oarsmen, turned hastily into light-armed men of their own, but it was a poor decision, as every dead man was that much less motive power for their ships.

The second day, our light-armed were tired. Only a few went out, and the enemy cavalry killed some of them. The balance was return-ing, and men shouted for Miltiades to lead us to battle. Muttering began that the army had voted for battle and now Miltiades was hesitating.

'Men are childish fools,' Miltiades muttered as he watched the beaten psiloi trudge up the hill. 'Don't they see? We've *won*! All we have to do is sit here and fill the plain with psiloi! And watch them eat – their horses will be out of forage in a day.'

But the hoplites didn't see, and the pressure to fight mounted.

The third day, the light-armed men went out together, and the barbarians stayed in their camp – they had to be feeling the same fatigue as our men by then. But in our camp, the hoplites boiled over. Sophanes – Aristides' friend, and mine – led the protest. He came up to Miltiades with fifty spearmen behind him and demanded that Miltiades lead us to the plain – there and then.

'Are we cowards, that we are letting our servants do the fighting?' Sophanes asked. 'What kind of city will we have, if my shield-bearer can tell me that he – not I – drove the Medes from Holy Attica?'

He had a point, as you all can see. If we are honest with ourselves, we hold citizen rights from our cities because we fight. True, eh? So if we – the armoured men, the heroes – were in camp, and the little men were fighting, then who was a citizen, really?

But Miltiades also knew he had a winning strategy. Men like Aristides worried about the consequences, but Miltiades was a fighter. And as we had put him in charge, his only concern was winning.

He took Sophanes aside, talked to him the way a man talks to his son and sent him back to his friends. He'd convinced the young men to give him another day or two.

Not that it mattered. The barbarians had had enough.

On the evening of the third day, the barbarians came out of their camp – and their army was unbelievably big. It was carefully planned, and they flowed out of their camp like water from a pot – and every contingent had its place. And then, having filled the plain from flank to flank, they came forward at a fast walk.

The psiloi ran for their lives. What else could they do? More than a few of them died, caught in the plain by the cavalry on the flanks or the bows of the Sakai and the Medes and the Persians in the centre.

Aristides had the hoplites on the plain that day, and he held his ground until the last of the little men ran past, and then, in good order, his hoplites walked back up the hill to us. But the barbarians didn't pursue. They turned about and walked back across the plain, fifteen stades back to their camp. The whole attack had taken less than the time it took for a speaker in a law case to give his argument.

I was getting into my corslet by that time, afraid that we were about to be attacked right up the hill, my eyes glued to the manoeuvres of the enemy. Miltiades came up next to me, jumped up on the wall and watched them as they retreated. He had Phrynichus with him, I remember, and Phrynichus had a stylus and a wax tablet.

'Persians on the right – cavalry and then infantry – their best. Just like us. Mounted Sakai on the left; then East Greeks. They look like the marines of all the ships – some Phoenicians there. And then the dismounted Sakai. Persians again in the centre – dismounted. Maybe

Medes. More Medes on the right.' He watched them carefully. 'They fill the plain, Arimnestos.'

Phrynichus wrote the Persian battle order carefully. I was looking at the fact that the Persian right would have all their best troops. It would be opposite our left. That would be the Plataeans. Like the day my father faced the Spartans at Oinoe, we would bear the brunt of their best men.

Of course I was afraid, young man. We were not the invincible hoplites of Greece. We were men who had lost every battle we'd tried with the damned Persians. But I swallowed my fears, like a man should. I nodded, and my voice barely caught when I spoke.

'About twelve thousand, give or take. Not as deep as we fight.'

'Deep enough, though.' Miltiades gave half a grin. 'We need to fill the plain, too.'

'Hah!' I said. I could see it – if our hoplites brushed against the hills and the sea, the cavalry had no way to slip around us – and no hoplite feared a horseman in front of him.

Actually, that's bravado. All men on foot fear cavalry – but a mass of spearmen who keep their nerve are not really at risk, however loud the thunder of hooves.

'Plataeans on the left, then the tribes in order or precedence,' Miltiades said. 'That puts your men on the far left and mine on the far right. You ready for five hundred new citizens?'

'What, tonight?' I quipped. But in my heart, I was afraid. My Plataeans, against the Persians. It was not just a matter of whether we could win. It was that I was taking my friends, my brother-in-law; by the gods, I was taking my city into action with the most dreaded foe in all the bowl of earth.

'I'm about to free every slave in the camp,' Miltiades said, and his eyes sparkled. 'Then I'll send them to you. The free men and the psiloi – I'll arm them and fill the back of my tribes with them.

'Half of them won't have spears,' I pointed out.

'They'll take up space,' he said. 'They can get up in the rough ground on your flank if you have to spread out – or help thicken your charge if you need. And if the cavalry gets around you,' he shrugged, 'well, they'll buy you time while they die.'

I nodded. 'Are we going to run at the barbarians? Or walk?'

Miltiades chewed on his moustache. 'I thought we might tell off the picked men to go at a run – starting at long bowshot. The way Eualcidas did it.'

337

I shrugged. 'Why don't we all run at them?' I said. 'I'm not saying anyone will shirk – but if we're all charging forward it's hard for anyone to take a step back.'

'We'd end up with holes in the shield wall,' he said.

'We'd scare the shit out of them,' I countered.

He sighed. 'This is a big risk, and you want to do something new,' he said. He nodded. 'I'll think on it. I'm going to free the slaves.'

'I'll get a feast together,' I said, and grinned.

The sun was still up when a crowd of poor men – recently freed slaves – appeared in our camp. Themistocles led them.

'Plataeans!' Themistocles said. 'Athens has freed these men, and asks your aid in enfranchising them.'

I had Myron right there. I had warned him, and he rose to it like – well, like the archon of Plataea.

'Freedmen!' he said, and they were quiet – probably still delighted to hear that they were freed. 'Many of you are, in your hearts, men of Athens. Perhaps you will always feel that way. But Plataea is honoured to have you – and if you will let us, we will make you feel honoured to be Plataeans. Welcome! Come to our fires, and let us feed you your first meal as free men and citizens.'

We had bread and olives, pork and wine all prepared, and we fed the poor bastards a feast. Our own men joined in. I went over to Gelon and tapped him. 'You're free, too,' I said.

He grinned. 'You're all right,' he said, and went to stand with the freedmen.

They ate the way starving men eat, and drank like men who never saw enough wine. Our citizens joined them, and moved among them – speaking to one, learning the name of another. And serving them, like slaves.

Makes me weep – sorry, honey bee. I need a moment.

When they were done with libations, and being blessed by our priests, and eating, I stood on my aspis.

'I was once a slave,' I said.

That shut them up.

'I was once a slave, and war made me free. Now I am the polemarch of Plataea. I know how well a freed slave fights. So I won't give you a long speech.' I pointed out of the firelight, towards the barbarians. 'Right now, not one of you has the value of a medimnos of grain. But over there, in that camp, are your farms and your ploughs and your oxen – your house and your barns – for some of you, your brides. Every Sakai wears the value of a Plataean farm on his back – some Persians are worth three or four.' I pointed at the men who had marched here with me. 'Tomorrow night, we will pool everything we take – every item we win with our spears, and men who fight will each take away a share. Everyone will share. Now,' I said, and I hopped off my aspis to stride among them, 'who has a spear? Stand over here. A helmet? Anyone?'

It took for ever – the sun slipped below the western rim and I was still trying to build my phalanx. My Plataeans were generous – men who'd picked up a good helmet offered their old one to the new men, and men with a spare leather hat traded it round, and so on. It went on and on. Men with two spears shared one. Men gave slaves a pair of sandals. A chlamys. Anything that would help the poor bastards to live a minute longer.

I received four hundred new citizens, give or take a few, and we managed to arm almost two hundred of them as spearmen, if not hoplites. Most had to roll up a cloak and use it as a shield. Many had neither helmet nor hat, and behind them stood men with a bag of rocks or a pair of javelins or a sling.

But when I had them all placed, and as well armed as I could, I sent them to bed. 'Sleep well,' I said. 'Dream of a rich farm in Plataea.' I hoped that they would, because I knew that it was as close as most of them would ever get.

18

I slept badly. I hope you won't think the worse of me if I admit that the night before Marathon, despite my head telling me that we had the men and the will to win, I lay awake and worried. Not about death. I never worry about death. It was failure that troubled me, and I lay on my bearskin with the sound of snoring around me, and nervous whispers, and probably the occasional fart – and wondered what I could do better.

The night raid haunted me. I'd been lost, and I hadn't told my men what I needed, and I'd made a dozen other errors. So I lay awake, thinking through my actions in the morning.

When you're in command, you worry about the damnedest things.

I worried about getting my armour on and needing to take a shit. I worried about what I should say – a polemarch is expected to give a speech. I worried about sleeping too late, about what my armour looked like. Gelon was free now and my helmet hadn't been polished since I left Plataea. A hero should look the part.

I worried about how to deal with the rough ground that would be on my left all day, and I worried about the effect of four hundred untrained men at the back of my phalanx.

Hades, friends. I can't even remember all the things I worried about the night before Marathon.

And when I thought of my wife – my glorious wife – all I could think was that if she were there, we could make love, and that would cheer me up. Except that she was well along in pregnancy by then, and they say making love when the belly is round is bad for the baby. I don't believe that making love is ever bad for anyone, myself, but people say these things.

I think that's when I fell asleep. Thinking of her.

No, that's a lie. My mind was its own traitor, and I'm here to tell the truth. My last thoughts were of Briseis. If we won ...

If we won, would I be closer to her? And where was she? I said Sappho's poem to Aphrodite in the dark, for Briseis. And *then* I went to sleep.

I awoke in the dark, and I could hear the snores – but as soon as my eyes opened, it all came in, the way animals come in an open gate when there's food in the mangers and they haven't been fed. All my worries.

I got up. The dog star was going down, and morning wasn't far off, and besides, I was cold.

Idomeneus had snuggled close in the night, and as I rose, he rolled over. 'Ares,' he said. 'Morning already?'

I tossed my heavy himation over him. 'Sleep another hour,' I said.

'Aphrodite's blessing on you,' he smiled, and went straight back to sleep, the Cretan bastard. Odd that he mentioned Aphrodite.

I stirred our fire – my mess group had a fire, of course – and added an armload of wood that someone had left ready, like a proper soldier. The fire sprang up, and I was warm.

My kit was neatly stowed under the leather cover of my aspis. Gelon had done it – he must have – after the muster of the freedmen. My corslet had been buffed until the scales shone, and the helmet was like a woman's mirror, and the reflected gleam of the fire danced on the curved brow and the ravens on the cheekplates.

Gelon came and knelt by my side. I hadn't seen him get up. 'Good enough?' he asked, as he had on other mornings when he'd done a half-arsed job. This wasn't half-arsed.

'Splendid,' I said. He'd even mounted my fancy plume – the one Euphoria had made me – and laid out the cloak, too.

'Might as well look the part, polemarch.' He gave my arm a squeeze. 'I gather from Styges that you brought my armour.'

'I did,' I said. 'But I haven't polished it for you.'

He laughed soundlessly. 'You're all right,' he said. 'In the baggage?'

'With Styges' mule. I didn't want you to find it.' I waved down the hill.

In the east, the black-blue sky was moving towards grey.

A thousand of us had only a few hours to live.

*

341

I ate alone – a bowl of hot soup and a big chunk of pork from the feast the night before. I dunked bread in the soup, and drank two big cups of water and another of wine.

Then, clad only in my arming chiton, a stained thing of linen that had once been white, I crossed the camp to where the strategoi met. The day was warm already, and promised to be as hot as my forge.

I was the first strategos there. Miltiades was second, which says much about the state of his mind, and Aristides was third. Then the rest came in a clump, and this time we stood together with no regard to who voted for battle and who voted against. In fact, I helped Leontus tie his thorax while Miltiades spoke. Leontus had a beautiful white tawed-leather cuirass with a heavy black leather yoke and scales on the sides, and his armour tied with scarlet cords.

'So,' Miltiades said. He looked around in the half-light. 'Today's my day, and today we'll fight. As soon as the boys have food in them, we'll go down the hill. I want the Plataeans down first. They get their leftmost man's shield up against the hills, and then we'll all form on them, so there's no gap. And friends,' he said, and he looked around, 'all we need to do to win is keep the line solid from end to end. No gaps. No spaces. Nothing. Shield to shield all the way from the hills to the sea.'

Everyone got it. We all nodded.

'You all know the order, left to right, yes? So each contingent goes down in order, and no rushing, and no pushing. Forming the line is the key to victory. Once we're formed, we're halfway to it. Fuck this up and we're all dead men.'

Aristides raised an eyebrow. 'We get it.'

Miltiades didn't crack a smile. 'See that you do. Next thing. When we reach the bowshot of the enemy – the range where they shoot – we charge. Understand? Dead run, and to Hades with the man who slows or falls.'

That got them talking. 'We'll fall apart!' Leontus protested.

Miltiades shook his head. 'It works in the east. Young Arimnestos there once charged a hundred Persians all by himself—'

'With ten other men!' I said.

'And the rest of the phalanx came in behind. It wrecked them – right?' Miltiades said.

I got the last of Leontus's ties done and faced the others. 'It hurries their archers,' I said. 'They lose time and space to shoot.' I looked around. 'We're the best athletes in the world, and we can cover that ground in no time, with the gods at our backs.'

'You're in command,' Leontus said to Miltiades. He shrugged. Then he smiled. 'All right. I'm fast. I'll run.'

'Just make sure the rest of your tribe goes forward too!' Sophanes said.

That was it – perhaps our shortest command meeting to date. Callimachus asked Miltiades where he should stand, and Miltiades nodded gravely. 'You are the polemarch,' he said. 'You take the right of the line.'

Callimachus bowed. 'I am honoured. But the place is yours if you wish it.'

Miltiades shook his head. 'When I'm polemarch, I'll take the place of honour,' he said, and that was that.

Then many of us embraced, and if my voice chokes to tell this – I embraced many men I loved for ever, and we all knew it. We all knew that win or lose, the price would be high. That is what a battle is – a culling. Except this time, instead of standing with strangers and 'allies', I was standing in an army with my friends in every rank, and every dead man would be the loss of someone I knew. It was all very personal.

More wine, girl. And this for the shades of the heroes who fell there!

So my friend Hermogenes, phylarch of the leftmost file of Plataea, was the first man down the hill, the first to form and the lynchpin of our line. And Callimachus was the last file-leader down the hill, and formed the farthest to the right in the front rank. Hermogenes' shield brushed against the trees, and Callimachus's right sandal was in the water, or so we used to tell the story.

Our Plataeans were twelve men deep and one hundred and twenty men wide. We took up a little more than a stade of the plain's width, and our rear rank was just twenty-four paces at normal order from our front rank.

The three tribes next to us had been 'bolstered' with light-armed men, and they, too, had twelve ranks. Many of the Athenian archers had also been put in the phalanx on the left. So they were deep, and they stretched three more stades.

We couldn't even see the middle as it started to form. Aristides was in the centre with his Antiochae, and they formed twice as wide as we did and only half as deep – just six deep – to cover more frontage.

That's where the richest, best-armoured men were, and Miltiades felt confident that they could take the brunt of the archery. At least, I hope that's what he thought. Because otherwise, what he thought was that the cream of the enemy's archers – the Sakai – would rid him of a world of political opponents.

There were three tribes in the centre, and they covered almost five stades.

And on the right there were three more tribes, double depth as we were, and they covered three more stades. So our line was twelve or more stades from end to end.

No one could keep a line that long from buckling and flowing and bending. But we formed it well, and even as we formed, the barbarians came.

They did what they had done the day before, but it all went mad, like a sudden thunderstorm.

First, the forming of the Persians was terrifying from ground level. Yesterday, I'd watched it from a hundred feet above the plain. It had been majestic and professional. At eye level, it was like a lion pouncing. They flooded out of their camp in silence, twelve thousand professional soldiers all running to their posts in about as much time as it takes to tell the story.

And then they came forward at us.

My end of the line had settled in position. Men were kneeling to tie a sandal, wiping the dew from their shields, laughing, resting their heavy shields on the ground, or on the instep of their left feet.

The onset of the barbarians blasted the laughter from us. They flowed over the plain like a sudden flood, and the horsemen on their flanks looked like gods in a blaze of sunlit gold. They came on without a sound except the ring and jingle of harness, of metal on metal, the hollow knocking of wooden shields on armoured legs.

Just as yesterday, they put their Phoenicians and Greeks on our right, so that I was opposite Persians, the front ranks armed just as we were armed, big men with heavy armour and shields – mostly oval shields, almost like our old Boeotians, with short heavy spears – but with six ranks of archers behind them. Opposite Hermogenes was a troop of Persian noble cavalry. Directly opposite me was a man in a helmet that seemed to be made of gold. As he came forward in the new sunlight, he called out a war cry and his men answered, all together, a single shout that carried to us like a challenge.

I remember my breath stopping in my throat.

To his right, from my perspective, were the Medes. The dismounted Medes were the second largest contingent after the Sakai, and they had armour, the best bows, sharp swords and axes. Beyond them, I assumed, were the Sakai, the best of the enemy's archers, in the centre, and then the enemy Greeks and Phoenicians on our right, facing Miltiades.

They were formed exactly the way they'd formed the day before. My Plataeans faced the cream of their army.

It steadied me. Being the underdog has its advantages. And in that moment I knew what I'd say.

They came closer, moving swiftly across the plain like hunting hounds or wolves. Hungry wolves.

I had Leontus on my right. I left my shield with Teucer and ran to Leontus – a stade each way, thanks. 'I'm going to charge them as soon as they reach bowshot,' I said, pointing down the field.

He was taken aback. 'Is that what Miltiades wants?' he asked.

'I don't know what Miltiades wants,' I said. 'He's five more stades that way, if you want to ask.' I shrugged, no easy thing in twenty pounds of scale armour. 'But as soon as they stop to shoot, I'm going at them.'

He was eyeing the Persians. His men would be in the arrow storm, not mine. 'I'm with you, Plataean,' he said.

I tapped his aspis by way of a handshake, and ran back to my place, and his tribe cheered me as I ran by. They were getting their shields off the ground, pulling their helmets down, and when I reached my own men, Idomeneus had already given the orders.

The enemy was still three or four stades away.

So I walked, forcing myself to take my time, all along my front rank. I met the eyes of every man there – some said a few words, some nodded their heads so that their plumes rippled, the horsehair catching the sea breeze. I walked all the way to Hermogenes.

'Fight well, brother,' I said.

'Lead us to glory, polemarch,' he said. I could see his grin inside the tau of his face slit.

By the gods, those words went to my heart.

Then I walked back – making myself walk, even while the Persians and Medes were slowing, closer than I'd expected – faster than I thought possible. Their mounted Persians – the best of the best – seemed close enough to touch, close enough to ride over and gut me before I could take shelter in our ranks.

I stopped in the middle of my line, turned my back to the enemy and raised my arms. Then, with the kind of gesture that Heraclitus taught us, a broad orator's sweep of my right arm, I indicated that I would speak.

'I could talk to you of duty,' I shouted, and they were silent. 'Of courage and arete, and of the defence of Hellas and all you hold dear.' I paused, and forced myself to look at my own men and not to turn my head and look at the enemy, who came closer and closer to my back. 'But you are Plataeans, and you know what is excellent, and who is brave. So I will say two things. First – yesterday, many of you were slaves. And for the rest – no one here expects us to beat the Persians. We are the left of the line and all Athens asks is that we take our time dying.' I paused, and then I pointed my spear at the enemy. 'Horse shit, brothers! We are Plataeans! Every man here is a Plataean! Over there is all the wealth of Asia! The gods have given us the Persians themselves, every one of them wearing a fortune in gold. You were a slave yesterday? Tomorrow you can be an aristocrat. Or be dead, and go to Hades with the heroes. Whatever you were, whatever you are at this moment, however much you want to piss or creep away – tomorrow is yours if you win today! All of that gold is yours if you are men enough to take it!'

My Plataeans responded with a roar – a sharp bark. Only then did I sneak a glance at our enemies. They were a stade away, or more. I returned to my place in the ranks. I put my aspis on my shoulder and grasped my spears – my fine, light deer spear in my right hand and my heavy man-killer in my left, sharing the hand with the antilabe of my shield.

I turned to Idomeneus. 'How was that?' I asked.

He nodded. He wore a Cretan helm that showed his face, and his smile was broad. 'Everyone understands gold,' he said. 'Arete is more complicated.'

'See the mounted bastard in the gold helmet?' I said. 'I'll take him. But he's got to go, and if I fall or I miss, you take him. Understand?' I tapped my spearhead against his, and saw his grin.

'Good as dead now,' Idomeneus said.

'Yes,' I answered.

He smiled his mad, fighting smile. 'Sure,' he said.

I turned to Teucer, who was tight to my back. 'Hear me, friend – do not take that man's life. I want his men to see him go down to *my* spear. In a fight like this – everything depends on the first few seconds.'

'Aye, lord,' he said. He was doubtful.

Opposite me, the whole enemy line – every bit as long as ours, and at least as deep – was slowing. It didn't stop all at once. It takes time for a line fifteen stades long to stop and straighten.

'Ready!' I roared. 'Spears up!'

Idomeneus hissed 'Close our order!' at me.

'I know what I'm doing,' I said.

The Athenians obeyed me as fast as my own men, and three thousand men raised their spears over their heads, spear-point just clear of the rim of your shield, spear-butt well up in the air so that it doesn't foul the man behind you or, worse, catch him in the teeth.

We were one stade from the enemy. The Persians were settling down, planting shafts in the ground. The cavalry were actually lagging behind their main line, with a few men trying to pick a way through the scrub to our flank and struggling. But giving me heartburn nonetheless.

I nodded to Idomeneus, and he blew the horn – two long, hard blasts, and the pause between them was thin enough for a sword blade to fit and not much more.

And then we were off.

Ever run a foot race? Ever run the hoplitodromos? Ever run the hoplitodromos with fifty men? Imagine fifty men. Imagine a hundred – five hundred – three thousand men, all starting together at the sound of a horn.

We were off, and by the will of the gods, no one stumbled in all our line. One poor fool sprawling on his face might have been the difference between victory and defeat. But no man fell at the start.

On my right, the Athenians moved as soon as I did, and the Persians and the Medes raised their bows and shot – too fast, and too far. Men in the rear ranks died, but not a shaft went into the front.

It's a tactic, honey bee. They halt at a given distance, a distance at which they practise, and pound the crap out of you – if you stand and take it. But if you move forward ...

Every step was a step towards victory. We were on the edge of a wheat field, tramped flat by psiloi over the last few days, and the hobnails on my Spartan shoes bit into the ground as I ran – full strides, just like the hoplitodromos.

That's why I didn't close our order, of course. Because men need room to run.

I was neither first nor last – Idomeneus was ahead of me by a horse-length, just heartbeats after he blew the horn. My old wound kept me from being first. But I was not last. I looked over the rim of my shield. We were facing Persians, Medes and a handful of Sakai, and every man had a bow.

Ten more paces and the Persians were loosing again – a rippling volley – and an arrow skipped off the gravel in front of me and ripped across my greave at my ankle and vanished into the ranks behind me. They'd shot low. This time, men fell – a few Plataeans, and more Athenians. And other men fell over the wounded. A man can break his jaw, falling with an aspis at a dead run, or break his collarbone or shield arm.

Just opposite me, and a little to my left, Golden Helm was bringing his Persian nobles forward. I saw him raise his hand, saw him order them forward – saw his hesitation.

We were charging them.

The Persian polemarch had spear-fighters – dismounted nobles – for his front two ranks. But he had sent them to the rear for the archery phase – his archers would shoot better and flatter if they didn't have to lift their shots clear of the front rank. The problem was, we weren't waiting to be pounded with arrows. And now his best fighters – killers, every one, like Cyrus and Pharnakes – were in the eleventh and twelfth rank.

If he rotated them again now, his men would have to stop shooting.

I read this at a glance, because there were no shields facing me, only round Persian hats and bright scale armour like mine.

A third volley flew at us. It is a fearful thing when the arrows come straight at you – when the flicker of their motion seems to end in your eye, when the shafts darken the sky, when the sound is like the first whisper of rain, growing swiftly into a storm.

And then they hit, and my shield took the impacts, like a hail of stones thrown by strong boys or young men. Two hit my helmet, and there was pain.

Then I was free of them and still running. More men were down. And the rest were right with me.

Golden Helm had made his decision.

He ordered his cavalry to charge us, slanting across our front

– horses take up three or four times the frontage of a man with a shield, unless they move very slowly. So suddenly the whole of the Plataean front was filled with Persian cavalry.

I altered my stride and ran for Golden Helm. My Plataeans didn't know any better, so they followed me.

The received wisdom of the ages is that infantry should not charge cavalry. In fact, it's about the best thing the infantry can do. Charging keeps men from flinching. Cavalry is only dangerous to infantry who break. I *wanted* their unarmoured horses in among our rear ranks, where they'd be swarmed and killed. I didn't want to fight them later – in our flanks, or our rear.

But to be honest, it was too late to change plan.

I ran at Golden Helm, and he became my world. He saw me, too, and he rode at me. He had a long axe in his hand, and his beard was saffron and henna-streaked, brilliant and barbarous. He was someone important. And the way he whirled the axe was ... beautiful. Magnificent.

I could say the battlefield hushed, but that would be pig shit. But it did for me. These moments come once or twice in a lifetime, even when you are a hero. As far as I know, we were the first to clash on the field that day. I saw no one else in those last moments. I saw the fine ripples in the muscles of his horse, the way the sun glinted like a new-lit fire from the peak of his helmet. The way his axe curved up from his strap – reaching for my throat.

I was perhaps five paces from him – one lunge of his horse, three strides of my legs – when I cast my spear.

The point went into the breast of his mount and sank the length of my forearm, and the horse's front legs went out from under it as if it had tripped.

He cut at me anyway. But the gods put him on the ground at my feet, and my second spear rang on his helmet, snapping his head back. He tried to rise, and quick as a cat I stabbed twice more – eye slit and throat. The first rang on his helmet and the second sank slickly and came out red. And then I was past him, and the world seemed to burst into motion as the rest of his cavalry slammed into us or slackened their reins – confusion everywhere, but the Plataeans ran in among them.

The Persians had balked, or most of them had. It happens to horses and to cavalry. Especially men who are riding strange horses. Many of them were just Greek farm horses, and they balked at the line of shields and the *eleu-eleu-eleu* shrieks from every throat.

And then they broke. They wanted a shooting contest, not a toe-to-toe brawl with men in better armour. The noble Persians broke away from us, leaving their dead, having accomplished nothing.

But we had. We were like gods now. We went after them, at their infantry, at the archers who had stopped shooting for fear of hitting their own.

The gods were with us.

I ran with a host of dead men – Eualcidas was there, I know, and Neoptolemus, and all the men who had died for nothing at Lade. I could feel their shades at my back, giving wings to my feet.

But Persians are men, too. Those archers were not slaves, nor hirelings, nor raw levies. They were Darius's veterans, and when we were ten short paces from their lines, they did not flinch. They raised their bows and aimed the barbed shafts straight at our faces, too close to miss.

And then they loosed. I remember hearing the shout of the master archer, and the grunts of men as they let the heavy bows release – I was that close.

I was in front. Men say that our front rank fell like wheat to a scythe. I know that the next day I saw men I loved with eight or nine arrows in them, men shot right through the faces of their aspides, through leather caps, or even bronze.

But not a shaft touched me. Perhaps the shades kept them from me. Or Heracles, my ancestor.

Nine paces from their line, I knew I would outrun their next volley.

Eight paces out, and men in the front rank were as plain as day – tanned faces. Handsome men, with long, black beards. Drawing swords.

Six paces out, and they were flinching.

This was not the fight at the pass. I didn't need to risk hitting them at full speed. I slowed, shortening stride, bringing my second spear up, gripping it short – just a little forward of halfway.

Three paces out, and my prayers went to my ancestors. There is no Paean at the dead run, but to our right, the Athenians were singing, and I could hear it.

I remember thinking – *This is how I want to die.*

One pace out, the man in front of me wouldn't meet my eye, and my spear took him while he cringed, but the man to his left was made of better stuff and he slammed his short sword into me. I blocked it on my aspis and then I put my shield into him. He had no shield, and I probably broke his jaw.

My strong right leg pushed me through their front rank. Left foot planted, shield into the second-ranker and I knocked him back – Ares' hand on my shoulder.

The second-ranker was a veteran and he knew his business. He and the man to his right got their swords up, into my face, points levelled, and they pushed back at me together. Then a rain of blows fell on my aspis as they tried to force me out of their ranks. I took a blow to my helmet and I went back a step, and then Teucer – already at my shoulder by then – shot one, a clean kill. I pushed forward against the other man, chest to chest, and he stood his ground, and our spears were too long to reach each other, close enough to embrace, to kiss, to smell the cardamom and onion on his breath. I thrust over his shoulder at the man behind him. He pushed me back – he was strong, and I remember my shock as he moved me back another full pace, but he was so dedicated to pushing me by main strength that I had time to throw my light spear into another second-ranker. My sword floated into my hand and I cut – once, twice, three times – at his shield rim, no art, no science, just strength and terror and the last shreds of force from my desperate run, and he raised his cloak-wrapped arm and ducked his head, as men will, and *pushed*. My fourth blow came as fast as the first three, stooped like a hawk on a rabbit, bit through his cloak and into the naked meat of his arm, so hard that it cut to the bone and my sword snapped as I wrenched it loose – falling, because even as I cut him, his push overcame my balance. I fell, and the melee closed over me.

Imagine – I had killed him, or wounded him so badly he couldn't fight, yet still he knocked me down. At my shoulder was Teucer, who had no shield. At my victim's shoulder was a smaller man who hadn't quite kept up – in a fight like that, a rear-ranker needs to be pressed tight to his front-ranker to help him at all, or his spear-thrusts are too far back. Teucer shot the next man, but the arrow skittered off his shield.

Suddenly we were fighting their killers, their front-rank men, who were pushing as hard as they could to get to their correct places. By all the gods, the Persians were brave. Even disordered, they fought, and their best men weren't finished.

I saw it all from where I'd fallen backwards, my back against Teucer's knees and my shield still covering me.

I had never gone down in a phalanx fight before, and I was terrified. Once you are down, you are meat for any man's spear. In falling, my chin had caught on my shield rim and I'd bitten my tongue – it may sound like a silly wound to you, thugater, but my head was full of the pain and I didn't know if I'd taken a worse wound.

'Arimnestos is down!' Teucer called. He meant to rally aid, but his words sucked the heart out of our phalanx. The whole line gave a step to the Persians and Medes.

I couldn't get an arm under me. My left arm, beneath my shield, was wrapped in my chlamys, and I couldn't get the rim of the shield under me – my right arm slipped on the blood-soaked wheat stubble and one of the enemy thrust at me. I caught a flash of his spearhead and turned my head, and his blow landed hard. His point must have caught in the repoussé of my olive wreath, and I fell back again, this time on my elbows. My aspis bore two heavy blows, and my shoulder felt the impact as my left arm was rotated against my will – I screamed at the pain.

Then Bellerophon and Styges saved my life. They passed over Teucer, their shields flowing around him in the movements we had taught in the Pyrrhiche. They stood over me, their spears flashing, the tall crests on their helmets nodding in time to their thrusts, and for a moment I could see straight up under their helmets – mouths set, chins down to cover the vulnerable throat – and then Styges pushed forward with his right leg and Bellerophon roared his war cry and they were past me.

I got a breath in me. Teucer stepped over me, close at their shoulders, and shot – and there were hands under my armpits, and I was dragged back. I breathed again, and again, and the pain was less, and then I was on my back and my shield was off my arm.

'Let me up!' I spat.

They were all new men – the rear-rankers – and they scarcely knew me. On the other hand, they'd been bold enough to push into the scrum and get my body. I finally got my feet under me and I rose, covered in blood and straw from being dragged.

'You live!' one of the new men said.

'I live,' I said. I pulled my helmet back and one of them handed me a canteen. I looked at the front of the fighting – just a couple of horse-lengths away. I could see Styges' red plume and Bellerophon's white, side by side, and Idomeneus's red and black just an arm's length to the right of Styges. They were fighting well. The line wasn't moving, either way.

I looked to the right. The Athenians under Leontus were into the Medes – but the fighting was heavy, and the Sakai in the rear ranks were lofting arrows high to drop on the phalanx, where they fell on unarmoured men, many of whom had no shields.

To my left, the Persian cavalry were pressed hard against the front of our shields, stabbing down with their spears and screaming strange cries.

A new man – little more than a boy – handed me a gourd. 'More water, lord?'

I drank greedily, pressed the gourd back into his hands and pulled my helmet down. 'Shield,' I said, and two of them put it on my arm. My left arm muscles protested – something bad had happened in my shoulder. 'Spear,' I growled, and one of them gave up his spear – his only weapon.

Behind me, the sound of battle changed tone.

I had to turn around to look – once I had my helmet on, my field of vision was that limited.

Beyond the Athenians fighting the Medes, something was already wrong. I could see the backs of Athenians – I could see men running. But they were two or three stades away – slightly downhill. It looked to me as if our centre was bulging back.

Remember that we had been fighting for only two minutes – maybe less.

I remember sucking in a deep breath and then plunging forward into the phalanx the way a man dives into deep water. I pushed past the rear-rankers easily – they were anxious to let me past. When I came to armoured men – our fifth or sixth rank, I suppose – I had to tap the men on the backplate.

'Exchange!' I called.

Rank by rank, I exchanged forward. This is something we practise in the Pyrrhiche over and over again. Men need to be able to move forward and back. I went forward – sixth to fifth, fifth to fourth, fourth to third. Finally, after what seemed like an hour, I was behind Teucer, and I could see Idomeneus, locked in his fight with a Persian captain.

They were well matched. And both of them were failing – their blows slowing. I've said it before: men can only fight so long – even brave, noble men in the height of training.

I stepped to the right, cutting in ahead of Idomeneus's second-ranker – Gelon. He knew me immediately.

I tapped Idomeneus on the shoulder.

He looked back – the merest flash of a glance, shield high to deflect a blow – but in that heartbeat he knew who was behind him.

He set his feet, and I put my right foot forward across my left, and allowed my knee to touch the back of his leg. He pivoted on the balls of his feet and stepped to the rear. I pushed forward and launched a heavy blow into the Persian's shield with my new spear, rocking him back.

He was tired. I could tell he was fading from that first exchange, and he crouched behind his shield and thrust low, at my shins, but I was having none of it. I had caught my breath, and I was as fresh as a man can be in a phalanx fight. I powered forward on my spear foot, and Gelon came at my shoulder, pounding away at the noble Persian with high blows to his shield and his helmet.

He gave ground.

'Plataeans!' I roared. 'TAKE THEM!'

I remember that moment the best, children. Because it was like the dance, and it was glorious – it was, perhaps, a taste of godhood. Enough men heard me – enough men in every rank heard the call.

I was Arimnestos the killer of men. But in that kind of fight, I was only one man.

But I was one *Plataean*, and together, we were *that thing*. I planted my right foot and around me every Plataean did the same, and though we had no pipes to call the time, every man crouched, screamed their war cry and pushed forward.

Apollo's Ravens!

The Persian officer was gone – knocked flat, or exchanged out of the front rank. I lost him in the moments when we pushed, and my new opponent's eyes were wide with terror. I swept my shield forward and caught the rim of his oval shield and flicked it aside, and Gelon's spear robbed the man of life as easily as if he was a dummy of straw.

Then we went forward. I had Styges at my left shoulder and Idomeneus was pressing up on my right. Gelon was at my back, and Teucer shot and shot from behind my left ear. We went forward ten paces and then another ten – the enemy stumbling away before

354

us. They didn't break, but suddenly there was less pressure on our front.

Leontus and his Athenians were keeping pace, and the Medes were backing away almost as fast as we pressed forward, but they were not yet beaten men. In truth, it was the hardest fighting I had ever seen. By this time, we had been spear to spear for as long as a man gives a speech in the Agora – or more – long enough that the sun was suddenly high in the sky. I was covered in sweat. My face burned from the pressure of my helmet and the blood and salt against the leather of my helmet pad. My shoulder was lacerated by the damaged scales on my thorax, and my legs ached.

The Persians flinched back again, and their front solidified. Men were calling to each other to hold their ground, and the Medes on our right got their spear-fighters into the front rank and locked shields, and we came to a stop, just a pace or two clear of their line.

I looked around – we'd pushed them back a stade or more. And as they recoiled, they were pivoting on their centre, so that we were facing their ships in the distance, far away by their camp.

All along the line, men breathed and stood straight, they switched grips on their spears, or dropped a broken weapon. Many exchanged, giving their place to fresher men.

'You live!' Styges said. He raised my shield arm – wrenching my shoulder as he did – so that the black raven on my red shield rose over the battlefield.

Men cheered. That is a great feeling, daughter, and worth all the pain in the world. When men cheer you, you are with the gods.

Opposite us, an officer called for the Persians to cheer and got a rumble – and no more.

'Plataeans!' I called, and Heracles or Hermes gave my throat power. 'Sons of the Daidala, *now is the time!*'

The spear came up again, and our cheer had the force of a crack of thunder, and we charged – not far, two paces, but the Persians were yielding before we reached them, their shields moving, so that every veteran in our line knew that we had beaten them – and with a long crash like the sound two boats make as they collide, the enemy gave way.

The first-rank man opposite me was brave, or foolish, and stood his ground. I knocked him flat. I threw my borrowed spear at the next man and it stuck in his shield, dragging it down. Gelon put a spear-tip into the top of his thigh and I stepped on his chest and pressed forward, reaching for a sword that wasn't there – a moment of fear – and I was into the third rank.

This part I remember as if it was yesterday, thugater. I had no weapon, and the next man should have killed me, but he cowered, and my right arm shot out as if it had its own life in combat, grabbed the rim of his scalloped shield and spun it to the left. His shield arm snapped. He went down. He screamed, and his scream was the surrender of the Persians to panic.

And the rest were running.

The screaming man with the broken arm had a perfectly good spear, and the gods gifted it to me as he let go and it seemed to leap into my hand.

I looked left – Hermogenes was coming into the flank of the Medes. No idea where the beaten Persian cavalry had got to, but the Persians were wrecked – men in front and the flank – and they ran, and the Medes started to run with them.

All in as long as it takes to tell the tale. After an hour of endless pushing, we were winning.

To my right, the Medes were backing fast, but they were not beaten, and their rear ranks continued trying to lob arrows high to drop them on our phalanx, and it was working. My men were still dying. But the Sakai had no shields, and our spears were hurting them.

I was no longer in command. We were no longer a phalanx. Plataeans and Athenians were intermixed along two stades, and men were plunging into the front of the Sakai, in groups or alone.

I remember that I stooped and picked up a Sakai axe and put it in my shield hand. Better than no weapon, I thought, if my short Persian spear broke.

I could hear a Mede demanding that his men rally – and they did. The Persians tried to form on them – they had lost many men. And the Persian cavalry came forward with a shout and a hail of arrows.

Hermogenes' men were still milling around, in no sort of order – but remember, he had twelve ranks of men behind him. The cavalry hit his front ranks, and they locked up – spear and aspis against horse and sword and bow. Our line moved back a pace, and then the men on my left ran at the flanks of the horses and started pulling the Persians from their saddles.

The Medes – like lions – came forward to take advantage of our confusion – or simply to save the Persians – I have no idea.

'On me!' I roared. 'Charge!'

The Medes were shocked as we ran at them again. Some stopped dead, and others kept coming, and they had no more order than we did.

That's when the fighting was the worst – the fiercest. They were shamed from their brief rout and meant to have our heads, while we already thought that we were the better men and meant to have theirs. Both sides lost their cohesion, and men died fast. Blows came out of everywhere and nowhere, and the only hope was to be fully armoured, as I was. I must have taken ten blows that should have been wounds, on my arm and shoulder plates, on my scale shirt, on my helmet. Some must have been from my own men, in the confusion.

Then, somehow, I was in among the Persian cavalry, not the Medes, though I have no memory of running at them, and that made my fighting easier – anyone on a horse was a target. Mounted men seldom have shields. I was like Nemesis.

Idomeneus must have decided to stay at my shoulder, and I had Gelon at my back – and we killed them. Ahh, I remember Marathon, children. That day, I was a god of war. My armour flashed and shone, and men fell under every blow of my spear. I ripped men from their horses. Mounted men have to fight to the front – they cannot face to the flanks or rear. Not against two rapid blows, anyway.

Idomeneus and Gelon were not much worse than me, though, and as the fight became looser, and ranks dissolved, we were more dangerous, not less. I had a simple goal – my usual goal in a melee – to burst out of the back of the enemy formation. So I killed and wounded, I knocked men off their mounts and stepped on them, and I kept going forward, and my little group stuck to me.

It is possible to get lost in a big fight, the way a man may get lost in the woods. Confined in the eye slits of your helmet, it is possible to take a wound or die simply because some bastard turned you around. It is essential to have men at your back whom you trust – men who will turn you back round, or kill the opponent who is circling outside the realm of your helmet. But with such men, anything is possible, and it is incredible how a man can move inside a melee if he has purpose and companions.

I went at a rider in a rich purple cloak and he turned and jammed his heels in – and when I followed him we burst free and then we were running in a hayfield, and the fight was behind us. The fleeing man took an arrow and fell back over the rump of his horse, and he rode away like that – a surprising distance, as I remember. Then Teucer, at my elbow, grunted and released another arrow, high, and it fell on him and he crashed to earth. He tried to rise, and a third arrow finished him.

Teucer came out from the cover of Idomeneus's shield, nocking an arrow, and the Persian cavalry folded up and ran – again – and this time they left half their men or more dead on the ground because we'd burst through them. Then the Medes broke and ran, shooting as they went. There were horses down in the brush, and men screaming, and horses bellowing. Ares, it was grim – blood on the ground, enough of it to splash over your sandals when the man next to you made a kill or died. So much blood that the copper-bronze smell fills your nostrils, more even than the stink of sweat, the smell that men have when they are afraid, the smell of men's guts like new-butchered deer. Only when you stop do you notice it – the stench of Ares – and then it makes you gag, especially if some unarmoured boy has been cut to death at your feet, his lips already blue-white and bled out, his eyes bulging from the horror and pain.

War.

But, as I say, the Medes ran, the Persian cavalry ran or died, and the Sakai, despite their leader's calls, had not been keen for the second engagement, and the whole mass went back. This time, they went back to the east, down towards the beach, trying to hide themselves among the Sakai of the centre, I think.

Teucer started shooting into them, and then he was out of shafts. It seems odd to tell it, but the only arrows I remember at that point were his, although I'm told that the Sakai kept shooting until the very end.

I had other concerns. The Athenians were pushing the Sakai, and the Sakai, whether by intention or by chance, where backing only at our end of the line – so that they swung like a gate, still linked to their centre two stades away.

At our end, we'd won. The Persians, cavalry and infantry were dead or broken, fleeing, throwing away their shields. Once a man discards his shield, he's done. The Medes ran, and the Sakai nearest us were – well, mostly they were dead.

Idomeneus was at my shoulder.

'Sound the rally!' I panted.

I could see it – by Ares and by Aphrodite – that's what I remember best of that whole glorious day. I could see what I needed to do, as if

Athena stood at my shoulder, or perhaps Heracles, and whispered it in my ear.

I pivoted my body to face the beach, twelve stades away, and spear my arms wide. 'Rally here!' I called. 'On me!'

Idomeneus went into his place, and Gelon and Teucer. In seconds, fifty more men were fitting in, and then a hundred. A long minute, and an arrow slew one of my Plataeans almost at the end of my spear, but by now the whole mass of them was forming up, fifteen hundred men.

Even the former slaves. Even when the old Plataeans had to show them where to stand.

The Sakai weren't stupid. They were shooting at us as fast as they could.

The far end of the line had Hermogenes and Antigonus. I ran down the front rank and counted off twenty files from the left end, and pulled Antigonus out of the ranks.

'Take them – wheel left, and pursue the beaten men. Stay close enough to keep them running and stay far enough that they don't turn and kill you. If you reach their camp – stop!'

Antigonus nodded. 'Pursue.' He gave me a tired smile. 'Have we won?'

'That's right!' I slapped his shield. 'Go!' If you think I was a good strategos, a just man – I'm no Aristides. I sent my brother-in-law and my closest friend away to a nice safe pursuit. They'd done their part, and Pen would not become a widow this day. I didn't think that the remnants of the enemy had any fight left in them – nor was I wrong.

Then back to my own – now formed facing the empty air that hung off the new flank of the Sakai.

'Slow and steady. Keep together.' I shouted these things. I wanted the Sakai to see us coming. 'Sing the Paean!' I yelled, and men took it up – all along the line. There had been no time to sing the Paean or give much of a war cry before our first charge. Now – now we had all the time in the world.

We sang, and our lines stiffened, bent, righted themselves – it is hard to keep the line on rough ground, and the plains of Marathon in early autumn are like farm fields the world over. We had to flow around clumps of trees, bushes, rocks – it was not like the painting in the stoa, children. There were no straight lines at Marathon.

But the Sakai saw us and gave more ground. They tried to run and re-form to face us, but the Athenians stayed on them, and they died. Those Sakai were gallant, and they tried, again and again, to make a stand and hold the line.

As we passed the edge of their formation, we saw why.

Our own centre was shattered, as if a herd of cattle had passed through. Where Aristides had stood, there were only victorious Persians, Datis's bodyguard and dead Greeks.

I cursed under my breath, trying to see. Had we lost? I faltered, and my voice roared 'Forward!' without my volition – some god took my throat, I swear. I went forward.

Then, as we turned the flanks of the Sakai, they folded as fast as a man can lose a boxing match. One moment they were outmatched, but still game, their line backing away but their men fighting hard, and the next they were finished, flying for their lives. They started to run in earnest because we were behind them. I didn't want to fight the Sakai anyway. I wanted to come to grips with Datis. The day was neither lost nor won, and with everything in the balance, my men were not going to stop and fight men in flight.

'Paean! Again!' I roared, and they obeyed – although as long as I have been a soldier, I have never heard the Paean sung twice in the same action.

Now I could see the Greek centre – well back, almost where we had started our charge, and only clumps of men. I could see horsehair crests there, and Persian felt hats. And men looking towards us.

It all happened in moments, heartbeats of time, too little for me to give an order or change our front. The Persian centre was killing the Antiochae – and then they were running, racing over the stubble of the hay for their camp. The sight of us behind them – however ill-formed our phalanx really was – terrified them the way our charge apparently had not.

The Sakai had held the flanks for Datis and his picked men to wreck the Athenian centre, and the dead were everywhere, or so it seemed. But by the gods, when they saw us coming behind, threatening to cut them off from the ships, I saw men grab the satrap – hard to miss in his scarlet and gold – and run him to a horse. His picked killers ran at his heels like dogs on a hunt.

They were too far away for my formed men to reach. They ran through the hole in our lines and down towards the beach. Some of their men ran west, away from the beach, following an officer. More – I didn't see this – ran west and north – around *behind* our lines.

The right wing – our right, Miltiades' men – had fought as hard as we had and been just as victorious, and even as we came up to the Persians, Miltiades' men began to form a new phalanx facing us – one of the strangest sights I've seen on a battlefield, two victorious phalanxes from the same side facing each other over three stades of ground, with Persians streaming away between us.

There was no holding my men then. It started with the rear-rankers – the freedmen. They saw their fortunes running by, hundreds and hundreds of gold-laced Persians running for their camp, and they left their ranks and started in pursuit. I called for them to halt – and more men joined them.

All my men streamed away after them. I stopped, popped my helmet on the back of my head, took a swig of water and spat it out, and bandaged my knee. By my side, Idomeneus was panting, bent double, staring fixedly at the stubble, and Teucer was humming to himself, scouring the grass for spent shafts.

When I raised my head, I could see all the way to the ships. There was haze in the distance, but I could see that the barbarians had formed again, well down the field, and there was fighting there, and over in the olive grove west of the swamp, too.

Most of my oikia – my own men – stood around me. Styges had a cut on his sword arm, Gelon looked as fit as a statue, and a dozen of my new freedmen had chosen to loot the corpses in the area. So I had maybe twenty men, and there were knots of fighting all over the field. Men were leaving the field, too – dribs and drabs of Greeks, wounded or just too tired too continue. Not everyone lived the life of the palaestra and the gymnasium. And there was no real discipline – man who felt he'd done enough could just turn and walk away.

But I was the polemarch of Plataea, and there was still fighting. The Greeks around me were saying 'Nike, Nike.'

Maybe. But to me, the sound from the north was an ominous one. It suggested that the battle wasn't over yet.

I tested my wounded leg, and it was solid enough. Pain is pain. Fatigue is fatigue.

'Zeus Soter,' one of the new men said. He had a wound on his hand with blood flowing out of it, despite the rag he'd put on it. 'I feel like shit!' he said. 'I need to sit.'

I grabbed his shoulder. 'You feel bad?' I asked. 'Think how they feel!' I pointed to the row of dead Sakai, naked now and their white bodies lying in a row where our rear-rankers had stripped them.

Idomeneus barked his battle laugh.

'More fighting,' he said.

We all drank our canteens dry, and then Greeks came up from the wreck of the Athenian centre – some ashamed, and others proud. Many had run, and others fought on until the Persians were forced back – and you can guess which group included Aristides.

'By the gods, Plataean, I think we have won!' he shouted as he ran up. He had the cheekplates of his helmet cocked back to give him a better view. There was blood flowing down his leg, and Idomeneus and I insisted he be bandaged before we went forward again. Aristides brought a hundred men with him – they were weary, but they wanted to be in at the kill.

We moved down to the beach. The fighting seemed heaviest by the ships, and we could see black hulls launching all along the bay. It seemed too good to be true, but one after another, ships pushed their sterns off the sand and their oars came out. Some stayed in close, rescuing men from the water.

Others simply fled.

That was when we knew we'd won.

The barbarians had formed a line by the ships – whether by intention or merely in desperation – and Miltiades' men were fighting there. Most of my men and many of Miltiades' went up into the camp and started to loot.

The fighting by the ships was deadly. Aeschylus's brother fell there, and Callimachus, the polemarch of Athens. Cimon, Miltiades' eldest son, took a wound there, and Agios was wounded when he leaped aboard an enemy ship and started to clear it.

We were walking – I can hardly call it a march – along the beach, passing over the wreckage of the Persians – corpses of men and horses as thick as seaweed after a storm, dead Medes cut down by Miltiades' men. And as clear as an actor on the stage of the Agora, I heard Agios calling. Then I saw him, on the stern of an enemy ship half a stade away.

I wasn't going to let him die while I had breath in my body. I started to run.

At my back, all my oikia followed me.

Aristides and Miltiades heard him, too.

And like a flood, the best spears of the army converged on the stern of that ship. We weren't far – a hundred paces.

How long does it take to cut your way through a hundred paces of panicked Medes and desperate Persians?

Too long.

I went through the remnants of the Medes with my trusted men at my shoulders, but then we hit the Persians, and we slowed. There were a dozen of them – not men I knew, thank the gods, but the same sort of men as Cyrus and his friends, and they fought like demons, and we slowed.

Agios probably died then, while I was face to face with an armoured Persian. The Persian fought well. We must have exchanged four or five cuts before my spear ripped his forearm and my next thrust sent his shade down to Hades. As I stepped past him, the Persians backed away, grabbing at a man with a hennaed beard. His helmet was gold and set with lapis, and I'd seen him before.

Datis.

I thrust at him and saw my spear drive home under the skirts of his armour, and then his men were all around him. I was an arm's length from the ship where Agios lay dying, pierced fifty times, shot with arrows and continuing to call the battle cry of Athens, so that the whole army heard him, and men pressed forward, possessed with the rage of Ares. The barbarians could have rallied – they certainly should never have lost a ship. But we cut into them the way the sickle cuts into the weeds at the edge of a garden.

Agios's shouts grew weaker, and my blows fell faster, and I got a Mede against the stern of the ship and punched my spear at him so hard that my spearhead stuck in the tar-coated wood. Then I dropped my shield and jumped. As I got my leg over the thwart a Sakai archer cut at me. His short knife caught in my chlamys and turned against my scale armour. With that axe in my right hand I cut into him, and he fell away, and I got my feet under me.

I could see the faces of the panicked oarsmen – and Agios, collapsed across the helm. A spearman stood over him, having just stabbed him, and my axe licked out and cut the back of his knee so that his leg gave way and he fell, spraying blood – but I hit him again, and again, and again, until the side of his helmet caved in.

Now the blows of five men fell on my armour, and I had no shield. I took a wound in the thigh – just a pin-prick – but enough to snap me out of the blood rage. Suddenly Aristides was beside me – using his spear two-handed – and then Miltiades came over the other gunwale, then Styges, Gelon, Sophanes, Bellerophon, Teucer, Aeschylus, and we stormed that ship, the living wrath of Athena.

Six more ships were taken and cleared before they could get to sea. The Athenians and the Plataeans were no longer an army – nor were the barbarians. They were a fleeing mob, and we were in the red rage of Nike and Ares, when men die because they care about nothing but more blood. Our fire burned hot, and many were consumed. Indeed, I've heard it said that more Athenians died by the ships than when the centre broke – but I've heard a great many things said by Athenians about the battle, and a few of them are true, but most are pig shit. We lost a lot of men, and so did Athens, although Cimon will tell you otherwise.

We burned like a bonfire in a high wind, and then their last ship was away, and we burned to ash. We were spent.

We came to a stop, so that a hush fell over the field. I suppose that wounded men screamed, and gulls screeched, and horses trumpeted their pain, but I remember none of that. What I remember is the hush, as if the gods had decided that all of us deserved a rest.

I leaned on the haft of my looted axe, and breathed. I don't know how long I was out of it – but ask any man who's been in the battle haze, and he'll tell you that when you are *done*, you don't cheer. You just stop. When I came back to myself, I was sitting on the blood-soaked planks of the marine box. My thigh wound was open and bleeding again, and Miltiades was beside me. We'd cut our way from the stern, by Agios's corpse, to the bow. I was covered in blood – sticky, stinking blood.

'I think we've won,' Miltiades said. He didn't sound proud, or arrogant, or in any way like the hero of the hour. He sounded awe-struck.

We all were, children. I don't think that we really believed we could win – or perhaps the issue was so much in doubt that we couldn't separate what we dreaded from what we hoped for.

But as we watched the last shreds of the Persian cavalry swimming their horses out, and the ships closing round them to save them, we knew that these Persians were not coming back. Especially when they abandoned their horses in the water.

I remember then, watching the ships creep past us from the north. Many had lost oarsmen as well as hoplites, and they didn't move fast. Behind me, the victorious Athenians had started to sing – some hymn to Athena I didn't know.

Out across the water, a ship's length away or less, I saw the scorpion shield standing on the stern of a light trireme. The enemy ship was going past us, picking men out of the water, bold as brass.

Teucer had an arrow, and he drew it to his chin, but I put my axe head in front of his arrowhead just when he went to loose, and he cursed.

Archilogos saw it all. His mouth formed an O and his head tracked me as my eyes must have followed him. He raised his shield.

'Tell Briseis I send my greetings!' I called across the water.

His men rowed him away and he didn't reply.

It was harder to leap down from that hull than it had been to climb aboard – my muscles were seizing, and I remember Aeschylus catching me as I stumbled. We were much of an age, he and I. He was a good man, despite his jealousy of Phrynichus's success.

Idomeneus had my shield. 'You alive, boss?' he asked. 'You've got a cut.'

So we bandaged my thigh again and then we looked after the dozen cuts he had – one in his bicep so deep I couldn't see how he could use his sword arm. Aeschylus helped. I didn't realize then that he was standing a few paces from the corpse of his brother.

Miltiades came up to me.

'I need the best men,' he said quietly. 'We're not done.'

Just north of the plain was an extensive stand of olive trees surrounded by a stone boundary wall. The Persians who had run north and west when their line gave way ran all the way around our army, but were cut off from the beach by the ruin of their camp. Being true Persians, they refused to surrender. They went into the walled olive grove and determined to die like men.

Half of our army must already have started back across the fields to our camp by the time Miltiades became aware of what was happening, and good men had died – some of them Plataeans – trying to storm the olive grove. The rumour spread that Datis was there, and the Persian command staff.

I gathered my oikia, and Miltiades gathered his, and Aristides his best men from the wreck of the centre, and we walked north along the beach and then through the Persian camp. We passed beautiful carpets and bronze urns and I saw silk and finely woven wool – but we had no time to loot. I did pause to pick up a silver-studded sword – that one, honey bee. Look at that steel. Too light for me, but so well crafted – Hephaestus's blessing on the hand that made the blade – that I would use it in preference to a better-hefted blade.

I found Hermogenes at the edge of the camp, with Antigonus, who had a wound in the foot. Peneleos and Diocles were there, although other men who should have been with them – like Epictetus – were missing.

'Those are some tough bastards,' Hermogenes said. He had four arrows in his shield. He looked sheepish. 'The Athenians tried to storm them and got in trouble – we just went in to help them out.' He looked as if he would cry. 'I lost a lot of the boys,' he said quietly.

'They beat us,' Antigonus said.

Miltiades took a deep breath. 'They're desperate men,' he said.

'Surround the grove and get them tomorrow,' Themistocles suggested. He had a dozen hoplites with him, and they looked as tired as the rest of us. 'Or burn it.'

'They'll break out in the dark,' Aeschylus said. His voice was thick. He knew by then that his brother was dead, and he wanted revenge. 'They'll break out, and every cottage they burn, every petty farmer they kill will be on our heads.'

It was true. Tired men have no discipline, and the Athenians were tired. Indeed, every man looked twenty years older. Miltiades looked sixty. Aristides looked – well, like an old man, and Hermogenes looked like a corpse. Ever been exhausted, children? No – you are soft. We were hard like old oaks, but there was little flame left in us. I remember how I walked, forcing each step, because I hurt and because my knees were shaking slightly. My sword wrist burned.

Miltiades looked around. The sun was setting – where had the day gone? – and we had perhaps two hundred men of all the army standing there at the north edge of the enemy camp. Others were looting. But most were sitting on the ground, or on their aspides – some singing, some tending wounds, but most simply staring at the ground. That's how it was – how it always is. When you are done, you are done.

Miltiades watched the ships behind us. 'Where are they going?' he asked suddenly.

The barbarian fleet was forming up out in the bay. And starting not east, towards Naxos or Lemnos or an island safely owned by the Great King, but south – towards Athens.

'They're making a stab for the city,' Cleitus said softly. I hadn't seen him since the fighting started, and there he was, covered in dirt as if he'd rolled in the fields. Perhaps he had. I had. His right arm was caked in crusted blood to the elbow, his spearhead dripped blood, and flies buzzed thickly around his head.

Miltiades took a deep breath. He was the eldest of us, over forty, in fact, and his face beneath the cheekplates of his Attic helmet was grey with fatigue, and below his eyes he had black lines and pouches like a rich man's wallet. But as I say, none of us looked much better apart from Sophanes, who looked as fresh as an athlete in a morning race, and Bellerophon, who was grinning.

'We have to clear the olive grove as quickly as we can,' Miltiades said. 'We can't leave them behind us – we'll have to march for Athens.'

There was a groan. I think we all groaned at the thought of walking a hundred stades to Athens.

Miltiades stood straighter. 'We are *not done*,' he said. 'If the old men and boys we left behind surrender the city to their fleet – and there are people in the town who might do it – then all this would be for nothing.' He sighed.

Phidippides, the Athenian herald, pushed forward. 'Give me leave, lord,' he said, 'and I'll run to Athens and tell them of the battle.'

Miltiades nodded, his face full of respect. 'Go! And the gods run with you.'

Phidippides was not a rich man, and had only his leather cuirass, a helmet and his aspis. He dropped the aspis and helmet on the ground and eager hands helped him out of his cuirass. He stripped his chiton off and put his sword belt on his naked shoulder.

Someone handed him a chlamys, and he gave us a grin. 'Better than mine in camp!' he said. 'I'll be there before the sun sets, friends.'

He'd fought the whole day, but he ran off the field, heading south, his legs pumping hard – not a sprint, but a steady pace that would eat the stades.

Miltiades turned to me – or perhaps to Aristides. 'I have to get the army ready to march,' he said. 'I need one of you to lead the assault on the grove.'

I'll give Miltiades this much – he sounded genuinely regretful.

'I'll do it,' I said.

'Then we do it together,' Aristides said. He looked at his men – the front-rankers of his tribe. 'We need to do this,' he said quietly. 'We broke. We must find our honour in the grove.'

Miltiades nodded curtly. 'Go with the gods. Get it done and follow me.' He took his *hyperetes* and began to walk across the fields. The boy at his side blew his trumpet, and all across the field, Athenians and Plataeans looked up from their fatigue, summoned back to the phalanx.

Many of my Plataeans were right there – perhaps a hundred men. They were a mix of front- and rear-rankers, the best and the worst, and the Athenians were in the same state, although there were more of them, and they had more armour and better weapons.

Mind you, the Plataeans were working hard to remedy that, stripping the Persians at our feet.

'They can't have many arrows left,' I said.

'Why not?' Cleitus asked.

'They'd be shooting us,' Teucer answered.

Aristides smiled a little sheepishly. Then he frowned. 'You have a plan, Plataean?'

I shrugged, and the weight of my scale corslet seemed like the weight of the world. Even Cleitus – bloody Cleitus, who I hated – looked at me, waiting.

The truth is, I didn't have enough energy to hate Cleitus. He was one more spear – and a strong spear, too. So I raised my eyes and looked at the grove. The precinct wall was about half a man tall, of loose stones, but well built, and beyond the wall the grove climbed a low hill – completely inside the wall, of course. It was a virtually impregnable position.

'Seems to me they're as tired as we are – and their side lost. Nothing for them now but death or slavery.' I was buying time, waiting for Athena or Heracles to put something in my head besides the black despair that comes after a long fight.

I remember I walked a little apart, not really to think, but because the weight of their expectations was greater than the weight of my scale thorax and my aspis combined, and I wanted to be free of it for a moment.

And it *was* as if a goddess came and whispered in my ear, except that I still fancy it was Aphrodite, whose hymn had been on my lips when I fell asleep. Because I turned my head, and there it was.

I put my helmet back on my head and my shield on my arm. I was only a few steps from the others. 'I see a way to distract them and save some fighting. I think you Athenians should go for them – right over the wall, at the low point by the gate. The rest of us – you see the little dip in the ground there?' I nodded my head. 'Don't point. If fifty of us go there, up that little gully, I doubt they'll see us coming.

The rest of you form up twenty shields wide and ten deep. When we hit the grove, well, you come at the gate, and it's every man for himself.'

Aristides nodded. 'If they see you coming, you'll be shot to pieces,' he said.

'Then we'd best hope they're low on arrows,' I said. 'No time for anything fancy.'

Someone shouted, 'Can we fire the grove?'

'No time,' I said. In truth, it was the best solution.

Let me tell you something, young man. I believe in the gods. One of them had just shown me the gully. And that olive grove was sacred to Artemis. And the gods had stood by me all day. To me, this was the test. It is always the test of battle. How good are you when you are wounded and tired? That's when you find out who is truly a hero, my children. Anyone can stand their ground with a full belly and clean muscles. But at the end of day, when the rim of the sun touches the hills and you haven't had water for hours and flies are laying eggs in your wounds?

Think on it. Because hundreds of us were measured, and by Heracles, we were worthy of our fathers.

'You man enough for this, Plataean?' Cleitus asked, but his voice was merely chiding – almost friendly.

'Fuck off,' I said, equally friendly.

'Let's get to it,' Aeschylus said. He put the edge of his aspis between Cleitus and me. 'This isn't about you, Cleitus.'

I remember that I smiled. 'Cleitus,' I said softly, and he met my eye. 'Today is for the Medes,' I said. I offered my hand.

He took it and clasped it hard.

Aeschylus nodded. 'I ask to be the first into the grove,' he said. 'For my brother.'

Athenians and aristocrats. Not a scrap of sense.

So the Athenians formed a deep block the width of the low wall. Behind the screen they provided, I took my Plataeans – household first – in a pair of long files and ran off to the south, around the edge of the low hill. I pushed my legs to do their duty. I think 'run' may be a poor description of the shambling jog we managed – but we did it.

We ran around the edge of the hill and there was the entry to the gully, as I'd expected. That gully wasn't as deep as a man is tall – but it was shaped oddly, with a small bend just before the west wall of the grove, and I trusted my guess and led my men forward – still in a file.

369

The Persians had formed a line – not, to be honest, a very thick line – facing Aristides' small phalanx. We could see them, and by a miracle, they still hadn't seen us. It was, well, miraculous. But on the battlefield, men die because they see what they expect to see.

Then Aristides and Aeschylus led their men forward. They were so tired that they didn't cheer or sing the Paean, but simply trotted forward, and all the Persians shot into them.

The clatter of the arrows on their shields and the solid impacts drowned the sound of our movement.

'Form your front!' I called softly, but my men needed no order.

The men behind me started to sprint forward. I didn't slow. The neatness of our line was immaterial. And by the gods, Aphrodite was there, or some other goddess, lifting us to one more fight, raising us above ourselves. Two or three times in my life I've felt this, and it is ... beyond the human. And at Marathon, every one of us at the grove felt it.

I was at the edge of the gully, and it sloped steeply up, head height, to the base of the stone wall. The Persians had assumed this part was too tricky for us to storm.

I was first. I ran up the gully lip – and at the top a Persian shot me.

His arrow smacked into my aspis at point-blank range, and then I was past him, over the wall in a single leap, and a flood of Plataeans poured in behind me. I have no idea who killed that man, or, to be honest, how I got over the wall – but we were in, past the wall, among the trees.

I crashed into the end of the Persian line – most of them never saw us coming, so focused were they on Aristides and his men to their front.

They died hard.

When they stood, we slew them, and when they ran – some in panic, more just to find a better place to die – we chased them, tree to tree. Those with arrows shot us, and those without protected the archers. Some had spears and a few had aspides they'd picked up from our dead, and many had axes, and they fought like heroes.

No man who survived the fight in the olive grove ever forgot it.

Desperate, cornered men are no longer human. They are animals, and they will grasp the sword in their guts and hold on to it if it will help a mate kill you.

The fight eventually filled the whole grove, and some of them must have climbed the trees – certainly the arrow that killed Teucer came from above, straight down into the top of his shoulder by his neck. And Alcaeus of Miletus, who had come all this way to die for Athens, went down fighting, his aspis against two axemen, and I was just too far away to save him.

A Persian broke my spear, dying on it, and another clambered over his body and his short sword rang off my scales, but didn't go through or I'd have died there myself. I put my arms around him and threw him to the ground, rolled on top of him to crush him, got my hands on his throat and choked the life out of him. That's the last moment in the battle I remember – I must have got back on my feet but I don't remember how, and then I was back to back with Idomeneus, but the fighting was over.

The fighting was over.

All the Persians were dead.

Idomeneus sank to the ground. 'I'm done,' he said. I had never heard those words from him, and never did again.

That was Marathon.

Equally, to be honest, I remember nothing of the march over the mountains to Athens, in the dark, save that there was a storm brewing out over the ocean and the breeze of that storm blew over us like the touch of a woman's cool hand when you are sick.

I must have given some orders, because there were nigh-on eight hundred Plataeans when we came down the hills above Athens to the sanctuary of Heracles. And as each contingent came up, Miltiades met them in person. That part I remember. He was still in full armour, and he glowed – perhaps, that night, he was divine. Certainly, it was his will that got us safely over the mountains and back to the plains of Attica. The Plataeans were the last to leave Marathon apart from Aristides' tribe, who stayed to guard the loot, and the last to arrive at the shrine of Heracles, and as we came in – not marching, but shuffling along in a state of exhaustion – the sun began to rise over the sea, and the first glow caught the temples on the Acropolis in the distance.

'We've made it, friends,' Miltiades said to each contingent.

Men littered the ground – shields were dropped like olives in an autumn wind, as if our army had been beaten rather than victorious.

My men were no different. Without a word, men fell to the ground. Later, Hermogenes told me that he fell asleep before he got his aspis off his arm.

I didn't. Like Miltiades, I was too tired to sleep, and I stood with him as the sun rose, revealing the Persian fleet still well off to the east.

'Even if they came now,' he said, 'Phidippides made it. See the beacon on the Acropolis?'

I could see a smudge of smoke in the dawn light. I nodded heavily.

'By Athena,' Miltiades said. He stood as straight as a spear-shaft, despite his fatigue. He laughed, and looked out into the morning. 'We won.'

'You should rest,' I said.

Miltiades laughed again. He slapped my back, grinned ear to ear, and for a moment, he was not ancient and used up – he was the Pirate King I had known as a boy. 'I won't waste this moment in the arms of sleep, Arimnestos,' he said. He embraced me.

I remember grinning, because few things were ever as precious to me as the love of Miltiades, despite the bastard's way with money, power and fame. 'Sleep would not be a waste,' I said.

He shook his head. 'Arimnestos – right now, this moment, *I am with the gods.*' He said it plain – no rhetoric. And he wasn't talking to a thousand men, feeding on their adulation. I honestly think every man in our army was asleep but us.

No – he was telling the plain truth to one man, and that man was me.

I remember that I didn't understand. I do now. But I was too young, and for all my scars and the blood on my sword arm, too inexperienced.

He laughed again, and it was a fell sound. 'I have beaten the Persians at the gates of my city. I have won a victory – such a victory.' He shrugged. 'Since Troy . . .' he said, and burst into tears.

We stood together. I cried too, thugater. I cried, and the sun rose on the Persian fleet, turning away in defeat. Many men were dead, and many more would die. But we had beaten the Great King's army, and the world would never be the same again. Truly, in that hour, we were with the gods.

Epilogue

A day later, the Spartans marched in on the road from Corinth. Their armour was magnificent, and their scarlet cloaks billowed in the west wind, and the head of their column was just in time to see the last of the barbarian fleet as it turned away from the channel by Salamis and started back for Naxos.

They marched over the mountains to Marathon and saw the barbarian dead, and then they marched back to Athens to shower us with praise. I think most of the bastards were jealous.

Many men died at Marathon – my friends, and men who had followed me. And worse awaited me at home, although I didn't know it.

As soon as our lightly wounded could walk, I took our men back over the mountains to Plataea. We still feared that Thebes might move against us. Indeed, Athens sent us a thousand hoplites to accompany us home, to show Thebes that they had backed the wrong horse. Athens could not do enough for us – to this day, thugater, the priestess of Athena blesses Plataea every morning in her first prayer – and within the year, we were made citizens of Athens, with the same citizen rights as Aristides and Miltiades, so that all those freed slaves were able, if they wished, to go back to Athens as free men.

We came down the long flank of Cithaeron, three thousand men, new citizens and old, and the valley of the Asopus was laid out before us, the fields like the finest tapestry a woman could weave in soft colours of gold and pale green.

At the shrine of the hero, Idomeneus halted his men – those who had survived – and we embraced.

'Good fight,' he said, with his mad grin.

We poured libations for the hero. Probably hundreds. It is odd, but one of my memories of that autumn day is the wine lying in pools before the hero's tomb. I had never seen so many libations poured there, and the image of wine filling the wagon ruts is, to me, one of the strongest I associate with Marathon. We did not commit hubris. We gave thanks.

Then we went down into the lengthening shadows of the valley, and we halted under our own walls and formed the phalanx one more time. Thousands of citizens came out to see us – indeed, they'd known we were coming when the first glint of bronze was seen on the passes, and runners had long since brought them the tale of the battle and the number and names of the dead.

We formed one last time, and Myron came out of the phalanx.

I took off my helmet and handed him my spear. 'We are no longer at war,' I said. 'I was the archon of war, and I return my spear.'

He took it. 'Plataeans,' he said. 'I return you to your city, at peace.'

And they cheered – the hoplites, and the new citizens, and the women and children and even the slaves.

It would be good if I could leave it there.

Pour me a little more wine.

I looked around for Euphoria – I hadn't really expected her, as she would have been in her ninth month – but I saw neither Hermogenes' wife nor my sister. I remember that Antigonus and I stood together, and I had a joke at the edge of my tongue, about how, for the first time, we were timely and our wives were late.

Before I could make that cruel jibe, one of my Thracians – the men I'd freed – came on to the Field of Ares. He told us his news, tears running down his cheeks. To be honest, I don't remember anything after that, until I stood by her bedside. I had missed her by perhaps three hours.

There was blood – enough blood that she might have died at Marathon. She had fought her own fight – a long one – and she had not surrendered or given way. She stood her ground until the very end, and pushed our child out, and died for it.

'I told her you were coming,' Pen told me. She held me tightly against her, and I felt nothing but the fatigue and the crushing lack of emotion that had dogged me since we stormed the olive grove. 'I told her, and she held my hand – oh!'

Pen wept. Antigonus wept.

I felt as if I had been wrapped in thick wool.

I drank some wine, and later I lay on some blankets, my eyes open.

Then, my choices made, I got to my feet. I lifted her – she weighed nothing – and carried her outside to the stable. I took a horse – no great crime with a brother-in-law – and I carried her body across my lap, as I had carried her over the mountains when first she was my bride.

I carried her home.

Of course, there was nothing left of my home but the forge. Cleitus and Simon had burned my house.

I laid her on the work table in my forge, and I put everything on her – every jewel Mater had saved from the house, every piece of loot I had taken from Marathon or been given by thankful Athenians, until she glittered like a goddess.

Then I lit my forge.

I prayed to Hephaestus, and I lit my torch from my forge fire.

Then I set my forge ablaze, and I left it to burn as her pyre.

It burned behind me, bright as a new sun. I rode down the hill, away from the farm and the fire. I rode steadily until I heard the crash as the roof-tree gave, and the whoosh as the rest of the building leaped into new flame – and then I pressed my horse to a gallop and rode away.

I never promised you a happy story.

If I tell you more . . .

If I tell you more, thugater, it will be another night. And then I'll tell you how I broke the mould of my life and cast it away – how I went with Miltiades and then to Sicily, and left Greece behind me.

For now, though, leave an old man to weep old tears. So many dead – and only me to sing of them now. I am the last.

But remember, when you pray to the gods, that men stood like the heroes of old at Marathon, and were better. And that they are still no better than the women who bear them.

Wine!

Historical Afterword

As closely as possible, this novel follows the road of history. But history – especially Archaic Greek history – can be more like a track in the forest than a road with a kerb. I have attempted to make sense of Herodotus and his curiously modern tale of nation states, betrayal, terrorism and heroism. I have read most of the secondary sources, and I have found most of them wanting.

The Persians were not 'bad'. The Greeks were not 'good'. And since both cultures grew from the same roots, 'Western' civilization would probably have been much the same had the Persians remained the world empire. Or so I believe.

And yet, and yet ... the complex web of decisions, betrayals and conspiracies in Herodotus somehow gave birth to the first real attempt at democracy – at least, the first of which we know. I have done my best to make this element of the story as essential as the fighting – to try and show how the small men gained political power, despite the overwhelming power of landowners and an ancient aristocracy.

It is nothing but facile error to see Athenian democracy as bearing any resemblance to the United States, Great Britain or any other modern democracy except in the most general way. There were no 'middle-class hoplites' in the front ranks. Aristocrats led the demos in every walk of life, and at war they served in front, in their superior armour, with their superior training, and the evidence for this is on every page of the literature, and only the most pig-headed myth-making can ignore it. In the period of which I write, the 'phalanx' as we now imagine it was just being born. Indeed, one possible reading of Herodotus would suggest that the 'phalanx' was born at Marathon. Archers and light-armed men still served in the front lines, and heroic aristocrats still fought duels – or so the art and literature suggest, however the idea is disliked by current historians, especially 'military' historians.

In fact, there were few middle-class hoplites because our modern notions of class didn't exist. A poor man, like Socrates, might still be an aristocrat to his finger ends. A rich man, like the former slave who gave a thousand aspides to support the rearming of Athens in the fourth century, remained a former slave. Unless the term 'middle class' has no other meaning than to stand as a group between the poor and the rich, it can't be made to apply.

And finally, or perhaps first, it may be that only the veterans among my readers will know the truth that military historians often cannot stomach – that all races and breeds are equally brave or cowardly, regardless of government, loyalty, race, creed or sexual preference. That all men lose combat effectiveness with fatigue and confusion.

That only a few men are killers, and they are supremely dangerous.

Really, friends, it is all in the *Iliad*. And when my inspiration failed, I always went back to the *Iliad*, like a man returning to the source of pure water. I have enormous respect for the modern works of many historians, classical and modern. But they weren't there.

I have seen war – never the war of the spear and shield, but war. And when I read the *Iliad*, it comes to me as being *true*. Not, perhaps, true about Troy. But true about *war*. Homer did not love war. Achilles is not the best man in the *Iliad*. War is ugly.

Arimnestos of Plataea was a real man. I hope that I've done him justice.

Acknowledgements

On 1 April 1990, I was in the back right seat of an S-3B Viking, flying a routine anti-submarine warfare flight off the USS *Dwight D. Eisenhower*. But we were not just anywhere. We were off the coast of Turkey, and in one flight we passed Troy, or rather, Hisarlik, Anatolia. Later that afternoon, we passed down the coast of Lesbos and all along the coast of what Herodotus thought of as Asia. Back in my stateroom, on the top bunk (my bunk, as the most junior officer), was an open copy of the *Iliad*.

I will never forget that day, because there's a picture on my wall of the Sovremenny-class destroyer *Okrylennyy* broadside on to the mock harpoon missile I fired on her from well over the horizon using our superb ISAR radar. Of course, there was no Homeric deed of arms – the Cold War was dying, or even dead – but there was professional triumph in that hour, and the photo of the ship, framed against the distant haze of the same coastline that saw battles at Mycale and Troy, will decorate my walls until my shade goes down to the underworld.

I think that the *Killer of Men* series was born there. I love the Greek and Turkish Aegean, and the history of it. Before Saddam Hussein wrecked it in August, my carrier battle group had a near perfect summer, cruising the wine-dark sea where the Greeks and Persians fought.

But it may have been born when talking to various Vietnam veterans, returning from that war – a war that may not have been worse than any other war, but loomed large in my young consciousness of conflict. My grandfather and my father and my uncle – all veterans – said things, when they thought I wasn't around, that led me to suspect that while many men can be brave, some men are far more dangerous in combat than others.

Still later, I was privileged to serve with various men from the Special Operations world, and I came to know that even among them – the snake-eaters – there were only a few who were the killers. I listened to them talk, and I wondered what kind of a man Achilles really was. Or Hector. And I began to wonder what made them, and what kept them at it, and the thought stayed with me while I flew and served in Africa and saw various conflicts and the effects that those conflicts have on all the participants, from the first Gulf War to Rwanda and Zaire.

The *Killer of Men* series is my attempt to understand the inside of such men.

This book was both very easy and very hard to write. I have thought about the *Killer of Men* series since 1990 in some way or other; when I sat down to put my thoughts into the computer, the book seemed to write itself, and even now, when I type these final words, I am amazed at how much of it seemed to be waiting, prewritten, inside my head. But the devil is still in the details, and my acknowledgements are all about the investigation and research of those details.

The broad sweep of the history of the Ionian Revolt is really known to us only from Herodotus and, to a vastly lesser extent, from Thucydides. I have followed Herodotus in almost every respect, except for the details of how the tiny city-state of Plataea came to involve herself with Athens. That, to be frank, I made up – although it is based on a theory evolved over a hundred conversations with amateur and professional historians. First and foremost, I have to acknowledge the contribution of Nicolas Cioran, who cheerfully discussed Plataea's odd status every day as we worked out in a gymnasium, and sometimes fought sword to sword. My trainer and constant sparring partner John Beck deserves my thanks – both for a vastly improved physique, and for helping give me a sense of what real training for a life of violence might have been like in the ancient world. And my partner in the reinvention of ancient Greek xiphos fighting, Aurora Simmons, deserves at least equal thanks.

Among professional historians, I was assisted by Paul McDonnell-Staff and Paul Bardunias, by the entire brother- and sisterhood of RomanArmyTalk.com and the web community there, and by the staff of the Royal Ontario Museum (who possess and cheerfully shared the only surviving helmet attributable to the Battle of Marathon), as well as the staff of the Antikenmuseum Basel und Sammlung Ludwig, who possess the best-preserved ancient aspis and provided me with superb photos to use in recreating it. I also received help from the library staff of the University of Toronto, where, when I'm rich enough, I'm a student, and from Toronto's superb Metro Reference Library. Every novelist needs to live in a city where universal access to JSTOR is free and on his library card. The staff of the Walters Art Gallery in Baltimore, Maryland – just across the street from my mother's apartment, conveniently – were cheerful and helpful, even when I came back to look at the same helmet for the sixth time. And James Davidson, whose superb book, *Greeks and Greek Love* helped me think about the thorny issues of ancient Greek sexuality, was also useful to a novelist with too many questions.

Excellent as professional historians are – and my version of the Persian Wars owes a great deal to many of them, not least Hans Van Wees and Victor Davis Hanson – my greatest praise and thanks have to go to the amateur historians we call reenactors. Giannis Kadoglou of Thessaloniki volunteered to spend two full days driving around the Greek countryside, from Athens to Plataea and back, charming my five-year-old daughter and my wife while translating everything in sight and being as delighted with the ancient town of Plataea as I was myself. I met him on RomanArmyTalk, and this would be a very different book without his passion for the subject and relentless desire to correct my errors.

But Giannis is hardly alone, and there is – literally – a phalanx of Greek reenactors who helped me. Here in my part of North America, we have a group called the Plataeans – this is, trust me, not a coincidence – and we work hard on recreating the very time period and city-state so prominent in these books, from weapons, armour and combat to cooking, crafts and dance. If the reader feels that these books put flesh and blood on the bare bones of history – in so far as I've succeeded in doing that – it is because of the efforts of the men and women who reenact with me and show me, every time we're together, all the things I haven't thought of, who do their own research, their own kit-building and their own training. Thanks to all of you, Plataeans. And to all the other Ancient Greek reenactors who helped me find things, make things or build things.

Thanks are also due to the people of Lesbos and Athens and Plataea – I can't name all of you, but I was entertained, informed and supported constantly in three trips to Greece, and the person who I can name is Aliki Hamosfakidou of Dolphin Hellas Travel for her care, interest and support through many hundreds of emails and some meetings.

In a professional line, I would like to acknowledge the debt I owe to Mr Tim Waller, my copy-editor, whose knowledge of language – both this one and Ancient Greek – always makes me feel humble. He's pretty good at east and west, too. Thanks to him, this book is better than it would ever have been without him.

Bill Massey, my editor at Orion, found the two biggest errors in this story and made me fix them, and again, it is a better book for his work. A much better book. Oh, and he found a lot of other errors, too, but let's not mention them. I have had a few editors. Working with Bill is wonderful. Come on, authors – how many of you get to say that?

My agent, Shelley Power, contributed more directly to this book than to any other – first, as an agent, in all the usual ways, and then later, coming to Greece and taking part in all the excitement of seeing Lesbos and Athens and taking us to Archaeon Gefsis, a restaurant that attempts to take the customer back to the ancient world. Thanks for everything, Shelley, and the dinner not the least!

I'm lucky that my friends still volunteer to read my manuscripts and criticize them: Robert Sulentic, Rebecca Jordan (who also maintains the websites at www.hippeis.com and www.plataians.org), Jenny Carrier, Matt Heppe, Aurora Simmons and Kate Boggs. Thanks to you, this is a better book.

Christine Szego and the staff and management of my local bookstore, Bakka-Phoenix of Toronto, also deserve my thanks, as I tend to walk in and spout fifteen minutes' worth of plot, character, dialogue or just news – writing can be lonely work, and it is good to have people to talk to. And they throw a great book launch.

As usual, this book was written, almost every word, at the Luna Café in Toronto, where I sit at my table, take up another table with Barrington's Classical Atlas, and despite that, get served superb coffee, good humour and excellent food all day.

It is odd, isn't it, that authors always save their families for last? Really, it's the done thing. So I'll do it, too, even though my wife should get mentioned at every stage – after all, she's a reenactor, too, she had useful observations on all kinds of things we both read (Athenian textiles is what really comes to mind, though) and, in addition, more than even Ms Szego, Sarah has to listen to the endless enthusiasms I develop about history while writing (the words 'did you know' probably cause her more horror than anything else you can think of). My daughter, Beatrice, is also a reenactor, and her ability to portray the life of a real child is amazing. My father, Kenneth Cameron, taught me most of what I know about writing, and continues to provide excellent advice – and to listen to my complaints about the process, which may be the greater service.

Having said all that, it's hard to say what exactly I can lay claim to, if you like this book. I had a great deal of help, and I appreciate it. Thanks. And when you find misspelled words, sailing directions reversed and historical errors – why, then you'll know that I, too, had something to add. Because all the errors are solely mine.